A Line of Provenance

Juliet Cromwell is the author of two novels. She lives by
the sea on the Essex coast with her best friend.

By Juliet Cromwell

A Perception of Sin
A Line of Provenance

A Line of Provenance

Juliet Cromwell

*

ISBN-13: 978-1979092876
ISBN-10: 1979092877

For those I Love

*

CHAPTER 1
Tuna Sandwiches

*

May 2023

"The first I knew of it was the fuck'n smell. 'Bloody 'ell,' I thought, 'that honks.' So I looked up to see where it was coming from, and there it was ... sort'f hanging there like a bloody great turd," says Stan Bishop.

D.C. Fry glances up at the large, black bag, dangling precariously off the digger bucket.

"Was the bag torn by then, Mr Bishop?" he asks, wanting to be clear on the facts before his new boss arrives.

"I'd say. Tibsey must've ripped it open with his last scoop."

"The bag, you mean?

"Yeah, the bag—bloody great thing. Anyways, it was just sort'f swaying there off the bucket-fork, when that fuck'n head thing dropped out."

"From the bag?"

"Yeah, from the bag. So I shouts up to Tibsey: that's him over there." Fry looks to where Stan Bishop is pointing and sees a man by the site hut, sitting on an upturned oil barrel. Even at this distance, Fry can see the distinctive, sharp, red glow of his cigarette as he drags on it deeply. "Mike Tibbet's his name. Poor fucker's really shaken up," Stan Bishop continues. "Don't suppose he'll want to dig again for a while. S'pect you'll be wanting to have a chat with him too?"

1

"Probably. You were saying about the head?" Fry prompts, checking the light on the Cam to make sure it's still recording.

"Dropped out. Just like that. Plop. Bounced around a bit before rollin' into the bottom of our 'ole. Round and hairy-like, and smelly. You wouldn't wanna smell that again in a month of Sundees."

"I'm sure you wouldn't," Fry agrees, finding the gentle waft of decomposing flesh on the morning air bad enough to stomach. "So, what happened next?"

"So I shouts at Tibsey to cut the fuck'n motor but he can't hear me on account of his 'eadphones and he's too busy singin' anyways. He's a bit of a Country and Western fan. So there I am, jumping about and waving my arms like a right loony, and that's when the head dropped out. I'll remember that sight to m' dying day."

"So, the head dropped out when you were waving at Mr Tibbet to switch the digger's engine off?" Fry confirms.

"Yeah, I said didn't I…though I did stop to puke." They both take an involuntary glance at the pile of lumpy vomit. "Tuna sarnies, Mrs made them fresh this mornin'. She's good like that," Bishop enlightens Fry, making him want to gag even more. Fighting the urge, he swallows hard.

"Is that when Mr Tibbet stopped the digger?"

"Yeah, must've seen somethin', or smelt it. You'll have to ask him. But it was either me jumping around or the bag or the stink, coz that's when he switched the motor off."

"And is that when you went to get the foreperson?" Fry asks.

"Yep, that's about the long and short of it. I went off to tell Ms Bragg and she called you lot in."

"Thank you, Mr Bishop. That's all we need for now, but you'll probably be required to make a formal statement."

"Okay, but it'll just be the same. It's not a thing you s'pect to see every day and that head, ugh, it's enough to give you the willies. Anyways, I'd best go and see how old Tibsey is, poor fucker."

D.C. Fry watches Stan Bishop trudge off across the building site before instructing the Cam to stop recording. Heading back to his car, he pulls on a set of white forensic overalls, pockets a pair of latex gloves and taking some police tape he sets about cordoning off the crime scene.

"Morning, Fry." Turning round, Fry sees a small woman wearing a matching set of overalls, tucked firmly into a pair of Wellington boots, and wonders why he hadn't thought of that.

"Morning, Boss."

"What have we got?" D.C.I. Logan asks.

"Looks like the remains of a body."

"Anything from the digger driver or his mate?"

"I've not spoken to the driver, he's in a bit of a state. But his mate, Stan Bishop, saw most of it and has given a full description." Fry tries not to think about the pile of sicked-up tuna sandwiches sitting a couple of yards away from where they're standing.

"What did he have to say?"

"Mainly how there was no obvious indication of a body being buried here. They were digging out foundations, and the bucket-fork punctured the bag as it brought it up to the surface. I reckon the weight of the body widened the rip." A large, muddy clod leisurely slides off the underside of the bag and falls with a wet thump. They both look down at the freshly dug hole then at the bag.

"It doesn't look very secure," Logan comments.

"Could go at any moment," Fry agrees. "What do you think? Body bag?"

"Could be. Military, hospital or private morgue. Look, on the edge… that might be writing." They both squint up at the mud-coated bag, bent double and secured by the remnants of a frayed rope that is dripping blackish water. Suddenly, the rip widens and a bony arm topples out, making Fry jump. It swings, pendulum like, before dropping into the pit next to the head. They both instinctively peer in after it.

"We'd better take a closer look," Logan says.

"Okay, I'll get the ladder."

"Be quick, I want a gander before the Fozies arrive."

Squelching across the furrowed track again, Fry nearly slips over in his office shoes.

"Damn," he thinks as he tries to wipe some of the mud off on a patch of grass before grabbing the collapsible ladder and carefully picking his way back across the building site.

Taking the ladder, Logan clicks it open and guides it down into the pit. Climbing down, she carefully steps around the arm and the skull. Fry gingerly follows her, balancing the Cam in one hand. "Okay Fry, Cam on, let's see what we've got," she says, bobbing down next to the bony remains.

CHAPTER 2
The Collector of Souls

*

A pale blue translucent light fills the pit as Fry instructs the Cam to configure. He checks the screen, commands it to narrow its field of vision until it encloses the head and arm bones, and then tells it to holo-record.

"Skull," Logan dictates, "partly covered in a thick coating of dark, mattered hair… is that a moustache?" Fry squats next to her, trying to breathe through his mouth while the Cam adjusts its focus to accommodate the change in angle.

"Could be, Boss, it's hard to tell with all that mud."

"Right humerus, radius and ulna, I think, plus carpals, metacarpals and- and what are the finger bones called?"

"Phalanges, right hand phalanges to be precise," informs a friendly voice from above them.

"We have company," Logan murmurs to Fry. They both stand and look up at the tall, slim-built man, whose dark hair catches the light from the pale spring sun. The arms of his forensic overalls are tied at his waist and he, like Logan, has Wellington boots on. In one hand, he is carrying a large hard-sided case and in the other, a collapsible ladder.

"Hello, Greyson," Logan greets.

"Thought it was you, Lo," Greyson replies, lowering the ladder and climbing down effortlessly.

"This is Fry, my new D.C."

"Hello, Fry," he says, extending his hand.

"Hi," Fry replies, shaking the offered hand.

"So, human and decomposing nicely from the smell of things."

"Yeah, been here for a while I'd say," Logan replies. "And we think that might be a body bag." They all gaze up at the dark shape hanging precariously over their heads.

"Ah ha, the Sword of Damocles. I hope the gods are feeling kind today. I don't fancy being underneath that lot when it comes down," Greyson says with a laugh, reminding Logan of why she prefers working with him to any of the other police pathologists.

"Suspicious, unless the dead have learnt to strap themselves into a body bag and bury themselves six feet under."

"Yes, suspicious alright," Logan agrees.

"We thought the body bag could be either military, hospital or private morgue," Fry states.

"Or BDSM," adds Greyson.

"What?" Fry asks.

"Bondage, discipline, sadomasochism," Logan replies, matter-of-factly.

"Oh," Fry murmurs.

"We'll soon know if this is edge-play gone too far, as their bags tend to have breathing holes," continues Greyson.

"Edge-play?" queries Fry again.

"Sex, using extreme manipulation, such as erotic asphyxiation," Logan informs him.

"As opposed to SSC or vanilla sex," Greyson adds.

"Safe, sane and consensual. Conventional sex," Logan translates, before Fry gets a chance to ask.

"Right. Thanks. That is-well-educational," murmurs Fry, poking the toe of his shoe into a lump of mud.

"We can pretty much eliminate a forensic bag. Ours are white for spotting anything that's dislodged from cadavers on their journey to the slab," Greyson says with a smile.

"Maybe male, as the head has possible facial hair," resumes Logan.

"Right, let's have a poke around and see what we can find. I'm guessing you'll want a good look, Lo?"

"Yes, and okay if we film?" she asks.

"Be my guest."

Crouching next to Logan, Fry aims the Cam back at the bones as Greyson pulls on a pair of latex gloves, unclips his case and takes out a stainless-steel probe. Poking the skull, he rolls it slightly so he can see inside the bone cavity.

"No brain to speak of, cerebral matter decomposed, closure of cranial sutures, teeth fully developed. At a guess, age at death over 30, under 60. Looks like a broken nasal bone."

"Can you tell when his nose was broken?"

"Only if it's an old injury, as then there'll be evidence of renewed bonegrowth. Hair still present. I'd say we have a ginger."

"How can you tell? It just looks dark to me," Logan says.

"See here, Lo," and Greyson lifts a matted lock of hair with his probe, on the right side of the skull. "See the roots this side? Ginger. I'd say he was lying on his left side. The right's pretty free from goo, though the left is a different matter. He was leaking on his left. And that arm," Greyson transfers his probe to the humerus and scrapes the surface. "See here. Clean apart from the mud; you could eat your dinner with those bones." Fry gags.

"Are you okay?" Logan asks, sympathetically.

"Yeah, just about," he mumbles, swallowing hard again.

"If you want to vomit, try to do it away from the evidence," she suggests kindly. He nods, and she smiles reassuringly at him.

"How long do you reckon he's been down here?" she asks, turning back to Greyson and the bones.

"Well at a guesstimate, give or take a few years, 20 to 25. I'll know more when I get him back to the lab. Did you know this was an allotment until very recently? And not just any allotment. This was the very allotment where the Allotment War took place," Greyson comments.

"The Allotment War?" Logan queries.

"Well, that's what the press labelled it. Though it was more of a scrap between Braxham Wick District Council and the allotment

7

holders. Though I do believe it came to blows."

"Really?"

"Expect the body would never have surfaced if the council hadn't sold the land for development."

A sudden gust of wind stirs the black bag hooked above their heads. It creaks ominously and another lump of wet earth slips down the plastic and plops next to the skull. They all automatically stand up and take a step backwards.

"Perhaps it would be prudent to get a move on," Greyson suggests.

"Okay. Thanks, Greyson," Logan says reaching for the ladder.

"Guess we'll hear from you soon."

"Sure, I'll let you know when we," he nods towards the bones, "have become better acquainted. Are you still on Grim's team?"

"Yeah, for my sins."

"Give him my regards and tell him he's still got an open invitation to my bowls club."

Logan smiles, "Okay. Bye."

"Bye Greyson," Fry says following Logan up the ladder.

"So that's Greyson Stonewalker," Fry remarks as they head back across the building site to their cars. He'd heard about the pathologist with the quirky name, whose reputation for living life to the full was often the talk of the station.

"That's him."

"Have you worked with him often?"

"A couple of times. Don't let his casualness fool you; he's brilliant at his job."

"Do you think he really plays bowls? I always thought bowls players were, you know…boring and old, and he's known to be some sort of party legend."

"I wouldn't put it past him. I know he and Grim have a running joke about it."

"And why do they call D.C.S. Reaper, Grim?"

"As in the Grim Reaper, the collector of souls."

"Yeah, I get the name but not why he's got it."

"He was a force to be reckoned with in his day, had a brilliant clear-up rate. I loved being his D.S. Never a dull moment. Let's go and have a word with the foreperson. What's her name?"

"Ms Bragg."

A rush of warm air greets them as they enter the portable site office. A few people sit at one end nursing hot drinks while, at the other, stands a woman dressed in a hard hat and high-visibility jacket, examining a hologram.

"Ms Bragg?" Logan asks.

"Yes?"

"Chelmsford Police, D.C.I. Logan, D.C. Fry. I think we have all we need for the moment but could we take a scan of the site map?"

"Yes," she says, standing back from the table. Logan nods at Fry who positions the Cam to capture the site hologram.

"Ms Bragg, is it usual to dig so far down for foundations?" Logan asks.

"This site is coastal, with a high sand proportion, hence three-metre footings," she states laconically, adding, "When will you be off my site?"

"Forensics will remove the body this afternoon and we'll probably gather any remaining evidence tomorrow. If there are no surprises, we should be out of here by tomorrow afternoon."

"Good. This has already damaged my schedule."

Leaving the portable office, a gust of wind catches at their overalls, making Logan wonder how Greyson is faring under the unstable body bag.

"Come on Fry, I'll buy you a coffee back at the station and then I think we should tackle the Allotment War, whatever that is."

9

CHAPTER 3
Shooting Stars

Easing her boots off, Logan removes her latex gloves and forensic overalls before putting on her shoes. Sliding into the driver's seat, she can just make out Fry hopping around, trying to scrape mud off his shoes.

"You'll learn," she thinks, smiling at her new D.C. and remembering all the times she'd turned up with inappropriate footwear to an outdoor crime scene.

Pulling away, she drives past the village green and along the small high street. It had been years since she'd last visited Godlinghoe.

"Not much has changed since Grim and I arrested that couple," she muses before remembering that Trev had been there that day too. This memory, like all her memories of Trev, cuts into her deeply, making her useless emptiness resurface. Angry tears prick her eyes, blurring her vision, forcing her to pull over. She parks in the small car park belonging to the church, grabs her jacket and gets out.

The wind, much stronger here than at the crime scene, catches at her short hair as she walks down one of the old grass paths. The ground is uneven as it weaves between sunken gravestones, whose eroded scripts have lost all meaning. Reaching up, she runs her hand across the spiky surface of her head; it still feels strange, almost naked, without her long ponytail. "I should just sign the divorce papers and get on with it," she tells the sleeping souls. "There's no reason not to; there's no going back now." She'd heard on the grapevine that Sharon was pregnant; it had made her cry. "Fuck you, Sharon Mulligan," she shouts now into the wind. "And fuck you Trevor Dillsworthy. It's so unfair."

Sharon had been her best friend, her maid of honour, on the day Trev had promised to love her and her alone, through sickness and health until death parted them. He hadn't added that if she couldn't conceive he'd have Sharon instead.

It had been on their third wedding anniversary when he'd proposed again, this time for a baby. They'd climbed Scafell Pike, not for the views across the Lake District but for the night sky—something he'd always wanted to show her.

"Lo," he'd said, "you've got to see it at least once before you die," his voice full of passion.

They'd lain near the top of the mountain, wedged in a dip between some rocks and snuggled deep in a double-sized sleeping bag. She'd stared up into the vast blackness filled with pathways of starlight while he'd pointed out the constellations.

"There, see those four stars? That's the Plough, part of the Great Bear, and if you follow the Plough it'll lead you to the North Star." His wonderment was infectious and she'd found herself absorbed in the starscape. When he'd finished, they had lain silently, until, quietly, he'd said, "Lo, there's something I want to ask you."

"You can ask for anything," she'd answered, "except for the last flapjack, that's mine!" They'd laughed as he'd tried, unsuccessfully, to wrestle the cake from her.

"Seriously, though," he'd said as they'd lain back down, "I want to ask you something."

"Go on," she'd replied, breaking the cake in half.

"Lo, I want to have a baby." She'd almost choked in shock.

"Well, why not? We've been married … what is it, I can't remember," and she'd hit him then and he'd laughed again.

"Stop it," he'd said, "you're such a husband beater. Oh yes, has it only been three years?"

"Yes. Three wonderful," punch, "incredible," punch, "fantastic," punch, "years!"

"But seriously Lo, imagine a baby, a little person made from both of us. It would be something, wouldn't it?"

"Maybe, I don't know. What about my job?"

"I know your job means the world to you; I wouldn't expect you to give it up. Loads of women stay on after they've had children, look at Trisha." Logan had wanted to say that Trisha was only part-time now and would never be promoted, but she didn't want to spoil the moment.

"Look. There," he'd said excitedly as an arc of light shot across the sky. "A shooting star. Quick, make a wish. Let's wish for our baby. Look another and another. It's the Perseid Meteor Shower. I'd hoped we would see it. How many babies is that?" and they'd laughed again as they watched the heavenly display.

"And that was a big, fat fucking lie, wasn't it," she tells the moss-covered tombs with tears running down her face. "There was no baby for me." Her only answer comes as the wind stirs an old yew tree, setting off a startled pigeon. "Right D.C.I. Logan, that's enough wallowing for one day." Pulling a tissue from her pocket, she blows her nose loudly and heads back to her car. Fastening her seat belt, she starts the engine and heads for the A12. Joining the motorway, she forces her mind away from Trev, short haircuts, babies and star gazing, and back onto the crime scene.

At Chelmsford Police Station, she swipes her security card and enters the building. Taking the stairs two at a time she reaches her small office on the third floor and sits behind her desk. It's warm and tidy. It makes her feel safe. It makes her feel in control.

"Afternoon Lo," says a smiling Grim, propping himself against her doorway with his arms folded.

"Hey Grim," she says, smiling back at him.

"What's the score?" he asks, tapping his thumbs rhythmically against his arms.

"One body, badly decomposed, probably male. Buried approximately 20 years ago."

"And do we suspect foul play?"

"Yes, we do indeed. It was buried in what looks like a body bag, bent double and secured with a rope."

"Dug up on a building site out at Godlinghoe, so I hear."

"Yeah, buried deep too. Whoever put it there didn't want it to be found."

"Who's the Foz?"

"Greyson."

"Ah, that should brighten the proceedings."

"Oh yeah and he said to tell you that you're always welcome at his bowls club."

"Fucker," Grim chuckles. "Where're you going to start while you're waiting for the post-mortem results?"

"Well, Greyson mentioned something interesting, an Allotment War. So as soon as Fry's back I thought we'd try the local press and websites. Also thought I'd get Chillies to give me a list of missing people from around the late 80s, say 88, to about 2010."

"Okay. How's Tristan Fry working out?"

"Fine. I like him."

"Good. He came with a glowing report from Hanson's team. Fancy a drink later?"

"Probs. Ah, speak of the devil. Like the trainers, Fry," she comments with a smile as Fry rounds the corner.

"Yeah, sorry. It's the only thing I had in the car to change into; they were in my gym bag."

"Should've put your shorts on too, your trousers look soaked," Grim says.

"Didn't think that would go down well in the office," Fry explains self-consciously.

"I don't care, but you'd have to watch out for Lo. She can't keep her hands off a man in shorts," Grim comments, walking off down the corridor.

"Fuck off," Logan shouts after him.

"See you later in the Jolly," comes the distant reply.

13

CHAPTER 4
Left Hook

*

"Here, Fry, sit at my desk next to the radiator and dry your trousers," Logan says, getting up from her chair. "I'll go and buy us a coffee while you search for anything on the Godlinghoe Allotment War." Returning a few minutes later with two steaming mugs, she hands one to Fry asking, "Found anything yet?"

"Masses, would you believe," he replies, before instructing the computer screen to change from Single Viewer to Group Viewer. The small cylindrical systems unit removes the dark shield, embosses the writing and enlarges the translucent field to fill the space above the desk. "It goes back to March 11th, 2019. But look at this." Touching the text, he scrolls down until he reaches April 10th, 2023 and clicks to open the article from the local newspaper, The Weekly Echo. The picture loads, showing an elderly woman throwing a punch. The photographer had timed the shot well, it was taken just after the punch made contact with a man in a suit wearing a hard hat. The man's head is caught in the process of reeling back from the impact while the elderly woman, dressed in a tweed skirt and a green quilted jacket, looks like she is going to follow through with a left hook. A crowd of people fill the background while a banner, sporting what looks like a picture of a pie, flies above their heads.

"Ouch, I bet that hurt," Logan winces. "What does the article say?"

"Uhmm… Tempers flared as the Allotment War drew to its

14

inevitable close. With the diggers revved up and ready to roll, council workers started to demolish the barricade. It was then that 83-year-old Mrs Tingle, a founding member of the MPC, Mud Pie Club, stepped forward and engaged Mr Jerkin in a final plea to save her vegetables. 'I asked him very politely,' Mrs Marjorie Tingle told me, 'And he said to stop being an obstinate old bat. Well really, that took the biscuit! And I have to say I lost my temper and gave him what for!'

'You hit him, Mrs Tingle?'

'Yes, and it was marvellous, haven't swung a punch like that in years. Used to be in the Ladies Amateur Boxing Team when I was RAF. Didn't know I still had it in me; must be all those years of digging!'

Sadly, the council had its day and, with the barricade removed, there was little the MPC allotment holders could do but watch as their well-tended plots were decimated. Mr Jerkin has declined to give us an interview, though the council has issued a statement on his behalf saying he will not be pressing charges against Mrs Tingle."

"And that was dated just over three weeks ago," Logan comments, sipping her coffee.

"Yes, it hasn't take them long to dig it all up. There was no evidence of any vegetable beds."

"Who's the reporter?"

"Colin Mercury. He has an office in Braxham Wick."

"Let's give him a ring."

An hour later, Fry, with considerably drier trousers, sits in the passenger seat of Logan's unmarked police car as she parks on Braxham Wick's high street. The afternoon light is dull as they get out and walk towards the glass-fronted office. Pushing the door open, a man looks up from a computer.

"Hi, Mr Mercury? Essex Police, we phoned earlier," Logan says.

"Yes, come in, I'm Colin Mercury."

"Hi Colin, I'm D.C.I. Logan and this is my colleague, D.C. Fry."

"You said on the phone you were interested in the Godlinghoe Allotment War? Is that right?"

"Yes."

"I pretty much covered the whole thing, apart from a couple of pieces by Shiny, but it was me mostly. Is there something in particular you wish to know? It's not Mrs Tingle, she's not in trouble, is she? Or…" Colin pauses as a smile reaches his lips, "is it the body? Dug up this morning, so I'm reliably informed."

"We are presently gathering background information on the site," Logan answers evasively.

"Any news on who it is?" asks Colin with a sparkle in his eye.

"I can't comment at the moment."

"I bet you can't. I'd be surprised though if it's anything to do with the Mud Pie Club. I know Mrs Tingle let fly the other day, but they really aren't violent people, just angry. How long do you think it's been there? Is it male or female?"

"We really can't give you any details at present," Logan asserts calmly.

"Fair enough. So, what can I do you for?"

"The Allotment War, can you give us some background details?"

"Sure."

"Do you mind if we record?"

"Okay." They wait as Fry sets the Cam to holo-record. "Right, it started about four years ago probably stimulated by the banking issues. A bit like the 2008 crisis… you'd think we'd have learnt a thing or two, but never mind, that's a whole different story. Anyway, with the austerity cuts in funding, Braxham Wick District Council, like many others, had to pull their belts in sharpish. They looked around at their assets to see what they could sell. As you are probably aware, allotment land was originally situated on the outskirts of most towns and villages, but due to expansions it's now, more often than not, at the heart of communities, making it very desirable real estate.

The trouble was that allotment land was protected in law until parliament decreed the Freedom of Council Act, with subsection 4 giving councils the right to seize vacant property and land for the purpose of revenue. This made it a prime target for developers and we mustn't forget the old boy network here, but that's another story and hard to prove. However, what many councils underestimated was the allotment holders themselves, and nowhere more so than Godlinghoe.

It all started in a civilised manner with petitions and meetings, before escalating into protests and demonstrations. Braxham Wick District Council was not going to back down and nor were the allotment holders. Rumours and accusations soon followed over who had what fingers in which pies. Alistair Cameron, our most honourable Member of Parliament, was shipped in to reassure the allotment holders that their interests were at the heart of the matter and a new site had been allocated for their needs, only five miles from the village. And yes, it was an old landfill site, but he could personally give absolute reassurance that the soil was wholesome.

The allotment holders hired Watlandsafe, a company that deals in testing rivers and farmland for poisons and pesticides, and their report stated clearly that the land was releasing methane, high in toxins and the water contained leachate liquid, making it, in their opinion, unsuitable soil for growing food. Another meeting was held, attended by Mr Jerkin from Braxham Wick District Council, Alistair Cameron and a fair number of allotment holders from Godlinghoe Allotment. And that was when the first mud pie was thrown. Unfortunately for Mr Cameron, he received a direct hit. Made the front page, brilliant photo, even if I say so myself.

After that, the mud pie became the symbol that rallied the troops, so to speak, and the Mud Pie Club was formed to fight their eviction. They brought a court case against the council, which failed, and the council set a date for the clearance."

"When was this?"

"Autumn of 2022. Anyway, the Mud Pies built a barricade at the allotment gates. It was quite a sturdy affair having been constructed by people who were used to improvising and recycling. It eventually stood ten feet tall with a platform running its whole length.

After that, it was a daily continuance of arguments with the council on one side and the Mud Pie Club on the other. There were a couple of altercations that got out of hand and ended in arrest but the stalemate lasted until April this year. Then the bulldozers arrived and though they were met by a barrage of mud pies and rotten vegetables, the inevitable happened. Old Mrs Tingle was so fired up she punched Mr Jerkin in the face."

"Yes, we saw the photo," Fry smiles.

"Anyway, that's it really, a storm in a teacup or the common man taking on the ruling class, whichever way you wish to see it."

"Do you have any more photos from the site?" Logan asks.

"Yes, quite a few. I popped in most days."

"Can we take copies?"

"Ah, perhaps a deal? You give me first dibs on the body story and I'll email my photos to you?"

"Okay, but it might be awhile until I have a statement and I need the photos now."

"Then I'll just have to take your word for it D.C.I. Logan, and seeing as you're an honest upstanding member of our fine police force, I'm sure you will keep your end of the bargain," he answers with a wry smile.

"Thanks Colin," Logan says, smiling back as Fry clicks off the Cam. "I'll send the photos over tomorrow and I'll look forward to hearing from you."

Outside it had started to rain again. "How useful do you think that was Boss?" Fry asks, pulling his jacket tightly around himself. "It's not as though our body is likely to be a member of the council knocked off by the Mud Pie brigade. It's been in the ground too long for that."

"I know, but there might just be something in those photos. And, if nothing else, we can get a feel of how the site looked before the bulldozers moved in," Logan replies, unlocking the car and gratefully sliding in out of the rain. "Tomorrow I think we should speak to Braxham Wick District Council and find out how long the site has been an allotment." Logan checks the time on her Noc, "It's gone 6:30 Fry, time for you to knock off."

"What about the data I recorded today?"

"It can wait until tomorrow. Leave the Cam with me; I'll lock it up."

Back at the station, Logan transfers the data onto her computer and locks the Cam into the SafeCage. She asks the computer to go to Group Viewer in 3D and sits back and watches the holo-recording from the pit. She's just finishing her notes when her Noc buzzes with a message from Grim:

Stop working. Drink's on the bar.

She smiles, swipes her forefinger across the 3D image to close the screen, grabs her coat and heads for the pub.

CHAPTER 5
Marry Me

Tristan Fry

Parking his car, Fry lets himself through the side gate into the garden and opens the back door.

"That you Tris?" his grandfather calls.

"Hi Frank, yeah just me."

"Mum's at Leroy's, don't expect we'll see her this side of the midnight hour. How was work?"

"I had my first body today."

"I suppose crimes, like hens, come home to roost. I bet that was a sight for sore eyes, seeing it in the flesh so to speak."

"Yeah, you could say that. But it was the smell more than anything. It didn't half make me feel sick."

"A bit of a humdinger?"

"Cor, yes."

"How'd your new D.C.I. cope?"

"Didn't bat an eyelid."

"Tough then?"

"I reckon. What's for supper?"

"Shepherd's pie. Mum's left it in the fridge. I've drawn up some designs for the telescope stand, do you fancy a butchers after we've eaten?"

"Definitely. I've just got to dry my shoes and change."

"Give them here, I'll do it while I'm warming the food."

"Thanks, Frank."

Logan

Logan pushes open the heavy door to the Jolly Fox pub and is met by a roar of noise as police, both plain clothed and uniformed, relax after their long shifts. Spotting Grim at the bar with Daff and Alisha she heads over.

"Hi," she greets them as they unconsciously move to allow her into their circle.

"Hey, Lo, here's the piss water you call a drink," Grim says, handing her a long glass of bitter lemon with ice.

"Cheers," she murmurs, sipping the fizzing liquid. "Ah, that's good. I hope you are not suggesting, D.C.S. Reaper, that I drink and drive."

"Never, D.C.I. Logan, but you could always have a proper drink and bunk at mine."

"I can't, got too much on. I don't know how you guys do it," she grins.

"Easy, it's all in the elbow," Daff answers, raising his beer glass in a salute.

"How'd you get on with the newspaper bloke?" Grim asks. It's his job to know what his D.C.I.s are up to. It should be kept in the office but Grim, being old school, tends to regard the Jolly as an extension of the station.

"Yeah, entertaining. But what he does have is photos of the original site when it was an allotment. He's going to email them over tomorrow in exchange for updates on our body."

"Good."

The chat turns to banter, and after a couple more drinks Daff and then Alisha leave.

"So how are things Lo? Signed those divorce papers yet?" Grim asks solicitously.

"Not yet. Did you hear about Sharon being pregnant?"

"Yep." He'd heard, everyone had. Only yesterday the cunt had been boasting about it in the locker room. Taking a mouthful of beer, he thinks, "Fucking Trevor Dillsworthy, he doesn't want to meet me in

21

a dark alley one night," but aloud he says, "Can't keep a secret in the Essex Police Force Lo, you know that."

"Yeah, I know," she replies resignedly.

"Sign the fucking papers Lo, and be done with the bastard. Move on. You can always marry me." And he grins at her with a big cheesy smile. She laughs.

"Cheers Grim, that's an offer that's hard to refuse."

"Better be quick, I've a queue of women waiting to be asked."

"I'm off, I'll catch up with you tomorrow," she says, finishing her drink.

"See ya in the morning."

"Yeah."

Driving home, the streetlights fade in Logan's rear-view mirror as she leaves the town and joins the A12. The rain splatters across her windscreen, mirroring her mood. She knows the only thing waiting for her is a sad, empty house in the back of beyond. A house she'd never really wanted; a house that Trev had insisted they buy.

"It's out of town Lo, in the middle of nowhere. Clean air, good living," he'd said when they viewed it. "We don't want Trev Jr to have breathing problems. Look at the garden. Perfect. Me and my boy will play footy while you bake cakes."

"Shut up," she'd said laughingly, and though she had known she'd never bake a cake, she'd wanted him to be happy, so she'd agreed to the purchase. They'd moved in and made love the moment the packers had left.

"That'll do it," he'd said afterwards. "That'll be the one." They'd been trying since that night on Scafell Pike. It had been fun, making love anytime, anywhere. But the months had rolled into years and she hadn't fallen pregnant.

"There," she thinks now, as her unmarked police car tears down the outside lane, "That's when I should've put my foot down and stood my ground. But I didn't want to ruin his dreams." Glancing down at her dashboard, she sees that her speed has crept up to 86mph.

"Fuck," she mutters, easing off the accelerator. Taking the next exit, she weaves her way through a small village until she turns down a narrow country road.

Pulling into the driveway, she switches the engine off. The house is shrouded in darkness with only the barest of outlines. She sighs and instructs her Noc to switch all the house lights on before getting out of the car into the damp evening air. Finding her key, she lets herself in at the front door, her footsteps sounding hollow on the bare boards. Once there had been a brightly patterned rug running the length of the hall but, along with everything else that hadn't directly belonged to her, Trev had taken it.

When he'd first left, he'd walked out of the house in just the clothes he was wearing.

He'd driven off in his car and she'd listened as the engine had roared through its gear changes as he'd powered away along the small lane. She'd waited all day and all night for him to return, but he never did. What she got instead was a text message saying:

I need some time to think Lo, some space to sort things out. You know I love you and if you love me you'll understand.

Three months later, he'd messaged again to say he wanted to come by for a chat. She'd agreed, thinking he was ready to come home, to her, to the house he'd loved so much.

"Hey, Lo," he'd said. "Hope you don't mind, but James and Toffee will be round soon with a van."

"Oh," she'd murmured as he walked in.

"Lo, could we have a chat before the others come?"

"Yeah, sure, that would be good. I'll make coffee," she'd responded warmly, trying to hide her hurt.

"No, sorry, I can't stop for coffee. Look, listen, there's no easy way to say this, but…" he'd stopped there, leaving that *but* hanging in the air between them. She'd looked at him, standing there, and she'd known.

"But what, Trev?" she'd challenged.

"Look, Lo, you'll be alright, you always are. You're one of the boys, right?" and her heart had sunk even lower. She'd hidden it by straightening her shoulders and lifting her chin.

23

"Just spit it out Trev," she'd asserted.

"Lo... I've sort've hooked up with someone else. Well actually more than hooked up, I'm moving in with her."

"So this break for you to find some space and sort it out, was all crap then?" she'd thrown back at him.

"Here we go, the hard-faced bitch," he'd yelled at her. "And as it fuckin' happens, I did sort it out. She's gentle, kind, she'll make a great mother." And there it was, the mother thing. The thing she couldn't do. Tears burnt her eyes. "Look, Lo, be honest, you never wanted kids, not really. You're married to the job. I want a wife, a proper wife, not some part-timer who'll fit me in between shifts."

"I am your wife, Trevor," she'd responded passionately.

"Oh, come on Logan, that's crap and we both know it," he'd retorted. "You're not that person, you're not like Shar..." She'd thought afterwards that he'd never meant to say the name, that it had just slipped out.

"Shar?" she'd muttered, etching the question with a sickening horror. "Sharon Mulligan? My best friend, Sharon Mulligan?"

"Yeah and so fucking what. She's got more heart in her little finger than you've got in your whole fuckin' body," he'd bristled defensively.

"Trev, I don't believe it." She'd cried then, her anger giving way to the pain of his betrayal with her best friend. It cut her to the quick. "How could you? How could she? All those late-night calls when I poured my heart out to her, told her how much I loved you and wanted you home. Told her..." She'd stopped then, the truth dawning on her. "Were you there? Oh fuck, you were there, weren't you? You heard it all, you bastard."

"Not such a good detective after all, are you, D.C.I. Logan? Anyway, don't blame Shar. It was you who rung her, going on and on. I don't know why she put up with it."

"She's my best fucking friend," she'd shouted, snot mingling with her tears. Using her sleeve, she'd wiped her face before adding, "I suppose you were tucked up in her bed, making a baby... OH MY GOD, you were!"

"Shut the fuck up Logan, it's none of your fucking business."

"None of my fucking business? You're my husband and she's my best friend … was my best friend. How can it be none of my fucking business?"

"Always the tough tart, aren't you D.C.I. Logan," he'd sneered sarcastically. "Always gotta swear, be one of the boys. Well here's news for you, Detective Bad Ass Logan, I wouldn't want you to be the mother of my kids even if you paid me. I want a proper woman!" She'd grabbed her car keys then and left.

Later, much later, she'd returned to find he'd stripped the house of everything that wasn't hers. Even the things they'd bought together. She'd walked into the sitting room and seen her old sofa abandoned in the large empty space. Upstairs was the same, but worse somehow was the bedroom. Only her clothes hung pathetically in the wardrobe, her old telly lay on its side next to a pile of bedding and a lamp.

"I can't believe you took our bed," she'd moaned, collapsing on the duvet and crying.

Now, walking through into the kitchen, she can't stop herself from glancing across at the table. The divorce papers sit where she'd left them over a month ago.

"Tomorrow. I'll sign them tomorrow," she tells herself, pouring a large glass of red wine and pulling a ready meal from her freezer. Removing the cardboard wrapper without reading the label, she slits the plastic film and heats it in the microwave. Dumping the contents onto a plate, she carries it and the glass through to the sitting room.

Curling up on her old sofa, she switches the telly on and picks at her food.

"Fish pie," she murmurs tasting the first forkful. The telly vibrates garishly around the barely furnished room as she makes herself eat. Giving up after a few mouthfuls, she drains the glass of wine, washes her dirty dishes and goes upstairs.

In bed, she forces herself not to think about Trev's warm, strong body snuggled next to Sharon's swelling belly. Instead she thinks

about the case, going over the facts as though counting sheep. Her Noc buzzes. Picking up the phone she reads a message from Grim:
The offer's still good, marry me :)
Smiling, she turns on her side and goes to sleep.

CHAPTER 6
Tangoed

*

The dawn light wakes Logan. She stays in bed until she can't bear it anymore. Grabbing a coffee, she pulls on her running clothes and lets herself out of the back door. Jogging up the lane, she cuts up the farm track to the small wood. The air is cold, it burns her throat, she pushes her body hard, then harder still, welcoming the physical pain as it smothers her broken heart.

One mile then two, three, four, she can't breathe, she stops. Bending over she rests her hands on her knees and sees mud splattered up her lower legs and over her pink-tipped trainers. Her muscles scream with pain as her chest fights for air.

"Go home," she tells herself and turns into the early morning sunlight.

Showered and dressed in a ubiquitous suit of black with a white shirt, she balances two coffees and a bag of croissants as she walks into her office.

"Hi, Boss, I've made an appointment with the Leisure department," Fry informs her.

"Hey, Fry. Leisure department?" she asks, handing him one of the coffees.

"Thanks. Yep, that's the department the allotments come under at Braxham Wick District Council. It's 10:30 with, would you believe, Mr Jerkin, the bloke that old woman punched. Remember, in the press coverage?"

"Yeah. Okay, that's good. Can you also ask Chillies for a list of missing people from Essex and Suffolk for the period of 1988 to 2010?"

"I'll give it to Andrea, she's pretty good at that sort of stuff."

"Fine, then we'd better get going."

At the council, a neat man greets them and shows them through to his office. Logan can't help but notice the mass of old bruising across his left eye.

"How may I help you?" he asks.

"I expect you've heard that a body was found on Godlinghoe's allotment site?" Logan says, trying not to look at the blackened eye.

"Yes, for a small place it seems to have had more than its fair share of troublesome residents."

"What we need is a plan of the site and the names of the allotment holders."

"I don't expect you'll be wanting a full history. What year are we looking at?"

"From approximately 1980 onwards."

"Let's see," says Mr Jerkin asking his computer for the Trinity Lane allotments, 1980–2023. "Ah yes. Any idea of which plots?"

"Not yet. If we could have a map of the site then we can match it against its current layout."

"You'll be pleased to know that the plot locations haven't changed at all since it was first opened in 1940." Logan is just about to tell Fry to open the Cam, expecting Mr Jerkin to instruct his computer to Group Viewer when he says, "Here we go, map drawer 62, room 12. This way."

They follow him through a series of dusty corridors before entering a long room with a large-paned window at the end of it. In the middle sits a rectangular table, mimicking the shape of the room, with four small paperweights sitting on it. Lining the sides of the room are huge chests of drawers made from solid wood. Each drawer is no deeper than 10 centimetres, though more than a metre wide, with handwritten labels slotted into tarnished brass handles.

"Wow," Fry murmurs in wonderment. "I've never seen anything like this before."

"You'll have to excuse us, we are a bit behind the times here at the council. Lack of funds for modernising. Now, drawer 62." Taking the drawer by the two handles, Mr Jerkin eases it open to reveal a stack of papers.

"Godlinghoe, Trinity Lane, yes," and he pulls out a sheet. Carrying it carefully to the table, he spreads it out, securing each corner with a weight. The parchment has yellowed with age but the diagram lines are still clearly defined.

"Can we take a holo, Mr Jerkin?" Logan asks.

"Yes, do." Pulling the Cam from its bag, Fry scans the map.

"So, what are we looking at Mr Jerkin?" Logan asks.

"93 plots, boundary lines, paths and water standpipes. Each plot is numbered; see here, number 1 then 2 and so on. Each plot is registered to a holder. When you know which plot you are looking at, I will be able to give you a list of the holders' names and addresses."

Out in the car again Fry says, "Cor, that was some room. Have you ever seen anything like it?"

"Would you believe when I first joined the Force, most things were still filed on paper and we still had document drawers like that."

"My grandfather would love that room. He's got a garage full of old stuff like phones, the big old things like bricks with aerials."

"I remember those too."

"I didn't realise you were that old, Boss," Fry smiles.

"Fucking watch it or I'll have you reassigned," Logan laughs back as her Noc and then the in-car computer beeps. "Can you get that, Fry?"

"It's Greyson. Want me to read it out?"

"Yep, maybe news on our body."

Hi Lo, slicing and dicing at 4 if you fancy a gander.

"Looks like we've got ourselves an invite to the P.M. Tell him we'll be there. Have you attended an autopsy before?"

"Yes. No, well sort of," Fry mumbles as he types in the message.

"I've been in the theatre just checking evidence before but never when they're actually doing their thing."

"There won't be any blood or guts I shouldn't think as our body is too far gone for that but it might smell. Will you be okay with that?"

"Hope so, but it was a bit, you know, choice yesterday. It did make me feel slightly sick."

"If you feel sick or faint just say so and leave. I'm not that brilliant at P.M.s either."

Back at the office Fry downloads the allotment map and overlays it with the building site plans. The computer resizes the two maps so they shadow each other, showing the plots beneath the new housing layout. The fit is not exact as the boundaries differ.

"Where do you think the body location is?" Logan asks him. Fry comes around to her side of the holo and thinks for a moment.

"There's the site hut," Fry says, pointing to an area by the entrance gates, "Which near enough lies over plots 1 and 2. So when we entered the site, we walked past the site hut. The end of the hut was at our backs for a while, that's approximately 240° degrees southwest. How far do you think we walked before turning left?"

"Uhmm, about 60 or 70 metres?"

Fry takes out his Noc and calculates the distance by centimetres. Then setting a light beam to 70cm, he lines the Noc to the site hut and pokes the 3D image, instructing it to mark the spot.

"That's a handy app," Logan says admiringly.

"Yep, I picked it up for Frank but he doesn't trust it. He still prefers to use his old tape measure. So, if we walked 70 metres before veering off to the left," Logan nods encouragingly, "How far do you reckon to the hole?"

"Ah, maybe 40 metres?"

Readjusting the Noc's light beam to 40cm, Fry points it at 150° southeast. Logan marks the spot.

"That gives us the top end of plots 41 and 42 and the bottom end of plots 5 and 6. It's a place to start," she says.

"Do you want me to email Mr Jerkin and get a list of plot holders for these plots?"

"Yes, but perhaps ask him for plot 40 and 4 as well." There's a knock at the door. They both look up.

"Hey, Andrea," Fry murmurs shyly. She smiles back at him.

"Hi. Boss, I have the photos from Colin Mercury," Andrea says. "And a list of missing people. I've got three possibles. I've sent the details to your computer."

"Thanks Andrea." Logan asks her computer to show the file. A 2D script immediately streams from her cylindrical systems unit, filling the air with words. "Can you talk us through it, Andrea?"

"Sure. Okay, so the first and most likely candidate, by a country mile, is Victor Martin. Walked out on his family Christmas 1997, aged 45. His description is a fairly good match for the body. Ginger hair, with a moustache. Family home was Ipswich, though his wife now lives in Braxham Wick. I've attached a photo." They all look at a stocky man with short wavy hair, sporting a bushy moustache and wearing a highly colourful flower-patterned, short-sleeved shirt. He stands with his family against a backdrop of bright blue skies and palm trees.

"Looks like a holiday snap," Fry comments.

"Next is Guy Abbott. Not such a good match. Aged 23, disappeared after a night out in 1992. Parents reported him missing." Again, there's a picture attached. This time it's of a long-haired, slim-built youth on a skateboard. "Lastly, Walter Whitcomb, aged 67. Lived alone in Podhamlea, Essex. Reported missing by a neighbour. Vague description, but what we have would only fit with a big push. No photo this time."

"Let's take a closer look at Victor Martin. Do you have an address and telephone number for Mrs Martin, Andrea?"

"Yes, I'll send it to Fry's Noc and give her a ring. Do you want to go now?"

Logan checks the time. "Yeah, if she's in, then we can go straight to the P.M. from there."

"Fuck, you've been invited to the autopsy?" Grim exclaims, coming into the office.

"I know, it's got to be a first," Logan responds, raising an eyebrow.

"Jammy fucker," he says with a snort. "How's it going anyway?"

"Good. Fry's pretty much worked out where the body was buried and Andrea's printed off the press photos."

"Let's see," he says, taking them from Andrea and shuffling through them. "Whoa, that's a corker. Alistair Cameron tangoed with a mud pie."

Logan looks. "Colin said it'd made the front page."

"Boss?" Andrea says.

"Yeah?"

"Mrs Martin is at home and I said you'd be there within the hour."

"We'd better go, Fry; you can email Jerkin for the plot holders in the car."

"Okay. See you later Andrea… maybe in the bar?" Fry says, his voice full of uncertainty.

"Uhm, yes, I'll be there," Andrea murmurs back shyly.

Grim smiles and adds, "So will I. Have fun with Greyson."

"Line that bitter lemon up. I've got a feeling I'm going to need it," Logan smiles back.

CHAPTER 7
Special Air Service

*

"I never imagined the Martins would live in such a rough area from the photo we have of them," Fry says.

"Yep, I know what you mean, but I bet there's a story behind this location," Logan replies, driving slowly along a street littered with burnt-out cars. She slows down even more as they pass a fenced area containing a bright red frame that had once supported children's swings. All that remain are six chains that dangle at different lengths.

"What number is it?" she asks, parking the car next to a block of rundown flats.

"49, level four." Slumped against the wall next to the entrance is an old, stained mattress, smelling of piss. They give it a wide berth as they enter. The inside is no more welcoming, with an even stronger stench of filth and an empty lift shaft.

"It'll be the stairs then," comments Logan.

As they climb the cold concrete steps, they hear an irregular thump-thumping ahead. Turning for the second flight, they see an old man dragging a battered shopping trolley up behind him.

"Do you want a hand with that, mate?" Fry asks. The man looks up. Grey flesh droops from his face like melted plastic, while his hooded eyes are tinged with milky cataracts and his nose runs with colourless snot.

"F off, you little bastard. You'll not rob me. I'm SAS, I could kill you with my bare hands."

"I wasn't going to…" Fry stammers back.

"Didn't you hear me? F off."

Logan pulls at Fry's arm. "Leave him," she says, adding quietly, "He's scared," and she steps around the defenceless old man who can barely lift his shopping trolley, let alone kill someone with his bare hands.

"But…"

"I know, Fry. It's just the way it is sometimes."

"But he's the same age as my granddad. He shouldn't be scared. We should report this to the council and get him rehomed," Fry argues, following her up the stairs.

"They won't help him."

"Why not? Surely that's why we pay our council tax to support people like him."

"You want to blame anyone, blame the people who voted for the austerity cuts." They reach the third floor and start climbing again.

"What flat number did you say it was?" Fry knows she remembers, but realises it's her way of moving things along.

"49, Boss." On the fourth floor, they find Mrs Martin's flat and knock at the door. A moment passes before a timid voice comes from the other side.

"Hello?"

"Hello, Mrs Martin. It's Essex Police, D.C.I. Logan and D.C. Fry."

A bolt slides back from its housing, accompanied by the dropping of tumblers as a key is turned. The door opens a crack and a middle-aged woman peeps around its edge.

"Hello, Mrs Martin, sorry to disturb you. We wonder if we may have a word with you?" Logan asks gently.

"Yes," she says, opening the front door and letting them in.

"Thank you," Logan replies brightly, holding out her I.D. card.

"Please come through to the sitting room," Mrs Martin offers, leading the way. They enter a small room with neat furnishing in muted colours. On the wall above the sofa is a large family portrait photograph.

"Please sit."

"Mrs Martin, would you mind if we recorded this meeting?"

"No, I suppose not," she answers cautiously. Logan looks at Fry who is already setting up the Cam.

"I need to clarify, for the Cam, that you are Mrs Christina Martin."

"Yes."

"And you are married to Victor Martin?"

"Yes," confirms Mrs Martin again, but this time her voice wavers nervously.

"Did you report Victor missing in 1997?"

"Yes."

"Have you heard from Victor since you reported him missing?"

"No, not a thing. Vic said he was going to buy a newspaper on Christmas Eve, 1997. He put his coat on, waved to the kids, who were watching telly, and walked out of the door. I was busy in the kitchen preparing our Christmas dinner for the following day and didn't think much about it until an hour or so had passed." Tears fill the woman's eyes and her chin puckers with emotion. "I sat up all night waiting. I was so worried; I thought he must've had an accident. I phoned all the local hospitals, then the police." She pulls a hanky from her sleeve and blows her nose. "Sorry," she adds.

"There's no need to be sorry, Mrs Martin," Logan reassures her while Fry vigorously nods his head.

"Of course, the police said not to worry and that he'd more than likely turn up, but he never did."

"That's very difficult for you, Mrs Martin," Logan acknowledges and Fry nods again.

"Yes, very difficult, but it's the children who've suffered. You see, they think it's their fault in some way, though they were only little, eight and five years old. They'd both been abandoned by their birth mothers already, then Vic left them… and they thought they were unlovable." Mrs Martin glances up at the huge photo on the wall as fresh tears trickle down her lined cheeks. "Poor little Kyra; she committed suicide in 2010."

"Oh, no," murmurs Fry as they both turn and look up at the little girl in the picture, who smiles eagerly at the camera while holding her father's hand.

"She was at university, had her whole life ahead of her, but she couldn't get over the fact her Dad didn't love her. I told her he did, that something dreadful must've happened for him to have left us. But it wasn't enough and she jumped in front of a train. And Danny," again they all look at the photo of a dark-haired boy who leans shyly against his mother, "he never gave us a day of trouble until Vic left. He's killing himself in another way, with drugs and alcohol."

"Where's Danny now?" Fry asks.

"In prison. Drug offences. It never helped him moving here."

"You used to live in Ipswich?" Logan asks.

"Yes, I lost the house when I couldn't pay the mortgage. We had plenty of insurance cover but the company refused to pay unless I had a death certificate. The council moved us here when I was repossessed. I suppose I should feel grateful for being given a flat to rent but it's quite a difficult place to live."

"Yes, it is," Logan acknowledges.

"I'm sure Vic never meant for all this to happen."

"Mrs Martin," Logan begins, keeping a steady voice. "You may have heard that we have recently recovered the remains of a man at Godlinghoe. We have been interviewing anyone who has reported a person missing who fits the description."

"Oh, do you think it could be Vic?" Mrs Martin responds with hope in her voice.

"We can't say at this stage. Would it be welcome news if it were your husband?" Logan asks, treading carefully.

"Oh yes, it would be such a relief if he'd been dead all this time."

"Why do you say that, Mrs Martin?"

"Because it would mean that he loved us," she cries, "It would mean that he never meant to leave us, that some kind of terrible accident took him from us."

Logan waits until Mrs Martin's sobs lessen before asking, "You said earlier that both children had been adopted?"

"Yes. I never seemed to be able to fall pregnant." Logan's heart gives a sudden lurch and then pounds uncomfortably in her chest. "Vic never complained. It was his idea to adopt and I was very happy to go along with it. First, we were given Kyra, then Danny came along six years later." Mrs Martin glances up at the photo again.

"Does Vic have any biological relatives?"

"No, his parents are long dead and his brother died a bachelor."

"Do you have anything of Vic's, say, like a hairbrush?"

"No, I must admit when we moved I tried to make it a new start for the children and I got rid of Vic's possessions. Is that a problem?"

"No, that's fine. Can you tell us where he grew up?"

"Birmingham, mainly, but he spent the first ten years of his life in Bristol. Is that important?"

"It could be," Logan says, standing and putting out her hand.

Mrs Martin clasps it tightly in both of hers. "Do you think it's him? I could tell Danny, and-and you never know, that might just help him."

"I'll let you know as soon as we have an identification," Logan assures her.

At the front door, Mrs Martin slides the bolt back and turns the key. Logan is about to say goodbye when Fry stops.

"Mrs Martin, if the body is Vic's, will the insurance company pay out?"

"Um, I suppose so, yes, because I'll have a death certificate. Oh, I could move and give Danny a better home, get him away from all the addicts that live here," she answers optimistically.

"It would solve a lot of Mrs Martin's problems if it is him," Fry comments back in the car.

"I know," Logan agrees as she starts the engine.

"Shame about the DNA. That's going to make it almost impossible to prove it is Victor Martin."

"Yes, but on the other hand, it won't rule him out either," she replies as they drive back past the sad playground.

CHAPTER 8
Mouldy Old Cheese

*

Logan and Fry walk through a set of double doors into a room lined with stainless steel floor-to-ceiling refrigerators.

"Hi," greets Greyson, from a small office at the far end.

"Hi, Greyson," Logan replies, smiling at the dark-haired man dressed in white scrubs walking towards them.

"Hello, Fry."

"Hi, Greyson," Fry mumbles nervously.

"Welcome to my office. Let me show you around." Logan and Fry follow Greyson down the line of fridge doors.

"These here," he says, indicating to their left. "Hospital stiffs. And these shiny fridges, which you can probably see are brand new, are for the fatties who can no longer be squeezed into Mr Average's drawers. I have the odd client stowed in there myself. On the right, we have the under eighteens and, last but not least, my section – suspicious deaths, clothing and items for forensic analysis."

Grabbing a trolley, Greyson wheels it to the fridge and opens the door. A swirl of cold air seems to wrap itself around them, drawing them forward towards the metal racks. Logan can clearly see three heads stacked one on top of the other and, next to them, shelves containing bagged items.

"Three customers pending. Here's our lad," says Greyson, jacking the trolley up to the corresponding height and sliding a stainless-steel tray containing a body covered by a white plastic sheet from the middle section. "Please come through." Swiping his security card, he guides the trolley through another set of double doors into a large room shining with yet more stainless steel. Five metal operating tables with blood gullies and sinks fill the main space. Above each table is a network of electronics and screens. Corresponding workstations, with knives, weighing scales and microscopes run the length of the far wall.

"It looks like a cross between an operating theatre and a space capsule," Logan thinks as she watches Greyson, with practised ease, slide the metal tray onto one of the tables.

"Roger, Wendy," Greyson calls. Two people decked in matching scrubs, aprons and scrub caps emerge from the office.

"You called?" says the taller of the two, humorously.

"May I introduce our guests today: D.C.I. Logan and D.C. Fry. And these are my partners in crime, Wendy Selby and Roger Chase."

"Hi," Wendy says with a friendly smile, while Roger salutes theatrically.

"Hi," Logan and Fry say in unison.

"Can you prep please?"

"We are here to serve," Roger states formally, though Logan sees the shared smile pass between the three of them. Donning full-face masks and disposable gloves, they set up a small trolley with knives, scalpels, tweezers and probes. A strong smell of mouldy, old cheese mixed with putrescent meat wafts up from the table when Roger removes the sheet. Logan's toes curl in disgust and she feels Fry shift next to her. She stills her emotions and looks at the body.

The skull, with its smashed nasal bone, sits at the top of the spine, tilted forward onto the jawbone. She can clearly see, now that its muddy coating has been washed away, that the hair is definitely red. A patch of shrivelled skin stretches down the left side of the face with the remains of a moustache still attached. But that's not what makes her take a step closer.

"That's weird," she remarks.

"Yeah, isn't it," Greyson acknowledges, smiling back at her. "I've only had a couple of others before. This ballooning of grey matter on the lower left side of the body is called adipocere or grave wax. It's a process known as saponification where subcutaneous fat is turned into a type of soap, creating a cast. Rumour has it that there was a character called Augustus Granville in the 1800s who actually made candles out of it for his dissection lectures." Logan hears Fry swallow hard and knows how he feels.

"That must've been fun," Roger states sarcastically, offering Greyson a mask and gloves before switching on the overhead Cam. "Consequently, we've named him Waxy." Both Wendy and Roger confirm this by nodding.

"Right, let's begin. We have a body in an advanced state of decomposition with clear adipocere formation, mainly left side, leg, buttock and torso." Greyson, taking a probe, taps the wax-like material causing a hollow tone. Logan's stomach lurches.

"Unfortunately, the adipocere gives no indication of the post-mortem interval, date of death, as it can persist for many years. But it may give us some idea of body type, injuries and burial conditions. Adipocere tends to develop in environments high in moisture and low in oxygen, which suggests Waxy was almost certainly wet before being placed in the body bag and buried at an approximate depth of 1.8 metres."

"Do you mean he could have been drowned?" Logan asks.

"There's not enough of him left to test that theory but maybe, though he would've had to have been fully submerged. He could equally have taken a shower just before he was killed and buried.

So, I.C.1, male. Germanic descent, skin tone fair, hair coarse in texture, light red, no male-patterned baldness, facial hair, a darker shade of head hair. I think we can presume his hair colour is natural. Once the D.N.A. and isotope results are back, we will have a more accurate picture. No new bone growth here as nasal bone was broken during or after death. Biological age at time of death I set between 38 and 50 from pubic symphyses wear. Again, I will be able to narrow it down when I have the results. Height," Roger picks up a Noc and holds it adjacent to the top of the skull as Greyson reads off the measurement at the anklebone, "1.76m. Weight is going to be a bit of a guessing game. I'd put his weight at between 98 and 115kg. What do you think, Wendy?"

"Yeah, I'll go with that."

"Roger?"

"Yep."

"So, definitely overweight with his subcutaneous fat lying heaviest around his lower torso, buttocks and legs, though breast fat here too. I'd say not a manual worker, probably someone who sat down to work. But here's something you don't see everyday," Wendy and Roger immediately peer closer. "The cervical and upper thoracic, humerus, radius and ulna, arm bones, and yes, look the hands, the metacarpus and phalanges have abnormal bone density. And, I wonder…" Taking hold of the skull, Greyson tips it back and eases the lower jaw open. "Yes, the mandible and temporomandibular joint as well all show signs of long-term stress." Roger and Wendy both murmur their agreement but all Logan can see is bones and teeth.

"What does it signify?" she asks.

"It means that although Waxy wasn't very fit and was certainly overweight, he exerted considerable and repeated physical pressure on his upper body, arms and mouth."

"Like a weight lifter or boxer?" Fry asks.

"In the way that their activity is repetitive and unvarying. But this activity is very particular."

"Can you be more specific?" Logan probes.

"Put it this way, the last time I saw this type of bone stress coupled with a larger lower body mass was on a middle-aged woman whose occupation was as a sex worker, with a speciality in oral sex."

"Could Waxy be a sex worker then?" Logan asks.

"Could be. Right, moving on. Roger, Wendy, can you lift the left leg? Now, see here where the adipocere formation has a clear indentation around the calf; that's where the rope ran around the outside of the bag."

"Would the rope have needed to be secured tightly to have done that?" Fry asks.

"Yes, very. Whoever tied this was physically strong. And knew their knots. To be more accurate, there were two ropes. One has decayed but the other is still pretty much intact. Which leads us to the nature of the rope. It is a specialised climbing rope."

"What, like rock climbing?" Fry interjects.

"Exactly. Diameter is 9mm, colour red. And the whole climbing aspect is collaborated by the knot. A standard grapevine bend. I think the two ropes ran in opposite directions, round the back of Waxy's lower leg and neck, which probably explains why the skull was partly detached and then dropped loose when the bag was dug up."

"So, the body was bent double," Fry states.

"To be more accurate, the bag was bent double, so the body inside was too."

"Anything on the body bag, Greyson?" Logan asks.

"Yes, I was saving the best for last," he answers, and she knows, somehow, he's smiling at her from behind his mask. "The body bag has stood the test of time and burial. It says Braxham Wick Hospital Batch ID-0659-AC3."

"Wow," exclaims Fry, "That's here, this hospital."

"I thought you'd be pleased."

"I don't suppose there's a date on that bag?" Logan pursues.

"And yes again, I think you'll like this. The bags were specifically designed for one purpose. When this hospital decided to specialise in the selling of organs for transplants they saw a need for body bags. This batch was ordered in 1996."

"That means Waxy was not buried before 1996," Fry smiles.

"Precisely. But, even better. Wendy checked and the following batch of body bags was ordered in 1999. Which kinda matches nicely and gives us a date of burial set between 1996 and 1999."

"Brilliant," Fry exclaims.

"Anything else?" Logan asks.

"Yes. He was virtually naked but for the remains of a binding tied around his neck." Addressing the Cam, Greyson asks it to show image 48. The holo flickers through the 3D stills until the headless corpse appears, with a gloved finger holding a dirty cord of some sort away from the vertebra. "This was tied around the neck."

"Could he have been hung or strangled with it?" Logan asks.

"I doubt it, too flimsy. And it was knotted in a neat bow. Wendy has cleaned and analysed the binding and it appears to be a fastening from a hospital gown, the sort used for surgery."

"Wow again," Fry exclaims enthusiastically.

"Too right," Greyson agrees.

"Do you think he could've been a patient here who died under suspicious circumstances. A cover up." Logan suggests.

"Maybe. We debated it," Greyson says, looking at his team who nod their heads, "but we decided that if he had been a patient here, why would anyone have gone to all that trouble of burying him out at Godlinghoe when all they would've had to do is register him as a John Doe and ship him out with the paupers' cremation collection."

"Is that possible?" Logan queries.

"Not now that all our cadavers are electronically chipped, but back in the 90s everything was done on paper making it easy to forge a document, especially if you worked here.

Lastly, along with the body was a bundle of clothes, well more fragments of corrupted cloth, but Wendy managed to discern good-quality denim, probably jeans, and a synthetic fleece material, the sort that would line jackets, for example a baseball jacket. Shoes, black leather, slip-ons, size 9. Not a cheap shoe but not handmade. Deep inside, which is probably why it has survived, was the remains of a white ankle sock, sports type. That's about it until I receive the test results back."

"Cheers, Greyson, that was really informative," Logan says, smiling at him and realising she's forgotten all about feeling queasy.

"I'll send you a copy of the P.M. report as soon as I've completed it."

CHAPTER 9
Rakey Thin

*

"How'd it go?" Grim asks, leaning against the bar, beer in hand.

"Do you know what, it was really interesting. Want another?" she says, pointing to his drink.

"I might just squeeze one in," he answers, draining his glass.

"Fry?" she asks.

"Pint of lager, please."

"Another in there," she says to the barman, pointing to Grim's glass, "And a pint of lager and a bitter lemon with ice too, please."

"Oh come on, Lo, it's Friday night. Why don't you stay and have some fun, be a real copper for a change? You can always stay at mine."

Fry takes his lager, thanks Logan and heads off towards a group of people, including Andrea, sitting in the far corner.

"I thought I'd work tomorrow, get going on building an I.D. for Waxy."

"Waxy?"

"Yeah, that's what Greyson has christened him."

"Hah, typical Greyson. Come on, let me put a fucking gin in that lemon. Look, even your D.C. is having fun." Logan glances across the pub and sees Fry deep in conversation with Andrea. She smiles.

"Fuck Lo, don't make me beg."

"Okay," she says and holds her glass out.

Several drinks later, her and Grim endeavour to walk back to his flat. She's had him in fits of laughter describing the moment she wasn't at all sure whether she'd be staying for the whole autopsy, what with the waxy soapy stuff. Swiping his electronic entrance key, Grim lets them in and makes straight for the American-style fridge. He grabs a couple of beers and flips the lids. Handing one to Logan, he settles himself into his Lazyboy chair while she sprawls across his huge black leather sofa, undoing the button on her suit trousers. Logan knows this sofa well. She's spent many a night on it over the years, sitting up drinking into the early hours playing one of Grim's latest war games on his massive 3D telly.

When she'd first started dating Trev, he'd not said much about her relationship with Grim, but after a few months he started to drop hints that soon turned into accusations.

"What's with you and Grim?" he'd asked accusingly.

"Nothing. Just mates," she'd replied honestly.

"That's not what I've heard."

"That's just the usual crap that goes around the station."

"But Jesus, Lo, it makes me look bad," he'd kept on.

"I don't see why," she'd snapped back, feeling irritated.

"Cause it makes me look like a twat. You off fucking about with Grim and me waiting around."

"Don't be a prat, Trev." After Trev had left her she'd virtually moved in with Grim. His flat had been a safe place for her when she hadn't wanted to go back to the house.

"I still can't believe Greyson let you sit in on one of his autopsies," Grim says, picking up the conversation again.

"Yeah," she answers thoughtfully, remembering his bright blue eyes smiling at her through the mask.

"What?" Grim asks light-heartedly.

"What?" she replies, smiling.

"You... you're smiling. I've not seen you smile like that in ages."

"I don't know," she murmurs, "I think it's Greyson; he makes me smile."

"From what I've heard he makes a lot of fucking people smile," and they both roar with laughter. "Oh, and by the way, I've made a new playlist. I've sent it to your Noc."

"More 70s hits?" she asks, raising an eyebrow.

"You know me too well, but in my defence, it's a remix."

Waking up, Logan squints her eyes against the early morning sun streaming in through Grim's sitting-room window. Crawling gingerly from her makeshift bed, she goes to the kitchen and makes herself a strong coffee. Opening the huge fridge for milk, she is reminded briefly of yesterday's adventure at the mortuary.

"No milk, typical," she thinks. Taking her mug and draping a blanket around her shoulders, she opens the glass door onto the balcony. Slipping through, she closes it quietly behind her. Sitting on one of the chairs, she sips the hot coffee. Clouds skate across the bright, blue sky and, like always when time hangs on her, her mind drifts towards memories of Trev.

"He loves this time of morning—fresh and bright. He'd be demanding we should get up and do something—go for a walk, plant a tree, make a baby," and there it was, her failure as a woman.

Abandoning her coffee, she leaves the flat. The streets are already busy with early morning shoppers and marketers setting up their stalls. She weaves her way through to the large chemist and buys a personal hygiene travel set. At the station, she goes to the toilet and brushes her teeth, cleans her face and sprays deodorant under her arms. Running her fingers through her short hair, she glances the mirror. A thin, dark-haired woman looks straight back at her.

"Not even fashionably thin," she murmurs at the image. "Just rakey thin."

Her Noc buzzes. She pulls it out from her pocket; it's a message from Trev.

Sign the fucking papers

Shoving the phone back into her pocket she leaves the toilet. The corridors are quiet, with just an odd detective at a desk. In her office, she starts to build a profile for Waxy but her mind just keeps flicking back to the text.

"Fuck it," she mutters, closing her computer.

Driving home she lets herself into the house, changes into some joggers and an old t-shirt.

"Link to speakers, Grim's remix," she orders her Noc. By the time she's done sing-sobbing her way through *Love to Love You Baby*, she's scrubbed out the kitchen and bathrooms, washed her clothes and microwaved a lasagne. Flopping onto her old sofa with the plate of food she really doesn't want, she replaces Grim's 70s hits with the telly. Her Noc buzzes; it's Greyson.

P.M. report completed and if you're kicking your heels tomorrow and fancy a cuppa,

I'll be on my allotment. It's Duck Lane, Little Marney. Just follow the road into the village, turn right at the pub. Allotment is on left.

She thinks, "Why the hell not?" and types back:

Thanks.

CHAPTER 10
Castles and Gods

*

The morning is chilled, though the scent of blossom fills the cold air. Logan runs along the narrow lane before cutting up the farm track to the small wood. The mud has solidified and small pockets of rainwater sparkle in the spring sun. The world feels still to her as she pushes herself beyond her physical pain. Reaching the wood, she stops and catches her ragged breath. After a moment she stands and rubs the cramp from her side. Then turning for home, she pushes herself hard. Her body fights for oxygen, blotting out her emotional pain.

At home she showers, slips on some jeans, a t-shirt and an oversized jumper that had once belonged to Grim. Grabbing a hastily-made sandwich, she gets in her car and tells her Noc to find Duck Lane Allotments, Little Marney.

Reaching Braxham Wick, the computer guides her around the large town and out towards the coast. Following the route, she turns off and weaves her way through ever-smaller villages until she sees the sign for Little Marney.

"God, and I thought I lived out in the sticks," she murmurs as she takes another tight bend and enters the village. Driving past an old-fashioned village green ringed by Tudor-beamed cottages, she turns right at the pub into Duck Lane. After a few more cottages, the lane narrows down into a series of twists and turns. Around yet another bend she sees three cars parked in a small car park and one of them is Greyson's dark-green Golf.

Pulling in, she stops and switches her engine off. She's just wondering where the actual allotments are when a woman appears through a gap in the hedgerow.

"Excuse me, I'm looking for the allotments," Logan asks.

"You're here," replies the woman. "Just follow the path and you'll soon see them, dear."

"Thanks." Through the hedge she finds a footpath, which is not much more than a narrow tunnel of arching trees and shrubs. Winding her way through, she makes out a patch of sunlight at the tunnel's end. Heading towards it, she emerges into an open space full of allotment plots.

There are a few people dotted about, but she easily spots Greyson and finds herself smiling as she looks at the man digging the soil. "He's not good looking in the way Trev is, but he has something. Well, he must have something according to station gossip," she muses. He stops and turns towards her, as though he has sensed her presence.

"Hey, Logan," he calls. "You made it then."

"Yeah, it's a bit of an adventure. Luckily, my Noc knew where it was going."

"Some tea to revive you?" he asks, indicating to a low table made from a tree stump next to a long bench made from a log.

"Sounds good," she replies and sits down. Pouring two mugs, he hands her one and sits next to her. She finds herself noticing a smell of fresh sweat mixed with a fragrance from either washing powder or shampoo. She'd quite like to lean closer and smell him some more.

"Logan?"

"Oh, sorry, I was miles away."

"Somewhere nice I hope."

"Sort of," she murmurs. "Nice allotment."

"Yeah, I like it. It's really quiet and good for my head, especially if I've spent the weekend partying."

"Is this where you live? The village I mean."

"Yep, moved out of London in 2015. Wanted a slightly more sedate lifestyle but still be close enough to London to enjoy the nightlife. Would you believe there's a railway station here? Not a direct line, but even so I can still be in London in 50 minutes. It's a good place for me to live."

"Do you have family here?"

"No," smiles Greyson. "They live on a remote island off Scotland in a sort of rundown castle that's barely habitable. Their ethos is live off the land and God will provide."

"Are they religious?"

"Nah, they just pray to whichever god suits their purpose at the time, Ēostre, Odin, Athena, Jesus, etc."

"I like that, a policy that covers all bases."

"I think that's the general idea. Believe in a god just in case you find out that there is an afterlife and, if not, there's no skin off your nose," he answers with a smile.

"And you, do you pray to a higher being just in case?"

"Nah, not me. I'm too much of a scientist, that's my religion. What about you?"

"I'm too much of a police officer," she smiles back. "Did you grow up in a castle then?"

"Yeah," he laughs. "The truth is it was very cold and damp and full of rodents. There are a fair few of us brothers and sisters. We all have names connected to some earth god or other, including the surname Stonewalker."

"Was that something your parents chose then?"

"Yeah, I blame the hippy existence and too much sci-fi. We all live across the world now but we try to get home en masse at Christmas. It's always a dash for the last ferry on Christmas Eve. What about your family? Are they local?"

"No. East London, one brother who has got a couple of kids. I moved to Chelmsford to join Grim's team." She sips her tea, it's hot and sweet and surprisingly good.

"I reckon that was a good move."

"Yeah. And while we are on the subject of Grim, do you really play bowls or is that something just to wind him up with?"

"Yes, for my sins," he answers, laughing again. "What about you? What's your thing? Are you a secret knitter or perhaps a bell ringer?"

"Me? I… nothing, work, run a bit, get drunk with Grim, play video games and argue over music." She watches him as he pulls on a jumper and cups his hands back around his mug.

"Sounds good to me. Do you know we met before I took the forensic job here?"

"Really?" she says, thinking, "I'm sure I'd have remembered you."

"You don't remember, do you? Go on, own up," he says, nudging her with his elbow.

"Okay, you're right, I don't remember."

"It was towards the end of my training. We were working on the 2009 London bombing. You and Grim were on the case and Adrian Trent sent me to Chelmsford with a report."

"I remember that case. That was the last time I was in Godlinghoe before Waxy." And Trev was there too she thinks, before changing the subject. "So, what do you grow here?" she asks.

"Some potatoes, legumes, the odd carrot, onion and beetroot. I'm not what you'd call fully committed but I love it here. I think some of the other allotmenteers think I'm a right lightweight but that's not really why I come here."

"Why do you come here?"

"It gives me a sense of life. Nothing here is hurried. I love the contrast to my job and social life." A picture of Greyson's long, lean body, naked and entwined around another human form flashes through her mind, making her redden.

"You okay?" he asks, looking at her quizzically.

"Yeah, yeah just thinking about the autopsy," she lies, hoping that one of his many talents isn't mind reading.

"Interesting."

"What?" she says in alarm.

"The P.M. on Waxy. I've only had a couple of adipoceria corpses before."

"Yeah, really weird stuff," she answers, relieved.

"How're things going with the investigation? Have you found an I.D. for him?"

"Maybe," she says hesitantly.

"Go on."

"Well, it's a goodish match. Victor Martin. Disappeared Christmas 1997. But it could be a bit of wishful thinking."

"Why?"

"It's just that if it is him, it will make such a huge difference to the family he left behind."

"In what way?"

"They've had a rough time. One child committed suicide and the other is an addict. If Waxy turns out to be Victor Martin it would explain why he left them. They lost their home too because the insurance company wouldn't pay out without a death cert."

"That's difficult."

"I know. The trouble is I can feel myself getting caught up in their story rather than sticking to the facts."

"Is that a bad thing?"

"Says the scientist," she smiles, poking her elbow into his ribs this time.

Another hour and two more cups of tea pass in easy conversation before she decides to head off. Back on the road, she smiles at the thought of what Grim will say when he hears where she has spent her Sunday afternoon.

CHAPTER 11
A Mad Murdering Religious Cat Woman

Monday morning is grey with clouds that are heavy with unshed rain. Logan parks her car in the police compound and takes the stairs two at a time up to her office. Her legs complain after the pounding she'd given them the day before.

"Morning, Boss," Fry greets her, looking happy.

"Hi, Fry."

"Mr Jerkin's list of holders is in and Andrea and I have been matching Colin Mercury's photos to our co-ordinates for Waxy."

"Good work. The P.M.s in too. Let's check it out and see if Greyson's placed Waxy in a similar position." Asking her systems unit to show the autopsy report on Group Viewer, she and Fry begin to read it.

"Isotope results show that during tooth formation he lived in the West Country, so that matches nicely with Victor Martin," Fry comments. "And age is a good match as well." She can tell Fry's pleased and she too is starting to feel that familiar tingle of excitement when answers marry up to questions.

"Right, here's Greyson's co-ordinates," she points to the sentence.

"Looks like he's run into the same problem we had plotting an exact location on the allotment site," states Fry.

"Yeah, looks like he's gone for …plots 42 and 5."

"Cor, we weren't far out."

"We'll focus on the 1997 plot holders for 5 and 42 first then. Let's see Mercury's photos of those plots."

"Here." Fry picks up four photos and lays them out. "Andrea worked out that this is plot 5 and this is 42." Logan notices he wants to give Andrea the credit; she likes that. "5 is sort of neat and tidy, all ordered, but 42 looks a bit messy."

"Who does Mr Jerkin say the plots belonged to?"

"Uhmm," Fry checks his Noc. "You'll never guess who had plot 5," he says, smiling broadly.

"Go on," Logan smiles back encouragingly.

"The notorious, ex-RAF, fist swinger herself, Mrs Tingle. Lives out at St Ella, 2 Chimney Street."

"That should make it interesting."

In the car, Fry asks his Noc to send the route to the in-car computer as they head out of Chelmsford.

"Good weekend?" Logan asks him.

"Great. Frank and I built a stand for our telescope."

"For the Mars launch on Thursday?"

"Yeah, we're really looking forward to it."

"We've got a girl going up, haven't we?"

"Asha Blackthorne," he says, and she hears the pride in his voice.

"Trev'll love all that," she thinks, with a stab of pain.

"Boss?"

"Nothing. Isn't she British Army?"

"Yeah, Army Major. She's captaining Maya-Daughter then Maya-Complete on the outward journey. Frank and I are going to India next year to visit the Satish Dhawan World Space Station." They chat about the Mars project until they turn off for St Ella. At 2 Chimney Street, they knock at the front door of a small bungalow.

"Good morning, Mrs Tingle? Chelmsford CID. D.C.I. Logan and D.C. Fry."

"I've already said I'm sorry for punching Mr Jerkin," she states defiantly.

"It's nothing to do with that, Mrs Tingle. It's about the body."

"Well in that case, you can come in." A cup of tea later, Mrs Tingle confirms she was indeed the holder of plot 5 but no, she doesn't know who the body is or how it got there.

Leaving St Ella, rain splatters the windscreen between the rhythmic arcing of the car's wipers.

"I can't see Mrs Tingle murdering anyone and burying them in her allotment," Fry says as the small village fades behind them in the grey afternoon light.

"She did give Mr Jerkin one hell o' a punch though."

"Yeah, but she's basically an honest person."

"I think she's mentally capable."

"What, of murder?" Fry questions.

"Mrs Tingle is ex-R.A.F., so she would've had to be prepared to take a life."

"Isn't that different?"

"Different in detail but no different in having the ability to kill. But she'd have needed quite a bit of assistance lifting that body, unless she'd had a winch."

"I had to help lift an inebriated man onto a bench once and damn, that was hard enough. And she'd have been in her sixties too."

"I don't think age has ever been a barrier to the likes of Mrs Tingle. Anyway, who's next?"

Opening his Noc, Fry reads, "Plot 42 was held by Maggi Drew at the time of the murder. Address 33 Peartree Road, Godlinghoe. I'll enter it into the in-car computer."

"Andrea given you anything on Maggi Drew?" Logan asks, glancing at the screen.

"Date of birth 21.7.55, which makes her 68."

"She'd have been approximately 42 at the time of the murder. Younger than Mrs Tingle."

"She does have a partner too, Jonathan Gifford. The electoral role has them living together from 1998."

"More promising by the minute. Anything else of interest?"

"Only that she held plot 42 from 1981 to 2017. Nothing more."

At the crossroads, they turn for Godlinghoe. As they climb the hill, Logan asks, "How's things going with Andrea?"

"Good. We're going on a proper date tomorrow."

"Where are you thinking of going?" she asks as they pass the church.

"Probably just the Jolly."

"You could always go somewhere different. What about the new club that's just opened in town?" she suggests, turning left.

"I'm not sure, I think Andrea likes the Jolly Fox."

"None of your business," she warns herself silently. "It's not as though you're some sort of expert on successful relationships." Changing the subject, she says, "Should be the next right."

"Yeah...there it is."

Logan brakes, taking the right turn. Peartree Road is tree-lined and residential with red-brick Edwardian houses. She slows the car as Fry points his Noc at the first house on the left. It immediately responds by displaying the full address and the owner's details.

"That's number 24, so it's a bit further down on the right... that one." Fry points to an overgrown garden with two entrances. Bringing the car to a virtual standstill, Logan tries to decide which of the two entrances would be the easiest to tackle. Both appear narrow with creeping vegetation and arching trees, thick with leaves.

"It looks a bit like her allotment plot – messy, if you know what I mean. I hope Ms Drew isn't a cat lover," Fry frowns.

"Why?" Logan asks, choosing the second entrance and manoeuvring carefully through the tight space.

"You know, one of those batty old women with a house full of cats. I had one of those before I joined your team. Me and Rowena Wilkinson, she's that P.C. who's a touch fiery."

"I know her." And Logan smiles at the understated description of the policewoman that the whole station is a little bit scared of. Even Grim tends to duck out of her way if he sees her coming.

"Well, the house was full. I mean bursting with cats and shit everywhere."

"And why would Ms Drew's house be like that?" she asks, parking the car next to a little, old, red Fiat that had definitely seen better days.

"Because it looks sort of the same," Fry answers, unclipping his seat belt and getting out.

At the side of the house is another car wrapped in tarpaulin. It is long and low, some type of sports car, and from the bleached appearance of the tarpaulin it is evident that the car has not moved for a very long time.

"See what I mean?" he says, nodding at it as they walk towards the porch, which shines welcomingly in the dull afternoon light. Logan presumes, as her feet crunch on the stony driveway, that the light must be coming from the hallway beyond the front door, but as they step into the porch they are met by a huge Christmas tree, covered in white lights.

"That's different Boss, a Christmas tree in May. Do you think it's some sort of religious thing like Easter and Jesus, you know, coz some people call his cross a tree?"

"Maybe, but I've never heard of it before."

"So, it could be a mad, murdering, religious, cat woman then," Fry states, finding the doorbell and pressing it. A loud chime rings deep inside the house, followed by a half-hearted bark.

"Probably not a mad, murdering, religious cat woman, but perhaps a mad, murdering, religious dog woman," she says, smiling at him, but he looks just as uncomfortable.

"What?" she asks.

"I'm not that good with dogs either, Boss" Fry confesses, fidgeting with his I.D. card. Logan wants to say, "You mean like first dates," but instead says, "Don't worry, you can always hide behind me."

An elderly woman opens the door. She gives the impression of solidness as her stout frame fills the space. In complete contrast, a sleek greyhound stands at her side, sniffing the air.

"Good afternoon. I am D.C.I. Logan and this is D.C. Fry. We are here to speak to Ms Maggi Drew," Logan declares, holding out her I.D.

"I'm Maggi Drew," the woman replies calmly. "I've been expecting you since the body was unearthed on my allotment at Trinity Lane."

CHAPTER 12
Hypnotic Beauty

*

Logan catches Fry's look of surprise out of the corner of her eye. She ignores it, forcing her own features to remain impassive and professional.

"Come in," the woman says, standing back from the door. Stepping over the threshold, Logan automatically starts to process the information on offer. The dog gives a single bark, making Fry jump nervously.

"Please don't mind Lobo, he is very old and nearly blind and has no idea what he's woofing at. 'Do you?'" Maggi remarks, ruffling the dog's ears. "Come through."

They walk along a tiled hallway, passing two open doors. Logan glances in. One room contains a single bed with a bedside table, lamp and stack of books. The other room has a deep sofa with mismatched armchairs, a large 3D Perspex television and a battered wood burner sitting in an original fire hearth. But what really catches Logan's attention is yet another incongruous Christmas tree, decked out this time in coloured lights.

At the end of the hallway, the elderly woman pushes open a door. "I tend to use the kitchen during the day when it's just Lobo and me. It's the warmest room in the house. 'Lobo, back to your basket'." The dog plods leisurely round the doorway and disappears to the right.

"She probably still lives with Jonathan Gifford then," Logan thinks as she follows Maggi into the room, which stretches across the back of the house. Daylight floods in through a huge set of bi-folding glass doors, illuminating the space. To the right is the kitchen, ordered and clean, though Logan is immediately drawn towards a row of hooks holding an array of crafted pottery mugs in pastels above a powder-blue range cooker. In front of the range is a cosy dog's basket, which the greyhound has now plonked itself in.

To the left is a circular, dark wood table, ringed by an assortment of chairs with brightly coloured cushions. On the table is an old, brown jug filled with red gerberas and two lumpy pottery shapes and yet another, much smaller, Christmas tree.

"Please sit. I'll put the kettle on, it's always a good place to start," Maggi says, making Logan feel as though it is less of an offer and more of a declaration.

"But of what?" Logan thinks. Turning to the table she stops and stares up at the far wall opposite the bi-folding doors. Fry checks his step too and looks to see what has caught her eye. A vast oil canvas, full of swirling patterns in vibrant greens and blues fills the whole of the back wall. Logan feels immediately drawn to its hypnotic beauty.

"It's something," Maggi comments.

"Yes," murmurs Logan. "Did you paint it?"

"No, I've never had any artistic talent. I have more canvasses throughout the house; they each have a different colour scheme. I rotate them, apart from Jonny's one. He's very particular about his painting, so it stays in his bedroom. And two more that are quite different, but I'm sure we will get to them later." And though the answer is stated almost matter-of-factly, Logan notes the emotional modulations in her voice.

"Is Jonny, Jonathan Gifford?" she asks, watching Maggi move around the kitchen with ease, confirming her first assessment of someone who is able-bodied and strong.

"Yes. But he didn't paint the canvas either."

"Is he out?"

"All day. He'll be back at five."

"We'll need to speak to him too."

60

"No doubt. Please sit." Choosing her chair with care, Logan places her back to the canvas so as not to be distracted by it. Her view is directed towards a chair that has been pushed back from the table and holds an indented cushion. On the table, in front of the chair, is an early version Gab Book laptop.

"Wow," Fry mutters in awe, taking the chair next to the computer. Logan catches his eye and silently reminds him they're here to investigate a murder.

In the kitchen, Maggi fills the kettle and places it on the gas hob. Striking a match, she lights the flame. By the time the kettle whistles into life she has laid a tray with a coffee jug, three of the pottery mugs, a milk jug and a sugar bowl.

"All odd," Logan silently observes. "Especially the clumsy mug in a primary green with an oversized lumpy handle and an even bigger red heart protruding awkwardly from its side." She glances at the two pottery lumps on the table.

"Yes, D.C.I. Logan, they're made by the same person," Maggi confirms, as she places the tray on the table and then settles herself back into her chair. Closing the lid on her laptop, she moves it to one side before looking first at Logan, then at Fry. Fry immediately responds by smiling brightly back at her.

"I expect you want to ask me about the body that was dug up on my allotment plot?" Maggi says, as though it's the most natural thing in the world.

Logan feels her heart rate quicken very slightly. "Do you know who it is?"

"Yes," Maggi replies, plunging the coffee and starting to pour.

"Who?" Fry almost yells, enthusiastically. Logan throws him another look.

"There are other people involved in the murder of this man and I wouldn't do them justice if I didn't tell you the whole story." Picking up the crude pottery mug, she places it in front of herself before adding, "Help yourself to milk and sugar."

"Did you kill him?" Logan asks, keeping her voice measured and calm.

"Again, I will answer that question, but not until I have explained why he died."

Hearing a hint of wistfulness in Maggi's voice, Logan wonders if it's remorse or regret.

"Right," she declares authoritatively, holding her hand up as though to stop traffic. "I am going to Caution you Maggi Drew and I strongly advise that, before you say anything else, you have legal representation. We can wait for your lawyer or arrange for one at the station."

Maggi shakes her head. "I don't need legal representation."

"In that case, I will Caution you and record your interview. Do you understand?"

"Yes."

"Brilliant," exclaims Fry, eagerly pulling the Cam from its bag.

"I must warn you though, Jonny will be home at five and I will need to stop by then," explains Maggi.

"That won't be possible. It will be up to us when the interview is terminated. If you refuse we will take you into the station," asserts Logan.

"I'm not refusing anything," Maggi retorts, stiffening her body and jutting her chin forward.

"Interesting," thinks Logan, registering the anger.

"You will understand better when you meet Jonny. Now, where would you like me to begin?"

"We'll start with formal identification. Fry," she nods at him to set the Cam up. He puts it on the table and asks it to configure. The translucent blue hue fills the room from corner to corner, wall to wall. He checks the screen and commands it to narrow its field. When the pale light shrinks, enclosing only the table, shrouding the three of them, he instructs it to lock and holo-record.

"Okay. Location: 33 Peartree Road, Godlinghoe, Essex. Present is D.C.I. Logan, D.C. Fry and Ms Maggi Drew." Turning now to Maggi, Logan recites the Caution. "You do not have to say anything but it may harm your defence if you do not mention, when questioned something which you later rely on in court. Anything you

62

do say may be given in evidence. Do you understand?"

"Yes."

"Please confirm your name, address and date of birth."

"Maggi Drew, 33 Peartree Road, Godlinghoe. 21.7.55."

"How long have you lived at this address?"

"42 years. We moved here in 1981."

"Do you reside with Jonny Gifford?"

"Yes."

"How long have you lived together?"

"Since 1998. He sold his house and moved in here."

"How would you describe your relationship with Jonny Gifford?"

"We are family."

"Is he your partner?"

"Not in the sense you mean."

"In what sense do you think I mean?"

"I think you are asking me whether we are lovers, sexual partners."

Logan notes the flare of irritation again as Maggi looks straight at
her.

"Are you?"

"No. Platonic. Family."

"Did you rent allotment plot 42 at Trinity Lane site from Braxham
Wick Council?"

"Yes, yes, yes and yes! You know I did," snaps Maggi. "Why don't
we stop wasting time with you asking me inane questions that really
aren't going to give you the answers you want? Why don't you just
let me tell you everything: who Jonny is, who I am, who the body is,
how and why it was buried there, etc., etc., etc.?" Fry, startled, looks
across at Logan. She thinks for a minute, gauging the situation. She's
not put out by the anger, but calculates that by letting this woman
talk she could get more information, even if it is the version that
Maggi wants presented. "Later," Logan thinks, "I can always rip it
apart through questioning."

CHAPTER 13
Lobo

Maggi

I look at the woman who sits directly opposite me. Even if I didn't know she was the one in charge, I could've easily guessed from her demeanour. She might be small but she radiates authority.

Over the years, I've imagined having this conversation with someone just like her. At first, I'd concocted varying versions with thin layers of facts, but as the years have dragged themselves by, the need to hide the truth has lessened to the extent that lying now would be a worthless waste of time, though goodness only knows I don't want to spend the rest of my life in prison.

"Okay, but keep it relevant," D.C.I. Logan states in a voice that leaves me with no uncertainty that she means business.

I breathe in deeply and try to steady my voice. "I was born in London and grew up by the Thames, in Erith. My parents were what you'd have termed working class. School was fine for me. I was no great shakes, just average. Average in everything really, apart from one thing, I was gay. Not that I knew the word or understood what I was feeling. I think now that my Dad must've known, because he kept telling me not to worry about what other people thought and to be proud to be myself. Anyway, the point is, I had a happy, untroubled childhood. At 16, the school careers officer decided I should be a nurse." I hear a sharp intake of breath from D.C. Fry. He's not much more than a boy really; it's not just his youthful appearance, it's something else, something in his manner. I catch the slightest of warnings as D.C.I. Logan shakes her head at him. Pretending I've not noticed, I carry on talking. "It seemed like a good idea to me, so after school I started my training at St Thomas' Hospital in London. It didn't take me long to realise I didn't want to be the type of hand-holding, bed pan sort of nurse, so when there was an opening for a position as a theatre nurse, I jumped at it.

It was the summer of 74. I was 19 and London was alive. One night at a party, my friend Amy asked me out…"

1974

The party is in full swing, people snogging in corners, Rocket Man belting out of a home-rigged speaker system, and Amy, leaning up against a hallway wall with a bottle of beer in one hand and a joint in the other, smiles at me. "Are you gay, Maggi?"

"Yeah, really happy…what's so funny?" I ask, as she doubles over with laughter.

"Maggi, you're so sweet. No one would think you'd lived your whole life in London. Gay means homosexual. I'm asking you if you're a lesbian."

"Oh, hmmm… why?"

"Coz I'm about to kiss you."

2023

"…We started a relationship and what a summer that was. The other amazing thing that happened that year was, out of the blue, my brother was born…"

1974

"What's his name?" I ask, looking at the ugly baby in my arms.

"Jim Bob," Dad announces proudly. "You know, like from the TV show 'The Waltons'."

"Really Dad…Mum? You can't do that to him," I exclaim.

"It's a great name. You'll see, he'll love it," Dad says enthusiastically.

I look down at the sleeping baby and whisper, "Sorry Bro, I tried."

2023

"…His name was Jim Bob. He called me Bigster. He was warm-hearted and clever, a much better version of me. He died in California in a car accident, in 2014…"

2014

Dragged under, I'm sinking in my own bed. The pain is suffocating. I want to die but I'm not brave enough to kill myself, though starving in my own personal wasteland, under my duvet, has masses of appeal.

"Maggi, NO!" Gwen orders firmly, pulling the bed covers back. Her face, seamed by age, is set with determination and I know I'm never going to win a battle with this old woman.

"Get up now and take a shower; you stink. I've made tomato soup and fresh bread. Jonny's cleaning the kitchen. Then we'll all sit together and eat."

Crawling out, I shower, letting the hot water pound my bereaved body. I cry in long, low sobs under the merciless water, then dress and go downstairs. Jonny has opened the bi-folding doors, flooding the kitchen with sunlight and bird song. Gwen makes me sit and thrusts a mug of hot soup into my hands. With every sip of the life-giving liquid, I feel my body betray me as it begs for more. Like an addict, I can't stop drinking it.

"It's not your time to die, Maggs, you have a job to do. You promised Norah," Gwen, always tiny but now shrunken with age, declares pragmatically.

"Why can't Jonny do it?" I snap back, glaring at him, knowing he must've recruited Gwen into getting me out of bed.

"Maggs," he says softly. "You know why. I'm getting worse."

"And there's another job to do as well now. A job that neither Jonny nor I can take on," Gwen adds, taking no notice of my resentment.

"What?" I challenge sulkily.

"It's Jim Bob's dog, Lobo, he's nowhere to go. Jonny said they were

going to kill him if he hadn't offered to take him. But we all know
what that really means, don't we?"
"I've got to look after him," I mutter back through clenched teeth.
"So, you see, Maggs, you can't die. Lobo needs a home. You owe
that to Jim Bob after what he did for you. You made a promise to
Norah and Jonny is going gar-gar."
Jonny bursts out laughing. "Gar-gar," he exclaims, "That's so
funny, Gwen."

2023

I feel my throat tighten. I swallow it down and carry on. "…That's
how I came by the dog. He'd belonged to Jim Bob. He'd rescued
him from some bloody awful racetrack. Jonny had him flown back
from America.

Anyway, the dog and I turned into grieving partners. I stuffed my
face with crap food while Lobo hid in a corner behind the sofa,
refusing to eat. Jonny looked after us both, even though he wasn't
well himself. He tempted Lobo to eat and built a bed next to him on
the carpet. It took him months to persuade Lobo to come out of his
corner. I tried taking him to the allotment but he wouldn't get out of
the car."

Tears burn in my eyes. "So much for being objective," I think, as
Lobo, always aware of my moods, comes and lays his head on my
lap.

"Maggi, we are here for a statement of facts concerning a murder,
not to hear about your dog," D.C.I. Logan says assertively.

"Fuck you," I think, but I wipe my eyes and order Lobo back to his
basket, though I do catch a look of concern on D.C. Fry's face before
I continue. "It was after that I handed my allotment plot back. I
hadn't really done much with it in years. After the body was buried
in 1998 none of us could bring ourselves to eat anything off the plot
anyway."

"The body was buried in your allotment in 1998?" D.C.I. Logan
reiterates.

"Yes. 31st of August 1998, under the shed to be precise."

"Did you bury the body there?" she asks.

"Yes, and it was my idea, no one else's."

"You must've had help burying him?"

"I did, Jonny and Jim Bob, amongst others, but I'll get to that part of the story later."

"Tell us about Jonny Gifford then."

"Okay. I was 20 and having the time of my life when I met Jonny. It was at a gay rights march. We were meeting up with some of Amy's friends from the hospital and among them was Jonny Gifford…"

1975

The street is full of people, flags and banners are raised and cracking in the breeze, joints are being passed and voices chanting in unison. And there he is, laughing and joking, the centre of everyone's attention. Beautiful Jonny Gifford turns to me and never looks away again.

2023

"…Jonny was everything I was not. He had the sort of looks that made people stare and then the personality to charm them. We hit it off straight away. I think, initially because there wasn't any sexual chemistry between us and that was a novelty for him. There weren't many people who didn't fancy Jonny: gay, straight, male, female. And Jonny was never one to turn away a good time, though he was hopeless when it came to relationships. That was his Achilles heel, his damaged core. He'd run a mile if anyone got too close to him."

"But you're close to him," D.C. Fry comments.

"I mean sexual relationships, partners. He couldn't cope with the responsibility; it made him feel trapped. But I did ask him once what he saw in me that day on the march and he'd said, 'You are who you say you are, Maggs …unlike me'."

"Did Jonny work at St Thomas' Hospital too?" D.C.I. Logan asks.

"Yes, he was an A&E nurse. Brilliant, as you can probably imagine. Everyone loved working with him, though most of them would have liked to have done more with him than just work…"

1975

Waiting for him after a shift in the hospital, I see him coming down the corridor being stopped by men and women alike. I watch as they stand taller, setting out their wares. It makes me smile.

2023

"...Jonny was the flyer and I was the plodder, if you like. So, picture us, handsome Jonny and me – short, round and never destined for success, but always up for a good night out."

"Does Jonny have any family?"

"Apart from me, not anyone to write home about." I hear the barely concealed acrimony in my voice. I try to push it back down into the place I store all my hate. I think D.C.I. Logan has registered it, as her next question hits the nail on the head.

"How would you describe his childhood?"

"Horrible. His mother, Julia Gifford, is still alive, living in a very expensive care home. She's far too spiteful to die. He has two sisters. One in Canada and another God knows where. I've never met them."

"Not a close family then."

"No, neither in distance nor relationships. I only met Jonny's parents twice. The first time I disliked them on the spot and the second they did nothing to persuade me that I was wrong."

"In what way?"

"His mother is a bully. She uses her power to wield control over other people's lives. Anyone who disagrees with her is ridiculed unmercifully. She has a spiteful tongue and knows how to use it. She's bullied Jonny all his life. She thought him weak and emotional."

"Because he is gay?"

"No, because he was a nurse, because he is innately kind and caring, because he has a gentle soul. The gay thing was the only part about Jonny that Julia liked as far as I could tell. She thought it very fashionably chic to have a gay son. So, no, the homosexual part of Jonny was fine, unlike the rest of him. And what his mother thought, his father, Edmund, thought too. He's dead now. He was a coward, scared of Jonny's mother, and hid his emasculation in the pleasure he took in killing."

"Killing?" questions D.C. Fry.

"Killing animals, not people. They have nothing to do with the body at Trinity Lane allotments. Neither of them would have broken a judicial law, but morally they broke the rulebook. Edmund hunted everything from elephants to pheasants. Never with a sporting chance, you understand. He'd employ beaters and dogs to drive the creatures into traps where he'd pick them off with his shotgun. I think the elephant was actually tied to a post. He kept a pack of hounds and would feed live fox cubs, deer fawns or rabbit kits to them for fun. Jonny doesn't like to talk about it. I think he's very ashamed."

"Let's get back to what's relevant here."

"I think it's pretty relevant," I retort, allowing my temper to surface again. I see the policewoman's eyes widen ever so slightly, but I don't care about what she thinks of me. I just want her to understand who Jonny is.

CHAPTER 14
Like a Real Woman

*

Maggi

I shut my eyes as silence fills the room, broken only by Lobo's struggle to get out of his basket again.

"It's alright boy, go back to sleep," I say, finding, as always, there's nothing like the battle of a loved one to nail my soul back down again.

"Anyway," I continue, "Jonny and I got a flat share. I had a couple of relationships after Amy, and Jonny had who ever he pleased. Then, the winter of 77. It was cold. I mean, really cold. Snowed every day and froze every night. A&E was inundated with broken bones, particularly wrists, where people had slipped on icy paths and tried to save themselves. It was the 24th of December, Jonny's birthday. I'd been in theatre for most of the day when orthopaedics phoned main theatres looking for someone to help mix in the Plaster Room as they were overloaded. I volunteered.

We'd just finished an ankle and Rosie, the plaster nurse, was cleaning the table down while I was in the adjoining wash room, elbow deep in plaster, when in walked Jonny pushing our next customer. I could hear the animation in his voice and knew instantly that he liked this patient. I carried on mixing, imagining some handsome, young lad hanging on Jonny's every word..."

24th December 1977

"Good afternoon, fellow workers," Jonny says in his most camp voice. "I have personally escorted this gorgeous, young person up

here to ensure they receive our very best plaster cast and not the third-rate stuff you usually dish out." There are three sets of laughter. I know Jonny's, and Rosie's is easy to identify, but what takes me a moment is the third; it belongs to a girl.

2023

"…But it wasn't a boy; it was a girl. Jonny introduced her." I pause, as my misery threatens to strangle my words. My fingers touch my lips. I don't want to say her name. I don't want it bandied about in police records like another statistic, another criminal. But I know I have no choice if I want her to be heard. Clearing my throat, I say, "Norah Montgomery." Neither detective responds. They just sit and wait, so I carry on. "Rosie joined in with Jonny's banter. I finished cleaning and walked through, taking a quick look at the patient to make sure she was finding it funny too. And there she sat, the most beautiful girl I had ever seen…"

1977

I stare at her, she's like some sort of mythical woodland elf conjured up to represent beauty. She wouldn't have looked any more out of place in the hospital treatment room if she had been wearing a gown of flowing gossamer and a wreath of flowers in her hair.

2023

"…I could describe her for you, but this is not what it's about. It's about the fact that I fell in love the moment I saw her. Jonny told me afterwards that he'd seen the look on my face and covered for me by babbling on to Rosie and Rah."

"Rah?" D.C.I. Logan questions immediately, reminding me that nothing is going to slip past her unchallenged.

"Short for Norah…Rah, it's what Jonny and I called her. Anyway, he made them laugh about how he had found Rah in A&E cradling her broken wrist, crying her eyes out and how he'd performed his best disco moves to cheer her up. Rosie had asked her if she was still in pain and Rah had said it wasn't the pain that had been making her cry. It was the fear of losing the movement in her hand. I saw her smile slip from her face as she explained that she was an oboist with the London Glass Orchestra and she was due to play on New Year's Day. Jonny and I would come to understand, many years later, what a devastating effect it was to have on Rah when she could no longer play, but, at the time, neither of us really had any idea about anything to do with classical music, orchestras or, in particular, oboes and oboists. Jonny, being Jonny, immediately said that we would come and see her orchestra play when she was better. Again, unbeknown to us, the LGO was, and still is, a highly acclaimed orchestra that tours all over the world and tickets are like gold dust as well as being extremely expensive. Rah had immediately understood that we didn't have a clue, but she never corrected us, only promised to send us tickets for their August Bank Holiday performance in the Glass Hall Theatre. To that, Jonny assured her that she wouldn't be able to wait that long to see his dance moves again and, seeing as she wouldn't be able to work, she should come out with us on New Year's Eve to experience his full repertoire. She'd laughed, saying she'd love to. They exchanged telephone numbers, and with her arm all plastered up Jonny wheeled her off to check her out. I hadn't said a thing, and really, I didn't believe she would come out with us, though I counted down the days to New Year's Eve.

Jonny had arranged for us to meet for drinks in Soho before heading to our favourite club. I was in a whirl of nerves and worried she wouldn't come, then if she did that she'd hate it. But Rah wasn't like that. Anything new, anything different fascinated her..."

New Year's Eve 1977
I stand back against the club bar with a bottle of beer in my hand while Rah and Jonny hit the dance floor. Boys join Jonny, embellishing their moves, strutting their stuff, wanting his attention.

2023
"...She danced with the best of them, even though her arm was in

plaster…"

1977

I recognise the moment Jonny's swallowed up by the sexual energy. I've seen it many times before. It's the moment when he lets pleasure stifle the darkness of his childhood. Stepping in, I join Rah on the dance floor. We laugh as 'Dancing Queen' fills the air, and I suddenly feel as though I can take on the world.

2023

"…Then midnight struck…"

1977

"Get ready folks, it's…it's n…ineteeeen seventyyy eiggght, Yabba Dabba Doooo," the DJ announces, and I feel Rah's small hand slip into mine. I turn and look into her dark eyes. Rah pulls me closer and I can smell her hair and feel the warmth from her dark skin as she says, "Happy New Year, Maggs." Something brave stirs inside me, pushing aside my fears I lean down and kiss her. And, as the club explodes around us, I feel her kiss me back.

2023

"…and I kissed her," I murmur, smiling through my tears. "After that night, Rah, Jonny and I saw each other quite a bit while Rah's arm healed, then less as she went back to work."

"Did either of you suffer any prejudicial problems?" D.C.I. Logan asks. I know where she is going with this question. It's to find out whether the body is some bigoted bastard we'd decided to rid the world of. And, in truth, he was homophobic, but that isn't why he died. So, I choose to ignore the real question and just answer what she has asked.

"I've never encountered any form of prejudice. Or, if I have, I'm just too pig-headed to notice. But I know my first girlfriend, Amy, did, and Jonny has had his fair share of abuse. So, when Rah and I first got together, I warned her of the dangers, but she just smiled knowingly back at me and told me not to worry about her. She said that growing up after the Second World War with strong Japanese features was enough to invite all sorts of comments and opinions.

Jonny and I still had no real idea about her career until, true to her word, she gave us tickets to the August Bank Holiday concert of the LGO."

"Is this relevant?" D.C.I. Logan challenges. I'm beginning to really dislike her.

"Right, let's get something straight here," I snap back. "I'm not telling you this for fun and, quite frankly, you'd be one of the last people I'd choose to share my personal life with, but if you want to know who the body is and how it got to be there, then you need to understand things that I doubt you've ever encountered before. So, yes, it is relevant, D.C.I. Logan." The woman just looks steadily back at me. Her bearing unruffled; her face composed.

"Okay," she acknowledges lightly, making me feel I've overreacted.

"Right," I mumble, breathing deeply, trying to calm myself. "I remember Rah's uncertainty when she phoned to tell us about the concert. It's one of those things that just made me love her more."

"Why?" Fry asks.

I smile at him. "Because the tickets she was giving us were like gold dust, unattainable unless you are on some sort of exclusive mailing list. I know at the time Jonny and I didn't understand that, but she did, and yet it was her who was humble enough to worry over whether we would want them or not..."

1978

Sitting over coffee in a late night greasy dive after the club, Rah reaches into her handbag and brings out a snowy crisp envelope. Its very presence feels alien in this place.

"I don't know if you remember, but ages ago when I first met you I said I'd wangle you some tickets for our August Bank

75

Holiday concert? Well, here they are, but don't feel you have to come if you don't want to," she says hesitantly.
"Yeahhh," Jonny replies enthusiastically, taking the envelope and ripping it open. Inside are two beautifully crafted tickets that wouldn't have looked out of place in an art exhibition.

2023

"…The tickets were so expensive that they looked more like invitations than tickets. I even offered to pay for them, not knowing I would've had to save for a year to afford them…"

1978

"Nothing Maggs, it would just be great to see you there, if you feel like it."
"I'm dressing up for this," Jonny declares with his usual zeal.

2023

"…But we did go and buy new outfits, though I've often wondered how appropriate they really were…"

1978

"What are you going to buy?" Jonny asks me on the bus to the West End.
"God, I don't know. Whatever fits, I suppose. And you?"
"A suit, tight and white, like…"
"Saturday Night Fever?" I finish for him.
"Exactamundo."
In Oxford Street, we meet up with Emmy, a friend of Jonny's who owns a designer shop for men, and it isn't long before Jonny has managed to squeeze his slim frame into a cream, three-piece suit that does nothing to hide his credentials. Even I think he looks amazing and Emmy nearly has a heart attack.
"Now you Maggs," Jonny insists, and Emmy, leaving the shop to his assistant, helps Jonny set about dressing me.

"God, I hate this," I moan inside the cubicle as they force me into ever-tighter outfits.

"We can go flouncy," Emmy shouts through the changing room doorway.

"Whatever," I shout back, waiting for Emmy's hand to appear around the curtain, holding another totally not-me outfit.

"Try this," he says, giving me a long, white, embroidered, cheesecloth dress.

"And these," Jonny adds, thrusting a pair of cork platform sandals at me.

Easing my feet into them, I slip the dress over my head. It floats around me as the embroidered hem drops to my ankles. I don't want to look in the mirror as I'm sure I will see some sort of monstrous troll dressed up as a princess. I turn and dare myself.

"Not a troll," I think, swaying the folds of fabric from side to side. I have a sudden urge to curtsy or pirouette because I feel like a lady. Holding the dress out in what I imagine is an elegant pose, I go to show the boys.

"Bloody hell, Maggs, you look gorgeous," Jonny exclaims.

"I know right, like a real woman," I answer, making us all laugh.

CHAPTER 15
Thinking of England

*

Maggi-2023

"August Bank Holiday came and we dressed up. When we arrived at the Glass Hall Theatre, it was buzzing with celebs and press. I think that was the moment when Jonny and I began to have an inkling of how much our tickets might have cost. Anyway, we were shown to our seats like honoured guests. I remember sitting there, knowing we were in prime position, waiting for goodness knows what to happen. Then it started." I hear my voice crack with pride as the hair on my arms stands on end. "If I tell you," I say with the palm of my hand unconsciously placed on my chest as though I'm about to recite the American Pledge of Allegiance, "we were blown away, that wouldn't even touch what we felt. Rah played first oboe. She was graceful and beautiful. She wove love and passion into her music, making me believe in every note." I know I should be sticking to objective explanations, not flowery descriptions, but I can't, not when it comes to Rah.

August Bank Holiday 1978
The auditorium lights rise for the interval and I find myself clinging to Jonny's hand. The woman in the next seat asks if I'm enjoying the music.
"Yes," I say, turning to her and gazing into Rah's eyes.
"Rah?" I respond without thinking, still stunned by the music.

"No," answers the woman, *"but if you mean Norah, yes, well, that is to say I am Norah's mother. It's our Japanese genes. It doesn't matter how much we dilute them, they're still very strong."*

"Oh, I'm sorry. I didn't mean to be rude. I'm Maggi and this is Jonny; we are friends of Ra...Norah's."

"Pleased to meet you. I'm Gwen and this is Norah's father, Minty. Norah told us to look out for you."

2023

"That was the night we met Rah's parents, Minty and Gwen Montgomery," I continue, rubbing the gooseflesh on my arms. I see D.C.I. Logan check the time. "Are these people rel..." she begins.

"They are if you want the whole cast of murderers. And I'll warn you now, there's more to come," I assert, truncating her.

"Okay," she states objectively again, showing no sign that my belligerence has affected her.

"Anyway, it was not long after that when Rah moved in with us. It soon became apparent the flat was too small and I can't remember who suggested it, but we decided to move out of London. Also, the rumours about HIV were starting to become a reality. Jonny and I would end up losing loads of friends to that vile virus.

Rah wanted to live near her parents, so that's how we came here, to Godlinghoe. Minty and Gwen used to live just up the road in Oyster Lane. Jonny bought a house on Pump Street and Rah and I bought this house."

"When was this?" D.C.I. Logan asks.

"1982. This house was a bit of a mess when we bought it, but Minty and Jonny helped me do it up over the years. Anyway, Jonny and I both got jobs at Braxham Wick's General Hospital and Rah went from an amazing oboist to a virtuoso. Her name became synonymous with oboe music and she was forever being head-hunted, though she remained a principal player for the LGO.

She was well liked too, which can't be said about many of their star performers. There's a huge amount of rivalry, some subtle, some blatant. And the bassoonist was known as a right tea leaf."

"Tea leaf?" D.C. Fry frowns.

"Thief," D.C.I. Logan informs him, dispassionately.

"Rah lost no end of personal stuff…"

1996

"*Maggs, I have to tell you something.*"

"*Okay. What?*

"*It's a confession.*"

"*Just tell me Rah.*"

"*Okay, but I feel awful.*"

"*Just say and then we can deal with the fall out.*"

"*Right… you know the Zuki gown you bought me a couple of Christmases ago?*"

"*Uhmm?*"

"*You remember… you wouldn't tell me how much you paid for it.*"

I remembered then; it had cost me an arm and a leg. "*Oh, was it black with a red swirly pattern?*"

"*Yes, silk, really beautifully made.*"

"*Yeah, I know the one,*" *and I did, she looked amazing in it, but then I think she looks amazing in anything.*

"*Well… it's missing. I wore it in Cardiff and I swear I packed it to come home but it's not here. I phoned the hotel and they haven't found it. I even checked with the dry cleaners just in case I'd inadvertently booked it in, but no…*"

"*I reckon it's that bloody bassoonist again.*"

"*It could be, but I don't want to say anything to her. Last time I did over the necklace Mum gave me, it caused such a row. There was a bad feeling for months between the wood-winders. I don't want that again.*"

"*I don't blame you,*" *I say, taking the opportunity to kiss her,* "*we'll just have to get another.*"

"*But it was a Zuki gown, Maggs.*"

"*I'm sure Mr Zuki…*"

"*Ms Zuki.*"

"Ms Zuki has loads more gowns for sale."
"But they're so expensive."
"Never mind. We'll sell one of your kidneys. You've got two and you don't need them both to play an oboe," I reason.
"Where do I sign up?" she replies laughingly.

2023

"…She was also a keen supporter of other oboists, encouraging them and giving them time and tuition." I can see D.C.I. Logan is about to ask her 'relevant' question again. Getting in first, I snap curtly, "And before you ask me again, D.C.I. Logan, whether this is relevant, I will tell you about Herrick Butler."

"Is Herrick Butler involved in the murder?" she questions objectively, again refusing to respond to my irritability.

"Yes. I'm virtually there with the whole cast. Apart from a couple of extras, but I'll get to them later," I state, trying to be equally objective and failing completely. I know I'm not doing myself any favours and, worse, I'm damaging those I love. I warn myself to be careful before carrying on. "Herrick played second oboe and that probably sums him up. He was quiet and unpretentious, happy to play second to Rah's first. He was never jealous of her standing; instead, he admired and loved her in his own way. When we got together and he knew that all his hopes of a romantic relationship with her were dashed, he just set about being the best friend he could be to her. After we moved to Godlinghoe, he came into some money through the death of his mother, I think, and used it to buy a house here, 16 Bosuns Road."

"Was that a bit… you know …weird, stalker-ish?" D.C. Fry asks.

"Not that way. I think he was lonely. He didn't seem to have much family to speak of. I think he had relatives in Germany. But he was just a really good friend to Rah, though, I must admit, Jonny and I used to find him more than a bit irritating and we'd laugh at him behind his back, which used to annoy Rah. Later, when we knew him better, we realised we'd seriously misjudged him, and that his love for Rah would push him way beyond his capabilities. He would go further than either Jonny or I gave him credit for.

Anyway, while I renovated the house Rah filled it with her creativity; the canvas is hers," I say, nodding towards the picture behind D.C.I. Logan. "She could've been anything – artist, potter, musician – but what she chose was me and then... a baby."
"A baby?" D.C. Fry interjects, "But I thought..."
"Just because she was in a lesbian relationship, it didn't mean she couldn't be a mother."
"Who was the father?" D.C.I. Logan asks bluntly.
"I think you can guess the answer to that."
"What, Jonny?" D.C. Fry interjects again.
"Yes, Jonny," I smile at him. "Don't get me wrong, Jonny's gay through and through. If you sliced him in half, he'd have 'homosexual' written right through his core like a stick of seaside rock. But there are other ways to make a baby without sexual intercourse."

1984

"Maggs," Jonny calls from the bathroom.
"Yeah?" I answer as he opens the door.
"Here," and he passes me a hospital specimen pot full of warm, live sperm. Bracing myself, I try to think of it in terms of science, not as my best friend's cum.

In our bedroom, Rah holds out the plastic cylinder of a sterile syringe and I carefully transfer the gluey semen.
"Oh my God Maggs, we are about to make ourselves a baby," she says excitedly.
"We won't if you don't hold that syringe still. I really don't want to be spilling this-this stuff."
"It's only a part of Jonny."
"Frankly not a part I like to think too much about."
"You are funny, Maggs."
"That should do it, give it here." Placing the rubber-tipped plunger into the neck of the cylinder, I hold the loaded syringe up between my fingers and thumb, trying not to look at the creamy fluid oozing

from the nozzle.

"Are you ready?" I ask unnecessarily. Scrabbling down onto the makeshift bed we've made on the floor, she rests her pelvis on a stack of pillows, tipping her uterus slightly upward. I didn't really think the position was needed, but never having artificially inseminated anyone before I wasn't going to argue.

"Ready," she answers, opening her thighs.

"Okay, but I've got to tell you, I'm finding this all a bit weird," I mutter, sitting in front of her.

"You do want a baby, don't you?" she says, smiling at me through her open legs.

"Not really," I think, slipping the syringe carefully in.

This wanting a baby had taken me completely by surprise. When she'd first put the idea to Jonny and me he'd jumped at the idea and I suppose I never said no, though I'd never really seen myself as a parent. But I said, "Yes," because what I do want is her to be happy. Pushing the syringe further, I can feel the muscular walls of her vagina grip the plastic body.

"Relax Rah, I need to get it as deep as I can."

"Okay, okay I'll try. Shall I think of England?"

"Fuck off and don't make me laugh," I say, laughing anyway.

"Right, I think that's as far as it should go." Applying pressure on the plunger, I press down. There's resistance and it's harder than I expect. Easing the plunger back a couple of times, I manage to send it home.

"Done." I gently remove the syringe and sit up. "Lie still and I'll tell Jonny and make you a cup of tea.

"Thanks, Maggs," she says as I head for the door, wanting to throw the syringe away as soon as possible. "Maggs?

"What?"

"Really, thanks. It means the world to me."

"I know," I tell her, thinking, "and you mean the world to me." Out on the landing, Jonny is already lurking with a tray of tea and toast. "Thought we could do with some sustenance after our hard work," he says grinning at me.

"Fucker," I banter back.
"Well, not in this case," he laughs.

CHAPTER 16
Higgledy-Piggledy

*

Logan

Lobo unfurls his long legs and eases his lean body into a stretch
before getting out of his basket and padding over to the kitchen door.
Turning his head towards Maggi, he looks at her expectantly.

"That'll be Jonny now," Maggi motions, and, sure enough, there's a
knock at the front door. She leaves the room and Logan gets up and
stands by the partly open kitchen door, wondering why someone
who has lived in a house for over twenty years doesn't own their
own front door key. Fry comes and stands next to her as she hears
the front door being opened.

"Hello Jonny, you've brought the sunshine with you." Logan notes
the warmth in Maggi's voice and, true enough, as she glances
towards the garden she can see that the sun has broken through the
grey clouds.

"Maggs … Lobo …hello boy," comes a gentle male voice in reply.

"We have visitors today, Jonny."

"Maggs…the Christmas tree lights, are they on?" the man asks, and,
though it's undoubtedly the same person, Logan can hear that a note
of desperateness has shaped the question.

"Yes, Jonny. All the Christmas tree lights are on. I've just checked
them."

"You've been on that loop all day, haven't you, Jonny? Worrying
yourself about the lights," another voice says. Logan guesses it

belongs to a younger woman.

"I know," answers Maggi. "It seems to have gotten worse lately. We just keep the trees lights on all the time now. I think it helps."

"Maggs, are the lights on? Orla needs the lights to see her way home."

"Yes, Jonny, and they look lovely. Did you see the Christmas tree in our porch?"

"Yes, we did, didn't we Jonny?" answers the female voice again. "We said how pretty it looks."

"Yes, pretty," replies Jonny in a calmer tone.

"And we can show Anya the one in the sitting room if you like, Jonny," Maggi offers.

"In the sitting room?"

"Yes, Jonny. Come and see."

Fry looks at Logan quizzically. "I'm not sure," she mouths back, "maybe a stroke or brain injury?" They hear Maggi guiding Jonny along the hallway. His feet shuffle slightly on the tiled floor until they reach the carpeted sitting room.

"See, Jonny, the lights are all on," states Maggi cheerfully.

"Aw, Jonny, they are really magical," Anya comments.

"Magical," Jonny repeats.

"You haven't eaten very well today, have you, Jonny? I think it's because you were a bit worried about the Christmas tree lights. But you've had a nice bath and a sing song. We enjoyed the singing, didn't we?"

"Yes, singing, very good. Were you there, Anya?"

"Yes, Jonny, and we had a good old time."

"Good old time, yes."

"I'll be off then. Bye, Jonny, see you tomorrow."

"Are you going? You can stay for tea if you like. There might be cake," Jonny says hopefully.

"I'd like that, Jonny, but I must go back to work now."

"Maybe another time."

"Yes, another time."

"Thanks, Anya, see you tomorrow," Maggi says. Logan and Fry

head back to their seats as Anya lets herself out of the front door.

"Shall we have a nice cup of tea?" Maggi asks Jonny gently.

"Cake?"

"Yes, cake as well, and you'll never guess what Jonny, we have two visitors waiting in the kitchen. Come on, Lobo."

"Visitors? Is Anya coming to tea?"

"Not today, but we have a nice young man called D.C. Fry and a woman called D.C.I. Logan."

"Nice. Perhaps they'd like cake. Have we got cake for tea, Maggs?"

The door opens as Maggi answers, "Yes, chocolate, your favourite," and in walks a tall, slim man with a head of heavy, silver-grey hair. Lobo eases himself around the man's legs and stands, wagging his tail.

"Hello," greets Logan with a welcoming tone, gaining a smile from Maggi.

"Hello, have you come to play? Don't mind me; I'm a bit higgledy-piggledy."

"This is D.C.I. Logan," Maggi says calmly, "she's come to have a chat with me. And this is D.C. Fry."

"Please call me Tris," smiles Fry.

"Hello, is that your Mum, Tris? Do you like cake?"

"Yes, very much," Fry replies happily.

"Let's have your coat Jonny and I'll make the tea." Maggi eases the coat off the elderly man before guiding him to a chair. Lobo immediately lays his head across Jonny's lap.

"Good boy, good dog Lobo," Jonny murmurs, patting his head.

"Maggi, I think we should go now," Logan says, indicating to Fry to pack the Cam away.

"Yes, I thought you'd understand when you met him. Anya calls for Jonny at 10:30, so any time after that."

"Okay, tomorrow. Goodbye, Jonny."

"Oh, aren't you staying for tea? There might be cake you know. Orla won't be long. Maggs, have you put the Christmas trees on yet?"

"Yes Jonny, the one on the table looks really pretty, doesn't it? Can you look after Lobo while I see D.C.I. Logan and D.C. Fry out?

Then we'll have tea and cake."

"Righty ho," Jonny says amicably.

"Bye, Jonny," Fry says and Logan sees him reach out and gently rest his hand on Jonny's shoulder. Jonny reaches up and pats Fry's hand in return.

"Goodbye, Tris. Come back another day and have tea when Orla's home. I'll see if we can have cake."

"I'd like that," Fry says. Then, grabbing the Cam bag, he follows Maggi and Logan to the front door.

"Has he been like that for long?" Logan asks.

"He was diagnosed with dementia five years ago, but we knew way back in 2014."

"When your brother died," Logan states.

"Yes," Maggi answers, thinking, "You don't miss a thing, D.C.I. Logan."

"We'll be back tomorrow," Logan affirms.

"I know," Maggi replies, shutting the front door behind them.

CHAPTER 17
Cannibals and Hobgoblins

*

Logan

"Looks like we might've solved our case, Boss, what do you think?" Fry says, as Logan, catching the gleam of the Christmas tree lights in her rear-view mirror, turns out of the driveway.

"I think it's going to be an interesting day tomorrow."

"I really like her. I hope she's not going to turn out to be a murderer."

"You know it's not a good idea to tell people you are questioning your first name. It diminishes your authority. You're meant to be a blank force, not develop a personal relationship with them."

"Yeah, I know that, but it kind of slipped out. Sorry."

"What made you want to join the Force?"

"Dad was a copper before he died."

"Oh, sorry Fry, I hadn't realised your Dad was dead."

"It's no biggy. It happened ages ago, when I was a kid."

"How did he die?"

"Cancer. Mum fell to bits. That's why we moved in with Frank – that's her dad, my grandfather."

"How's your Mum now?"

"Yeah, fine. She's got a partner, Leroy, been with him for years. Frank and I really like him and can't understand why they don't get married, or at least move in together. I think she thinks we can't survive without her."

"What does Frank do?"

"He was an engineer, retired now though. But he's got a shed full of stuff he tinkers around with. He'd love that computer that still works off a cable. I can't believe anyone has something that old. And did you see those match things she lit the gas with? I've seen them on telly but never in real life. Frank'll never believe me. Did you see the TV though? It's got to be the latest Vellapennic."

"It's big. You seemed alright with the dog at the end there."

"Yeah, he was okay, not vicious or anything. Interesting that Maggi and Jonny worked as nurses."

"That's what I thought. It could account for the body bag and hospital gown."

Back at the station Logan parks the car.

"If you want to get off, Fry, I'll put the Cam in the SafeCage."

"Thanks, Boss. I said I'd try and be back in good time tonight as Frank and I are setting up the telescope stand in the garden, ready for Thursday."

"Huh," she utters under her breath, as she thinks of how Trev will be setting up a scope too.

"Boss?"

"I'm fine. See you tomorrow, have fun with your stand."

"Are you sure, coz I can stay if you need me."

"No, I'm fine." Then seeing the look of concern on his face she adds, "Honestly Fry, go."

"Bye then."

"Bye." Gripping the steering wheel, she watches him weave his way through the car park. Once he is out of sight, she drops her head onto her arms.

"Fuck, fuck, fuck," she moans through gritted teeth as she remembers how excited Trev was when they'd announced the mission.

2020

"Just bloody brilliant, Lo, we've got to see it. We'll have TJ by then," he says, kissing her.

90

"TJ?"
"Our little PC Trevor Junior."

2023

"Fuck," she mutters again before hunting for a tissue and blowing her nose. Grabbing the Cam, she locks the car and heads into the station. Unlocking the door, she takes the lift up to the third floor.

The station feels empty as she walks down the quiet corridor. Suddenly, there's a roar of laughter and she spots Grim in the coffee room chatting with Daff. Turning the corner into her office, she's instantly aware of a dark figure leaning back in her chair.

"Fuck Trev, you made me jump, I wasn't expecting to see anyone in here."

"Hey, Lo," Trev answers, in a false-friendly voice.

"Hi," she mutters back, trying not to sound needy.

"Yeah, well, it seemed like as good a place to catch you as any… seeing as you're always working," he comments, twisting in her chair.

"He's nervous," she thinks, before saying, "What do you want, Trev?"

"Look, Lo, it's been, what, 18 months since we broke up? You must know by now I'm not coming back. It's over."

"So what do you want? You've taken everything," she says, keeping her head down as she keys in the code to the SafeCage. Her throat feels dry and her hands shake slightly as she places the Cam inside.

"You know what I want, Lo," he states querulously. "You've had those divorce papers for weeks now. I need you to sign them. I need to sort the house out… Shar and I…"

"Go fuck yourself, Trev. I'll sign them when I'm ready," she lashes back, her anger masking her pain.

"Oh, here we go, the hard-faced bitch D.C.I. Logan," he sneers, rising from her chair. "I don't know why it took me so long to see it. Shar always said you were right up yourself, always wanted to be the best cunt on the block, can't bear to lose. Do you know what we Plods call you and that fat twat of a friend of yours? Top Cat and

Officer Dibble. Well, here's the thing, you've lost me, so get over it Top fuckin' Cat. I want to be married and have the house ready by the autumn."

"Oh my God, you want our house for when you and Sharon have the baby?" she utters in horrified realisation.

"What if I do? You never even wanted that house. It was what I wanted. You'll get your bloody dosh back, so I don't see what your fuckin' problem is."

"No, you don't, do you Trev?" she expresses quietly before turning away from him and walking out of the office.

"JESUS FUCKING CHRIST LOGAN, JUST SIGN THE FUCKIN' PAPERS!" he shouts after her.

She can hardly hold back her tears as she strides fast along the corridor to the toilet. In a cubicle, she bangs the door shut. It bounces back and catches her fingers. She grabs it angrily, slams it, bolting it tight. Pulling down the toilet lid, she sits and cradles her head in her hands as her pain bursts from her in violent sobs.

"Fucking Trev, fucking Sharon. It was meant to be our house, our home. I was the one who was meant to have the baby, not fucking Sharon Mulligan," she shouts silently.

Knock, knock, knock.

"Lo, are you in there?" Grim calls through the door.

"Yeah," she sobs back.

"Trev?"

"Yep."

"I thought I heard his dulcet tones. Come on, let's get out of here. I'll cook you supper and if you're really lucky, I'll let you play my latest computer game, Cannibals versus Hobgoblins. It's guaranteed to make anyone smile."

"'kay," she answers, sniffing loudly.

"There's nothing like clearing your passageways out, D.C.I. Logan."

"Give me a mo, and I'll be out."

"Right."

"And Grim?"

"Yeah?"

"Did you know that uniform call you Officer Dibble and me Top Cat?" A great roar of laughter comes from the other side of the thin door.

"Yeah, but what really pisses me off is you're Top Cat and I'm Officer fucking Dibble; how'd you manage that? I want to be Top Cat. That's a really cool name … or Benny the Ball even, but fucking Officer Dibble, now that's shit." Logan feels a smile creep across her lips as she gets off the seat.

"Fuck off, Benny the Ball, and give me a minute," she says, feeling the shift in her emotions.

"Right, T.C., I'll be outside." She hears him singing the theme tune as he leaves the bathroom. Unlocking the door, she looks in the mirror above the row of basins and sees her dark, cropped hair standing on end, her thin, pale face suffused with blotches, her eyes bloodshot and glazed.

"Jeezus," she mutters, turning on the taps and washing her face.

"Oi, Top Cat, how's it going?"

"Move it, move it, move it, Benny," she says in her best Manhattan accent, coming out of the bathroom. "So what are you cooking? And Cannibals and Hobgoblins? You don't half play some crap games."

"Don't knock it, T.C. until you've played it."

CHAPTER 18
Giant Terrorist

*

Logan

"Out bloody manoeuvred," Grim declares smugly a few hours later, as his Cannibals eat the last of her Hobgoblins. "It's got to be said, the best cat won!"

"Fuck off," she laughs, putting down her console and picking up a beer.

Maggi

The cold slaps hard against my waist, biting into my flesh. The howling wind whips the salt water violently, stealing the words I desperately scream. I turn frantically, looking for something ... anything to save myself, but I know for certain in my horrified mind that I'm going to drown.

Bee-beep. Bee-beep. Bee-beep.

The pressure-alarm pulls me back. I fight to wake up. As my nightmare drains away, I'm refilled by my waking companions: anger and hate. They steal my breath and render me incapable.

"In ... out ... in ... out," I make myself think. "In ...out ... in ... out."

Lobo is already up, waiting and watching expectantly. Gulping air, I check the monitor and see that Jonny is out of bed. The clock reads 2:30. Pulling back my duvet, I slip my feet over the side; the sensation of freezing cold saltwater briefly returns.

"Don't go there," I warn myself sternly as I find my slippers and pull on my dressing gown. Lobo nudges my leg. Reaching for him, I want to sink to my knees and bury my face in his warm fur, but instead we go downstairs.

The Christmas tree lights from the porch and sitting room light the hallway. They poke at my camouflaged anger that I work so hard to conceal. I quickly switch the hall light on, blotting them out, and knock gently at Jonny's bedroom door.

"Jonny, it's only us, Maggs and Lobo. Is it alright if we come in?" I call warmly.

"Yes, yes, come in, Maggs. I was just about to check the Christmas tree lights."

"Oh Jonny," I sigh softly as all my angst evaporates at the sight of him standing there marooned in his jumper with one arm stuck through the neck hole and the other pinned inside.

"What's the matter, Maggs?" He starts to panic.

"Nothing, I just couldn't sleep." But I realise I'm not quick enough, as his body stiffens and his eyes dart around the room.

"Maggs, is it Julia? Quick, we must hide Lobo," he shouts, frantically looking for a safe place. Choosing the bed, he stumbles towards it.

"It's alright Jonny, she not here. We are safe and no one will hurt Lobo, I won't let them."

"But, Maggs, she's really big. She'll kill him."

"I'm really big too and I won't let her. Lobo is safe ... safe as houses."

"Safe as houses?"

"Yes. Safe as houses."

"Safe as houses," Jonny repeats again, his fear fading as quickly as it had come. "Why are you here, Maggs?"

"I couldn't sleep and I thought I would make a hot chocolate and I wondered if you would keep me company?"

"Yes, I'll just get my jumper on. Do you know where it is?"

"Here, Jonny," I smile, easing his arm into his sleeve.

"Maggs, I just need to check the Christmas lights. Orla will need them to find her way home."

"The lights are all on and Orla is safe as houses. I promise."

"Safe as houses."

"Safe as houses. But I think Lobo needs to go out. Can you take him while I put the kettle on?"

"Come on old boy. Clickerty clack." Stopping to check the two large Christmas trees on the way, I guide him through to the kitchen. On the dining room table, the smallest Christmas tree casts a pool of light across the wooden surface, illuminating the pottery lumps. I look away, not wanting my hate to infect Jonny. Instead, I make myself see the garden lights that twinkle beyond the glass doors. I love this trail of stars that marks my pathway to the only place I truly want to be.

"The tree looks lovely, Maggs. Orla will like it."

"Yes, she will."

"Maggs, is there any cake?"

Later, after I've persuaded Jonny back into bed, I grab the mobile monitor and, with Lobo at my side, I take the starlit path to the end of the garden. At the summerhouse, I wrap the old dog in a thick blanket to keep his bones warm before settling into my favourite chair. This is the best part of the garden. I know every inch of the tiny meadow Orla and I planted with wildflowers. And even though darkness cloaks the blossom trees and the full-size bronze sculpture, I know they are there.

"Fucking Julia Gifford," I tell the bronze figures. "I hope she rots in hell." Unlike my nightmares, which centre solely and selfishly on my own fears, Jonny's fractured mind is always trying to protect others. When his mother storms his brain, like some sort of giant terrorist, he is convinced she is hunting Lobo.

I let my anger flow unchecked before reeling it in as a robin calls, announcing the first rays of dawn light. It grows, casting a rosy glow onto the figures, catching first their faces, before sliding down their metal bodies to their bare feet.

I think about the day ahead. A feeling of dread fills me. Sighing, I turn to Lobo, whose trusting eyes are watching me

"Let's go and get Jonny his breakfast and run the vacuum cleaner around the house before the police arrive," I tell him.

Logan

"Morning, Lo," Grim says, waking Logan with a mug of coffee.

"Morning," she answers, sitting up and running her hand through her hair. The feel of the short spikes still takes her by surprise.

"You okay?" Grim asks.

"Yeah, I'm okay," she replies, taking the coffee with a smile. "No milk then?"

"Nah, didn't know I was having visitors, but come round Thursday for the Mars launch and I'll promise you I'll buy some. Daff, Cheng and Tom are bringing pizza and beer."

"Sounds good."

"How's the investigation going?" Grim asks, sitting down with his mug. "Got anything yet to prove Waxy's Victor Martin?"

"No, but nothing to say he isn't either. We interviewed allotment holders yesterday and one of them reckons she knows who Waxy is and how he got there, but she won't spill the beans till we've heard her story."

"Is she a time waster?"

"Not sure. She doesn't seem the type."

"It's not always obvious. Do you remember that hit and run with… bollocks, what was his name? Donald-Donald Man… something, claimed he'd seen the whole thing. We believed him too. Seemed like a reliable witness."

"Yes, I remember. Donald Manford. Oh, he was a right one! We followed his lead, white transit, partial plates, IC3 driver. Turned out to be a figment of his imagination. We spent hours on it."

"Yeah," Grim laughs, "and do you remember when we threatened him with wasting police time, the fucker claimed he'd been…"

"…brainwashed by aliens," they both say together.

"Jeszus, what a cunt," Grim muses.

"Yeah."

"Are you bringing her in?"

"Nah, I've got a feeling if we let her do it her way, we'll get more

97

out of her. But she's got plenty of attitude. Also, there's a care situation going on. I'll check in with you for a Charge when it's clear what her involvement is."

"And don't forget that Pro-Ass on Tristan Fry. It's due in by the end of the month. What?"

"It's just that I can't make my mind up about him."

"I thought you liked him."

"It's not that."

"Is he a bit of a thicko?"

"No, he's really smart, but I can't help feeling he's too nice for the job. He keeps wanting to help people rather than nick them."

"Bollocks, Lo, you're going soft in your old age. Just write the assessment and give the bloke a chance for promotion. If he can do the job, that's all that matters."

"Yeah, you're right," she nods, before checking the time.

"Fuck, I better get my skates on. Can I use the shower?"

"Knock yourself out."

Tristan Fry

"Hi, Boss," Fry says as he sees Logan rounding the door into the office, munching on a croissant.

"Hey Fry, you all set? Got the Cam?"

"Ready when you are," he answers. Taking the lift down, he sees her eyeing the paper bag he's got in his far hand. He was hoping she wouldn't notice.

"What's in the bag?"

"Oh, just something I picked up."

"What is it?"

"A cupcake."

"Cupcake? Who for... Andrea?"

"No," he mumbles back.

A second passes and he can almost see her brain clicking into gear.

"It's not for Jonny, is it?" she demands.

He'd been queuing in the bakery waiting to buy his morning coffee when he'd spotted the cupcakes with chocolate flakes decorating their tops. It had reminded him of Jonny and then of the old vulnerable man they'd come across on the stairs at the flats in Braxham Wick. That encounter had left him feeling frustrated and powerless. It had made him question the job. He'd stared at the cupcakes, knowing full well that he shouldn't buy gifts for a potential criminal, but he reasoned, "If my life was as severely narrowed as Jonny's, I'd want to fill it with cake too. And, anyway, Jonny isn't a suspect yet... and a cupcake is just a cupcake after all."

"Is it?" Logan asks him again.
"I just thought..." he tries to explain.
"Well, just think again. That constitutes bribery."
"I don't see how. He's an old man with dementia, why would I bribe him?"
"Throw it away or give it to Ducksworth on the front desk. He'll eat anything."
"But..."
"Don't but me, it's against police procedure and you should know that."

The lift stops with a jolt and the doors open. Logan keys in the security code to let herself out as Fry heads for the desk.
"Hey, Ducksworth, fancy a piece of cake?"
"Cheers, mate."

In the car, Logan asks him about the telescope stand. He knows she is just trying to soften the situation, so he tries to sound enthusiastic.
"Great. We've got the tilt sorted for the trajectory, and I'll be able to get the live feed on my Noc, so we can watch the crew and track Maya-Daughter at the same time."
"Sounds good," she answers, negotiating a roundabout. He wonders if he should ask her if she wants to come and join in. He doesn't really want her to, but he knows about the divorce. It's one of the main topics of station gossip, along with Sharon Mulligan's pregnancy and Trevor Dillsworthy's wedding plans.

Andrea had told him there had been a big row in the female

changing rooms last week between Sharon and Rowena Wilkinson, and Rowena didn't hold back by all accounts. She'd had a right go at Sharon, not so much for the Trevor part but her disloyalty to her best friend. Sharon had put in a complaint to Personnel, but Andrea said they'd pretty much ignored it due to a combination of liking Logan and being wary of crossing Rowena. "You can join us if you like," he says tentatively.

"Thanks for asking," Logan replies, joining the A12, "but I'm watching at Grim's. Where's the launch again?"

"Satish Dhawan Space Centre in India," he answers, feeling relieved. "You can take a virtual video tour on their website. See inside Maya-Complete, the launch pad and operation rooms."

They chat about the Mars project until they turn into the overgrown driveway and Fry sees the Christmas tree lights shining out, reminding him again of defenceless old men.

CHAPTER 19
Unzipped My Soul

*

Maggi

Hearing the doorbell, I get to my feet. Laid out in front of the warm oven, Lobo can hardly bring himself to bark. He barely manages one woof and doesn't even lift his head.

"Really Lobo, is that your best shot?" I ask him lovingly. He looks at me, twitching his tail with the beginnings of a wag. "Never mind boy, it's not a burglar, only the police."

As I walk towards the kitchen door, with thoughts of the day ahead, my legs feel like lead and my mood darkens. I can see the shadowy outline of the detectives. It makes me feel afraid, makes me want to run away, but I know that's impossible and, "Besides," I think, "you owe the dead."

"Hello, Maggi," greets D.C.I. Logan as I invite them back into my home. And though her words are casual, I can hear the formality in their delivery. In contrast, D.C. Fry smiles brightly at me.

"Hi, Maggi," he says, following his senior officer in.

"Hello, D.C. Fry."

"How's Jonny this morning?"

"His normal lovely self, thinking about cake." I answer, trying to conceal my worries behind a smile, though I catch D.C.I. Logan's look of attentiveness.

"Where does he go during the day?" D.C. Fry asks as we enter the kitchen.

"Fellowfield House."

"That's in Great Tilling, isn't it? I've heard it's a good place."

"Fry, set up the Cam," D.C.I. Logan orders sharply, taking the chair she'd occupied yesterday.

"I'll make coffee," I say, lighting the hob, trying to put the truth off for a moment longer. I can feel D.C. Fry watching me as he sets out the Cam. With the coffee made, D.C.I. Logan asks for the last two minutes from the previous session.

"Holo," Fry instructs the Cam. "Last. Scroll. Stop. Play."

The tinted 3D image springs to life, hovering just above the table. I see the three of us: me nervously fiddling with my mug, D.C. Fry on the edge of his seat as though he might spring off at any moment, and D.C.I. Logan completely composed. I hear myself explain that Rah wanted a baby.

"Okay, Fry. Record," D.C.I. Logan instructs before turning to me. "Are you ready, Maggi?" she asks rhetorically.

"Ready?" I want to yell back at her, "How am I ever going to be ready to explain what hate makes you do?" But instead I bury my pain and begin. "Rah and Jonny were over the moon when Rah's pregnancy test came back positive. I was okay, happy for them, but no more excited than if we'd been planning on buying a puppy. Children weren't my thing. I knew I'd never have one myself, though that is not to say I didn't love Jim Bob, and I'd spent time with him when he was growing up. But I thought that was different. He was my brother, my flesh and blood, my kin. And if I thought about the baby at all, I thought about it in terms of it being Rah and Jonny's baby, not mine. So how wrong was I…" I pause, my fingers touching my lips, waiting for my lungs to relax. Taking a breath, I force them to work, "…when Orla was born."

"Date?" Logan asks succinctly.

"10 minutes past midnight on the 6th of September, 1984. She came into the world, unzipped my soul and stepped right in."

14 minutes past midnight, 6th September 1984
Her tiny body lies across Rah's belly. Her perfect miniature spine is

curled, with her limbs tucked beneath her. I watch as the oxygen-rich blood, flooding through her vascular system, turns her skin from ivory grey to creamy pink while Jonny and Rah hug each other and cry tears of joy. They'd both previously agreed to each choose a name.

"Do you think the name Orla suits her?" Rah asks, looking up at us.

"Definitely," Jonny says through his tears, "and I choose Éowyn."

I bend down and look into her dark eyes. Her Japanese DNA is already evident in her perfect features and her crowning mass of black hair.

"Hello, Orla," I say gently to the tiny baby girl and she gazes right back at me.

"Maggs, you choose a name too," Rah says.

"Yes, Maggs, what do you think?" Jonny agrees.

"Faith," I murmur, "because she makes me believe."

2023

"What's her full name?" D.C.I. Logan asks.

"Orla Éowyn Faith Montgomery. It was going to be Montgomery Gifford but Jonny couldn't bear to give someone so precious such an evil name."

"I like that," D.C. Fry smiles. "It reminds me of that really old film, *The Lord of the Rings*."

"And you'd be right. It was one of Jonny's favourite books. I think he fancied himself as a Rider of Rohan."

"Is that the complete list of people involved in the Trinity Lane murder?" D.C.I. Logan asks, getting straight back to the point.

"Near enough," I answer.

"So, can we get to the murder?"

"Real life is never that simple, D.C.I. Logan, as I'm sure you know. We didn't all just decide to club together one day and murder someone for fun. If I edit this story much more, it won't make any sense."

"Well, keep it relevant."

"Relevant? This is my life, my family we are talking about, not some

TV drama," I fling back at her. She doesn't respond. She just sits there, patiently watching me. I shut my eyes and feel Lobo's bony head on my lap. I'd not heard him leave his basket, but, as ever, I'm grateful for his love.

Calming myself, I open my eyes and say, "As Orla grew, she became more and more like her mother and grandmother, Gwen. Their Japanese blood, though diluted by several generations of Anglo-Saxon DNA, shone in their appearance. All three had beautiful long, dark hair, liquid brown eyes, olive skin tones and petite frames..."

24th December 1990

"Don't be ridicules, Jonny. That half-breed hasn't got an ounce of Gifford in her, it can't be yours," Julia Gifford declares, in her stupid over-pronounced lady fuckwit voice that makes me want to punch her lights out, as she stares across at six-year-old Orla who is on tiptoes at the ice-cream counter with Rah.

We have tickets for 'The Lion King' to celebrate Jonny's 43rd birthday, and the Giffords have insisted on meeting up for a drink beforehand. It's the second time I've met them. The first time for Rah and Orla, who, luckily, are out of earshot.

"Quite, Jonny old man. If the brat's not yours, you don't have to pay for it." Edmund endorses.

"You really take the fucking biscuit," I snap back at them.

"Maggi, my dear, you are oversensitive. I suspect it's your working-class background. You must learn to control your emotions," Julia caws insidiously.

"Let's go," Jonny says, rising to his feet. "Orla," he calls to the small girl dressed in her smartest party dress with her hair, plaited like her mother's, down her back. She turns at her name.

"Yes, Daddy?"

"I know the theatre has a much better selection of ice-creams. And they come in little tubs with teeny-weeny spoons. I think we should go and buy our ice-creams there." Rah, looking across at me, raises her eyebrows. I nod towards Julia, trying to restrain myself from

*making a wanking gesture, and she nods back, grinning. "I'm going
to have chocolate, what would you like?" Jonny asks his daughter.
"Chocolate too," she answers excitedly, which makes me smile.
"Oh, that sounds delicious, but I'm having raspberry. I bet Maggs
will have coffee though," Rah chats affably while pushing Orla's
small arms into her coat and pulling her hat on. "Say goodbye to
your grandmother and grandfather, Orla."
"Goodbye, Grandmama and Grandpapa, I hope you have a nice
Christmas. Maggs, do you think Simba likes ice-cream?"
"Of course," I smile and kiss her as I button up her coat and Rah
pulls on her own.
"Goodbye, Julia, Edmund," Rah flings over her shoulder as she
takes Orla's small hand and heads for the cafe door.
As I follow, I hear Jonny quietly say, "Thank you for my birthday
card. And since I know what bigoted arseholes you are, I'll forgive
you this time, but if you ever call my beautiful daughter a half-breed
brat again, or refer to Maggi's background as something
demeaning, I won't a second time."*

2023

"…Orla was a miniature copy of her mother; Jonny's contribution
seemed not to have made much of an impression on her make-up,
apart from perhaps his sense of humour. She'd also inherited Rah's
gift of music and love of art. I've seen you look at my mug and the
pottery figures on the table – they're Orla's. My mug was my
Christmas present from her when she was six. Jonny and Rah have
one too. Rah had a pottery room at the end of the garden. She made
all the pottery in this house, the beautiful mugs, coffee pots, bowls,
plates, you name it and she made it. Orla would spend hours down
there with Rah creating all sorts. The figures on the table are some of
the first creations and are by far my favourites. But, like her mother,
it was music that filled her soul.

I don't remember a time when she was unable to play. Of course,
there must've been when she was very small, but right from a
toddler she'd climb onto the piano stool and bang away at the

keys…"

1986

*"Maggs, listen," Rah marvels as we stand just beyond the doorway
to the music room, watching two-year-old Orla through the crack
between the door and the hinges. All I can hear, if I'm honest, is a
steady plink plonk as she presses the keys down with her tiny chubby
fingers.*

"That's cute," I reply.

*"No," Rah whispers, "I don't mean that. Obvs she's cute, she's
ours. But listen."*

"Uhmm, to what?"

*"Oh, Maggs," she says, punching my arm playfully, "It's virtually in
time."*

2023

"…Rah always said she was a natural talent, she understood stuff
without having to be taught. Anyway, after the piano, Rah taught her
recorder until she was old enough to play the oboe. The problem
came when Orla wanted to push through the conventional and
interpret the music in her own way.

And that brings my story up to 1997, when Orla was thirteen."

"1997?" D.C.I. Logan questions.

"22nd December 1997 to be more precise."

"What happened?" D.C. Fry asks, and I can tell from his tone he
knows it's nothing good.

"Orla was thirteen, which apart from being a brilliant oboist she was
also testing her boundaries. Rah had given Orla her old oboe when
she'd passed her grade seven with a distinction, which was no great
surprise as she'd had passed all her music exams with distinctions.
What you may not understand is that this oboe, to buy new, would
probably have cost in the region of £7,000."

"£7,000?" exclaims D.C. Fry.

"I know, it's a lot of money. Rah's parents had bought it for her
when she'd graduated from music uni. Anyway, what I didn't really

106

understand, though I probably should've after living with an oboist for years, is the value of the instrument, and I'm not talking financially here. Rah loved that oboe and knew it intimately. Orla instinctively understood its worth and knew the value of the gift. As I've already explained, Orla was like a miniature copy of Rah and they were very close. They looked like each other, they laughed and cried at the same things, they liked the same food, the same movies, the same music, but, when they clashed, they clashed and at that particular moment it was over Orla's oboe lessons.

They'd had a big row over a grade eight piece that Orla wanted to play in her own style, but Rah knew that she needed to perform it within the conventional manner to gain the marks…"

1997

"I don't care about the exam," I hear Orla shout in frustration after Rah has stopped her mid-phrase. "I know you want me to play it all wooden and hard, but that's not how I hear it."

"Orla, it's not what I want, it's what is required," Rah patiently explains for the umpteenth time, though I can detect her exasperation. And so can Orla.

"You don't understand," she cries, running up to her bedroom and slamming the door. Going into to the music room, I find Rah battling with her own frustrations.

"The trouble is, I do understand, I understand completely, but if she wants to gain entry to a major music school, she needs a distinction at grade eight. I remember feeling exactly as she does at her age, trapped by traditional constraints. In fact, I still feel it sometimes now, if we are working under an orthodox conductor. I've been thinking for a while that I'm going to have to stop teaching her."

"Why?" I ask. "You're brilliant and she learns so much from you."

"I think it's an age thing, this anger at me, taking my instruction as a personal criticism. She might respond more objectively under another teacher. I don't want to ruin her chances of a career in music over a stupid mother/daughter thing," she expresses, biting her nails.

"Do you have anyone in mind?" I ask, automatically moving her hand away from her mouth.

"Sorry," she motions with her hand. "There's Roxanne Agnew, she's a brilliant tutor but she only takes on a few students at a time and I know there's a waiting list."

"If you asked her though she might consider Orla."

"Maybe. But in the meantime, I wonder if Herrick would fill in for me."

"Do you think that's a good idea? Orla's not that keen on him."

"She's not that keen on me either, but Herrick is a really good oboist, he knows his stuff and he has the patience of a saint."

"That's true," I murmur, knowing Orla will hate the idea.

2023

"…That argument confirmed Rah's worry that Orla's attitude was translating itself into her playing. She decided to find her another oboe teacher, but with the grade exam looming, she asked Herrick, who taught occasionally, if he'd mind stepping in to help. Herrick, as always, said yes. I think if she'd asked him to fly to the moon, he would have gone straight home and started to build a rocket." I pause. Gripping the edge of the table, I feel the old, wood solid under my hands, unlike my life, that's shifting quickly now, like sand slipping through a timer. I feel more than see D.C.I. Logan looking at me expectantly.

"So, here it is," I continue, surprised by the strength of my voice. "The 22nd of December 1997…"

CHAPTER 20
Creepy Freaky Frankenstein
*

Maggi

"…I woke early and pottered around the kitchen. It was still very dark outside, but I could see the first part of the garden lit by the kitchen lights. There'd been snow in the night, carpeting the garden path and the trees with a pure white. I was making porridge and thinking about Jonny's birthday party. I smelt Rah's Riva perfume and knew she'd come into the kitchen. I turned and, like always, she took my breath away with her beauty. She was wearing her blue dress with her dark hair plaited in a single braid down her back. She was off to London as her oboe needed to be serviced before the Christmas Eve concert…"

22nd December 1997
"You look fanbloodytastic," I say as she snakes her arms around my waist and lays her head gently on my back.
"Thanks, girlfriend," she answers.
"Are you still meeting Lucy?"
"Yes. I'll drop my oboe in, then I'm shopping for Orla's Christmas present and Jonny's birthday present before I meet her."
"Oh, I thought we were giving him that enormous canvas you've been working on for the last six months?"
"Yeah, but… I'm not sure. Do you think it's good enough? Do you think he'll like it?"

"Bloody hell Rah, he'll love it! Jesus, you know he's been eyeing it and dropping hints forever."

"Okay, but shall I look for his Christmas present from us?"

"If you see anything that shouts, 'I should belong to Jonny Gifford' then get it, but if not, don't worry because I've bought that thing he wanted for his car."

"And me…? Have you bought that thing I wanted for my neck?" she asks sweetly.

"Shut up," I laugh back, "and eat your breakfast. It's cold out and the porridge will keep you warm."

2023

"…We sat at this table and she switched on the little Christmas tree that Orla had bought that year with her pocket money. As I am sure you are aware that since Orla was very small she has a love of Christmas tree lights.

Anyway, I served the porridge and coffee in the mugs Orla had made. It was so peaceful; it was the last time we were truly happy…"

1997

"So, are you still thinking about the latest Spice Girls CD for Orla?" I ask between mouthfuls.

"Yes, what do you think? And some clothes? I've heard of a new fashion store that's opened on Oxford Street catering for young teenagers."

"I think that's great, you're always good at picking stuff for her. Do you remember those Spice Girls trousers you bought her last year with the crop top to match?"

"Oh God, she loved them, pranced about all Christmas in them. Do you remember they were the clothes Jonny's mother was so rude about, when he sent her the photo?"

"Do I. Fucking Granny Cunt."

"Maggs!" Rah says in her 'I'm sort of shocked but at the same time that's really funny' voice.

"What?" I answer innocently.

"You can't call her Granny Cunt."

"Yes, I can... Granny Cunt, Granny Cunt, Granny Cunt," I repeat through my laughter.

"Stop it," she says laughing too, "My make-up will run."

"Granny Cunt," I mouth back at her as she tries to dab the corners of her eyes with a tissue.

"Stop it. I've got to be a sensible mother now. I need to talk to Orla before I go, make sure she knows what she's doing today."

"What you are saying is... can I go and get her up," I say knowingly.

"Pleeease, you are always so good at it."

2023

"…Rah wanted to have a chat with Orla before she left for London, to check whether she'd remembered she had a lesson with Herrick. I don't think Rah thought Orla had forgotten, I think she was more concerned that Orla might pretend to have forgotten and, by reminding her, she was letting her know that she couldn't get out of it on the grounds that she'd forgotten.

I was always better at getting Orla out of bed, so I went to wake her…"

1997

"Good morning, Sunshine," I sing in my not-very-good singing voice, while balancing a mug of coffee in one hand and opening Orla's bedroom door with the other. Putting down the mug on her bedside table, I pull back the curtains. Weak winter sunlight fills the room, illuminating the varying Spice Girls posters stuck to her walls.

"Maaaggs," Orla moans dramatically from under her covers. "It's the holidays. I don't need to get up."

"I know sweetheart, but Mum wants a quick word with you before she goes to London. You can go back to bed afterwards."

"Do I have to?"

"Yes, I think you do love. Come on, here's your dressing gown, all

warm from the radiator. And Orla..."

"Yes?" she answers as though my question is bound to be something totally unreasonable.

"Try not to get annoyed with Mum. She's always a bit edgy before a big concert and she only wants what's best for you."

"What, like having to go to Creepy Freaky Frankenstein's house for a music lesson," which makes me chuckle, though I know I shouldn't. "Okay," she says resignedly, sitting up in bed and grabbing the coffee, "I'll try, but you've got to admit, Maggs, he is creepy and he does look a bit like Frankenstein."

"If I admit that, then you and Jonny will only do that Frankenstein shuffle thing with your arms out behind Herrick's back on Christmas Day and I won't be able to keep a straight face and Rah will have my guts for garters."

"Oh no, Creepy Freaky isn't coming on Christmas Day again?" she says with an exaggerated sigh that only a teenager can pull off.

"Only for lunch. Minty, Gwen and Jim Bob, plus his latest girlfriend, will be here too."

"Oh, I love Funcle Jim Bob, do you think he'll get drunk again and do his Irish dancing?"

"Probably, and that's bound to impress his girlfriend," I chuckle again. "Come on down and don't be long, as Mum has a train to catch."

"Okay ... and, Maaaaggs?"

"Yes?"

"Can you put the Christmas tree lights on, pleeease, pleeease, pleeease? I love coming downstairs when the Christmas tree lights are on. They look all twinkly and pretty."

"It's a deal, I'll put the lights on and you come downstairs and be nice to Mum."

"Deal," she says happily, climbing out from under her duvet.

After switching on the Christmas tree lights in the porch and the sitting room, I go back to the kitchen. Rah looks up expectantly.

"Is she coming?" she asks calmly, though I can see she's been biting her nails.

"Yes, she'll be down in a mo and stop biting your nails."

"Sorry. I just know it's going to be a battle getting her to go for her lesson today."

"Have you spoken to Roxanne thingy about teaching her yet?"

"Roxanne Agnew. Yes, she said she might be able to do something in the New Year."

"That's good." The kitchen door bangs open and in wanders a tousled Orla, one long messy plait hanging over her left shoulder, looking just like her mother does when she climbs out of bed.

"Hi Mum," she says sweetly, hugging Rah before slipping her tiny frame into the chair next to her.

"Hello, sweetheart," Rah replies. *"I'm off to London Christmas shopping today for my most favourite person in all the world."*

"That will be me then," I say, getting the smiles I wanted from both of them.

"S'pose you want to talk to me about my lesson with Creepy Freaky Frankenstein today," Orla says, glancing up at me. I try to hide my smile but she sees it and smiles back at me.

"Yes, and please don't call him that, it's not very kind. Herrick will help you get the distinction you need for your grade eight, if you do as he says. He's a really nice person, if you just give him a chance."

"Minty and Jonny don't like him," Orla retorts. I give her my stern look.

"I know, but I do. He's a nice bloke and he is giving you his time and advice for free, so the least you could do is be thankful."

"Alright," she answers, looking back at me. I wink a thank you.

"Your lesson is at..."

"11, I know," she interjects.

"Great, I'll see you when I get back. Maggs is working an afternoon shift but Jonny's around if you need anyone."

2023

"...Orla came down and Rah reminded her about the music lesson. Orla moaned a bit and called Herrick Creepy Freaky Frankenstein, which always upset Rah."

113

"Creepy Freaky Frankenstein?" queries D.C. Fry.

"A stupid name her and Jonny called Herrick. They'd stand behind him with their arms out like Frankenstein's monster and pretend they'd got bolts through their necks. I don't really know why. Anyway, I must admit I kind've found it funny, but it used to piss Rah off.

Then Orla asked if she could go and see her best friend after her lesson…"

1997

"Can I go to Chante's this afternoon? I can take the bus, no one'll have to drive me."

"You know I don't like you going over there, Orla," Rah says, trying to keep her tone reasonable.

"Why not?" Orla snaps back, though I know she knows perfectly well why not.

"You know why," Rah answers, her calmness fraying at the edges.

"You just don't like Chante because her family is poor and live in a flat."

"No, I do like Chantelle, I just don't like the way her parents are always drinking and I don't like the people that hang out there. But if you put in a good lesson and practice, Chantelle can come over here for the night if you like. And I'll make pizza and popcorn and you can hire some movies."

"S'pose," Orla answers grudgingly, but I see her stroppiness already diminishing.

"Good. Okay, I've got to go." After grabbing her coat, bag and oboe, Rah kisses and hugs us both.

"Don't forget my present," I say, making Orla laugh.

2023

"…Rah didn't want Orla to go to her friend's flat as the family were notorious for drugs and alcohol. I know coming from a family that commits murder that sounds pretty lame, but at that moment we were all still innocent…"

CHAPTER 21
A Musical Heathen

*

Maggi

"…So Rah invited Chantelle over to ours for a sleepover. After she left, I cleared up while Orla dressed and started her practice. Just before 10:30, I popped my head around the music room door to let her know I was off to work. Her hair was scraped back from her face in a high ponytail that snaked down her small back. I noticed she was dressed in her Spice Girls t-shirt, tracksuit pants and trainers..."

1997

"You look like Sporty Spice," I tell her, knowing it'll make her feel good. "I'm off in a jiff. And remember…"

"I've got Creepy Freaky at 11, I know," she says, though she is smiling.

"Do you want me to drop you off?" I offer.

"Nah, it only takes me 10 minutes on my bike."

"Orla, you know Mum doesn't like you riding your bike with your oboe, especially the way you balance it on the handlebars."

"I won't tell her if you don't," she jokes.

"Cheeky monkey," I say, blowing her a kiss before leaving the room.

2023

"…I offered to drop her at Herrick's but she said she was taking her bike. As I walked to the front door, I heard her starting the first

movement of Mozart's Concerto in C Major. You might wonder
how a musical heathen such as myself knew that, but I'd often spent
time lurking in the hallway, just outside the music room door,
listening to Rah and Orla's endless practices. That day too I leaned
against the hall wall listening to Mozart's perfect sonorous rhythms
and, as if to add to the magic, I could see snowflakes falling
gracefully through the glass of the front door. After a few minutes I
pushed myself off the wall and went to work.

My day started with an emergency RTA. We had three on the
table. Two we saved but the third was hopeless. He was only young,
no more than twenty. His airways were compromised and although
Mike and I worked tirelessly, we couldn't save him.

Cleaning the theatre afterwards I was feeling subdued. It affects
all of us when we have a patient die on the table. Some people joke
around, some snap and others, like myself, become introverted. I'd
just finished disinfecting the floor when a phone call came through
for me…"

1997

*"Hey, Maggi," I look up and see Terry's big burly frame filling the
doorway, "there's a call for you."*

*"Cheers, Terry. Jo, do you mind?" I ask, not wanting to leave her
with the rest of the cleaning.*

*"Take it," she replies. Pulling off my gloves, I calmly walk through
to the adjoining anaesthetic room where the phone, attached to the
wall, has its receiver sitting on the worktop.*

*"This is not going to be good," I think as I pick up. "Hi, it's
Maggi."*

*"It's Orla," Rah's frightened voice answers me, "I don't know
where she is."*

*"Okay, have you just got in?" I ask, trying to sound confident, but
my gut twists nervously.*

*"Yes, half an hour ago. I was able to pick my oboe up, so I got an
earlier train home. But she's not here. Jonny says he's not seen or
heard from her. He's on his way over but he's got a nightshift*

116

tonight." I can hear the panic rising in her voice; it matches my own.

"Rah, look she's probably gone off to see that friend of hers, Chantelle. She was pretty pissed off with you this morning over her lesson and she knows you don't want her to hang out at Chantelle's house," I say, attempting to keep my own voice level.

"I know, I know ... but I did say Chantelle could sleep at ours," she pleads.

"She's a teenager now Rah, and she probably thought that if she had her lesson she'd earned the right to do what she wanted. Have you phoned Herrick?"

"Yes, almost straight away."

"What did he say?"

"That she'd left his just after 12 and they'd had a really good lesson and she seemed herself. But I know she's not been home; everything is the same from when you cleared up this morning and, anyway, her oboe isn't here." Rah's voice is reaching new highs of distress. Looking at the clock on the anaesthetic room wall, I see it's just gone five. "Fuck," I think, "where is she?"

"Maggs?"

"It's alright, I'm here. Listen, it's ten minutes past five. My shift finishes at eight. Sit tight and I'll be home and if she's not back by then I'll drop by Chantelle's and pick her up," I answer, striving to sound rational.

"Fuck, Maggs, I'm really worried," she cries, tearing at my heart.

"Okay, okay, listen," I say desperately, trying to stop myself from tumbling into the rapidly widening pit of panic I'm feeling. "I'll see what's next on the list and I might be able to get someone to cover for me. Then I'll be there as soon as possible."

"Thanks, Maggs, but hurry, please," she begs.

"Hang on, Rah, Jonny will be there any moment now," and with that I hear him in the background. Ringing off, a wave of dread sweeps through me, leaving me breathless and sick. I lean against the worktop trying to reason it out.

"Look, you were feeling bad before you picked the phone up, Orla's

117

probably at Chantelle's right now getting up to naughty stuff like all good teenagers." Forcing my nausea down and taking a deep breath, I go back into the theatre.

"Crikey Maggi, you look like shit. What's happened?" Jo exclaims as I walk back in.

"Nothing ... maybe ... or something, I'm not sure."

"I'll give it to you girl, you know how to deliver a concise answer."

"Sorry ... it's just Norah, she phoned to say Orla's not come home."

"That's bloomin' teenagers for you. If she's anything like my Tilda, she'll turn up when she's hungry."

"Yeah, that's what I told Norah, but I can't help but feel worried."

"Probably 'coz we lost that lad earlier. It's always shit when that happens."

"Yeah, I thought that too."

"Do you know what's next on the list for this theatre?"

"A knee. I could do with more practice on knees. How about you go home and then cover for me one afternoon?"

"Cheers Jo, I was hoping you might say that."

"Go Maggi, I'll clear it with Terry."

"Thanks, I owe you one."

"No worries."

2023

"...It was Rah on the phone panicking because Orla had not come home. So I left work without even stopping to change out of my scrubs and headed back to Godlinghoe. The roads were already icing up causing the traffic to slow to a snail's pace, making me feel irritated and anxious. As I crawled along with the other vehicles, I tried to force myself to believe it was a storm in a teacup. That Orla would be at home when I arrived. Pulling into the driveway, Rah flew out of the front door with Jonny behind her and I knew my prayers had not been answered..."

CHAPTER 22
Toe Rag

*

Maggi - 22nd December 1997

*"Maggs, she's not here, she's not home," Rah cries, burrowing
herself into my arms, making my heart pound with fear.*

*I look at Jonny. The snow is gently falling all around him, his face is
taut, his eyes wide with dread. He shrugs his shoulders at me in
despair.*

*"Okay, have you got a phone number for Chantelle?" I say, taking
Rah's hand and leading her out of the cold.*

"Yes, but there's no answer. I've tried ringing and ringing."

"Do you know where she lives, Maggs?" Jonny asks.

*"Sort of. It's a block of flats in Braxham Wick. I picked Orla up from
there last summer."*

"Do you want me to go?" he offers.

*"No, by the time I've tried to explain where I think it is, I'd be
halfway to Braxham Wick."*

"I'll come with you," he says.

"I'm coming too," Rah demands, grabbing her coat.

*"Maybe it would be better if you stayed here, just in case she comes
home?" I suggest.*

"No, I'm coming," she almost shouts.

"Jonny?"

*"I'll stay," he says with his usual grace, because I know he wants to
come too.*

119

2023

"...We decided that Rah and I should head back to Braxham Wick to see if Orla was at Chantelle's, leaving Jonny at home just in case she turned up. Rah was rigid and silent in the front seat. She sat staring wide-eyed at the road, and I felt her willing me to go faster. At one point, on the main road, we got stuck behind a gritting lorry and I thought she might burst with frustration, but she didn't say anything. I tried to tell her it was going to be alright but she shut her eyes and said, almost in a whisper, not to tempt fate. After that, we were both wordless with just the whir of the heater and the swish of the wiper blades breaking the silence.

In Braxham Wick I had to really think about where Chantelle lived. After a couple of false starts I found the block of flats. I tried to conjure up that summer's day when I'd picked Orla up. I remembered climbing the concrete stairs, as the lift was broken. The stairs had stunk of stale urine and vomit and I was pleased Rah wasn't with me or she'd have had a fit..."

1997

"I'm pretty sure this is it," I tell Rah as we get out of the car.
"Do you know which flat it is?"
"Not exactly. It was either floor 3 or 5. I know it's an odd number. Do you remember what Chantelle's surname is?"
"Uhmm," Rah frowns, biting the nail on her index finger,
"Chantelle Mo-Mollon, yes Mollon."
"Right." One of the double-entry doors hangs awkwardly while the other swings and bangs in the wind. We step gingerly into the small entrance hall that's lit by a dim overhead light that randomly flicks up and down its long fluorescent tube. The same 'out of order' notice is still stuck on the lift door, so we round the corner and start to climb the concrete stairway.
At the third floor, I glance along the grim landing.
"Does it look familiar?" Rah asks.
"Could be. Let's try." I begin knocking on doors. By the fourth flat, I get an answer. A waft of stale cigarette smoke and fried food seeps

out from behind a woman in her late thirties.

"Wot?" she demands.

"Sorry to bother you, but I'm looking for a teenage girl called Chantelle Mollon," I say calmly, though I'd really like to match the women's aggression.

"Wat you wan' dat li'le toe rag for?" she barks back at me.

"I'm here to pick up my daughter and I stupidly forgot the address," I answer, trying to keep my temper in check.

"Dat one, 37," she says, pointing further along the landing before slamming her front door shut.

"Thanks," I mutter at the closed door. Rah races to 37 with her fist raised ready to knock but stops and stares. I catch up with her and see the problem. Much of the door's surface is fractured glass or gapping boarding. Choosing the least likely place to cut her hand, she knocks loudly. A dog barks, deep and guttural, an interior door opens, flooding the flat corridor with light. A fuzzy, human shape distorted by the shattered glass, fills the space and a man's voice, rough and pitted, shouts through the locked door.

"Oow's it?"

"It's Orla's Mum," I reply trying to keep my voice level and friendly.

"Oow?"

"Orla's mum. Orla Montgomery. She's a friend of Chantelle's."

"Ow 'er," he mutters walking away from the door. My panic rises and I'm about to shout again when I hear him yell, "Chantty, Chantty get your fuc'in' arse down 'ere. Dat snobby friend 'f yours's mum's 'ere." The frayed man disappears into the lit room, shutting the door and leaving us in darkness. Rah lifts her hand to bang again but another light goes on and a moment later, Chantelle opens the front door.

"Hi," she whispers.

"Hi Chantelle, we are looking for Orla, is she here?"

"No. She was meant to come over this afternoon but she didn't come." A rush of adrenalin tears through me, my heart explodes, suffocating me. I cough and splutter trying to regain my breath while

Rah begins to slide down the wall.

"Chantelle love," I say, struggling to get my words out. "can you remember when you last saw her?"

"I don't know... last week ... maybe ...Thursday but I spoke to her on the phone Friday."

"Did she say she was going anywhere today?"

"Yeah," I'm rooted, statue still. "Music lesson and then 'ere."

"Thanks, love," I mutter as failure swamps me, driving out my hope. I look down at Rah, whose now sunk onto the dirty floor.

"Is..," Chantelle begins cautiously, "Is she okay?"

"I don't know, Love, we can't find her," I murmur through my tears.

"Oh," Chantelle murmurs back as I bend down and put my arms around Rah, lifting her to her feet.

"Let's go home," I say, "and call the police."

2023

"...We found the right flat and spoke to Chantelle Mollon."

"Mollon?" D.C.I. Logan immediately queries.

"Yes, Chantelle Mollon, Why?"

"Just a surname that is well known to us."

"Anyway, Chantelle hadn't seen Orla and I believed her. She might have come from a shitty family but she was a nice girl.

So we left and if I thought it had taken me ages to drive to Braxham Wick, it was nothing compared to the journey home. The smaller un-gritted roads were now frozen, cars were creeping along and the snow was falling in driving sheets. Rah sat with her face in her hands, rocking back and forth. At last I turned for Godlinghoe. I took the hill in second gear but the back of the car slid and twisted nearly sending us off the road. I managed to keep going and made it to the top.

As we entered our road Rah took off her seat belt and got ready to dive out of the car. I knew why. She was hoping the nightmare would be over, that Orla would be there saying something like, 'I'm sorry Mum, I was only at so-'n-sos.' But it was Jonny who opened the door shaking his head. His face was bleached white and I saw his hand shake as he shut the front door behind us.

"Nothing?" he asked me, though I knew he knew the answer. I told him I was calling the police and he agreed. Herrick was there too and he said Orla had left his about 10 minutes or so after 12. So I picked up the phone and dialled 999…"

CHAPTER 23
Ashes of the Dead

*

Maggi - 1997

Jonny comes to my side and holds my hand as I grip the receiver and dial. I can see Rah now in Herrick's arms. They all listen as the call is answered.

"Which service do you require?" the operator asks.

"Police," I answer struggling against the syllables.

"Please hold while I put you through."

"Police. How may I help you?"

"My daughter is..." stumbling, I feel Jonny take the receiver from my hand and I hear him say, "Our daughter is missing. She has not been seen since 12 p.m." I feel sick as I wait for Jonny to speak again.

"Please can you repeat the number while I write it down?" Jonny asks. We all watch him write the code for Braxham Wick followed by a telephone number.

"How long should we wait?" I can hear his stress in his question. The seconds seem to turn into minutes before Jonny speaks again.

"I'm not sure we should. This is out of character for her; she has never not come home before," he explains, pausing for the reply.

"Right. I'll ring if she comes home." Putting the phone down he turns to us. "He said all the usual stuff about teenagers going missing and how they inevitably turn up. How we shouldn't worry. And give it till tomorro..."

"Tomorrow?" Rah pronounces in a horrified voice.
"That's what he said but ... what's the time now?"
"7:34," Herrick says, checking his watch.
"Let's give it till 8 then I'll ring the local station in Braxham Wick, he gave me the number."

2023

"...In the end, Jonny made the call and they fobbed him off with the usual crap about teenagers always turning up sooner or later. But he did get the phone number for Braxham Wick police station and we made a decision to give it half an hour before phoning them. I decided to go and make tea and toast, not that I wanted to eat but I knew I needed to and so did the others. I boiled the kettle and toasted the bread, then put it all on the table next to Orla's tree. Herrick said he had to go but he'd check in later. I felt immensely grateful to him that he'd cared enough to take it seriously, unlike the police.

Jonny phoned the hospital and cancelled his shift and we sat and watched the hands on the clock laboriously tick towards the hour. At eight, Jonny picked up the phone and called Braxham Wick police. We huddled again in the hall and waited with baited breath but it pretty much followed the same pattern as the first call. He tried again at 9 p.m., then 10. Then I phoned at 11 and demanded a response. At 12:40, the police arrived. Jonny let them in. P.C. Bird and P.C. Doran. They sat where you are sitting now. Dark, and covered in equipment.

Jonny and I went right through all the details again while Rah, frozen in a state of shock, bit through the last of her nails, adding nothing..."

1997

"What was your daughter wearing when you last saw her?" P.C. Bird asks.
"Her hair was tied into a ponytail, held by a white band. A pink, collared Spice Girls T shirt over navy track suit pants that have a white stripe down the outside of the leg and black trainers," I tell

him, silently thanking the gods that I'd noticed that today.

"The trainers have a white line around the sole," Rah adds, speaking for the first time. I look at her. "She always wears those trainers with the track suit bottoms and pink t-shirt," she explains flatly to me before saying to P.C. Bird, "She wants to look like Sporty Spice."

"I know, I've got a daughter of my own," the police officer replies. "Can we have Herrick Butler's address?"

"16, Bosuns Road," I tell him. "It's about five minutes in a car, 10 on foot."

"Was your daughter walking?"

"No, bike," I say glancing over at Rah and feeling I'm betraying Orla's trust.

"Bike?" Rah murmurs jumping up and shooting out the front door. A rush of guilt sweeps through me.

"What if it's my fault for letting Orla take her bike?" I think. Out loud I voice my fears. "Perhaps she's come off and is lying in a ditch somewhere? Maybe she's unconscious and now with this weather...Oh my god," I mumble, feeling mortified at the idea.

"I don't think so Maggs, coz there's not really any ditches on her route," Jonny reasons, but my guilt doesn't let up.

"What if she fell off her bike and broke her oboe and is now too scared to come home?" I whimper pathetically clutching my hand to my mouth.

"Is that likely?" P.C. Doran asks.

"No," Jonny states firmly. "There's no way she wouldn't have come home and told at least me or Maggs, even if she'd been worried about telling Norah."

"Where has Norah gone?" P.C. Bird asks.

"To the garage," Jonny answers and I wonder why I hadn't thought to look there myself. Moments later Rah returns, she stands in the doorway, her face twisted with pain and washed of colour, her brow crumpled, her dark hair flaked with snow like a biblical mourner whose covered their head in the ashes of the dead.

"No," she cries, "it's not there."

"Well, it's a place to start. Do you know the route she would have taken from Bosuns Road home?" P.C. Bird asks.

2023

"…We gave them a description of Orla and her bike as well as Herrick's address. The police left saying they were going to check out her route. After they'd gone, I couldn't sit there any longer doing nothing so Jonny and I decided to go out and search the streets…"

1997

"I'm coming too," Rah insists.

"Rah, you're too tired," I tell her, looking into her exhausted face. "Besides I need you to stay here and listen for the phone and answer the door to the police. Make some tea and more toast so you're strong when I get back, I'll need you then to…"

"Don't fob me off Maggs, I'm not a child," she throws back at me.

"No, you're not," I answer just as sharply before taking her hands in mine and looking into her eyes. "So here's the thing… you're tired out. You haven't eaten or drunk anything. You'll be useless out there in the cold. Jonny and I can split up and search properly, you'd just slow us down."

"I see that," she surrenders, her tears running freely down her smooth cheeks. Taking her sweet face into my hands, I kiss her gently.

"Rah, you must eat and drink so you can concentrate on helping. I know you don't want to but you'll be by manning the phone and answering the door." She nods. "Jonny, are you ready?"

"Yeah," he answers pulling on his boots and buttoning his coat.

"You'll need hats, gloves and torches. I'll get the hats and gloves," Rah volunteers, dashing to the cupboard under the stairs.

"Did you eat anything, Jonny?"

"No." Riffling in the kitchen cupboard, I find some energy bars that Rah uses when nerves stop her from eating before a concert.

"Here," I say tossing one to him. "Eat it." I peel the wrapper off my own bar without looking at the flavour. I don't give a shit what it is,

I just know I need to fuel myself for the night ahead. I take a big bite. It feels like glue in my mouth, my throat closes and I want to spit it out. I swallow, it sticks in my gullet, I wash it down with a mouthful of cold tea. Another bite, then the next. I manage three before I know if I push it any further, it will all come shooting up again. I look at Jonny chewing away determinedly and know he isn't fairing much better. Stuffing the rest of my bar into my coat pocket, I see Jonny do the same.

"Here," Rah hands us each a hat, scarf and gloves. "And I've found a torch too. I think Minty left it here when he was checking the meters. What the fuck does that matter? I don't know why I said that. For god's sake, I can't speak, and then when I do, crap falls out of my mouth."

"Better crap than nothing," Jonny comments kissing her gently, "You take that torch, Maggs, I've got another one in my car."

2023

"…As we left to start our search, I could hear my voice organising Jonny and Rah. I sounded assertive and calm, but inside I was sick with nerves and there was something else too, something I didn't want to admit to. A darkness… no, more a blackness that filled my chest and crept up my throat making me want to curl into a corner and disappear from the world. I swallowed it back down because I knew it was never going to help me find Orla. Jonny and I left, it was about 1.30 in the morning…"

1997

Stepping outside and pulling the front door shut behind me, the cold bites into my face. I tighten the scarf around my mouth and smell Rah's Riva perfume impregnated into the fabric. The wind has dropped, making the snow fall softly from the dark sky.

"Which way?" Jonny asks.

"I'll take Isaac's Cut, then Thomas Avenue, down Sail Street and into Bosuns Rd."

"Right, I'll do the Isaac's Cut with you but turn down Trafalgar

along the High Street then meet you outside Herrick's. If neither of us have found anything, I suggest we both search Lead Lane together."

"Yes," I say gratefully as I don't want to do either the Cut or Lead Lane on my own. Both will be pitch black with bushes and waste ground. It isn't that I am scared for myself, it is because I'm scared I could miss something really important.

2023

"…We agreed to search a footpath together that Orla would most likely have taken, then split up and meet at Herrick's. Herrick's house backs onto a lane, which is less of a lane and more of a pot holed track. It has no lighting and is bordered by an overgrown hedgerow with fields on one side and back gardens and out buildings on the other. Orla could have easily taken the lane to the High Street. It is not any quicker in distance but it misses out the traffic on Bosuns Road…"

1997

Setting out, I can feel snow crunch softly under my feet. Ghostly white shapes loom out of the darkness at us. The world feels vacant and dead. Isaac's Cut is empty apart from the odd dog turd and a couple of empty cans. Splitting up, I begin to search every front garden, every bush, every bin. Nothing. As I reach Bosuns Road, I see a pool of light ahead. It is leaking from Herrick's front door. I can see him illuminated by his hall light, while two dark shapes head out of his front gate. I guess rightly; they are P.C. Bird and P.C. Doran. I don't know why but I feel as though someone has brushed my fur up the wrong way. It makes me stay hidden in the shadows where neither Herrick nor the police can see me.

"Goodnight, Officers," Herrick says, raising his hand.

"Goodnight, Mr Butler, and sorry to have disturbed you so late."

"No problem, really, anytime. If I can do anything to help, please just ask." I watch Herrick watch the Officers get into their squad car. I linger until he's about to close his front door before stepping

into the light.

"Hey, Herrick," I call.

"Goodness, Maggs, is that you?" he exclaims, patting his chest in fright. He is wearing a dark, tartan dressing gown over pyjamas, with matching slippers. He looks as though he has stepped right out of a 50's dressmaking pattern.

"Yeah, just thought I'd have a look about, you know, just in case," I say trailing off.

"It's cold and," checking his watch, "it's nearly 3 in the morning. Come in and let me make you a hot drink."

"Nah, but thanks anyway. I'm meeting Jonny here. He should be along in a minute."

"Do you want me to come and help? It'll only take me a jiffy to get my clothes on," he volunteers sincerely.

"You're okay, but thanks."

"Where's Rah? Is she out too?"

"At home, waiting," I trail off again. I just can't think about her right at this moment. I know if I do, I'll want to go home and make sure she is…. what? Alright? Well, that's stupid, I tell myself.

"I can keep her company, if you like," he offers.

"No need, I'll be home soon. What did the police ask you?"

"Maggs, it's freezing out here," he says, wrapping his arms around his body, hugging his dressing gown close, "I don't mind helping but I need to get dressed."

"Don't worry, we'll talk tomorrow."

"Fine. I'll come round and tell you in the morning. But if you want any help, Maggs, just bang on the door. Goodnight."

"Night, Herrick," I murmur as I watch him close his front door. Standing in the snow, surrounded by darkness, I see his house lights switch from downstairs to up and then out.

"Maggs?" It's Jonny.

"Hi, anything?"

"No."

"Let's start on Lead Lane."

"Okay." Lead Lane is as dark and difficult as I imagined it to be. We

130

each take a side and point our torches into every possible ditch or out building. I find myself searching in pointless places where it would be hard to conceal a mouse let alone a thirteen-year-old girl.

I stand up after looking under an old bucket and two large luminous opaquely white eyes stare back at me.

"Ahrr," I scream. My heart exploding in my chest with fear.

"Maggs, what? What? Have you found something?" Jonny shouts, running to my side.

"Jesus, fuck," I moan, leaning against him, trying to catch my breath. "It's a pony. Fuck, it gave me a fright. Sorry, Jonny, that was stupid of me."

"No more stupid than I'm being. I startled a cat earlier and I nearly jumped out of my skin."

We trudge on looking until we are back on the High Street. I feel as though my feet are encased in lead boots, and my back weighed down by a ton of bricks. My head throbs and my eyes sting. The nearer to home I get, the heavier my load becomes.

"Where to now?" I ask Jonny. Stopping, he looks up and down the street before turning to me. He stands below a streetlight in a pool of orange radiance and a shaft of glittering snowflakes.

"Let's split again," he suggests. "You walk back via Boleyn St and I'll go Tamatave Rd. Then meet me back at yours."

"Okay," I agree, trying to keep the despair out of my voice. I have the shortest route and it doesn't take me long before I am home.

2023

"…Jonny and I searched for hours. But there was no sign of Orla or her bike. We returned home as other people were starting their day. Rah must've heard the front door when I let myself in as she flew into the hallway with hope written across her face. I shook my head and she crumpled onto the floor. I sank down and took her in my arms and we cried together. Jonny arrived.

'No,' was all he could say as he hugged us both. I said that we'd look again in the light and that the police will be looking too by then. I also told them Herrick would be around in the morning and I'd find

131

out the exact direction Orla took when she left his house. I wanted to give us something to hold on to, something to do..."

1997

"I'm going to call Minty and Gwen," Jonny says.
I take Rah's hand to lead her towards the kitchen. Stopping at the sitting room door, she looks in. The multi-coloured bulbs on the Christmas tree illuminate the room with a gentle light and though I'd only switched them on a few hours ago, it feels like a life time has passed.

She clasps my hand and says in a sort of dreamy voice, "I don't think she's coming home." I look at her and see her silent tears rolling freely down her face. I feel shocked by what she has said; I want to tell her she is wrong, that of course Orla will come home and that it'll all be just some stupid mistake, but the smothering blackness in my chest tells me Rah is right. I squeeze her hand and mumble back, "I know."

CHAPTER 24
Flock Wallpaper

*

Maggi - 2023

"…We sat around the table pretending to drink coffee. Jonny and Rah looked like shit, so I knew I did too. I caught Jonny's eye and saw my own dread mirrored back at me. Minty and Gwen turned up about eight o'clock and Jonny and I went out hunting again. I left Rah curled under a blanket on the sofa. She'd slid into a sort of stupor, just lying stock-still and barely breathing, as though her life was leaking out of her.

Jonny and I scoured the same route we'd taken the night before. We'd stopped at Herrick's and knocked on his door…"

1997

"Perhaps he's not up?" Jonny says as we wait for what seems like ages. I knock again and we both stand back and look at the house. The curtains are still shut upstairs, which is really out of character for Herrick.

"I guess he was late to bed last night. It was 3 a.m. when I spoke to him."

"Let's do Lead Lane again and call back after?" Jonny suggests just as Herrick opens the door. He still has on his dressing gown and slippers but no pyjamas. We must've caught him dressing.

"Hi, Herrick, sorry if we've disturbed you," I apologise.

"No, Maggs, no problem. I didn't sleep that well anyway and I bet

133

you guys haven't either. Can I make you some breakfast or at least a strong coffee?"

"It's okay Herrick, but thanks."

"How's Rah? Is she...?"

"Not good," I tell him. "She's under a blanket in the sitting room. Minty and Gwen are with her."

"I'll pop round in a bit, I can always sit with her too, if you and Jonny are out."

"Thanks, Herrick," I say gratefully. "Herrick would you mind just going over Orla's lesson again and when she left?"

"Sure, but come in out of the cold," he says turning away and heading down the corridor towards his kitchen. I really don't want to follow him but Jonny steps over the threshold. As I walk down the hall, I can smell damp and see the flock wallpaper peeling at the corners. Looking in at his music room, I see the piano against the wall and the music stand next to it. I know instinctively that's where Orla must've stood yesterday. The thought makes me reel and I grab the doorjamb.

"Maggs?" Jonny asks, turning in alarm.

"Fine, I'm fine," I reassure him quietly, clutching at my chest.

"I've put the kettle on," Herrick calls the kitchen. Jonny shuts his eyes and I know he is trying to summon up some patience.

"I'm fine," I say again to Jonny. Farther along the corridor the smell of fustiness seeps from Herrick's sitting room, I try to ignore it and move on. In the kitchen, Herrick has made the coffee and is now pouring it.

"Do sit," he offers kindly.

"No, it's alright Herrick but thanks for the coffee. I know you've told the police and Rah everything already but please could you go through it again for me?"

"Of course, Maggs, I'd be glad too. We had a really good lesson. Orla was focussed and responsive to all my suggestions. We finished up just after 12. I offered her a drink and a biscuit but she said she was having a friend over and wanted to get home to do her practice then get ready. Something about a Spice Girls' party night. Anyway,

*I let her out of the back door, she pushed her bike down the garden
and out into Lead Lane."*

"Which way did she turn?"

*"I don't know," Herrick answers. His voice wobbles slightly. "I'm
so, so sorry, I just shut the front door."*

"The front door?" Jonny queries.

*"Sorry, no I mean the back door. I just shut the back door and didn't
think to look. If only I'd watched her... I'm so sorry, Maggs, Jonny...
I feel wretched and tired..." and he begins to cry.*

*"Don't be sorry Herrick," I say gently, "It's not your fault, you
weren't to know," and I think, God forgive me for taking the piss out
of you all these years.*

*"Herrick, would you mind if we went out of your back door and
down your garden path to Lead Lane?" Jonny asks.*

*"No, of course not." Unlocking the back door, we step out into the
snow. The path is well trodden with footsteps in both directions; in
places I can make out the track of a bicycle wheel heading to or from
the house, I can't tell.*

"There's loads of foot prints out here," I observe.

*"Yes, I've been up and down several times and the police had a look
too."*

*"Thanks, Herrick, we'll head out this way." I hand him back the
mug of untouched coffee.*

*"Okay, I've got something I need to attend to this morning, but I'll
be round this afternoon. I'll sit with Rah if you like, give Minty a
rest."*

*"Yeah, that would be good, I don't think she should be on her own at
the moment."*

*"Okay, I'll be there around 2. Also, I was wondering do you think I
should let L.G.O. know that Rah's not playing tomorrow?"*

*"Shit, I'd forgotten about the Christmas Eve concert. Yes, Herrick I
think that's a good idea. There's no way she'll be taking part."*

*"No problem. See you later." I start down the path and there's
suddenly a massive crash. Turning around, I see Jonny has turned
back too.*

"It's the kids next door," Herrick explains. "Bless them, they're so excited for Christmas." My face must've registered my anguish as he quickly adds apologetically, "Oh, I'm so sorry that was a thoughtless thing to say."

"It's not your fault, Herrick, life goes on," I utter, turning back and walking down the garden path to Lead Lane as another loud crash cuts through the cold morning air.

2023

"…Herrick invited us in. I've never really liked Herrick's house though it has virtually the same lay out as Jonny's, except Jonny's has an extended modernised kitchen. It's clean but it smells of damp and decay, probably because it's stuffed with his mother's old furniture. It's like someone tidied up in the 1950s, walked out and never came back.

Anyway, I tried to avoid going in there, if at all possible. But that morning, I wanted as much information from Herrick as possible, so I accepted a cup of coffee. He patiently went through Orla's lesson, her attitude, that she was looking forward to inviting Chantelle over and that she'd left on her bike, just after 12, via Lead Lane.

We walked through Herrick's garden, which is pretty bare apart from a couple of sheds and a garage at the end. Passing the garage, Jonny looked through the windows but all he saw was Herrick's silver Sierra. We searched Lead Lane again, then all the likely routes that Orla could have taken. At home Gwen made us drink a mug of hot tomato soup and eat a slice of bread. I stood in the kitchen with my coat and boots still on, ready to go again…"

1997

"How's Rah? I ask Gwen, though I know the answer.

"Silent. She won't eat, drink or sleep. She just lies there. Minty is sitting with her. He's cut the wood and lit the fire."

"Thanks Gwen," and she leans forward and puts her arms around me. I feel her chest heave with quiet sobs and my own tears, never far away, burst from me.

"Where next, Maggs?" Jonny asks, coming into the kitchen. I pull away from Gwen, wiping my eyes and blowing my nose.

"I'm thinking we should extend our search," I tell him.

"I was thinking the same thing, perhaps the roads around my house just in case she was coming to me before going home."

"That's a good idea," I say swallowing my soup down in big mouthfuls. "Gwen, Herrick said he'd be here around about 2ish to sit with Rah, if you guys want to go or just want a break."

"We might take a walk along the sea front but I don't think we will go far, if that's alright with you, Maggs?"

"Of course. The spare bedroom is yours to use. Stay as long as you want to."

I stick my head around the sitting room door. Minty is leaning back in an armchair with his elbows on the arms-rests and his hands closed as though in prayer. His eyes are shut but I know he is neither asleep nor talking to a holy deity. I can see Rah's small shape curled on the sofa. She stares blindly into the fire.

"Let's go," I say to Jonny, who is already buttoning his coat. We trudge around every road, corner, alley way and rough ground on Jonny's side of town. By mid-afternoon darkness begins to fall making me realise it's been over 24 hours since Orla went missing.

"Maggs," Jonny calls to me. "My tiredness is making me useless. I'm looking in the same place I looked in only a moment before. I'm worried I'm going to miss something." I know what he means; I'm shattered too.

"Let's go home, get some food, a shower and sleep. We'll tackle Farrierfield tomorrow."

2023

"...We searched all day, found nothing and decided to rest, then try again the following day. We still hadn't searched the top end of the town. There's a football field and a large housing estate there called Farrierfield. There's no reason Orla would've gone that way, as it is not on her route but we were desperate.

At home, we found not only Herrick but the police too. They had

137

obviously decided to take our claim a bit more seriously as this time they'd sent a sergeant as well as a P.C. Doran. Minty and Gwen were talking to them in the kitchen, while Herrick was making tea…"

1997

"No, she has never runaway before," Gwen tells the officers. Minty looks at me as we start striping off our wet coats and boots. I just shake my head. He stands and helps us with our wet gear, putting them by the range to dry. I go and sit at the table.

"Maggi, Jonny, this is Sergeant Sycamore," P.C. Doran explains, "Serge, this is Orla's other mother, Maggi Drew, and her father, Jonny Gifford."

"I've made tea," Herrick says, putting it on the table. He pours; hands each of us a cup before taking Rah's through to her in the sitting room.

"Has Orla got a boyfriend?" Sergeant Sycamore asks.

"No, not that we know of," I answer. "But I think her friend, Chantelle, might know if she has."

"Was she being bullied, maybe over your family set up?"

"No. I'm sure she would have told us if she was, not about a boyfriend maybe, but definitely about any bullying."

"Why do you say that?"

"Because she was bullied for a while when she first started secondary school. Well, I say bullied but more the target of one particular girl. It really affected her, and we knew something was the matter. When she told us, we gave her strategies and spoke to her form teacher. I'm pretty sure it died down after that."

"Can you give me the name of the girl?"

"Is that necessary?"

"Any information, however trivial, can be important at this stage."

"Okay, Hannah Brack, I don't know her address but the school will."

"We also need a photo of your daughter, the more recent, the better." Jonny pulls his wallet from his pocket.

"Here," he offers, "This was only last week." I look at the snap of

138

Orla caught almost straight on. It's one of those you get in a photo booth. "We were in Braxham Wick, shopping for Christmas and we wanted to take some silly photos to put on our presents but this one..." his voice falters as he gazes down at the image, "caught her unexpectedly. She wanted to throw it away, and I had to promise not to show it to anyone if I kept it." He hands it to P.C. Doran. The lump in my throat threatens to suffocate me. Gwen looks at the photo now laying on P. C. Doran's folder. She makes a small inaudible noise, then rises from the table and leaves the room.

"Thank you," Sergeant Sycamore says. "Also, can we have the full names addresses of her friends, particularly Chantelle?" I pull a piece of paper towards me and a pen from the pot on the table, and start writing. When I finish, I hand it over.

"Chantelle Mollon is a nice girl, but her family is a bit..." I begin

"Mollon, 37 Braxham Towers?" P.C. Dorian queries.

"Yes. Norah never liked Orla going there."

"Did Orla often hang out with people like the Mollons?"

"No, but like I said, Chantelle is a nice girl."

After Jonny lets the officers out of the front door, he sits back down and buries his head in his hands.

"Fuck, Maggs," he mutters through his fingers, "What have I done?" Minty, Herrick and I look at him.

"What do you mean, Jonny?" I say.

"I promised Orla; I said I won't show anyone that photo and now the world is going to see it. I've betrayed her," he cries.

"No, Jonny, you haven't," Minty states calmly.

"He's right, Jonny," I endorse, "You've got nothing to feel guilty about, but I do understand. I feel bad that I told everyone Orla had taken her bike, it was meant to be our secret. And then I started feeling it was somehow my fault she's disappeared because she might have fallen off the frigging thing."

"I know, I feel it too," Herrick adds. I'd forgotten he was here. "If only I had watched Orla longer and seen which direction she took or who she met."

"None of you are to blame," Minty asserts gently.

"I've got to go," Herrick says rising from the table. "I've let L.G.O. know, and it's no problem. Obviously Rah will be missed, but I'm standing in for her. I have told her, but I'm not sure how much she's taken in. I'll be in London till Christmas Day if you need me."

"Thanks, Herrick," I follow him into the sitting room, where he kneels next to Rah and holds her hand. Her tea sits on the coffee table, untouched.

"Love you, Rah," he says, before tenderly kissing her head.

Opening the front door the snow is heavy again, carpeting the driveway in white. The Christmas tree in the porch casts a white light across the frozen landscape.

"Are you driving to London, Herrick?" I ask as he zips his jacket up.

"Yes. It'll be fine once I'm on the main roads."

"Drive carefully, Herrick. Have a good concert."

"Thanks, Maggs," he says, burying his hands in his jacket pockets and hunching his shoulders forward. Closing the door, a wave of hopelessness sweeps through me, it battles against the tiny voice that tells me not to give up, to fight for Orla, to fight for my family. Minty comes to stand next to me.

"Go and shower, Maggs. Get into something comfortable, and then you and Jonny are going to eat, for Orla's sake as well as your own." His words remind me of how, just a few hours before, I'd said the same thing to Rah.

"What a fucking useless joke you are, Maggi," I think, but I say, "Okay," and drag myself upstairs. Passing Orla's room, I force my feet to keep moving. In mine and Rah's bedroom, I shed my clothes and climb into the shower. The powerful water drums on my shoulders and I shut my eyes.

It's then that I hear the scream. A long, low wail of pure agony that fills the shower cubicle. It takes me a moment to realise that it is coming from me.

140

CHAPTER 25
Porridge and Little Dens

*

Maggi - 2023

"...The police sergeant wanted more information about Orla and a photo.

After that Herrick went home and Gwen made Jonny and I eat and sleep. Jonny took the armchair in the sitting room next to Rah, who still hadn't moved from under her blanket and I went to bed. I didn't see how I was ever going to sleep, but I must've as I jumped awake at 5 a.m.

It was now the 24th December, Jonny's birthday, and Orla had been missing for 47 hours..."

1997

My heart is beating like a drum as a deepening sense of reality starts to swamp me. I feel sick and start to gag. Scrambling out of bed, I make it to the toilet as my body convulses. I retch and retch again. With nothing in my stomach, only bile and saliva drip pathetically from my mouth. Eventually the spasms pass; I sit on the toilet floor wondering how I can hold so much horror inside of myself and keep breathing.

2023

"...In the bathroom, I puked and then sat on the floor overwhelmed by my fears. I think we have established that I'm not a creative person, but I had a sort of vision of a blackness that swirled, filling my chest, tightening my throat and suffocating my mind. So, if that was what was happening to me, God only knew what terrors were crippling Rah.

Eventually, Gwen knocked on the bathroom door and asked to come in. I said yes, and she pushed the door open. She looked at me, defeated and broken, and ran a basin of water. Taking a flannel, she washed the sick from my face and hands…"

1997

"Maggs," Gwen soothes, "I need you, Norah needs you, please don't disappear."
"You know she's not coming home, don't you, Gwen?" I wail.
"I'm not sure. I think there's still hope. But I'm telling you, Maggs, if you give up you will lose Norah too." I hear her and know the truth of her words. "Clean your teeth and dress. I'm going to make you some porridge with fruit. If you eat, Jonny will too."
"Rah?" I ask.
"No, she's not eaten or drunk anything since you made her yesterday."
"Okay, I'll have a go."

2023

"…Gwen persuaded me to pull myself off the bathroom floor, metaphorically and physically. I dressed in fresh clothes and forced myself downstairs. Minty was still with Rah and Gwen was in the kitchen with Jonny, who sat at the table with his head buried in his arms.

She ordered me to sit; then pushed a bowl of steaming porridge with chopped banana slices on top in front of me and Jonny. I pulled mine to me and began to eat. Each spoonful felt wrong in my mouth…"

1997

"Drink," Gwen orders again as she places a glass of orange juice in

front of both of us, which was quickly joined by a pot of coffee. She sits with her bowl and coffee and looks at me, then pointedly nods her head towards Jonny. I know what she wants.

"Jonny."

"Yes," he breathes through his arms.

"We're going to search Farrierfield this morning."

"Yes. I'm ready when you are."

"You need to eat. You're no good to me if you're exhausted."

"Okay," and I see his valiant effort as he sits up and forces a spoonful of porridge into his mouth.

"Drink the juice too," Gwen adds, and he obediently obeys. I force mine to my lips and tip the liquid into my mouth.

"Swallow it," I silently shout at myself.

    The doorbell rings. We hold our breath. I hear Minty's footsteps and then the door latch.

"Hello," Minty says, and I try to analyse his tone. Is it an official 'hello' or a casual 'hello'? Does he know the callers? Do they have news?

"Hi, we are friends of Jonny's. I'm Seb and this is Paul. We thought extra hands on deck might be useful."

"Good. You are most welcome. Please go through to the kitchen; you will find him in there."

Rising from the table, Jonny stands as the boys come through the door. They immediately enclose him in their arms. Then, somehow, I'm there too, along with Gwen.

"Right," announces Seb, breaking our circle of grief, "What's the plan?"

"Farrierfield and the football ground," answers Jonny, wiping his eyes.

"Just give me a minute and I'll be ready to go," I say, picking up my orange juice and porridge and taking them into the sitting room.

Minty looks up and smiles. The Christmas lights still twinkle brightly in the dull winter light.

"Maggs," he acknowledges.

"I'm back, Minty," I tell him.

"Thank you," he murmurs.

Putting the juice and porridge down on the coffee table, I go and sit next to Rah. Gently easing her blanket back, I pull her into my arms. Her beautiful hair is knotted, her eyes sunken and her skin grey.

"Rah, listen to me. I promise you I will never stop looking for Orla; I will find her and bring her home. But to do that, I need you to live. I can't do it without you."

"Promise, Maggs?" comes a broken whisper that tears at my heart.

"I promise, Rah," I swear as I lift the juice to her lips. "Drink this now." She takes a sip, and I see how hard it is for her to swallow. After a couple of tries, it goes down, only to be followed by her gagging reflex.

"Keep it down," I warn her, and force a second, then a third mouthful.

"I can't," she moans, shaking her head.

"And I can't go out and search until you have drunk this." Taking the glass, and in an act of sheer will, she forces it down. I hear and see the vomit fill her mouth. She clamps her hands over her lips and swallows it again.

"Now, at least three spoonfuls of porridge," I order, just as Gwen had ordered me. She manages two before I can't bear to watch her fighting to swallow the regurgitating food.

Gwen appears with a bowl of hot, soapy water, a flannel and a towel.

"Go, Maggs; I'll do the rest. Minty you too, go and eat," she says. I kiss Rah's head and find the boys who are ready in the kitchen. Grabbing my outdoor gear from the clotheshorse by the range, I pull my coat and boots on. Jonny hands me a torch and walking stick.

"Ready?" he asks

"Ready," I reply.

2023

"…After we'd eaten, two friends of Jonny's came round to help us. And yes, D.C.I. Logan, these are the last of my cast of criminals. Sebastian Gold and Paul Storrie. Not that they in anyway have anything to do with the Trinity Lane body.

We split up and searched the Farrierfield housing estate, meeting later outside the town's football ground. The football ground is really a large field with two goal posts surrounded by a lot of rough grass and dense bushes. From a distance the whole place was bathed in white, but as I drew nearer, I could see foot tracks ringing the boundary. I knew it was a popular dog-walking area as well as a shortcut from the town to Farrierfield estate. As we entered I saw a woman throwing a red ball for her dog. And I wondered, as I have for the last 26 years, how the world just keeps on spinning for some people, while others desperately search for a lost child..."

1997

I feel my breath stick in my gullet, making me cough.

"Maggs?" I look at Jonny and the boys. They are staring at me expectantly, as though they'd been talking to me or asking me a question.

"Sorry, what were you saying?"

"Seb is suggesting we each take a quarter of the field, then swap our quarter with our neighbours. That way, we will have covered the rough ground twice," Jonny explains.

"Good idea," I agree, trying to keep my mind on the job and not let it drift back into darker places.

"Maggi, you go this way," Seb points to the right. "I'll take the bottom end. Paul take the top-left and Jonny bottom-left."

2023

"...We all took sections of the field; I had to shout at myself to keep focussed. Paul must've heard, as he asked if I was alright. I told him I was and carried on poking my stick under the bushes before pushing myself between the cold, wet branches. Little of the snow had penetrated through the closed packed thicket and, at the back by the boundary fence, I found evidence of hidden life. Empty bottles of alcohol, cigarettes butts, used condoms next to little dens children must've made during their summer holidays.

145

I stood and looked at one such den; an old blanket draped over branches, another on the ground. A small, wooden crate upturned, maybe for a table. Memories of dens I'd built with Orla filled my mind. Long, hot summer days, lemonade and suntan cream. I was just imagining how lovely it would be if I crawled into that abandoned den and never come out again when an excited shout punctured my thoughts.

If I'd struggled to get into the thicket, I certainly didn't struggle to come out again. A new surge of adrenalin-fuelled energy surged through me as I charged through the branches and back out onto the football ground. Paul was waving his arms frantically and, as I ran, I glanced around and saw Jonny and Seb running full tilt across the field…"

1997

"Oh God, please let it be her," I pray, hoping that all my heathen thoughts are wrong and there is some sort of fatherly figure who loves us all. "Oh God, let it be her. I'll pay back anything if it's her. You can have my life, my anything, just let it be Orla." My legs pump as I race across the white expanse. "Please God, please let her be alive, hurt me, take me," I plead, pathetically expecting to drop down dead there and then as I pull up next to Paul.

"I think I've found something," he gasps an octave higher than his usual voice.

"What?" I breathe, my lungs shredded by adrenaline.

"Is it her? Is it Orla?" I hear Jonny shout, as he almost crashes into us.

"Sorry. No mate, not her," Paul apologises, shrugging his shoulders. "And it might be nothing, but there's a bike in there, a blue, newish bike, a good bike." Jonny tears through the bushes. I follow with branches whipping my face and hands. At the back, leaning against the fence is Orla's bike. Jonny and I stand and stare.

"Is it hers?" Paul asks desperately. I look at Jonny and tears roll down his handsome face.

"Yes," I say.

CHAPTER 26
A Broken Deal

Maggi - 1997

Sinking to my knees, I reach out my hand to touch the frame of Orla's bike.

"Don't," comes a sharp command.

I look over my shoulder and see Seb, puffed from his run. "Don't touch anything," he repeats, trying to catch his breath. "The police will need to fingerprint it and we might be treading on evidence, so let's back out carefully."

Taking a last, longing look at the bike, I try to take in every aspect of it as though it's Orla herself before rising from my knees and following the others out.

Paul is holding Jonny's hand while Seb taps his teeth.

"I THOUGHT WE HAD A FUCKING DEAL GOD," I scream uselessly up at the cloud-filled sky.

"Maggs," Jonny calls, reaching out to me.

"Paul, have you got your mobile phone on you?" Seb asks, ignoring my stupid outburst.

"Yeah," Paul replies, letting go of Jonny's hand and pulling his phone from his pocket.

"Okay, dial 99..."

"No," Jonny interrupts, "dial 01206712234. It's Braxham Wick police station. Ask for Sergeant Sycamore." Paul dials.

The call is answered, and he's put through to an extension

*number. A muffled voice sounds on the other end of the phone and
Paul explains the situation.*

*"Okay, we will and no, no one has touched it," Paul tells the officer.
Finishing the call he turns to us. "They're on their way. I think
they're bringing in C.I.D. now and a forensic team too. He said not
to touch the bike and to keep anyone else away from the surrounding
area until they arrive."*

2023

"…What Paul had found was Orla's bike. We phoned the police and
waited for them to arrive.

All of a sudden I felt deflated and empty. I began to feel my aches
and pains now that the adrenaline had left my body. The cuts on my
face, from the branches, stung and my hands burnt with cold. Paul
asked if I was alright and if I wanted to go home. I told him I was
fine and I wanted to stay and confirm to the police that the bike
belonged to Orla. I didn't trust them not to fob us off again.

We stood, the four of us, in a strange huddle, waiting. I remember
a man walking by with a dog on a lead. He looked at us, then looked
away. I wanted to shout at him, take my anger out on him for just
living and being normal. Eventually, in the distance, we heard sirens.
The layered wails grew, and I mentally tracked their progress as they
entered the village. We all turned as two squad cars appeared in the
club's small car park followed by a plain vehicle and a white van.
Paul said what we all thought, that, at last, they were taking it
seriously.

Two detectives, Sergeant Sycamore and the two P.C.s crossed the
field to where we were standing. One of the detectives introduced
himself as D.S. Crumble and his partner as D.C. Houghton. He
wanted to know who we were.

I stood back, my tiredness drowning me, and watched as the
police teams set to work. They only talked to Jonny and me briefly,
to check our story. We went over the details of Orla's disappearance
again and why we were searching. When it was obvious I was just in
the way, I said I was going home to tell Rah…"

1997

"I'll come," Jonny utters in a voice that reflects my own weariness. We all trudge back along the snow-covered pavements as the day starts to fade. We pass house after house with Christmas lights glowing in the dwindling dusk. The iron-grey sky seems endless as the cold air wraps itself around me, freezing me down to the bone. Outside our house, Seb stops.

"Paul and I are going to head off now, but just give us a ring if you need any more help."

"Thanks, mate," Jonny replies, hugging them both.

"Thanks," I manage before dragging myself up the driveway and letting myself in through the front door.

"You've been gone ages," Minty declares, trying to hide the worry in his voice. "Here, let me take your things. Come in by the fire. Gwen, they're back," he calls over his shoulder.

"We found her bike, Minty," I murmur and I feel my hot tears burn my cold flesh as they roll down my cheeks.

"What, up by Farrierfield? But that's way off."

"I know. What the hell is it doing there?" Jonny angrily asks. I recognise his useless rage after my own futile screaming fit. "Paul called the police; they are taking it seriously now at long bloody last. I think they'll be here soon," he adds.

"Okay, we'll deal with it together. Now, come and warm yourselves. You look frozen."

In the sitting room, I sit next to Rah and Gwen pushes a hot cup of sweet tea into my hands.

"Your face Maggs, I'll need to do something about that when you have warmed through," she comments. I try to say it's nothing as I wipe away the blood seeping from the cuts, but my throat is clogged, and no sound comes out.

Minty looks at me enquiringly; I instinctively know what he wants. I nod in agreement.

"Norah," he articulates with such love and tenderness it causes yet another crack in my heart, "Norah, Maggi and Jonny are home. They've found Orla's bicycle. The police are checking it for clues

now."

2023

"…And do you know what Rah did? She didn't rave like some demented banshee, screaming at a supernatural being like I had. No, she fucking thanked me with all her heart, as though I'd given her Orla back, whole and alive. But it was what she said next that finished me off. She asked if I thought the police would be able to find her body now.

The terribleness that had weighed me down just plummeted to a new and even more awful low. I struggled to breathe, my lungs felt rigid. In truth, I'd always known Orla was dead, but her question smothered me. I gasped, my lungs sucked dry and refused to fill.

Jonny pulled me onto the floor and put me into the recovery position, reassuring me that it was only my diaphragm that had gone into spasm. It was the first panic attack I'd ever had, but it certainly wasn't going to be the last…"

1997

"Calm yourself, Maggs; your breathing will return. You know this. That's it, calm, calm, calm. I'm here." Slowly, the spasms pass. "Breathe properly. In …out …in…out."
Then, the doorbell rang.

2023

"…D.S. Crumble and D.C. Houghton arrived, and Gwen showed them through to the kitchen…"

1997

"She doesn't want them in here with Rah," I think, gasping to regulate my breathing.
"Maggi, are you up for this?" Minty asks.
"Yes." I drag on the last of my will to breathe properly and make myself stand. Leaning on Jonny, we go through to the kitchen. The two officers fill the room in their dark suits.

150

"Sit," Gwen orders. "I'm making tea." We sit – Jonny, Minty and I – as the two officers take their chairs.

"I believe you have already had contact with us?" D.S. Crumble begins. I look at his thin face topped off by a balding dome and, like some sort of ridiculous joke, one huge wiry eyebrow that snakes across his forehead.

"You're fucking unbelievable..." I start.

"Maggs," Minty cuts me off, gently laying his hand on my arm, "that won't help now."

"Want a bet?" I scoff, unable to contain myself. "If you'd got your fucking arses into gear two days ago we might have Orla, not just a fucking bike." But D.S. Crumble either doesn't hear or, more likely, chooses to ignore me as he carries on with his stupid questions.

"And you have not had any contact with Orla since the morning of the 22nd, is that right?"

"Yes" Minty says, shooting me a warning look. It was just as well because, at that moment, I wanted to punch D.S. fucking Crumble's lights out.

"I am sure you have been told that most teenagers..."

"Yes Officer, we have been told all of that. Now, the bicycle?" Minty asserts.

"Forensics are doing their thing. We will have to take all of your fingerprints to eliminate them, and we would like a sample of Orla's DNA."

"Why, have you found blood?" Jonny blurts out.

"No, nothing like that," D.C. Houghton shakes her head. "It's more to do with profile building, the more information we have, the better. Perhaps you can give us Orla's hairbrush and toothbrush and we might need to take saliva samples from her biological parents."

"Yes. But what are you actually going to do now to find her?" Minty persists.

2023

"...They informed us that now they regarded it as a full-blown 'missing child investigation' and that they would be taking over the

151

hunt for Orla and all we had to do was sit tight and wait.

'Jesus f-ing Christ,' I remember thinking, 'sit tight and wait.' I was fuming. All my tiredness seemed to evaporate in a surge of anger, and I could've hurled all sorts of abuse at them. But I was to be proved completely wrong about D.S. Crumble and D.C. Houghton. They were really honourable and they worked tirelessly to solve Orla's disappearance."

"I think this is a good moment to break for lunch. Fry, the Cam," D.C.I. Logan says briskly, jolting me and, by the look of things, D.C. Fry out of the story. "We'll resume at 2 p.m."

"Fine," I nod, but there's a part of me that doesn't want to stop. It's not that I want to tell these Officers my story, Jonny, Rah and Orla's story, but if I could keep going then at least it would be done and over.

CHAPTER 27
Cola and Chips

Logan

Shutting the front door, Logan clicks the key fob and opens the car. Climbing in, she waits till Fry has stowed the Cam and put his seatbelt on.

"I bet there's a good chippy here," she says, starting the engine.

"I'll look." He asks his Noc. "There's one on Kipling Road. Take a right out of here, then head towards the harbour."

Moments later, Logan parks the car. The smell of frying mingles with the sea air; it reminds her of summer holidays at Butlins. The nostalgia adds to her sadness.

"I'll get it, Fry," she says, and orders two bags of chips with cans of cola. After adding salt and vinegar, they walk to one of the harbour's benches.

All traces of yesterday's heavy rain clouds have vanished, and the wooden planking on the bench feels warm and comforting. Iron-grey waves roll lazily up the pebbled beach, lapping at moored boats. A mild breeze catches at their rigging, causing the metal strands to chime like tubular bells. Fry eats his chips with relish, while Logan picks at hers.

"Don't let this get personal," she thinks, as Maggi's emotions tug at her own pain.

"Nice chips, Boss, thank you," Fry says between mouthfuls.

"What do you think?" she asks him, watching the waves break leisurely against a rotting groyne.

"I'm not sure. She's got a temper. I don't mean like Rowena Wilkinson. I think her mood is more to do with defending the people she loves than attacking…" he's about to say "you," but quickly changes it to "us."

"Yeah, there's that," Logan nods. She'd watched Maggi, seen the moments when something had struck a deep chord, not just the obvious, but the hidden emotions too. Maggi, she is realising, is far from a closed book. This is a woman who, however hard she tries to hide it, wears her heart on her sleeve. Her body language betrays her thoughts.

"Still, it's hard to imagine her digging a grave under her allotment shed with her brother and Jonny. And she wanted us to know it was her idea, not theirs like she's protecting them. Why do you think she dug it there?" Fry continues between chips.

"It's quite a clever place when you think about it. No one can see what you're doing because you're inside your shed, and any piles of earth aren't going to attract much attention, being an allotment."

"But why wouldn't you dig it in your garden? It's got to be easier to carry a body to a hole in the garden than to an allotment."

"Unless he was killed at the allotment," Logan comments, giving up on the chips.

"Don't you want those, Boss?" Fry asks, eyeing the abandoned bag.

"Nah, help yourself."

"Cheers," he replies, stuffing the last of his chips into his mouth, balling his paper bag, and taking hers. She smiles and pulls the ring on her can.

"And if it hadn't been for the housing development, Waxy would never have been found."

"Yeah."

"You don't seem scared of the dog today."

"I'm just not. I kinda like him now," he answers, finishing the second bag and opening his cola. After a moment, Logan pulls her Noc from her pocket.

"Can you remember all the names she gave us off the top of your head?" she asks, before instructing the Noc to find Ron's e-mail address.

"Yes, Jonny Giff…"

"Hang on, tell me in a minute." With the blank email ready, she dictates:

"Hi, Ron, how's the family? Growing up quickly now I bet. I'm after a favour. I need some info on a group of people involved in a murder case. If you've got time, could you check them out for me? Cheers, Logan."

"Okay Fry," she says, holding her Noc out to him.

Taking it, he shuts his eyes and recites. **"Maggi Drew, DoB 21.7.55. Address, 33 Peartree Road, Godlinghoe, Essex. Jonny Gifford, same address. Norah Montgomery, same address. Orla Éowyn Faith Montgomery, DoB 6.9.84, same address. Jim Bob Drew, brother of Maggi Drew, born 1974, died in California in 2014. Herrick Butler, 16 Bosuns Road, Godlinghoe, Essex. Minty and Gwen Montgomery, address Oyster Lane, Godlinghoe."**

Opening his eyes, he hands the Noc back to her.

Pressing 'send' she asks, "Where did you drag all that from?" genuinely impressed by his recall.

"I'm quite good at remembering stuff, especially numbers," Fry replies, before asking, "Who's Ron?"

"A mate from my Met days; works in Logistics. He's spent years doing this stuff and has all sorts of contacts and resources."

"You know Andrea is brilliant at researching data too."

"We could get Andrea on to it as well, two reports are always better than one." Checking the time, she adds, "We'd better head back." Fry gulps down the rest of his cola then tries to burp quietly, making her smile.

CHAPTER 28
I Give You My Sword

Maggi

Dappled light filters through the trees, creating shaded patterns on the path. I stand still and tilt my head towards the clear blue sky. Closing my eyes, I hear the faint hum of bees and feel the sun's soft warmth on my tired skin. There's a gentle nudge on my leg, and I look down into the dark, faithful eyes of the old greyhound.

"Oh Lobo," I sigh, "I'm going to have to kill you, aren't I?" The old dog just looks lovingly back at me. The betrayal of his trust brings me to my knees, and I bury my face in his warm fur.

There's a knock at the door.

"That'll be them," I tell him, wiping my tears with the hem of my t-shirt and running my hand down his bony spine. "We'd better go and let them in."

Around the table again, D.C. Fry sets the Cam up. I wait, feeling my old anger shimmer, like oil on water.

"So, where were we?" D.C.I. Logan asks.

"Orla's bike had been found at Farrierfield football ground, and D.S. Crumble and D.C. Houghton had opened a missing child investigation," Fry informs us chirpily, earning him yet another look from D.C.I. Logan.

Ignoring the look, I soldier on.

"That night was Christmas Eve.

After we'd all pretended to eat an evening meal, Jim Bob turned up. Jonny made a bed on the floor next to Rah, who had returned to her catatonic state. Minty banked the fire up before he and Gwen went to bed in our spare room. I sat at this table with my head in my arms, drifting in and out of sleep while Jim Bob kept me company..."

25th December 1997

I jerk awake just after 4. My heart explodes with a burst of adrenaline.

"It's alright Bigster, I'm here," Jim Bob says soothingly.

"I can't find her," I tell him. He shuffles his chair over and puts his arms around me. They're big and muscular. Like me, his build is short and stocky with a core of strength, but unlike me, he works out. No one else in my life feels and smells like Jim Bob. I've known him since he was born. He has traces of my parents and traces of me mixed with his own solid personality. I bury myself into his chest and cry. After the tears comes the anger and I beat my fists against his rock-hard muscles. He says nothing until, at last, my useless temper burns itself out.

"Come on Bigster, get your coat and boots on. Let's go down to the sea."

The snow has stilled in the night, the sea is calm and the moon hangs like a globe of effulgent light casting a rippled road across the lapping waters.

"Whatever happens Bigster, I'll help you. You won't carry this alone," Jim Bob states.

I think about that for a while. I know I'm not alone – there's Rah, Jonny, Minty and Gwen – but then it dawns on me what he is saying. I've tried to take the load upon my back, shield Rah, protect Jonny, not burden Minty or Gwen.

"Thanks," I murmur gratefully. We stop at Tillman's Tower and look at the moon.

"Do you remember the tale of Ariadne and Theseus you used to read

to me when I was small?" he asks.

"Uhm," I mumble back, trying to search my brain.

"You do, Bigster. Ariadne falls in love with Theseus, who is doomed to die, lost in the labyrinth and killed by the Minotaur. She gives him a sword and a ball of thread so he can find his way out."

"Yes, I remember now."

"Well, remember this too, I give you my sword and I will never let go of the other end of the thread. I will always be there to guide you out of this horrendous labyrinth."

"I'm not sure there's going to be an exit, Bro."

"That's the nature of the labyrinth; you can't see the way out. But just hang onto the thread and know you are not alone when you are stranded in the depths of its darkest tunnels."

2023

"…By Christmas morning, Orla had been missing for 68 hours. I felt battered and bent. I could hardly string two words together. I completely got Rah's static state, her mind filled with horror, her body shut down. Herrick arrived in the afternoon and sat with Rah, holding her hand. Jonny and Minty were just as stunned as they tried to fill the hours with meaningless jobs. Gwen was the only one of us who truly believed Orla was alive. She clung to the notion that the British Police Force was invincible and a daring rescue was only moments away.

She also felt very strongly that we should inform the Giffords. Jonny, not surprisingly, felt we shouldn't, and I agreed. I just couldn't see the point in inviting more shit down on our heads. But Gwen was insistent…"

1997

"I think you should, Jonny," Gwen says passionately. "They're Orla's grandparents, and I'm sure they love her dearly, even if they have a funny way of showing it. And they're going to see it on the news sooner or later."

"Would you like me to phone for you, Jonny?" Herrick volunteered.

"It would be better coming from family. I'll do it," states Minty.
"Okay," Jonny reluctantly replies. Minty and Gwen take themselves into the hallway, leaving the rest of us in the sitting room with Rah. We hear Minty's voice, calm and measured, as he explains who he is and then why he is calling. There's a long silence before Minty speaks again.
"I can assure you I am not making it up. Orla is mis..." again there is a silent space before Minty speaks again, though this time his timbre is low, strong and precise as he articulates his words.
"Again, I can assure you that neither I nor the police believe that it is in anyway Jonny's fault and..." Silence, "I don't ..." silence...
"I'm sure someone will let you know when she has been found. Goodbye." Putting the phone down, Minty speaks quietly to Gwen, too quietly for me to hear. Then they enter the sitting room. Herrick, Jim Bob and I look up, but Jonny just stares into the fire.

2023

"...In the end Minty made the call. When he returned to the sitting room all he said was, what a very strange attitude she possesses. I never asked what Julia had said to him, I didn't need to, I could easily imagine.

Jonny decided to head off for a shower and change his clothes. I think he needed some space after the phone call. Herrick stayed for a while telling Rah about the Christmas Eve concert, talking seamlessly about the pieces they'd played..."

1997

"It went well, Abraham was pleased, the audience was receptive but you were really missed, Rah. I struggled to fill your shoes. Technically, I just about held on, but artistically I couldn't touch you. Everyone sends their love and says they are thinking of you. May and Tarquin gave me flowers for you. I've put them in the kitchen, we can arrange them later, or I can do them in a minute myself. I'll ask Gwen for a vase."
"Bless you, Herrick," I think, as I wearily climb the stairs, leaving

him to look after her.

2023

"...The rest of the day dragged itself by. The sun had risen, and then it set, but the phone did not ring until the following day..."

CHAPTER 29
Wizen Skeleton

*

Maggi - 26th December 1997
Loud trills echo down the hallway, like a call to arms. I come to attention as the rings cut through the still afternoon. Rah, curled lifelessly under her blanket, doesn't move but I hear her breathing change from low, torpid pulls to short, sharp gasps. I look at Minty as he rises from the armchair.
"I'll go," he murmurs.

2023
"…There was nothing I wanted more than news of Orla, but while that phone remained silent, I tried to believe that there was still hope. I didn't want it to ring, but I wanted it to ring more than anything in the world. So, on Boxing Day afternoon, with darkness creeping in at the windows, Minty went into the hallway and answered the phone. It was D.S. Crumble…"

1997
My heart leaps. I look across at the others. Jonny's hands are rigid on the arms of his chair, his knuckles showing white. Jim Bob and Herrick sit bolt upright staring at the doorway. Getting to her feet, Gwen moves towards the door. I leave Rah and follow her out into the hall. We stand next to Minty. He moves the receiver so I can hear.

"It is Minty Montgomery, Orla's grandfather," he says steadily into the phone, but I feel the tremor in his hand as he slips it into mine.

"Mr Montgomery, we have some news for you."

"Yes?" Minty manages. I can hardly breathe as I feel my panic rising.

"This is it," I think, *"this is what it feels like to hear that your daughter's body has been found. That she's dead, murdered, raped violated, tortured..."*

"We have arrested someone and brought him in for questioning."

"What... sorry, but have you found Orla?" Minty asks reeling from the unexpected news.

"No, not at this stage, Minty, but we do have a suspect," D.S. Crumble answers.

"A suspect? What does that mean?" Minty asks.

"It means we are closer to finding your granddaughter's whereabouts. We will let you know as soon as we have any news."

"But who is he? Did he take Orla? Does he know where she is?"

"We cannot divulge his name or give you any more details at the moment, but if we Charge him we will let you know."

"Yes, okay, thank you," Minty mumbles, defeatedly.

"We will be in touch," D.S. Crumble says kindly before terminating the call. Minty and I just stand there with the receiver between us. Gwen looks at us enquiringly.

"They've arrested a suspect," Minty tells her.

"Thank God," she exhales as her hands clasp together as though in prayer, *"Soon, they will bring our Orla home."*

"Gwen," Minty sighs, leaving me and putting his arms around her. *"Gwen, I don't think it necessarily means that."*

"Arrested someone?" questions Jonny from the doorway. I nod.

"Did they say who?" Herrick asks, coming to stand by Jonny.

"No, they wouldn't say," Minty tells them.

"I better tell Rah," I murmur.

"Right, I'm making tea and sandwiches, and we must get something down Norah," Minty says assertively.

"I'll help," Jonny offers following Minty into the kitchen. Gwen and

I go back to Rah.

"Rah," I call, gently stroking her hair, "sweetheart, that was the police on the phone." She doesn't reply, and Gwen and I look at each other.

"Norah, love, it's good news, Orla will be ..."

"Don't Gwen, we don't know that," I interrupt her.

"But..." she begins with hurt in her eyes.

"Don't give her false hope, that's not fair," I plead.

"I only..."

"I know, Gwen," I say pulling Rah to me. "Rah, the police have arrested someone."

"Orla?" she murmurs.

"No," I answer as calmly as I can. "No news of Orla, but they are questioning someone."

2023

"...D.S. Crumble said they'd arrested someone.

It was strange how that phone call had such a different effect on us all. Gwen was sure it predicted good news and Orla would soon be coming home, while Jonny, Minty and I were floored by the news.

Jonny, if it was at all possible, looked worse. I felt sick and trapped by an inescapable inevitability while Minty tried to divert his misery by being useful to others by making a massive plate of sandwiches. None of us wanted to eat, but we couldn't very well force Rah to eat if we were refusing food too. I saw Jim Bob brace himself as he sized up a sandwich in his hand. I picked up one and forced it into my mouth, then washed it down with tea. Minty encouraged Rah to eat and drink, but she barely managed a few sips of tea..."

1997

"Sorry," I say to Gwen hugging her hard at the front door before she and Minty head home for a change of clothes and probably the space to talk.

"Maggs, we are fine. I'll be back in the morning with soup and

bread." Outside, the lights from the Christmas tree catch the snowflakes falling from the now dark sky. I watch as Minty and Gwen walk, hand in hand, into the night.

2023

"…Later, after the others had left, Jonny and I decided to help Rah into a bath. We virtually carried her up the stairs and undressed her carefully, but neither of us could hide the shock on our faces when we saw her emaciated state. It had only been five days since Orla had disappeared but Rah had turned from a healthy forty-two-year-old woman into a wizen skeleton with protruding bones and paper-thin skin.

We got her into the warm water and I un-plaited her long hair. Chunks of it came away in my hands making me silently cry. I shampooed and rinsed it gently, but it just kept on falling out. After she was dressed and sat by the fire in the sitting room, I tried brushing it but with every stroke, the brush just came away caked in hair. I knew I was crying again, but I couldn't stop it. It wasn't the hair as such, though I loved Rah's long, dark hair, it was the watching her dying by inches. I knew we were all dying inside, if I could've pulled my heart from my chest it would've been cracked wide open, and Jonny too was adrift in his own personal sea of horror. But Rah was literally dying in front of us…"

1997

Jonny reaches across and stills my hands.
"Rah," he says gently, "Your hair is falling out. I'm going to get some scissors and cut the rest of it off."
"Yes, that's a good idea," she murmurs and then sits placidly as Jonny cuts the remainder of her long hair away.
Afterwards, she runs her hand over her head. "Thank you," she says so sincerely as though we've given her the latest in fashionable hairstyles.

CHAPTER 30
Senseless and Stupid

*

Maggi - 2023

"…The next twenty-four hours passed slowly as we waited for some news. Minty and Gwen returned with thick tomato soup and home-made bread. Herrick, Jim Bob, Seb and Paul came and went. No one mentioned Rah's hair.

Then, on Sunday afternoon, six days after Orla had gone missing, D.S. Crumble arrived. I answered the door…"

27th December 1997

"Maggi, may I come in?" he asks gently.

"Yes," I say, standing back from the door. I lead him to the kitchen and call the others. We all sit around the table. I can feel my heart pounding in anticipation for what he is about to tell us. I feel like a taut elastic-band that could snap at any moment. I want to shout at him, tell him to get on with it.

"As you know, we took a man in for questioning because we had a strong suspicion that he might in be involved in the disappearance of your daughter."

"What made you think that?" Jonny questions.

"He has previous… He's been on our radar since he was relocated to Godlinghoe."

"Are you saying he has a previous conviction for abducting children?" Minty utters incredulously.

"Not as such, he has previous convictions for burglary, assault, motoring offences."

"I don't understand, why is he on your radar for taking our daughter?" I can hear the cynicism in Jonny's tone.

"Because in 1995 he stood trial on 3 counts, abduction of a minor over the age of thirteen and under the age of sixteen, false imprisonment and rape of said minor."

A stunned silence fills the room. I try to compute what Crumble had just told us. It doesn't make any sense. "I don't understand?" I mutter, "Why isn't he in prison? What's he doing here?"

"The jury failed to reach a verdict. He was released and relocated here, to protect the child involved."

"To protect the child? What about our child?" I slam back at him, my elastic band has well and truly snapped now. "You," I hiss, pointing an accusing finger at him, "knew that this sick fuck was living here, in Godlinghoe, and you didn't think to mention it to the community?"

I see the blood leave Crumble's face, but he answers calmly, "Yes. But our hands are always tied by the law in these cases, all we can do is monitor this type of criminal."

"Monitor? Well, you did a fucking good job of that, didn't you? And come to that, how many other fucking pedos have you got stashed away here that you are monitoring?" I snarl sarcastically. I see Crumble shift uncomfortably in his seat, but I don't give a shit.

"Maggs," Jonny murmurs next to me, putting his hand on my arm to stop me. My blood is pounding in my ears, my heart is raging, I'm ready for a fight, and I want blood, but Jonny's hand stems my aggression. "Let's get the info before we sound off," he says and I know he's right so I shut my mouth but continue to glare at Crumble across the table.

"Who is this man?" Gwen asks.

"His name is Hamilton Hoyle, known as Hamy Hoyle."

"Never heard of him," I snap back as though I'm some sort of authority on local nonces.

"He used to work on the door as a bouncer at Tall Tom's, the

*nightclub on Braxham Wick's high street until he got sacked a
couple of months ago."*

*"Where does he live and, more to the point, where's Orla?" asks
Jonny reasonably.*

*"Spinner's Drive, Farrierfield, the estate beyond the football club.
We haven't found any evidence of your daughter's whereabouts,
apart from her bike."*

"And we found that," I mutter again.

*Crumble ignores my comment and carries on. "But we are searching
his flat thoroughly."*

"So Hamy Hoyle hasn't told you where Orla is?" questions Minty.

*"No, he's denying even knowing your daughter." I am just about to
fire another question into Crumble's face, but Jonny puts his hand
on my arm again.*

*"D.S. Crumble, what evidence have you against this Hamy Hoyle
that makes you believe he is responsible for Orla's ..." Jonny voice
breaks as he adds, "dis-disappearance?"*

"We have a partial fingerprint from Orla's bike."

"Fuck," I moan through gritted teeth.

*"You've got to get Hamy Hoyle to tell you where Orla is," Gwen
asserts. "We must rescue her." Crumble has the good grace to lower
his eyes, I know what he is thinking, it's written all over his face.*

*"Like I said, he's not talking. The Crown Prosecution Service has
agreed that we can go ahead and Charge him on four counts:
Abduction, Rape and ..." he hesitates ever so slightly before clearing
his throat, "Uhm, Murder, but that's just a formality."*

"Murder," mouths Gwen.

*"The murder charge is just a formality. If we don't charge him with
murder now, we cannot keep him in custody, and therefore, it will
damage our investigation."*

"It what way?" Minty asks.

*"In the way that with such a significant Charge we will be able to
prevent bail, apply for any court orders to search his property, bring
in any of his known associates and order extensive forensic analysis.
It might not mean he has actually...uhmm, killed her but it gives us*

the upper hand."

"Why don't you just tell us the truth, you think she's dead, don't you D.S. Crumble?" I accuse.

"Let's not jump to any conclusions. Orla might be found alive and well."

"Bull fucking shit," I mutter getting up and going to the kitchen. I lean against a cabinet with my arms folded defensively. I know targeting my anger and frustration at Crumble is senseless and stupid but he is all I've got to lash out at.

"What's the fourth?" Jonny says coldly.

"Fourth?" puzzles Crumble.

"You said you were charging him on four counts," I hear the barely disguised contempt.

"Oh yes, Disposal of Evidence."

"Shhhit," I mutter again from the kitchen.

Crumble clears his throat. "Hoyle is due to answer the Charges by Virtual Court on Tuesday 30th December. You are welcome to attend."

"Virtual Court?" Minty queries.

"It just means that he will appear via video link rather than in person. But apart from that, in all other aspects it remains the same. As it's an Indictable Offence, the Magistrate will direct the case to be heard at Crown Court. That will either be either Chelmsford or Ipswich."

"When will that be?" asks Minty.

"That I'm not sure of. I estimate the earliest is June, but it could be anything up to a year. We have evidence to collect..."

"But what about Orla?" Gwen entreats, widening the crack in my heart to a fucking great chasm. Minty puts his arm around her as I turn to leave the room, not wanting to hear any more.

And it is then I see Rah. She is leaning against the door frame, her hair short and spiky, her body bowed, her eyes large and bruised. Even through my tears I see the blood on her hands where she has bitten her nails to the quick. My anger shifts, making room for pity.

"Rah," I murmur, causing everyone to turn towards the doorway.
"Rah... did you hear?"
"It's alright, Maggs, I know she's dead." Coming into the room, she
clasps my hand and turns to Crumble. "Just bring her home, D.S.
Crumble, give me her body back to bury."
"I'll try," he says gently.

2023

"...Crumble came to tell us that they were charging someone with Orla's Abduction, Rape and Murder."

"Who?" Fry asked eagerly.

"Some scum bag called Hamilton Hoyle." I watch D.C.I. Logan to see if the name means anything to her but her face is literally expressionless, so I guess not. "He had a Virtual Hearing. It was the first time I saw him. He was smug and all puffed up, I could tell he thought he was The Man, King of the World. I hated him on spot. He sat there unconcerned, picking his teeth. The magistrates denied him bail and sent him for trial at Chelmsford Crown Court.

After that, we all waited with bated breath for news of Orla's whereabouts, but no real news ever came. Just the odd call from Crumble saying the Crown Prosecution Service were working hard to build a solid case against him, followed by a Plea and Case Management hearing, where, to no ones' surprise, he pleaded 'not guilty'. Then finally, the trial date was set for August 4th, a Tuesday, at Chelmsford Crown Court.

The weeks that led up to the trial seemed to drag on endlessly. Jonny and I took compassionate leave from work, he, more or less, moved in here with us while Minty, Gwen and Jim Bob returned home. Everybody else seemed to resume their normal lives while we balanced precariously on a knife-edge.

I'd watch Rah's daily struggle to eat and drink, to stay afloat in her fight for Orla. I'd often find her curled on the floor in Orla's bedroom, clinging to some piece of clothing that had once belonged to our daughter. I'd cradle her in my arms, and we would cry together until exhaustion made her sleep. She'd lie quietly for a few precious hours before her nightmares would rip her apart again.

For me, the walls of the house seemed to shrink. I began to feel I couldn't breathe. I spent hours hunting for Orla in the streets of Braxham Wick and the surrounding towns. I don't even know why, maybe it was just the urge to do something, to be actively engaged instead of passively accepting her loss.

A few times, I'd catch a glimpse of her in a crowded street or a busy shop. I'd shout her name and run to her, touch her shoulder or hug her only to find a stranger's face staring back at me. The last time it happened an irate father had me up against a wall. I tried to explain, but he still threatened to 'punch my lights out' and called me 'a dirty fucking perv.' That hit home because I knew I was perverted now, not in the sense he'd meant it, but in the sense that I would never view people in the same way again.

After that, I spent more and more time at the allotment, digging and planting. People would stop and want to chat about potato blight or clubroot as though my world was still turning. The only thing that turned and turned again in my head was how I would make Hamy Fucking Hoyle pay for what he'd done.

I dreamt of buying guns and blowing his balls off or smashing his kneecaps in with a sledge hammer. Eventually, I couldn't stand the allotment small talk anymore and after telling nice, old Mr Andrews to, "PISS OFF," I stopped going during the day and only went at night.

Sometimes I'd just sit on my bench with a cup of coffee, tracking the stars across the heavens, waiting for the first streaks of light before heading home to sleep. As the weeks slowly passed, the nights shortened turning spring into summer. Then the day came when the trial began.

Gwen refused point blank to attend court. She couldn't bring herself to look at the man who'd robbed Orla of her life. Though, in truth, she still carried a small flame of hope that Orla would be found alive."

"Did anybody else think she was alive?" asked D.C.I. Logan.

"No, Gwen was the last of us to believe that. The rest of us knew she was dead."

"How come?"

"I don't really know. I think Rah knew there was never really any hope. For me, it was just a sort of growing darkness, followed by an unequivocal belief. I'm not sure about Jonny and Minty."

"But you said you'd been out searching for her," Fry interjected.

"I know and I did. And I knew it was pointless, desperate, like digging an allotment in the middle of the night. None of it makes sense, it's-it's just what happened.

So, the trial…Jim Bob took holiday leave and came down to stay with us and every day we drove to Chelmsford and sat in courtroom 4…"

CHAPTER 31
Henry the Eighth

*

Maggi - 4th August 1998

"…The back of my t-shirt feels damp as the August heat invades the courtroom. The air is still and heavy with human sweat. I can see beads of moisture gathering on the foreheads of Rosengrette, our Crown Prosecutor QC and Vane, Hoyle's Defence QC. Even Judge Lea reaches up and scratches under her wig. Rah just looks like a wilted wallflower, slumped in her seat next to me and Jonny, Minty, Herrick and Jim Bob aren't fairing much better either.

The only person who looks relaxed and comfortable sits in the dock. His chin flab oozes over his shirt collar, virtually hiding the knot of his tie. His blank eyes, knob-shaped nose and scant lips look lost on his fat face, reminding me of another ginger tosser, Henry the Eighth.

The day is long, laborious and full of technical jargon as the court officials set the case in motion.

"You're a first-class wanker," I think as I stare daggers at Hoyle. "Sitting there in your suit won't fool anyone, you piece of shit." I scan the jury's faces for the hundredth time: 12 good men and true, though they aren't all men as over half are women.

I take Rah's hand as we leave the court at the end of the first day, guiding her through a smattering of reporters. They make half-hearted attempts to get us to comment, but we ignore their offers. Walking towards the carpark, I feel something is giving for the first time in weeks, like a dislodged log in a river jam. A renewed energy pushes at my depression, and as Jonny drives his Aston Martin along the A12, I open the window of the sports car and let the air fill my lungs.

Back home, the front door stands open. I guess Gwen is eagerly waiting for us to return, though she tells us it's to let a breeze through the house.

"Breeze," I think, "that'd be a fine thing."

"How'd it go?" she asks as she pours us a cup of tea.

"Okay," I tell her.

"What's he like...the man ... Hamilton Hoyle?" she questions hesitantly. I understand why, she wants to know but doesn't want to hear.

"Heavy built, fair skinned, calm," Minty tells her objectively.

"Calm? He's not calm, he's just a fat narcissistic cunt," I snap.

"Bigster," Jim Bob warns gently with an understanding smile, "stick it in your hurt locker."

"Sorry," I mutter, taking a gulp of tea.

"Hoyle's just putting on a show of indifference; it's a front for the jury. Most of them look like they're the sort of people who will see through his lies though," encourages Jonny.

"Guys, I've got to go. I've got to put some practice time in, but I'll join you tomorrow," Herrick says, finishing his tea.

"Sure, Herrick, and thanks for coming," Jonny says, standing to shake his hand.

"See ya, Bud," Jim Bob nods.

"Bye, Herrick," I mutter as he leans past my shoulder and hugs Rah.

"See you tomorrow, Sweetheart," he murmurs, gently kissing the top of her stubble head.

"Thanks, Herrick," she murmurs back.

After tea, Rah's siblings, Arthur and Amelia, phone followed by my parents. That evening, we actually eat properly. Even Rah manages a few mouthfuls. Later, much later, I let myself quietly out of the back door and walk through the garden. Nature has already started to reclaim the space. Clematis and honeysuckle tendrils fill

174

the overhead canopy, while shrubs reach new branches across the pathways. The small meadow at the end of the garden that Orla and I planted three years ago as a birthday present for Rah, is tall and filled with seed heads. Opening the double doors to Rah's pottery room, I pull a wicker chair outside and sit with the waxing moon above me.

"Maggs?" Rah calls quietly.

"Here, Love," I answer and turn to see her walking through the grass. Her shaved head is bent and the moonlight catches her cheekbones. She looks breathtakingly beautiful to me.

"I thought you might like a cup of coffee," she says, placing a steaming mug in my hands.

I find her a chair, and we sit and talk about everything and nothing until she says, "Maggs, please come to bed, I need you there. Please don't spend another night away from me."

"Oh Rah," I murmur apologetically, "I'm sorry, I never thought... I just haven't been able to sleep, and the house makes me feel trapped."

"So it's not me?" she asks softly.

"No, of course not. It's just that..."

"Your misery is so vast; you don't know how you can contain it?"

"Yes, that mixed in with an overwhelming sense of anger and powerlessness. I want to make it better, right, I want vengeance, justice. I want to rip Hamy fucking Hoyle apart and make him suffer. When I'm outside, somehow, it feels more manageable. I don't feel that I'm so likely to explode at any moment."

"That's okay then, Maggs. As long as my grief isn't suffocating you."

"No Rah, never. I love you, and I love Orla too."

"Me too," she says, slipping her small hand into mine.

Wednesday, *the courtroom feels stuffy and airless. Hoyle, sits behind his toughened glass, grinning confidently as Rosengrette sets out the case against him. He calls the first witness, who places Hoyle in the vicinity of Bosuns Road at approximately midday on 22nd December 1997. There's a bit of to-ing and fro-ing as Vane tries to* discredit her testimony, but I think her evidence is sound.

That evening, after we've eaten, Rah, Gwen and Minty disappear for a while. I don't think anything of it until Rah takes me by the hand and leads me through the garden to the little meadow. Her pottery shed doors stand open with a lantern throwing a gentle light across a blow-up mattress and two sleeping bags.

"I thought over what you said about feeling trapped by the house, so I thought, let's sleep out here instead. That way you can be outside, and I can sleep with you."

"Oh Rah, thank you. But how though?"

"Gwen really," she says leading me to the bed. "I spoke to her, told her why you were always out at night and she suggested this. It was her who lugged all this stuff down here today. I only helped Minty and her move the potters' wheel."

We lay in the shelter of the shed watching the stars remembering how we'd played camping with Orla in the garden. We both cry and sleep until Rah's nightmares return to wake us.

Thursday, Paul, then Seb take the stand. Rosengrette questions them about finding the bike hidden at the football ground. After which a forensic expert explains the process of fingerprinting, showing the court photos of Hoyle's prints and how they indisputably match the prints lifted from the handlebars of Orla's bike. Vane makes no effort to challenge either Paul and Seb or the forensic bloke. Hoyle, the fat twat, just looks bemused.

"Fuck, I hate him."

On Friday, Rosengrette, looking decidedly damp, calls a witness who I know nothing about, a Mr Seal. I feel Rah sit up as the Clerk ushers in a respectable looking, middle-aged gentleman. Placing his right hand on the bible, he swears to tell the truth, the whole truth and nothing but the truth.

"Mr Seal," begins Rosengrette, smiling encouragingly at the man, "Do you live next door to Hamilton Hoyle in Spinners Drive, Godlinghoe?"

"Yes, I do," answers Mr Seal confidently, though I see him give a furtive glance at the dock before turning away quickly. I look at the *cunt sneering derisively back at Mr. Seal.*

"In fact, your bungalow is attached to Mr Hoyle's, is that correct?"

"Yes, it is."

"Consequently, you sometimes hear Mr Hoyle through the adjoining wall."

"Yes, frequently."

"Were you disturbed by Mr Hoyle in the early hours of Tuesday, 23 December 1997?"

"Your Honour, a point of law," Vane injects, rising to his feet.

"Yes?" Judge Lea asks, looking over the top of her glasses at him.

"My learned friend is leading the witness," Vane says pleasantly.

"Quite, Counsel please rephrase your question," Judge Lea states.

"Of course, Your Honour. Mr Seal, will you tell the court what happened on the night of the 22nd of December, or to be more precise, the morning of the 23rd?"

"I was woken up at about 2 o'clock in the morning by a high-pitched scream coming from next door." My heart lurches in my chest, and I feel Rah shudder beside me, I grip her hand as Rosengrette continues.

"Did you think it was Mr Hoyle screaming?"

"No, definitely not, it was a girl's scream. I'm sure of that."

"In your mind, was Mr Hoyle hurting an innocent thirteen-year-old girl, for example, Orla Montgomery?"

"Your Honour, a point of law, Supposition," Vane interjects again.

"Yes, yes, be careful Counsel," warns Judge Lea.

"Sorry, Your Honour," Rosengrette apologises with a small bow of the head, but I think he's got what he wanted, an idea implanted in the jury's minds. "What did you do next, Mr Seal?" Rosengrette continues politely.

"I phoned the police."

"Did they arrive to investigate?"

"Not until the following day, when I suspect he'd disposed of any evidence." A surge of anger travels down my spine as I hear Orla being described as evidence.

"Thank you, Mr Seal, no further questions," Rosengrette says,

sitting down. Judge Lea invites Vane to cross-examine. He takes his time to stand ,as though he can hardly be bothered. I add his name to my hate list.

"Mr Seal," he starts in a voice edged with sarcasm. "We've heard you say loud and clear that you were woken by a girl's scream from Mr Hoyle's bungalow in the early hours of 23rd December 1997, is that correct?"

"Yes, that's right," Mr Seal answers steadily, though I hear a slight inflection in his tone.

"And sequentially, you phoned the police, is that right, Mr Seal?"

"Yes."

"If Your Honour permits, I would like to play the police recording of that phone call."

"Go ahead, Mr Vane." Producing a C.D. from the files in front of him, Vane hands it to the Clerk who inserts it into the court's player. After a few clicks and stutters, a voice asks, "What's your emergency?"

"There's a girl being murdered next door; I can hear her screaming," Mr Seal answers desperately.

"Oh fuck," I mumble under my breath because in the background I swear I can hear it too.

"What's your name, sir?"

"Mr Seal."

"Address please, Mr Seal?"

"11 Spinners Drive, Godlinghoe."

"And would that be 9 Spinners Drive where you can hear the disturbance?"

"Yes, that's right. I'll put the phone to the wall, and you will hear it too."

A series of loud bangs sounds, then a roar and a male voice shouting something aggressively.

"Can you hear it? I can't sleep with all that racket going on. Goodness knows what he's doing in there!"

"Mr Seal, an officer will be with you shortly." Vane indicates to the Clerk to stop the player.

"Now, let me play for the court two more police emergency recordings, dated 14th and 20th of December 1997. Both are from Mr Seal, concerning Mr Hoyle," Vane says, addressing the jury. They pretty much followed the same pattern, though neither mentions a girl screaming, only the noise coming from Hoyle's side of the dividing wall.

"Mr Seal, is it true there's been a long-standing neighbour dispute between yourself and Mr Hoyle concerning noise disturbance, in particular, the sound of computer games?"

"Yes, but..."

"I suggest, what you actually heard in the early hours of 23rd December was not a young girl in distress but a computer game called Gals, Guns, and Quickdraw being played by Mr Hoyle and his friend, Mr Wheeler. A game they played until gone 4 in the morning. Something of a regular habit for Mr Hoyle, wouldn't you say, and something you have spent months complaining about to the police on an emergency number?"

"Yes, but this time it was different. I definitely heard a girl screaming." And though Mr Seal's voice has now modulated to a falsetto, there's still a firmness to his answer.

"Couldn't the scream have come from exactly the source my client says it comes from, that of a sound effect from the computer game?"

"But this scream was different. It sounded human."

"Thank you, Mr Seal, that will be all." I look at the jury, and I'm sure a number of them believe Mr Seal's account.

"Fucking tosspot, Seal," Hoyle shouts, making a wanking gesture with his hand as Mr Seal leaves the courtroom.

"If the defendant shouts out again, I will have him removed from my court," Judge Lea sternly reprimands.

"Yeah, that's it, you make a tit of yourself Hamy Fucking Hoyle, then they'll see your true colours," I think gratifyingly before Judge Lea adjourns for the day.

CHAPTER 32
Guilty as Charged
*

Maggi - 1998

The weekend feels pointless; I just want to be back in court. We spend it aimlessly, waiting for each hour to pass. Monday arrives, it's hot and muggy. The others sit in the waiting room, Rah chewing her fingers with Herrick next to her, Jonny staring at his hands, Jim Bob and Minty in quiet conversation while I try to read the notices on the pinboard.

"Case no. T20160293, Hamilton Hoyle, court 4," announces the Clerk and I have to stop myself from running for the door.

The courtroom is as hot and airless as the previous week. I feel sweat dripping down my back as I automatically sit in the same seat as I'd sat in last week, like it's a normal part of my life now to have a chair of my own in courtroom 4.

Vane sets out the case for the defence and I think, "You don't stand a fucking chance, Vane. You've got nothing to prove that the cunt's innocent." He calls Graham Wheeler as a witness for the defence. Wheeler swaggers into court, giving Hoyle a thumbs-up. He looks pretty normal until he opens his mouth to reveal a couple of blackened stumps that must've once passed as teeth. He swears on the bible, and I think, "Bullshit, you wouldn't know the truth even if it slapped you in the face."

"Mr Wheeler, are you a friend of Mr Hoyle's?" Vane begins.

"Yeah, known him for 'bout a couple of years."

"Would you say you're good friends?"

"Yeah."

"Do you often hang out together, for example, go to pubs together?"

"Yeah."'

"Were you together on 22nd December 1997?"

"Yeah."

"What were you doing?"

"Drin'ing in The Albert from opening till kick out."'

"What time would that be?"

"Bout lunchtime till 11.30, I'd say."

"What happened after that, Mr Wheeler?"

"We left the pub and found a bike."

"Where did you find the bike?"

"In Godiva Gar'ens. It was sort'f just there like, leaning against a tree."

"What type of bike was it?"

"A gal's bike, you know without the bar fing at the top, and I fink it had a basket or somfing on the front."

"What happened next?"

"Hamy decided to try to ride it home but what with the beer and the snow 'e kept on falling off. In the end, we dumped it at the footy ground."

I look at Hoyle who sits there smirking. "Guilty as fuck," I think, but no one in the jury is looking at him, they're all watching Vane and Wheeler.

"Then what did you do?"

"Wot we normally do, played a computer game."

"Did anything else happen?"

"Na...oh yeah, if you mean that old geezer from next door banging on the wall shou'ing sumfing about calling the pigs... sorry police."

"Then what?"

"Went 'ome 'bout 4, I'd say."

"Is that 4 a.m.?"

"Wot?'

"4 o'clock in the morning, Mr Wheeler, is that what time you left Mr

181

Hoyle's house?"

'Oh yeah, that's it, yeah. I left Mr Hoyle's 'ouse at 4 a.m. in the morning, yeah."

"So, at no time between the hours of 11 a.m. on the 22nd of December until 4 a.m. on the morning of the 23rd of December 1997 did you see Mr Hoyle talking to a young girl?"

"No, never."

"Thank you, Mr Wheeler. No further questions."

"Let's break for lunch and resume at ten past two," Judge Lea instructs.

"All rise," announces the Clerk and the room begins to empty. I see the toothless wonder smirk at the cunt, and I think, "Just give me an excuse and I'll whack the last of your teeth out."

After lunch, Rosengrette gets purposefully to his feet and squares up to Wheeler.

"You're in for it now, pus mouth," I think as Rosengrette rips into him, proving that he's a liar with a criminal record as long as his arm. Wheeler starts to sweat. I see him wipe his face with his sleeve.

"Do you and Mr Hoyle often drink the Albert?"

"Yeah."

"So one day is pretty much like another."

"I didn't say that," Wheeler answers.

"How can you be sure it was the night of the 22nd of December when you were drinking with Mr Hoyle at The Albert then?"

"Coz we were celebrating Xmas."

"On the 22nd?"

"Yeah, coz our benny had just come in."

"Benny?"

"Dole, benefit. Our Xmas giro. We'd cashed it in and 'ad gone on a litool celebration."

"So, you don't work for a living then Mr Wheeler?'

"So wot if I don't?"

"And Mr Hoyle... does he work for a living?

"Na, but that don't mean he's done noffing, do it?"

"So, what you're saying, Mr Wheeler, is that you think Mr Hoyle is

182

guilty and he has done something?"

"Wot? Na."

"Your Honour, a point of law," Vane interjects.

"Yes, yes, be careful Counsel not to confuse the witness," warns Judge Lea.

"Of course, Your Honour, my apologies. Can I direct the court's attention to the Discovery File, page 104?" Rising from his seat, the Clerk hands the relevant document to Wheeler who looks more confused than ever, while Judge Lea, Vane and the jury find the relevant page.

"Page 104, Mr Wheeler," Rosengrette repeats.

"Wot?"

"Page 1-0-.4," Rosengrette repeats again.

"Twat," I think, laughing to myself.

"Got it? Can you see this is a photocopy of your giro, issued on the 22nd of December 1997 in your name, Graham Wheeler?"

"Yeah."

"Now, check the date of when the giro was cashed at Godlinghoe post office."

"Wot?"

"The date, Mr Wheeler, when you cashed the giro was the 23rd of December 1997, so how could you have spent it at the pub on the 22nd if you didn't cash it until the 23rd?"

"I don't know," Wheeler snaps petulantly. "Might've been Hamy's giro we spent. How's I'm meant to remember, it was ages ago."

"Hook, line and sinker," I think.

"And what about the bike story, Mr Wheeler?"

"Wot about it?" he sneers back.

"Well, it doesn't add up, does it? If you and Mr Hoyle were innocently playing around on a bike, why would you hide it so well?"

"Coz we knew we shouldn't 'ave ta'en it even though it was just lying there in Godiva Gar'ens just asking to be rid'en." He shrugs his shoulders at the jury as though he would've been stupid not to have taken the bike.

"But you didn't ride it, did you?"

"Wot?"

"Well, if the bike was just there asking to be ridden, why didn't you ride it? Why was it just Mr Hoyle who rode it?"

"I don't know; I can't remember, it was ages ago."

"I don't think you were even there, Mr Wheeler. I think you're just covering up for your friend."

"I was there."

"But you don't even know what day it was, you've told us a tall story about a giro cheque and a bike. I think you're lying, Mr Wheeler."

"Fuckin' not," snaps Wheeler with his mouth hanging open.

"No more questions, Your Honour," Rosengrette says, sitting down gracefully.

"Whoop bloody whoo, well done, Rosengrette," I yell silently, stopping myself from pumping the air as Judge Lea dismisses the court for the day.

Tuesday, Vane calls Hoyle to the stand. His voice is full of casual contempt as he answers Vane's questions, pretty much repeating what his halitosis side-kick said the previous day. Vane shows the jury a map of Godlinghoe, with a black line tracking Hoyle and Wheeler's supposed journey from the pub, along Pye Road, into Godiva Gardens. There's a large X marking the spot where they claim they found Orla's bike. Then there's a sort of squiggly pattern through the Gardens, across Godiva Road, right onto North Close, into the football ground. Another X marks the location of where we found Orla's bike before the line continues into Farrierfield Estate, arriving at Spinners Drive.

Hoyle then makes derogatory remarks about Mr Seal before Vane asks, "Did anything happened on the morning of the 23rd, Mr Hoyle?"

"I was asleep and then, the next thing I know the porkers are banging on m' door."

"You mean the police?" Vane pointedly asks.

"Yeah, that's what I mean," Hoyle mutters back.

"What time did the police arrive?"

"Don't know, about 9, I reckon."

"What did they want?"

"The usual. Tosspot Seal had rung them complaining about the noise."

"Is this something that happens regularly?"

"Like clock-work, mate."

"Did the police check your property?"

"They came in and had a snout about, but they knew the situation with the old git next door."

"Thank you, Mr Hoyle. No more questions." Rosengrette declines to cross-examine.

"No need, everyone can see he's a lying bag of wank," I think, as Judge Lea dismisses the court for the day.

On Wednesday, both counsels sum up. Rosengrette tears apart the defence and I don't think Vane has a leg to stand on when he addresses the jury. Then, Judge Lea dismisses the jury, after directing them on the points of law, to consider their verdict. She reminds them that the burden of proof lies in the balance of probabilities rather than solid evidence as Orla's body has, as yet, not been recovered.

Before we leave the court, I see Jonny and Minty speaking to Rosengrette, then briefly on their own. Their exchange seems intense, "But why wouldn't it be?" I think, "We're all fucking intense."

"Do you think Hoyle will tell us where Orla is after he is convicted?" Rah asks me as we lay under the stars that night.

"Rosengrette said he might use it as a bargaining tool for a shorter sentence."

"Do you think he will?" she says, turning to me. I can't see her face, but I know it is hollow from the weeks of starvation. Just as I know her eyes are sunken and smudged by dark circles. I want to lie to her and to myself. I want to say, "Definitely. Why wouldn't he?" but instead I say, "I don't know, Rah, he might if he thinks it will help his case. But I will never give up looking for her, I promise."

185

The temperature rises with the sun on Thursday morning. The atmosphere in the court waiting room is sweltering. Rah leans against me, exhaustedly. Jonny sits across from us staring into space. Earlier in the week, he'd looked as drained and grey as the rest of us but not today, well, not now. He catches me looking at him and smiles back. His eyes are bright and his skin glows with that Jonny kick-ass look of his.

"Jonny, what did Rosengrette say to you and Minty yesterday?" I ask him.

"Usual stuff; got to wait for the jury now. Could be today, could be tomorrow or next week."

"What did he think?"

"Might be a quick one. He thinks it's best for us to hang around, though he did say there's no real telling."

"Nothing else then?"

"Not really."

Nothing happens as the morning wears on. It makes me jittery. Rah is continually sick every time she tries to eat or drink. Minty and Jonny are remarkably composed, and Herrick and Jim Bob just pass the hours chatting quietly. As the afternoon sessions start, I'm just beginning to wonder if it will go the same way as the morning, when I hear a call over the tannoy for Case no. T20160293, Hamilton Hoyle, court 4.

"This is it," I say to Rah, taking her hand. As we enter, Rosengrette nods to us. I sit on the edge of my seat as we watch Hoyle enter the dock. The jury retake their seats. I can hardly breathe as the Clerk first asks Hoyle to stand then the foreperson of the jury.

A small woman climbs to her feet. My eyes flicker back and forth from the foreperson to Hoyle. I want to see her answer, but I also want to see Hamy fucking Hoyle's cocky expression wiped off his face when they convict him of murder.

"Have you reached a verdict on all four counts upon which you all agree?" asks the Clerk.

"Yes," the foreperson answers.

"Guilty as charged, Tosser," I mutter, predicting the verdict.

"Count 1, Abduction of a Minor over the age of thirteen and under the age of sixteen?"

"Guilty," I breathe.

"Not Guilty."

"What?"

"Count 2, Imprisonment of a Minor over the age of thirteen and under the age of sixteen?"

"Not Guilty."

"Count 3, Rape of a Minor over the age of thirteen and under the age of sixteen?"

"Not Guilty."

"Count 4, Murder of a Minor over the age of thirteen and under the age of sixteen?"

"Not Guilty."

CHAPTER 33
A Cloudless Sky

*

Maggi
"YES," Hoyle roars, punching the air triumphantly while Wheeler, sitting a few seats behind us, cries out, "I fucking knew it mate," as Judge Lea dismisses the jury and Hoyle.
"Not Guilty. How can you be so fucking stupid?" I shout angrily at their disappearing backs, horrified by what they've done.

2023
"…The trial was short, only eight days and the jury was back very quickly with a verdict of not guilty."
"Not Guilty? But…" Fry exclaimed, mirroring my original disbelief.
"I know right, you could have knocked me over with a feather, especially as we knew he had previous convictions. I was convinced he was going down, but unbeknown to me some of the others had read the trial very differently…"

1998
"Maggs, Maggs, it's not over, get it together," Jonny says pulling me out of my seat. "It's only just begun. Come on, let's get out of here and I'll explain."
"Rah," I remember, looking wildly around for her.
"It's okay Maggs, Minty and Herrick have got her. They've left the court. But I need you."

"Why? What do you mean?" I ask, stumbling after him as he pulls me through the crowd.

"Not here," he answers firmly as flashbulbs go off around us. I hear reporters shouting for statements, asking questions, demanding answers.

"Margret Drew, have you got anything you would like to say about Hamy Hoyle?"

"Maggi, do you think the verdict is right?"

"Jonathan, do you think your daughter is dead?"

"Is it because you're all poofters?"

"Fuck off, mate," Jonny growls as he pushes a reporter aside and barges a passageway through. In the car park, he elbows a camera out of my face and thrusts me into his car. Getting in the driver's side, he locks the doors.

"Jonny," I begin.

"Not here, Maggs," he says firmly again. We drive out of Chelmsford, taking the A12. Before long he turns off onto a slip road and we find ourselves weaving our way along ever smaller lanes, through tiny villages until the horror of the courtroom is left behind.

Pulling over, he parks the car in an entrance to a farm track. I get out. I feel sick. Vomit fills my mouth as I start to retch.

"Here," Jonny says, offering me some water as I struggle to stand upright. I stare out across the never-ending fields of golden wheat. The air is still with the humming of insects, the sky cloudless, the sun bright. I shut my eyes and lean my back against Jonny's car. Hot tears slide down my face as I feel the car jolt and know Jonny is leaning next to me.

I hear him light a cigarette and instantly smell the acrid tobacco. He sucks the toxic fumes into his lungs and exhales slowly.

"Here," he says again, but this time when I open my eyes, I see he is holding the cigarette out to me. I haven't smoked in years, but I take it anyway and drag deeply. My lungs explode, and I cough till I start retching again.

When I can speak, I say, "I don't understand, Jonny," and I didn't just mean the verdict, I meant him. I'm filled with rage and

189

confusion, but Jonny isn't. He's focussed, pumped and alive. I've
seen him like this many times in the past, mainly before Orla's birth,
when he was ready for a night out, ready to conquer the world.

"Did you think Hoyle would get convicted?" he asks, taking another
drag from the cigarette.

"Yes," I retort, still reeling from the verdict.

"I knew he'd get off," he says almost nonchalantly.

"Wh-what? I stutter back.

"You thought it was in the bag, didn't you?"

"Yes, pretty much... what with the fingerprint evidence, him being
I.D'd. in Bosuns Road and Rosengrette demolishing the defence and
Wheeler's obvious lies."

"Minty and I both thought it wasn't enough to persuade the jury."

"Why?"

"We thought Seal came across as vapid, but it was Hoyle's alibi,
Wheeler, that clinched it. I knew the jury believed him; I could see it
written all over their faces."

"Fuck, I didn't see any of that. I thought the jury knew he was a
lying piece of shit."

"Anyway," Jonny carries on, "It doesn't matter coz I wanted the
bastard to get off."

"What? Hoyle?"

"Of course Hoyle. Come on, Maggs, I need you to get your fucking
act together," he snaps at me.

"Sorry," I murmur, "I'm just a bit shell-shocked."

"Well, suck it up and switch on."

"Okay, okay... So, you wanted Hoyle to get off?"

"Yeah, that's exactly it, and Minty too."

"Why would you want the cunt to get away with it?"

"Because, Maggs, it means I get to find our daughter."

"Right...I'm lost again. How can Hoyle getting off help us to find
Orla?"

"Because I'm going to make Mr fucking Hoyle wish he'd never been
born. I'm going to make him tell me where she is," he explains
calmly enough, but I hear the venom in his voice, something I'd

190

never heard before.

2023

"…Jonny, Minty and Rosengrette, our QC, had pretty much guessed which way the verdict was going. On the way home Jonny explained he'd cooked up a plan with Minty to force Hoyle into telling us where he'd hidden Orla's body. I knew he meant it too. He had a manner about him that I'd never seen before, a cold, calculating vengeance. Me, I am easily riled, but Jonny was always the placid one, the voice of reason, the calm in my storms…"

1998

"Jonny, why would that bag of wank tell us where Orla is? It would incriminate him when he's just got away with it," I state rationally.
"The police have their methods, and I have mine," he answers methodically, as though he's repeating a well-oiled thought.
"Okay, are you saying if we hurt him in some way he'll talk to us?"
"Yes, that's exactly what I'm saying."
"Jonny, if you want to kill Hamy fucking Hoyle or just skin him alive, I'm your woman. Don't think I haven't thought about it, but I just kept hitting a brick wall. I've considered shooting him, but getting a gun is near on impossible. Smacking him with a hammer, but he's a big man, I'd never get nea…"
"I've got a plan," he states firmly, cutting me off.

2023

"…He told me he and Minty had already got an idea. I think he wanted to sound me out, see if I'd be up for it…"

1998

"Go on then, let's hear it," I say sceptically.
"It's really Minty's idea and it's more about finding Orla, not about killing Hoyle. Though I'd be up for that too. But I'll need your help, Maggs."
"I'll help, you know I will. What's the plan?"

"First, a meeting. Minty and I need to put our idea across to all of you."

"All of us? You mean Rah too?"

"Yes, there's no way we'll be able to keep Rah out of this. Besides, she'll never forgive us if we tried."

"You're right there," I say, staring out across the acres of wheat, knowing that if I went behind her back, even if it was to protect her, she'd never speak to me again. "When are you thinking of having this meeting?"

"As soon as we get back. Minty said he'd be waiting for us. I've already hinted something to Herrick, and he's on board."

"Gwen?"

"Yeah."

"Jim Bob?"

"Goes without saying."

"Seb and Paul?"

"Nah, I'd rather leave them out of it unless we need them. I don't think they'd want to get into anything illegal and the less they know, the better. Not that they would ever drop me in it."

"What about Arthur and Amelia?"

"Minty said not. Arthur's filming on location and Amelia has the children. Besides, it would mean bringing in Amelia's husband too."

"Best get back then."

"My thoughts exactly."

Two miles down the road we see a sign for the A12. Back on the dual carriageway Jonny puts his foot down. His old Aston Martin's engine roars into life as we fly down the fast lane. He winds his window down, and I watch as his blond hair twists in the wind. We zoom past normal people going about their normal business while I contemplate the intricacies of how to first torture and then murder someone.

CHAPTER 34
Full of Awe

*

Maggi

Back at Peartree Road, Rah is waiting on the doorstep. She rushes to me as we pull up. "Maggs," she says hugging me tightly, "Has Jonny told you? We are going to get Orla back."

"Yes," I murmur, hugging her back. She was always small, but now I can feel the ridges of her spine and the bowing of each of her ribs. "Yes," I say again, "we are going to bring Orla home."

Joining the others at the table, I sit between Herrick and Rah. Gwen places my mug into my hands, and I trace the lumpy clay heart motif with my thumbs. Beyond the table the bi-folding doors stand open letting in the evening birdsong. I suddenly have a memory of Orla standing there asking me for more water for her paddling pool. My breath sticks in my throat and my eyes cloud with tears.

"Maggs, are you alright?" asks Herrick quietly.

"Fine, thanks," I smile back at him, remembering he doesn't have to be here, he's doing this for love.

"Okay," Minty announces looking at me, "I'm guessing Jonny has probably told you something of why we are here," I nod. "I spoke to Norah just now and Jonny and I have sounded out Gwen, Jim Bob and Herrick." Minty smiles sadly at us all. "So, I had a feeling by Monday, after Wheeler's evidence, that the jury was softening towards Hoyle. They, of course, didn't know what we'd been told about Hoyle, that he is an un-convicted child rapist."

The words hang in the air like poisonous gas, invisible and deadly, making me recoil. I see Jim Bob flinch and Gwen sit back from the table. I hear Rah give the slightest of moans and feel Herrick shift in his chair. "Jonny said as much to me as Wheeler left the dock. By Wednesday, we were pretty sure of which way the verdict was going. So after the court session we asked Rosengrette what he thought, and he conceded that we might have a point. That evening Jonny and I met at his place and it soon became apparent that we shared the same opinion, though he, unlike me, was far from worried." Turning to Jonny, Minty says, "Jonny, you need to speak for yourself, I think."

"Okay. Minty's right when he said I wasn't worried, in fact, I was pleased."

"Why Jonny?" asks Gwen.

"Because I realised Hamy Hoyle was never going to give us Orla back unless I made him do it. If he'd been convicted it would've been years before I could've got my hands on him. But now he is acquitted; he's ours for the taking."

"You mean like kidnapping?" Gwen asks, her voice edged with shock.

"Yes, kidnapping," Jonny answers firmly.

"Oh," she responds slightly shaken.

"Brilliant," I exclaim.

"I want to kill him too," Rah declares enthusiastically, as though we are adding an extra tour to an already action-packed holiday. We all turn to look at her. She sits bolt upright in her chair, her eyes bright, her body taut, her fingers bitten. She's more alive than I've seen her be for months.

"I won't kill anyone," Jim Bob asserts softly. "I will do anything to help you find Orla's remains, but I will not kill."

"Nor I," seconds Minty.

"Me neither, I won't take a life. I won't be brought down to Hoyle's level. I'm better than that and so are you, Norah," Gwen adds to her daughter.

"No, I'm not," states Rah defiantly.

"Well, we all know that I would be lying if I said I didn't want to kill him. My moral compass points straight at death, with as much pain as possible as far as I'm concerned," I say vehemently.

"This isn't about killing Hoyle, it's about bringing Orla home," Jonny asserts calmly. "I understand why you want to kill him, Rah and Maggs; God knows I feel the same. But we need everyone on board if we are going to make this happen. So if Minty, Gwen and Jim Bob are willing to help if all of us agree not to kill, then I'll go along with it. Do you agree, Rah? Maggs?" There's a moments silence.

"I'll kill the cunt later," I think, and nod an acceptance. I look at Rah. She stares down at her damaged hands, they are clasped around her mug. A minute ticks by.

"Rah," I murmur, trying to convey the deal I've made with myself. "Yes," she utters at last. "Alright, I agree, I won't kill Hoyle."

"Good," says Minty. "Right Jonny, you'd better set out the plan."

"'kay. I... we, don't have a plan yet of how to kidnap Hoyle but it will certainly take quite a few of us as he is a well-built..."

"... Fat cunt..." I mutter.

"... man," Jonny states, ignoring my empirical analysis. "What we've worked out is a means of torture." Again, I feel the tension around the table ripple as the word 'torture' hangs in the air. No one moves or says anything. I imagine myself dressed in a medieval leather cap and apron, brandishing hot irons while Hoyle, chained tight to a rack, squeals in fear. I smile to myself. "Somehow," continues Jonny, "I can't see myself cutting Hoyle into little bits or punching him hard..."

"I can," I think but I don't say anything this time. I don't want to upset the others.

"...then Minty made a suggestion. He said we should think about what we are capable of, what our assets are, where our skills lie, what we have at hand. And, what I have is a house that I hardly use... so there's our Kill Room..."

"I thought we'd agreed no killing," Gwen jumps in.

"I just mean a room we can prepare in advance, then disassemble

195

afterwards. It's a turn of speech, Gwen, a telly thing."

"You must watch some strange programs, Jonny, Kill Room indeed, huh," Gwen replies.

"Let's get back on track, shall we?" Minty asks rhetorically. "Go on, Jonny."

"Right, so we can use my house. Prepare it in advance, hold Hoyle there, question him, release him and clear the evidence. Next, and this is the biggest part, is how. My skill base is nursing and Maggs is as a Operating Department Practitioner..."

"So?" I question.

"So, we both deal in powerful drugs. There are a whole bunch of drugs that can render a person useless, but there is one particular group of drugs, used every day in theatres, that does more than render a person useless, it paralyses them."

"Rocuronium?" I question.

"Yes, Rocuronium among others. I think there's quite a few;we use Suxamethonuim in A&E. Anyway, it is a neuromuscular blocking agent that works by interfering with the normal action of acetylcholine, a neurotransmitter chemical."

"Sorry, Jonny, I'm lost." Jim Bob looks puzzled.

"Me too," I say, but not for the same reason Jim Bob is confused. I know the family of drugs all too well, I use them daily. I know too how they work and why they are used, but I can't understand why Jonny is off down this road. It's not like the drug can be used to capture Hoyle as it has to be administered intravenously. However clever we are, I know there's no way we are ever going to persuade the cunt to put out his arm while we insert a cannula into it.

"Right, Rocuronium is a drug that works by relaxing the muscles to the extent that once given to a patient, the patient is unable to breathe for themselves and they need to be ventilated using an Ambu-bag, a self-inflating bag. You must've seen them on telly, the type with a face mask and bag that is manually operated."

"Yep, I get the picture," Jim Bob says.

"Why would you do that to a person on purpose?" Gwen asks.

"To ventilate a patient and deliver anaesthetic vapour during an

operation you need to insert an endotracheal tube down the trachea, windpipe. But to deliver the endotracheal tube into the correct place the muscles of the throat need to be paralysed, otherwise, the patient would automatically gag. Also, while the patient is undergoing surgery, it prevents them from twitching," I explain, adding, "But I still don't see the relevance, Jonny."

"Here's the thing...these drugs do not knock a patient out, they remain fully conscious, these drugs only paralyse them, leaving the patient completely helpless and at the mercy of whoever is operating the Ambu-bag. Obviously, in cases of normal day to day surgry, the patient is anaesthetised, they know nothing of this. But now consider if a person was not anaesthetized, they would be fully conscious of the fact that they are unable to move, breathe, speak or cry, but they will be able to see, hear, feel pain as well as..."

"Fear," I complete for Jonny, full of awe as the horror of what he is suggesting dawns on me.

"Precisely. No blood, no violence, just incredible fear that can be maintained for as long as we need it too."

This drug is something I help administer on a daily basis, almost like clockwork but never in a million years have I seen it in terms of torture, only in terms of assistance. I look around the table at the others. Rah has a sort of mad sadistic look of glee on her face, Gwen looks appalled, and Herrick and Jim Bob just stare at Jonny in disbelief.

"That is fantastically clever, Jonny," I say, breaking the silence.

"It's more clever than you think," Minty remarks.

"Oh?" I'm really curious now.

"Jonny was telling me about a study he'd heard of, where a group of anaesthetists tied the arm of a volunteer with a tourniquet, injected him with the Rocuronium and proceeded to ask him questions. The volunteer, whose entire body was completely paralysed apart from his lower arm, was able to answer their questions by writing them on a piece of paper. He could see, hear, feel and respond."

"Just so I'm clear about what you are suggesting, we get this Hoyle bloke, tourniquet his arm, give him this muscle-relaxing drug,

197

Rococumin or something, and ask him where Orla is?" Jim Bob reiterates.

"Yes," Minty and Jonny answer in unison.

"Wow," I murmur.

"Okay, I'm up for that," Jim Bob says, as though he's agreeing to a night out.

CHAPTER 35
Lonely Old Slapper

*

Maggi - 2023

"...The plan centred around torturing Hoyle using hospital drugs."

"What kind of drugs?" D.C.I. Logan asks.

"There's a group of muscle relaxant drugs that, once given, renders a patient immobile, so they need assistance in breathing, though they remain fully conscious."

"Meaning you could threaten a person with suffocation?" she replies, getting the picture much quicker than I ever did.

"Basically, yes."

"Whoa, nasty," Fry says, making me smile.

"Very," I add. "Put it this way, the drugs we were proposing to use were commonly combined, before abolition, into a three-drug cocktail for use in executions by lethal injection." I see Fry's face give a slight wince and find myself liking him even more. "Anyway, we all agreed to Jonny and Minty's plan."

"Who's we?" D.C.I. Logan asks.

"Jonny, Rah, Minty, Gwen, Jim Bob, Herrick and me."

"I need clarification for the Cam. Jonny Gifford, Norah Montgomery, Minty and Gwen Montgomery, Jim Bob Drew, Herrick Butler and you, Maggi Drew."

"Yes. Anyway, after we'd all agreed to the plan, we worked out what we needed and how we were going to steal it."

"From Braxham Wick General Hospital, I presume?"

199

"Yes, D.C.I. Logan, you presume right…"

1998

"In the hospital basement, there's a corridor full of broken trolleys and wheelchairs; perhaps we could 'borrow' one?" I suggest.

"Yep, that's a good idea, I don't mind doing the 'borrowing' part. We'd better sign back into work, Maggs," says Jonny.

"Okay, I'll give Terry a ring and book a shift for tomorrow."

"I'll hire transport and be the driver. It better be a van if we are stealing a trolley," volunteers Minty.

"Good. Maggs, can you steal an electronic tourniquet and the Rocuronium?" Jonny asks.

"Yes," I say, thinking, "How the fuck am I going to steal a tournie machine, it's not as though it's something you can slip into a pocket like the Roc."

"I'll do the sharps and Ambu-bag."

"And I'll do the Kill Room stuff… sorry Gwen, the-the …" Jim Bob stutters.

"It's okay, I know what you mean," Gwen sighs resignedly.

"I think you should buy rolls of plastic sheeting, duct tape and anything else you can think of," advises Minty.

"Cable ties," Herrick suggests.

"Good thinking," I smile.

"What about a heart monitor too? We could scare the shit out of him, pretending his heart is failing," I add, really getting into it.

"Like it, Bigster," Jim Bob grins.

"For that matter, we'd better add in a defibrillator, just in case we need to start his heart again, I'll do both," Jonny offers.

"Fantastic, that's something else that should frighten the bastard," I smile, imagining myself again dressed as a torturer, but this time waving the heart paddles in the air and shouting, 'clear' like they do on the telly.

2023

"…After we'd decided on our means of torture, we discussed how we were actually going to kidnap the bastard. He wasn't what you might call petite being nearly 6ft and fat.

Jim Bob was the only one of us who knew how to throw a punch, as he had done a bit of boxing. Jonny was physically strong, but none of us could imagine him hitting anyone. Minty maybe, as he'd seen action in World War 2, but he was an old man by then. That left Rah and Gwen, who, quite frankly, weren't even worth considering being so small and Herrick who was just a pussy. Me, I was tough enough, though nowhere near as big as Hoyle, but I had hate on my side and,quite frankly, I couldn't wait to bring the bastard down…"

1998

"Best place to start is with what we know about him." Minty says.

"That he's a fucking bag of wank," I mutter.

"Yes, he is that," Minty says, as though I've made a sensible suggestion. "But what do we know of his habits, how can we trick him?"

"To start with, he doesn't know who I am," Gwen pipes up. "I never went to court. I could do the tricking part."

"Gwen, I don't think…" begins Minty

"Nonsense, I might not want to kill him, or come to that torture him, but I'm perfectly able to trick him for the sake of finding Orla." I look at her: tiny, bright-eyed and kind, the spitting image of her daughter and granddaughter, just an older version. I now add brave to my list of adjectives to describe Gwen. "I could knock on his door and pretend I am a social worker," she continues.

"That won't work, he'll shut the door on your face," Jim Bob states flatly.

"What if I said I was assessing his social needs and I might be able to get him financial assistance? He might go for that. Then, perhaps I could ask for a cup of tea and slip drugs into his cup."

"There are just too many things that could go wrong with that. He might not let you in. If he does, why would he make you tea? If he did, when could you doctor his cup? He might not drink it, etc, etc."

Jim Bob states again.

"Yes, but I like the drug idea," Jonny ponders. "If I could get a needle into him, I could topple him with Midazolam or Ketamine."

"That would be difficult to nick, it's a CD drug," I say.

"CD drug?" Minty asks.

"Controlled drug," Jonny answers. "They're locked up and monitored but I've a good record, and I doubt anyone would suspect me, though there'll be an inquiry. The problem though would be getting him in a position where I could jab him."

"From the trial, it was evident that Hoyle and Wheeler drank regularly at The Albert. That could be a good place to nab him. Maybe catch him off guard and spike his drink somehow?" Jim Bob suggests.

"Does anyone know the pub?" Minty asks.

"It has a reputation of being a druggy dive from what I hear," Jonny says, "But spiking his drink is as unpredictable as calling round as a social worker. What if you were spotted dropping stuff in his drink or he passes out in the pub, the landlord would have to call an ambulance."

"Yes, but what if I got him really drunk, bought him loads of drinks, kind of flirted with him..."

"That could work, Gwen," Jim Bob says excitedly. "There's always a lonely, old slapper hanging out in those sort of pubs looking for.."

"Jim Bob," I exclaim.

"I wasn't going to say sex, Bigster, I was going to say company."

"No, Jim Bob is right," Minty wades in, taking me by surprise. I'd have thought he'd be horrified by the idea of Gwen posing as a lonely, old slapper. "Do you think you could pull it off, Gwen?"

"I'd have to dye the grey out of my hair and buy appropriate clothing, but I don't see why not. I'd be nervous, but a couple of gins for a bit of Dutch courage and I'd be away. I could ply him with alcohol and suggest I go home with him, then you could all jump out and knock him down, and Jonny could inject him," Gwen reasons.

"I'll help you, Mum," Rah offers quietly. It's the first constructive thing she's really said if you don't include the murder idea.

"Yes, Darling, I think we should team up," Gwen replies, smiling at her daughter.

"Right then, I'd say we have a plan," Minty declares, adding, "Let's re-meet in 48 hours and refine it?"

"I can't do Saturday, it's LGO, but I can manage Sunday," Herrick offers.

"Oh Herrick, I'm sorry," Rah says, "I can't believe that I've been so selfish. And don't you teach Annabelle's son on Sundays?"

"It's fine, Rah, really. Anyway, I've already arranged for Malcolm to take on my pupils, as you know I don't have many, just Simon, Adam and Louise and he has welcomed the work." It's then that I think about how subdued Herrick has been.

"Herrick," I say quietly, turning to him, "You don't have to do this, you know."

"It's alright, Maggs, like Gwen, I'm sure I won't be of any use with the torture stuff, but I'll help carry or drive or whatever is needed."

"Are you sure? Don't if it goes against your principles or conscience."

"I am sure; I want to, really, I do." A massive wave of guilt sweeps through me as I remember all the bad stuff I'd thought and said about him over the years.

I look away and mumble, "Thanks, Herrick."

CHAPTER 36
Phantom Axe Murderer

*

Maggi - 2023

"…We decided to nab Hoyle on his way home from the pub. Gwen volunteered to be the plant, as she was the only one of us that Hoyle hadn't seen before. The plan was for her to pose as, in Jim Bob's words, 'a lonely old slapper looking for company' and ply him with alcohol. I didn't like the idea much of using Gwen as bait and I'm sure Minty didn't either, but neither of us said anything. We arranged to gather again on the following Sunday to finalise the plan.

First thing Friday morning, I phoned the hospital to say I'd like to return to work. They booked me in for a shift that afternoon. Then Rah and I headed round to Jonny's house to help choose a room to hold and torture Hoyle in."

"Is that Pump Road?" D.C.I. Logan asks.

"Yes, 27 Pump Road…"

1998

"Did you ring the hospital, Maggs?" Jonny asks as he makes a pot of coffee.

"Yeah. You?"

"Yeah, I said I'd take the weekend night shift, starting tonight."

"That'll keep them happy."

"Should do and give me a chance for a bit of a recy too. You?"

"Late shift today. I'll let you know how I get on before you start."

Coming into the kitchen, Minty and Gwen catch the tail end of our conversation.

"Maggs, if you're back at work, do you think it might be a good idea to start sleeping in the house again?" Gwen suggests kindly.

"S'pose." I know she's right, but the thought of it makes me feel claustrophobic.

"Which room do you think would be best for the Kill Room?" Minty asks, changing the subject. I'm not sure if it's to stop me from snapping at Gwen or to stop Gwen from nagging me, probably a bit of both.

"Well, there are two empty bedrooms upstairs," Jonny says.

"I think an upstairs room might be difficult. Trying to force a person up a flight of stairs, awake or asleep, will be a struggle," reasons Gwen.

Jonny nods. "Yeah, good point Gwen. And the stairs have a bend in them too. Okay, it's the dining room/come dump room at the back or the sitting room/come smart room at the front."

"Backroom, away from prying eyes." Minty chooses. "Also, if you have a visitor, you will still have a sitting room to take them into."

"The dump room it is." Like our house, Jonny's kitchen and dining room sit at the back, overlooking the garden. When he'd bought the house, he had great plans to convert it into one long room long similar to ours. But the years had drifted by and with him either working, climbing, partying or at ours, he'd never got around to doing much more than painting a couple of rooms and adding a bit of furniture.

"I mainly use it for the computer and my climbing gear," Jonny explains as we all stand gazing around the room. It's large, with the original Edwardian mouldings on the ceiling and tiles surrounding the fireplace. Light from the garden streams in through an old sash window, whose wooden frame and plaited cords have seen better days.

In the middle of the room sits a table with a huge computer screen, spectacular speakers and a printer that looks as though it could cook dinner and find a cure for cancer if asked. Apart from that, just as Jonny said, is a dark green rucksack, a bright blue climbing harness and a number of neatly coiled ropes in reds, yellows and greens with a pile of carabiners and a helmet.

"Let's start by clearing the room," I suggest. It takes time to haul the table up to one of the spare bedrooms proving Gwen's words about carrying a body upstairs. With the computer re-set up and the climbing gear stowed, the room is empty. My voice echoes around the space as I tell the others I've got to go to work.

Jonny hugs me. "Fine, have a good shift. Jim Bob will be here soon with the DIY stuff and we'll start prepping the room."

"I'll ring you with an update if I've managed to filch anything."

"Good hunting."

2023

"...So, I turned up for the late shift. It was the first shift I'd had since the trial had begun. Everyone was really considerate, no one mentioned the trial, but a couple of people gave me a hug, while others just reached out a hand. In a way I was pleased to get back to work, to do a job that I knew back to front, that was methodical and routine. After a couple of small cases, I asked Terry for a break. He said it wasn't a problem and to take as long as I needed and that he'd book me back in for the 7:30 slot..."

1998

I pull off my overalls and gloves and push them into the clinical waste bin as I walk out into the theatre corridor. It's quiet, a couple of people are chatting in the coffee room, but they don't look up as I walk by. Slipping my hand into the pocket of my scrubs, I feel the piece of folded paper. Passing theatres 3 and 4 I can see they are occupied, but 5 is empty. I saunter in, trying to look confident, unplug the tourniquet machine and casually wheel it out. Passing the coffee room, I feel the sweat gathering on the back of my neck as my heart pounds uncontrollably. Suddenly, theatre 4's doors swing open.

"Hi, Maggs," Jo's muffled voice comes from under her mask.

"Hey Jo, busy?"

"Could say. Got to go and find Mr Silco, another Exter implant, he's flung the first," she raises one of her eyebrows. Even with half of her face obscured by the surgical mask, I know that look well. It's one that conveys ironic amusement mixed with respect and care. It makes my heart rate drop.

"He's always fun to work with," I reply smilingly.

"Catch you for coffee later?"

"Sure, I'll be here till 9."

"Okey dokey," and she heads off to Supplies.

Swiping my security card to exit the theatres, the doors pop as the rubber seal opens. I walk through, pushing the tournie and hear the familiar swish as they shut behind me. No one I know is in the corridor. At the lift, I try leaning one shoulder nonchalantly against the wall with my back to the corridor I'd just walked down. Feeling stupid, I stand up properly. When the lift arrives, the doors seem to take forever to open as I crane my neck to see if there's anyone inside.

"Empty, thank fucking phew for that," I think, getting in and pressing basement, the doors rattle shut. Breathing out, I feel weak. Never in my life have I stolen anything and I know now, without a doubt, why—I'm useless at it. My palms are sweating, my back is wet, and I bet my face is the colour of a beetroot.

"Thank goodness for the mask," I think, before realising I'm going up not down. "Shit," I mutter, attacking the buttons. But too late, the lift halts on floor 4, maternity. A couple get in and smile at me.

"Down?" I murmur from behind my mask.

"Yes, thank you, ground floor." Shielding the buttons from their sight, I press basement again. The lift reaches the ground level then clonks and clanks as though it has never really had to descend as low as the basement before. Coming to rest with a jolt, the doors open. Unlike the corridors above that are decorated with pastel colours and artworks, this corridor is built of dark grey, concrete blocks that would suit any film company looking for a prison of war location. Stark lights set far apart run along the corridor's ceiling,

207

leaving intermittent pools of darkness. Dusty pipes wrapped in old cladding grace the walls and coldness fills the air. I feel the couple draw back from the door, but I don't look at them as I walk out of the lift into the strange, eerie corridor. I hear the lift doors shut behind me and breathe a sigh of relief.

"That's the hardest part over with," I tell myself encouragingly. Not far into the dingy passageway is a set of old-fashioned double doors with porthole windows. Only darkness shows through them now, but once they were permanently lit, as this was the hospital's original morgue.

I've never been scared of the dead, though I'm not that keen on the living corpses on floor 9, but down here every hospital ghost story I've ever heard comes flooding back to me. Stupidly spooked, I find myself glancing back over my shoulder to check there's no phantom axe murderer swooping down the corridor after me.

BANG.

"FUCK," I yell, my heart exploding with adrenaline before I realise I've pushed the tournie machine into the exact thing I am looking for, the row of broken trolleys.

"Fuck," I breathe again as I walk past a few before choosing one. The trolley's framework looks reasonable, but the mattress is torn in several places, exposing a layer of nicotine-yellow foam. I pull it out, try wheeling it about. The wheels are sound, though the stench of stale urine mixed with bacteria and chemicals wafts gently around me.

"It'll do," I think and place it three trolleys down, in the shadowed darkness between two lights, with the tournie machine next to it, pushed back against the wall. Pulling the paper from my pocket, I stick it to the machine and stand back. I doubt anyone would even notice the tournie here, but if they did, they'd read the sign saying it was out of order and not to be removed.

Back in the lift, I stop on the ground floor and step into the main concourse. It's full of people looking in shops or buying coffees. At the public phones, I pick one up and dial our number. Minty answers.

"Hi Minty, it's Maggs, is Jonny there?"

"Hi Maggs, yes, hang on, and I'll fetch him." A moment later, Jonny comes to the phone.

"Hey, you okay?"

"Yep, fine. In the lower corridor, three down, you'll find what you are looking for."

"Do you mean the basement?"

"Yes."

"And a trolley?"

"Yes, and more."

"Right, I'll arrange pick up."

"What sort of time do you reckon?"

"9:30 ish."

"Okay."

CHAPTER 37
Sandy Cat

Maggi - 2023

"…I managed to steal a theatre tourniquet machine and leave it with a trolley for Jonny and Minty to collect later."

"Is that like a blood pressure cuff?" D.C.I. Logan asks.

"It's on the same lines but a much larger machine that can completely stop the flow of blood to a limb. It's no small thing…"

1998

The rest of my shift passes easily, and no one mentions the missing machine, though I jump every time the theatre door opens unexpectedly. Afterwards, I catch up with Jo in the coffee room. It's what I'd normally do, if there was such a thing as normal in my life anymore, but it also gave me a reason to hang round the hospital till 9:30.

"Criks Maggi, it's shit," Jo exclaims after I've tried to describe something of the failed trial.

"I know, it is shit, and it will always be shit now for the rest of our lives."

"Are you going to keep working?"

"Yeah, I have too, even if I don't want to, Rah will never work again. Anyway, I like work; I think it will be good for me in the long run."

"I'm thinking of maybe doing something with my Sign Language."

"Why? Are you fed up with the job?"

"No, it's not that. I'm not sure I like the hospital's new fundraising scheme."

"You mean the state of the art transplant unit?"

"Yeah. Have you been in there yet?"

"Not the theatre, only floor 9. It's a weird one, all those bodies hooked up."

"I call them the Living Dead. Blooming beds of them now. Terry said they're looking for theatre staff, it's good money, but I don't fancy it. It kinda goes against the grain selling your relatives so the rich can have a ready supply of organs, while the rest of us have to wait for free donations. It's weird in there too."

"I know what you mean." And I did. The dimly lit ward exudes a miasma of human waste, gases and sterilisation fluids, while monitors, ventilators and feeding tubes flash and beep atonally, keeping the organs viable. "It's not my cup of tea either, but I'll stick around at Braxham Wick. I can't see us ever moving, we couldn't leave our links to Orla. So, training as an interpreter? You'd be good at that."

"Yeah, but it means going back to education, and I'm not sure I'd qualify."

"I think they'd snap you up."

"We'll see... Y'know, mate, if you ever want to beat the cunt up, I'll be your wingman."

"Thanks, Jo, that's the nicest thing anyone has said to me in a long time." Finishing my coffee, I get up and rinse my mug. "I've got to go Rah will be waiting. See you Monday?"

"Sure thing."

2023

"...When I left the hospital that evening it was already dark, but I spotted them across the car park anyway. A white transit van pulled up near the disabled exit. Jonny emerged, pushing the trolley with a long mound, covered by a white sheet laid on top of it.

I thought, 'that'll be the tournie,' as I admired his brazenness. I watched as he took his time to position the trolley in line with the

211

back doors of the transit van, which were set open. Herrick appeared around the side of the van and between them they heaved it in.

I started to walk towards my car, but I couldn't help glancing back towards the transit, which I fully expected to see driving away. But no, it was still stationary; then I caught sight of Jonny re-emerging out of the hospital, pushing a wheelchair with Rah in it. Balanced on her lap were some large objects, which I knew instantly were the defib, heart monitor and the manual resuscitator…"

1998

"Fuck, Jonny, what are you thinking? This wasn't in the plan, Rah was never meant to be involved," I mutter angrily to myself as I watch him leaning forward and chatting with her, just as he always does with all his patients.

2023

"…Realising how stupid I must look standing stock-still and staring, I forced myself to open the car door and get in. Moments later I saw the transit van weave its way through the car park to the exit. My heart flipped as I waited for some sort of alarm to go off, which was a complete overreaction, it wasn't as though we were stealing the crown jewels.

Anyway, of course, nothing happened, so I pulled myself together and drove back to Godlinghoe, parked the car and walked around to Jonny's to help unload…"

1998

"Hi, Mag..," Minty begins getting out from behind the steering wheel.
"Why was Rah there?" I snap at him.
"Not now, Maggi," he warns me. "Have you got the house keys?"
"Yes," I retort.
"Good. Open the front door then." I do as I'm told, pegging the door ajar as Minty climbs into the rear of the van. I follow him around and see Minty, Gwen, Herrick and Rah.

"Maggs,' Rah says smiling at me. It's months since I've seen her look that way.

"Rah," I smile back.

"Look," she says, pointing at a collection of odd-shaped packages. The wheelchair, defib, heart monitor and tournie have been wrapped in cardboard, disguising their shapes but the trolley is another matter. Its bed-like length, metal posts and chunky wheels are not so easily disguised by a bit of cardboard.

"Great job, though the trolley is a bit..." I trail off, not wanting to extinguish her enthusiasm.

"I know. We tried wrapping it this way and that but..." she shrugs her shoulders.

"It'll do," Minty says with a touch of uncustomary truculence, which makes me realise how much strain he's keeping hidden under his usual calm exterior. "You take this, Maggi," he says, pushing the tournie towards me, "and I'll take the chair. Be ready you three. I want the trolley out in one swift movement, no dilly-dallying," he instructs, before grabbing his package.

Taking the tournie, I carry it into the house and plonk it in the Kill Room. Minty joins me with the chair.

"Minty, I thought we'd agreed to keep Rah out of this," I say, trying to keep my voice low and reasonable.

"Have you seen her, Maggi? She's more alive than she has been in months. Are you really going to rob her of this?"

"S'pose not," I mumble back.

He rubs his chin then wraps his hand around the back of his neck.

"Sorry, Maggi, I know you only want to protect her."

"I just want to keep her safe."

"I know, she's my daughter, and I'd do anything to keep her safe too, but we all know it's too late for that now."

"Yeah," I say with a sigh.

"Come on, let's tackle the trolley."

Back outside, we stand at the rear of the van as Herrick and Rah push the trolley forward. Minty and I take a leg each and step backwards. The body starts to emerge. All is well until Herrick and

213

Rah are left holding the whole weight at their end, with the wheels in mid-air.

"It's slipping," Herrick mutters, and Rah makes grunting noises as it starts to slide through their hands. With a massive rattling clatter that reverberates up the street, the trolley hits the road, bounces once, then skids, crashing into the van. I look at the other three, they're standing statue still with shock written across their faces. Minty shoves my shoulder.

"Get that end," he commands as he grabs the end nearest to himself. I get hold of it and try to push, but there's a jarring up my arms accompanied by a grinding noise. Looking down, I see one of the trolley wheels is buckled at an odd angle, and it's refusing to roll. I hike the corner up and try again.

Minty reverses with his end, lifts it over the doorstep and is inside. Then I am too.

"Phew," I mutter.

"Yes, phew," Minty says grinning at me and we burst out laughing, breaking the tension between us.

Once we start, we can't stop. I lean against the wall as I bend double, my sides splitting with stitches, my eyes glazing up with tears. Minty's deep roar is doing nothing to help and, as I glance up, he points to the trolley, and we start again.

Eventually, between great gusts of laughter, he manages to splutter out, "Let's get it into the Kill Room." Lifting my end, we push it along the hallway but try as we might we cannot get it around the corner and through the door.

"Shall I call the others?" I suggest.

"Best not, it would defeat the whole purpose of leaving them hidden in the back of the van." I knew what he meant. Jonny's street is even quieter than ours. It's one thing having a van pull up to make a delivery but quite another to have five people climb out of it. That would constitute rave status for Pump Road.

"We could leave it here in the hall, then get the others to help on the weekend."

"Good idea."

2023

"…Having actually done something constructive towards getting our daughter's body back seemed to galvanise us, not just our actions but our emotions too. Like I said, Jonny, who's probably one of the nicest people you'll ever meet, became calculating and objective. Rah turned from a zombie into a coiled spring of manic energy while my emotions swung precariously from one extreme to another. One minute, I'd find myself laughing hysterically and the next, I'd be crippled under the weight of my pain."

"How'd you mean?" asks D.C. Fry.

"It's like the trolley incident. After we'd got it into Jonny's house, Minty and I had a moment where the ridiculousness of us trying to surreptitiously manoeuvre such a large, ungainly item suddenly seemed hilariously funny. And we burst our sides with laughter. But as I was walking home from Jonny's, I saw Sandy Cat, a pet that used to belong to Molly Wilbur, our neighbour." I feel my voice falter as a familiar lump fills my throat. Swallowing hard, I push it back down.

"Grief is a funny thing," I say after a while. "All day, all night, I wear it like a coat of lead. I have never been able to take it off. It has morphed into me; it is who I am. Yet it's the smallest of memories that can fell me, like Sandy Cat on that day.

There I was walking along, Sandy Cat was sitting on Molly's wall and bang, it hit me, like a punch in the solar plexuses. My lungs seized, I couldn't breathe and I dropped to all fours, paralysed by memories of Orla as a small child insisting we stop and talk to Sandy Cat every time we passed…"

1998

"Maggs, Maggs," Rah calls as she runs towards me.
Sandy Cat jumps down from the wall and winds her soft body around mine, purring. Rah falls to her knees and holds me.
"Shh, Maggs," she coos, "shhh, my Maggs."
"Rah," I gasp.
"I know," she says, "You don't have to explain, it's Sandy Cat."

215

2023

"… You see," I cry, unable to control my tears, "I can still feel her small hand in mine as we'd walk to the shops or to her primary school and even when she'd squat down to stroke Sandy Cat, I never let go, just in case…. though I let go, didn't I? When she was thirteen."

CHAPTER 38
Up the Field and Between the Goal Posts

Logan

Logan sees the moment when Maggi is unable to breathe. It's not dramatic; she doesn't throw herself around gripping her throat, it's much more subtle than that. She gasps almost silently, as she tries to pull air into her lungs. The dog immediately leaps up from his basket and paces agitatedly around her.

Jumping to her feet, Logan grabs Maggi as she falls to the floor. "Maggi, stay calm. Breathe, breathe, breathe," she instructs, stating each word clearly. Slowly, Maggi's diaphragm re-sets, and she manages to suck oxygen back into her lungs.

"See what I mean?" she tells them, sitting back in her chair. "I can talk about the loss of my daughter but mention Sandy Cat and I'm back on that pavement again, suffocating."

"I think we should end the session here Maggi, give you a chance to recover properly," Logan decides, nodding to Fry.

"Are you alright, Maggi?" Fry asks packing up the Cam.

"I'll be fine," Maggi assures him, wiping her tears away and stroking Lobo, who's laid his head in her lap.

"We'll be here just after 10.30," Logan reminds her before saying goodbye.

In the car she pulls her Noc from her pocket and dictates another email to Ron:

Hi, I've got another name to add to the list. Hamilton Hoyle, Godlinghoe. More than likely he has a criminal record. Cheers, Lo.

"Do you think she'll be okay?" Fry says as Logan pulls out into the road.

"From what she's said, it's happened before, and she probably has her own way of dealing with it. She can't die from it but I think it must feel really frightening not being able to catch your breath."

"I bet," Fry mumbles back.

"Can you send that list of names to Andrea?"

"Already done it."

"Thanks." The in-car computer buzzed at the same time as Logan's Noc.

"You've got a text from Greyson. Do you want me to open it?"

"Sure."

"Okay: **Hey, I'm planting runner beans this evening,**" Fry's voice falters as he realises this isn't anything to do with the case, though he continues to read. "**There'll be falafels and strawberries.** Do you want to answer?" he asks.

"Yes." And he holds the Noc out to her. "**Sounds good,**" she replies, feeling something she can't quite put her finger on. After Fry has pressed 'send', she adds, "The evidence from the P.M. is starting to stack up now, what with the hospital stuff."

"Yeah, but it's a really sad story."

"Yeah," she agrees. She's found it hard to watch Maggi's raw emotions. She knows Maggi's pain is on a whole other level to her own, but the essence of loss stabs at her professional exterior. "It's difficult sometimes not to be touched by other peoples' tragedies. The trouble is if you get too involved in the emotional side, you start to miss information and mistakes can happen."

"I get that, but even so."

"Our job is not to judge but to collect evidence. And being emotional can make a person bias too."

"I guess," Fry acknowledges. After a moment, he says, "There must've been more evidence against that Hoyle bloke for the C.P.S. to have charged him with murder."

"I thought that too. It'll be interesting to see what Ron and Andrea come back with. How are you feeling about your date tonight?"

"To be honest, I'm a bit nervous. I don't know why, it's not as though I don't know her."

"Are you still going to the pub?"

"Actually, I spoke to Frank about it, and he said the same as you, that I should take her out for a meal or go to a club."

"Did he," Logan says, trying not to smile.

"Yeah. We're meeting at the pub, then I'll ask her if she wants to go to that club you mentioned."

"Good thinking."

Arriving at the station she offers to lock the Cam in the SafeCage. "Are you sure, Boss?"

"Yes, go. And have fun tonight."

"I will, see you tomorrow. Bye."

"Bye," she says, picking up the Cam and heading into the station. At the front desk, Ducksworth is eating what looks like a small, iced cupcake.

"Evening T.C.," he says, between mouthfuls.

"Piss off, Ducksworth," she answers jokingly, knowing he means no harm, though the name still stings.

Driving home, Logan changes out of her work clothes, showers and dresses in jeans and Grim's jumper. At the Little Marney allotments, she parks and walks through the tunnel of small trees and sees Greyson leaning on his fork. A small shiver runs down her spine as he raises a hand and smiles at her.

"Nice to see you, Lo," he says, pushing his fork into the ground, "I've just brewed some tea, fancy a cup?"

"Sure. How's the planting going?" she asks, sitting on the old tree log.

"Good. I'd have had it done by now if I didn't keep stopping to chat," he smiles, pouring her a mug of tea. "But that's all a part of it, the nattering, well it is for me."

"What kind of people are allotment holders, apart from you?" she asks, taking the mug.

"All sorts," he says, spreading out a mixture of falafels and strawberries on a plate. "Having said that, I have categorised them as I'm wont to do, being a scientist."

"How?" she asks, eyeing the brown balls and daring herself to try one.

"Okay, there's the Old Codger, retired, doesn't do house-work and spends most of his day, and it is usually a he, pottering around and spraying chemicals everywhere. His plot will be immaculate with everything planted in military rows. There's the Hardy Old Soul, who's never shunned a duty in their life…"

"Mrs Tingle," she thinks.

"Their plots are usually in rows too, though not quite so tidy. There's Mother Earth, who scatters love as they sow. Their plots tend to be a bit random but very successful. Then there's Healthy and Hearty, who grow organically, can see the point of rows but can't quite be that well organised. And lastly, there's The Twit Brigade, who follow the latest celebrity TV chef-cum-gardener and arrive in their massive 4x4s, throw a bit of dirt about, disappear never to return again. I think that about sums us up." Picking up a falafel, he takes a bite. "Umm, not bad. It's my Mum's recipe."

"I've not had them before. They're really tasty, what are they made of?" she asks, taking another one.

"Chickpeas, garlic and spices."

"So, which category do you fit into?"

"Ah, probably somewhere between Mother Earth and Healthy and Hearty, I reckon. Why? Are you thinking about Waxy?"

"Yeah, we've been interviewing a long-term allotment holder, and I'm trying to get the measure of her."

"Which category do you think she'd fit into?"

Logan thinks for a moment before speculating."Uhm… not the Twits or Codgers, maybe a cross between Mother Earth and Hardy Old Soul."

"Interesting."

"Are you into the Mars Project?" she says, not really wanting to think about Maggi anymore.

"Definitely, it's another one of my many science obsessions," Greyson laughs. "How about you?"

"Yeah, I'm really looking forward to it, especially as we've got our girl going up too."

"I know, it makes it more personal somehow. I love all that space stuff. That's one of the reasons I bought my cottage; it's in the middle of nowhere with a pollution-free night sky. I'm even nerdy enough to have built my own observatory in the garden."

"What, like a hut with an open roof?"

"Exactly. I built the roof on a circular wheeled rail, so I can point my scope in any direction."

"That is serious stuff."

"Yeah," he laughs again. "I'll be glued to my computer and scope on Thursday night. You can come over and watch with me if you like?" She feels again the same small shiver she'd felt when she'd seen him leaning on his fork earlier. "Yeah, okay," She answers with a smile. It's only later, on the drive home, she realises she hasn't thought about Trev all evening.

Tristan Fry

Fry carries a lager and a glass of white wine over to the table. The pub is busy for a Tuesday night and he weaves his way carefully through the crowds. Andrea is texting on her Noc but looks up and smiles at him when he puts the drinks down.

"Thanks," she murmurs.

"How's your day been?" he asks.

"Pretty average. I started on that list you sent. Then Emma got a text from her boyfriend dumping her, so we're all planning a girl's night out to cheer her up. But Sharon Mulligan is trying to get her baby shower off the ground, though Rowena wants us to boycott it."

"Will you go?"

"Probably, got to keep the peace and all that. I think everyone else will go too, apart from Rowena and her mate, Kady, though I expect the whipround won't amount to much."

"Because it's anonymous?"

"Yep. No one really likes Sharon for what she did. Talking of which, look who just walked in." He looks up and sees Trevor Dillsworthy and his mates heading for the bar. Fry can tell that he's already pumped up, as he's mouthing off.

"I don't know what Logan saw in him," Andrea comments.

"Yeah," Fry agrees. "Where do you go for a girl's night out?" he asks, changing the subject, as he doesn't want to end up talking about Logan behind her back.

"West End clubs in London, mainly. Do you like clubbing?"

"Yeah, but I've only been to Lords and Tall Toms in Chelmsford, never Lon ..."

"I told Top Cat or Top Cunt," Trevor's voice resounds spitefully above the chatter, making his mates laugh.

"Let's get out of here, Fry," Andrea suggests.

"Yeah, let's." Grabbing their things, they leave their drinks and start crossing the pub towards the door. As they pass Dillsworthy and his mates, Fry, and everyone else in the pub, hears him say, "Top fucking Cunt's going down, you can bet on it." Stopping, he looks at his shoes for a moment, then turns to the large police officer.

"Don't call her that, Dillsworthy," he says coolly.

"Well look who it is, T.C's little playmate. What do you want, baby-face Fry?" Dillsworthy sneers, squaring up to him.

"You might have personal issues with Logan, but that doesn't entitle you to call her names," Fry voices calmly, ignoring the jibe.

"Fry, let's go," Andrea says quietly.

"Oh, and remind me why I should give a flying fuck about what you think, baby-face?"

"Do you know, people like you only call women names because they're frightened of them. You need to grow a pair of balls and man up."

A chorus of "Whoa," and "Ouch Dilly, that's got to hurt," sounds off behind Dillsworthy as his mates jeer, egging him on.

"Fry, don't," Andrea mutters, pulling at Fry's sleeve while

Dillsworthy's face turns from alcohol ruddy to fucked-off vermillion red.

"You little wanker," he sneers. "We all know you'd like to crawl inside her knickers. I'll let you into a little fucking secret, baby-face, Top Cunt's got a twat made of..."

"See, that's exactly what I mean," Fry expresses, shrugging his shoulders. "Have to use derogatory terminology to make yourself feel like a man."

"Fry..." Andrea mutters with clenched teeth.

"Ouch Dilly. Up the field and between the goal posts," crows his crew.

"You need to watch yourself, baby-face, or I'll..." but Fry never hears what Dillsworthy is proposing, as he has walks casually away. He's not scared of the likes of Dillsworthy; he'd met enough of them at secondary school, all mouth and no trousers. He's almost sure his intercession won't stop Dillsworthy spouting crap about Logan, but he hopes that some of the others might think twice.

"Do you know what, Fry, I think I might call it a night, I'm feeling quite tired," Andrea excuses herself, outside the pub.

"That's okay, Andrea, but let me walk you to the taxi rank at least?"

"Are you sure?"

"Of course." After seeing Andrea safely into a taxi, Fry pushes his hands in his pockets and begins the long walk home. He could've have taken the next available taxi but the thought of bouncing around in the back of someone else's car, breathing in their extra strong air freshener with all his romantic hopes dashed, just makes him feel even more cheesed off.

CHAPTER 39
Holy Bloody Smoke

*

Maggi

Lobo and I help Jonny back to bed after the alarm has pulled me from yet another sea scenario, where I fight helplessly to stop myself from drowning. Making a coffee, I carry it with the monitor and my laptop into the garden. Loping stiffly, Lobo follows me along the star-lit path under the honeysuckle archway into the wildflower meadow. The sky is clear tonight, the moon fully formed and bright. I stop at the bronze sculpture as the old greyhound presses his head lovingly against my leg.

"I know, boy," I tell him. "I need to get on with it."

At the summerhouse, I tuck him deep into his warm blanket before opening my computer and typing an email.

From: Maggi Drew magrah@gmail.com
Subject: Jonny Gifford
Date: 10.5.2023
To: aluntrudyfellowfieldhouse@gmail.com
Dear Mr Trudy,
Sorry to sound desperate, but due to a change of circumstances, I am unable to care for Jonny at home any longer. I am hoping you might be able to offer him a permanent place...

I feel my tears slide down my face and see them plop onto my keyboard. "Is there no end to how much I can cry?" I mutter angrily, wiping them away and sniffing loudly. Lobo looks up enquiringly from his blanket. "It's alright, boy, go back to sleep," I tell him and type on.

... possibly by the end of the week? He will not require financial assistance.

Best wishes

Maggi Drew

Picking up my precious mug, I drink my coffee and watch as the first rays of the sun touch the bronze faces.

Logan

"How'd your date go with Andrea last night?" Logan asks as she drives towards Godlinghoe. Like Maggi, she'd been up early. She'd watched the sunrise as she'd run down the farm track. She'd pushed her body hard and felt a strength she'd not felt for a while returning. When the sun was fully risen, she'd stopped to catch her breath. Leaning over her pink-tipped trainers, she'd seen a beetle scuttle past. It had made her smile. Then she'd stood and turned for home.

"Not so good. I don't think I'm her cup of tea," Fry states pragmatically but Logan hears the underlying regret in his voice.

"Oh?"

"Yeah, never mind. But I did catch up with her this morning, and it's all cool."

"You're an idiot, Andrea," thinks Logan.

"How were the falafels and strawberries at the allotment?"

"Great," she answers, feeling the beginnings of a smile.

"And ... what are falafels exactly?"

"I know," she laughs, "I had no idea either. It turns out they're like brown balls of spicy chickpeas."

"What, like chicken balls?"

"No, chickpeas are a type of vegetable, a pulse."

"What?"

"Like uhmm ... you know, baked beans?"

"Frank and I live on them when Mum's not looking."

225

"Well, they're made of a pulse bean too."

"So, were they nice?"

"Yes, surprisingly they were."

Reaching Peartree Road, the Christmas tree lights feel strangely welcoming as they knock on the door.

Maggi

I hear the door and brace myself. Lobo looks up at me. I touch his back and go and let the police officers in.

"Hello, Maggi," D.C.I. Logan says as she steps over my threshold.

"Hi, Maggi. Hi, Lobo." D.C. Fry smiles warmly at me before stopping to stroke Lobo's back.

"Come in," I reply and watch them walk down my hallway into the kitchen. At the table, D.C. Fry pulls the Cam from its bag and sets it up while I make the coffee. The blue light fills the space as we watch the last minute where I recount my meeting with Sandy Cat. I feel a knot of pain clawing at my throat; I swallow my coffee, forcing it back down.

"Name and date of birth," D.C.I. Logan asks.

"Maggi Drew, 21.7.1955."

"Okay, Maggi," she orders dispassionately. I glance at D.C. Fry, who's already on the edge of his seat.

"Sunday morning came, and we all gathered here again. Jonny brought everyone up to date, adding syringes and needles to the items we'd already nicked, before asking for help in stealing the Midazolam. As I'm sure you're aware, when drugs like Midazolam go missing, the police are always notified, and everyone is searched. So he needed to get rid of the Midazolam as quick as possible before he was searched…"

1998

"It's got to be the kharzi, so I reckon that'll be me," Jim Bob states.

"The kharzi?" questions Gwen.

"The men's loos, Love," Minty tells her.

"Oh," she murmurs, "That's a new one on me."

226

"If you're caught with it, Jim Bob, you'll be in the shit," Jonny warns.

Jim Bob just looks at Jonny. I know his face well enough to read it easily, and his expression is one of total disbelief before he starts to laugh.

"Holy bloody smoke, Jonny, I'm about to kidnap and torture another human being, I don't think I'm going to worry too much about stealing drugs from a hospital."

I feel my own lips curl, I really don't want another hysterical moment like the last one I'd had with Minty, but there's no helping it as Minty's great roar hits the room. I think some of the others join in but mostly they just stare at the three of us.

"Sorry, sorry," I gasp between giggles. "Sorry, Jonny, go on."

"I can probably take the Midazolam or Ketamine, whatever's easiest, on my drug rounds Monday evening. It'll be about 8:30. I'll take it to the men's toilets on Constable Wing. If you're not there, I'll wrap it up in a plastic bag and stick it in the water system, say, the first cubical."

"I'll be there, Buddy, in the next cubicle," Jim Bob says, getting his laughter under control.

"I don't really want to be calling out your name."

"What if I sing something? I know...Put it, Put it, Put it where you know it needs to go," I glance across the table at Gwen.

"Don't be silly, Maggi," she responds, "I'm about to dress up as a slut and invite Hoyle to screw me." This time we all laugh, though Minty's roar is a little more subdued.

"Okay, you've got a date. But you might be inviting some unwanted attention hanging around in the Men's, singing, Put it." Jonny advises.

"I'll be okay, don't worry about me," smiles Jim Bob.

"Also, I need help getting the trolley into the Kill Room."

"I can do it this afternoon," Minty offers.

"Fine. Can we make it about 5? I've just come off night shift, and I need to grab a few hours of sleep."

"Sure."

"I'll help," I say.

"Me too," adds Rah.

"Me as well," Herrick offers.

"Can't do it this afternoon," Jim Bob says.

"That's okay, we should have plenty of hands on board. Next meeting then?" Minty asks.

"I'm shopping Tuesday for hair dye and clothes with Norah," Gwen informs us.

"Anytime Friday is good for me," Jonny states.

"I'm fine for that," I say after checking my rota.

"Count me in," Jim Bob seconds.

"I can do Friday, after 6," Herrick offers.

"Friday at 6:30 then, for the kidnap plan and final run through," Minty confirms looking at all of us individually.

Later, Rah and I walk to Jonny's. Herrick is already there; he looks shaken and pale.

"Are you okay?" I ask him.

"Yeah ...yeah, fine," he answers, but I see small beads of sweat glistening on his forehead.

"Herrick, you really don't have to do this."

"Everything okay?" Jonny asks, coming to stand next to us.

"I'm fine, just a bit of nervousness. I don't want to get it wrong or let Rah down."

"You won't, Love," I say, giving him a hug. When we break apart, he wanders off to find Rah.

"Jonny, I think we have misjudged Herrick, he's actually a really decent bloke."

"I know, but he's a bit wobbly. When he arrived, Minty and I were putting up the plastic sheeting. He was fine at the door, but when I brought him into the Kill Room, I thought he was going to faint."

"I suppose we shouldn't be surprised; I'd probably be the same if it wasn't our child. Maybe we should stop calling it the Kill Room, it kind of makes it sound worse."

"Yeah, you're right. I'm pretty sure I wouldn't be doing this if it wasn't for Orla. Come on muscles, let's try and get the trolley in..."

whatever you want to call the room," he says, punching my arm lightly.

We push, shove, lift and twist, but the fucking thing won't go through the doorway. In the end, Jonny cuts one of the crossbars off, and we manage to slide it in on its side.

"Looks a bit unstable," comments Jonny, as we all stand and gaze at it.

"Just as well it's not going to have to do much of a job then," Minty comments and I hope he's right. I hope Hoyle will cough quickly and we can get on with finding Orla.

Arriving on Monday morning for my shift, I find the lists are busy like usual. Mr Silco is banging off, Terry is up to his neck in timetables and rota teams, and I'm with lovely Mr Polly who, though slow, is a delight to work for.

"Perfect for stealing the Rocuronium," I think as I purposefully underestimate the Teeco while setting up my instruments trolley.

"Maggi, we seem to be low on the Teeco, would you mind popping out and getting some more?"

"Of course, sorry Mr Polly, it's my fault."

"Not a problem, Maggi, but I do need to get this hip cemented."

Pulling off my gloves and overall, I leave the theatre. In the anaesthetic room I slip six bottles of Rocuronium into my pockets and re-arrange the stock to hide the theft, before collecting the Teeco.

After the op, I transfer the bottles into my bag and go back to work. For some unknown reason, I haven't even broken out into a sweat.

"Must be getting used to this thieving lark," I think.

That evening Jim Bob knocks on our door.

"Evening, Bigster," he says, striding in.

"How'd it go?"

"Great. I was there, singing away when Jonny knocked on the cubical wall and passed me these," he hands over four glass vials of Midazolam.

229

2023

"…On Monday I stole the Rocuronium, and Jonny took the Midazolam which caused a stir. But by the time the police were informed Jim Bob had already collected the drug from Jonny, and it was sitting on our kitchen table.

Arriving home after a long shift on Tuesday I walked in to find Minty leaning against the kitchen sink, staring out of the window…"

1998

"Hi."

"Oh, hi Maggi, good shift?" he asks turning to me, though I can tell he's distracted.

"Not bad. I managed to pick up a box of latex gloves and a couple of theatre gowns. I know I shouldn't care with my job and all, but I really don't want to have to deal with Hamy fucking Hoyle naked," I say, flicking on the kettle. "Do you want a cuppa?"

"That might be a good idea." I make a pot and set the mugs out. "Are the others about?"

2023

"…He told me that Rah and Gwen had been out shopping for Gwen's outfit and she'd also had her hair dyed too…"

1998

"Oh," I say, not really knowing how to comment. I can tell from the way he is hunched over that he isn't feeling good about the whole thing. Bringing the tea tray to the table, I sit kicking off my shoes, and pour us both a mug. "Ah," I murmur as I sink back into the seat just as the kitchen door opens and Rah walks in.

"Da-dah," she announces gesturing towards her mother who follows her in, tottering on high heels and wearing a very short, black dress. Shock shots through me as I take in the transformation of Gwen from a beautiful 64-year-old woman into a 50 something sado.

Her long hair is all puffed up and dyed raven black; her beautiful, soft, brown eyes are circled with a hard kohl and her mouth, a ghastly gash of red. The dress is obviously designed to show a great deal of cleavage and for some reason, Gwen, who always appeared to me to have a less than average bust size, now seems to be sporting something that might grace a porn site. Rah must have seen me staring, because she begins to explain, "It's a special bra. It's called a Magic Bra to make you look as though..."

"Yes, we get the picture," Minty utters through gritted teeth.

"I think you look great Gwen, in the way you want to look great. You look the part," I try to say encouragingly.

2023

"...Rah asked Minty what he thought of the outfit when they came and showed us. Minty tried to cover his shock by saying that he'd never seen or thought of Gwen in that way before. And she reminded him that it wasn't about them, it was about Orla. After they left to clean the make-up off and change, he turned to me, shaking his head in disbelief and said... 'You think you know someone inside and out and then, they surprise you'..."

CHAPTER 40
A Yellow Ribbon

Maggi

"…In the early hours of Wednesday morning I woke to find Rah missing. This wasn't unusual. Before I returned to work I'd wake as soon as her nightmares began, but being back on shift I was tired and tended to sleep for longer periods. Getting up I went to where I was sure she'd be, Orla's room. I pushed the door open expecting to see her sitting on the floor or the bed, cradling something of Orla's, but the room was empty. I called her name into the darkness and she answered, opening the door to her studio. Really, it's just another bedroom, small and box-like, though the light is always good in there. Since Orla had been gone the room had been unused, the door shut with an unfinished canvas abandoned on the easel…"

1998

"Hey, are you painting?"

"Yes. When I was out shopping with Mum I was a bit tense, so she insisted on buying me some new canvases and acrylics. At the time I couldn't see the point, but now I think she might've been right. Come and see." Entering the lit room, I stare at the new canvas propped on the easel.

"Jesus, Rah," I exclaim, stunned by what I am looking at. Walking closer, I examine the darkness oozing from the picture. I don't know how she's done it, all I know is she's painted my pain.

2023

"…The following Friday, we were all back around the table again, this time to make a plan to ensnare Hoyle…"

1998

"First, I think we should set a date for the kidnap," Minty suggests.

"After this weekend we'll have everything in place, what about next weekend? It's a bank holiday too, so it sort of follows there'll be different people about in the pubs," proposes Jim Bob.

"I can't do Saturday, it's the LGO's Bank Holiday Concert at the Glass Hall, with rehearsals Thursday," Herrick says quietly.

"Of course," Rah murmurs, smiling at him.

"I'd rather do it sooner than later anyway. What about Friday night?" I urge.

"Friday's good for me," Jonny says.

"Fine with me, Bigster," Jim Bob concurs.

"So are we pretty sure he'll be in the Albert that Friday evening?" Minty asks.

"No, but I'd put money on it. One, it's a Friday night, two, it's a Bank holiday weekend. And if he's not there, we can postpone till Sunday and use it as a dry run," Jim Bob puts forward.

"Gwen?" Minty asks.

"Yes, I agree with Maggs, the sooner, the better."

"Okay, Friday the 28th August it is."

"Friday," I murmur.

"Friday," smiles Rah.

"Friday," mouths Herrick.

Unfolding a map of Godlinghoe, Minty points to the road junction of Pye Road and Albert Street. "The pub sits on this corner, and from the court case we know Hoyle's likely route home will be up Pye Road, cut through Godiva Gardens, along Godiva Road, turn right onto North Close and cut through the football ground into Farrierfield. I think the obvious place to snatch him would be Godiva Gardens. It's dark – plenty of trees and bushes to hide behind and unless there's other people actually in the gardens,

233

there's no one to hear any kind of scuffle or shouts."

"Yeah, and if it doesn't go according to plan we can, perhaps, have a second crack at it at the football ground," I suggest.

"Maybe, but let's not get ahead of ourselves. What time's kick-out from the pub?"

"Usually 11 for last drinks and I reckon at least 12 for kick-out," Jim Bob says.

"I think I should be in the pub by 10:00 then," Gwen suggests.

"That'll give him time to be quite drunk, and I can buy him more drinks, chat him up and suggest we carry on at his." The thought of little, innocuous Gwen standing on her own in that pub having to deal with the likes of Hoyle and Wheeler makes me shiver.

"I'm going too," I declare.

"You can't," Minty, Jonny, Jim Bob and Gwen say, all at the same time.

"Hoyle and Wheeler know who you are, Bigster. At best they'd smell a rat, at worst you might end up in some sort of fight."

"Maggs, the whole point of me doing this is because he doesn't know who I am," Gwen argues, taking my hand. "I'll be fine, I promise you. I'm not as innocent as you may think and besides, this is about finding my granddaughter, and that makes me feel very brave."

"Alright," I acknowledge grudgingly, "but I'm going to lurk outside in the car par..."

"Bigster," Jim Bob snaps.

"No one will see me. I'll stay hidden and then I'll follow you Gwen, when you leave the pub."

"That might just be a really good idea. You can help bring him down from behind," Jonny agrees, to my relief. "I'll be in the Gardens, presumably with you, Jim Bob, Minty and Herrick?"

"Defo,"'

"Yes."

"Uhm, yes," Herrick mumbles. I look at him sitting there like a rabbit caught in a car's headlights. I'm not the only one who notices, as Rah turns to him and takes his hand in hers.

234

"Herrick," she says, with such tenderness it hurts my heart, "you've already done so much to help, you don't need to do this too."

"I want to Rah, I'm just a bit...I'm just... well, I'm just not really cut out for this sort of thing."

"I understand. We won't think less of you if you don't want to come."

"No Rah, I'm definitely coming to help. I'm not sure how good I'll be."

"Oh Herrick," she murmurs into his shoulder as she cuddles him gratefully.

2023

"...We set the date for the snatch on Friday 28th August. It was the Bank Holiday weekend and we guessed Hoyle and his mate, Wheeler, would be out drinking. The place we chose to tackle him was Godiva Gardens, which, before you ask, is no longer there, having been sold off for housing by the council..."

"Why the Gardens?" D.C.I. Logan asks.

"It was the route he'd said he'd taken during his trial, so we reckoned it was his regular way home after the pub. If the plan worked Gwen would be with him, I'd be trailing them, and the others would be hiding in the bushes..."

1998

"By the way, I'll be there too," Rah adds, letting go of Herrick's hand.

"Rah..." I begin. What I really want is for her to stay at home. Out of harm's way.

"No, Maggs, I am going to help," she asserts determinedly, adding "I'll pull the bag over his head so he can't see you all."

"Bag?" Gwen questions, mirroring my thoughts.

"Yes," and she lifts a large piece of square, dark fabric from her lap, showing us all. "I sewed it up today." I look at her in amazement, sitting there, with her skinhead haircut and hollow face, holding out a neatly sown bag designed to rob Hoyle of his vision,

and remembered how Minty had commented on Gwen surprising him. At the time, I thought I'd understood what he'd meant but only now do I fully appreciate his sentiment.

I look at Minty as he stares first at the bag then at his daughter. After a moment he says, "That seems to be settled then. Norah, you will be with us in the gardens and when we have him down, you'll pull the bag over his head."

2023

"…Jim Bob suggested we should practice taking down Hoyle, which was never going to be an easy task, as he was a big, fat bastard…"

1998

"You'll have to be Hoyle, Maggi," Jonny says, as though he is offering me a leading role in a Hollywood blockbuster.

"Why the fuck should I be Hoyle?" I retaliate childishly.

"Bigster, think about it. Gwen and Rah are too small and the rest of us will be doing the tackling, so that just leaves you."

"I'll be tackling too," I snap.

"Yeah, but for this to work, for us to get some idea on the forward tackle, you need to be Hoyle."

"S'pose," I reluctantly agree, though the thought of being associated with that cunt makes me feel revolted.

"How are we going to do this?" Jonny questions.

"Mmm," Minty mumbles, rubbing his chin, "Gwen and Maggi, you walk up the hallway into the kitchen, as though you are walking along the path."

"What side does Hoyle need to be on?" I mutter, still feeling really pissed off at playing Hamy fucking Hamster.

"I'm probably the strongest and I punch better with my right, so if I'm hiding on the right, I'll get a better swing at him. That means Hoyle will need to be on your right, Gwen," reasons Jim Bob.

"I'll take the left side then," Jonny says. "Gwen, you'll have to be ready to move out of the way, so I can grab his arm as Jim Bob swings the punch. Will you go for the gut or the head, Jim Bob?"

"Probably the gut. I'm less likely to miss, and it should double him over."

"Okay. Herrick, you can grab his other arm. So you'd be best on the right too, but behind Jim Bob. Jump out as soon as you see him swing his punch."

"Fine," Herrick murmurs, sounding anything but fine to me.

"With us holding his arms, Rah you put the hood on and Jim Bob can force him down. Minty you'll have to help pin him to the ground while I get the kit and inject him." I look at Minty, he's fit and healthy but no spring chicken at 75.

"The last thing we need is a geriatric broken hip," I think, before saying, "I'll rugby tackle his legs and hold him down too."

"Good, Bigster, coz I've got a feeling he'll be a fighter."

2023

"…We positioned ourselves and went through the plan in slow motion. I stood in for Hoyle. Jim Bob made out he'd punched me as Jonny grabbed my left arm; I doubled over as Herrick gingerly took my right arm. Rah was as quick as lightning with the hood while they all brought me crashing to the floor. Then Minty held me while Jonny pretended to jab me with the Midazolam.

All went well until we speeded it up. Then it became brutal; it hurt like fuck. I cried a few times and ended up covered in grazes and bruises. Each time the boys wanted to stop, but I brushed my tears away and insisted we carried on. Only when Gwen got knocked down did I jump to her defence…"

1998

"Don't be silly, Maggi," she cries, cradling her hurt arm, "if you can do this, so can I. But I wonder if it would be prudent to mark your hiding place somehow so I know when to expect the attack. Perhaps we could visit the gardens tomorrow and earmark a good ambush site."

"Yeah, but I'm not sure how you can mark the place, we can hardly tie a yellow ribbon around the old oak tree," Jim Bob says.

237

"Why not?" Rah pipes in. "Hoyle probably wouldn't even notice, and if he did, he wouldn't think much about it. Probably just think it's some sort of memento."

"I could go to the florist on that Friday and pick up a bunch of flowers with a yellow ribbon tied around the stems, then just place them a yard or two from where you are going to hide. I know I'll know where you are, but everything will be different in the dark, and I'll have to be attentive to Hoyle too," rationalises Gwen.

"Good idea, Love," Minty agrees, helping her off the floor.

2023

"...But Gwen insisted we carried on. We practiced a few more times, making our moves faster and faster. The boys' accuracy improved and I even began to feel Herrick's grip tighten as his confidence grew too. After that, it was just a matter of deciding on the time..."

1998

"Gwen you'll be in the pub by 10:00 with Maggi in the car park, and I'd like to be in place just after 10 o'clock too," Minty proposes.

"It's a bit early; we'll have to hang around the gardens for two hours. That might look odd," says Jim Bob.

"I agree with Jim Bob, Minty; it's too early. I know you don't want to miss him. Maybe we should come up with some sort of warning that he's on his way," Jonny says.

"I could shout something?" Gwen offers.

"Um, that could draw unwanted attention."

"What if I hang around at the top end of Pye Road and when I see him coming, I'll run back and tell you," Rah suggests eagerly.

"Good idea," I say, though what I really want to say is why don't you go home, out of the way of any danger.

"That's sorted then. So, what time at the gardens?" Minty asks.

"I'd say 11 ish. I bet Hoyle won't leave the pub until kick-out," advises Jim Bob.

"No, I need to be there earlier, 10:45," Minty asserts.

"Okay, 10:45 it is," Jim Bob agrees.

"And when we have him out for the count, how are we going to get him to the Kill Room?"

"Easy," pipes up Rah again, "We'll put him in the wheelchair, wheel him back through the Gardens, cross over Pye Road, up Well Street and into Pump Road. We'll bring the chair with us, I'll ride down in it, so it doesn't look odd and we can hide it in some bushes."

CHAPTER 41
Cowardy Custard

Maggi - 2023

"…On Saturday, Rah and I took a leisurely walk through Godiva Gardens with Minty and Gwen. Rah and I pretended to play a game of jumping out on each other and then twirling around on the path with our arms extended while Minty and Gwen sat on a bench and watched. We narrowed it down to two likely spots but dismissed the first one for being too public. The latter snaked between two bends in the path. An old hawthorn tree grew on the first bend with a huge weeping willow tree approximately five paces beyond it, making it an excellent hiding place. Opposite was a patch of grass with a bed of dogwood bushes, which gave enough coverage for one person in the dark.

Monday came and I went through the motions of work, I felt agitated and distracted, but if anyone noticed they didn't say anything. By Thursday my concentration was shot to pieces; I kept dropping instruments or having to recount swabs. In the end Terry sent me home. That evening I helped Jonny finish setting up the room. It was now covered in sheets of plastic, the window was blanked out and there was even a plastic curtain over the doorway. The trolley sat in the centre of the room, next to a small table covered in plastic, laid with Rocuronium vials, syringes, needles, swabs, cannulas, scalpel blades and Jonny's stethoscope. We plugged in the tournie."

"Plugged in? Like with electrical wires and stuff?" D.C. Fry asks incredulously.

"Yes, this was quite some time before wireless technology. That night Jonny went to work and Rah was painting. I couldn't sleep, so I sat with her for a while and watched as she turned her thoughts into tangible colour. She said she could hardly contain herself and she thought she was going to burst waiting for Friday to come. She just wanted it to be over, wanted Orla to be home. She said that was all that really mattered now. I told her I understood and that I wished it was over too.

But they say be careful what you wish for don't they? And they were right…"

1998

I can't settle, the house is hot, and I feel trapped and stifled. After making Rah a sandwich and a cup of coffee, which she promised she'd have, I kiss her and go out.

Unlocking the gate on the side entrance of the allotment, I let myself in. The path is pitch black but I know my way after my many nights of trudging up here. Silhouetted shapes of beanpole structures and fruit cages loom out of the darkness; everything is ghostly quiet as I walk towards my plot. In my shed I find my fork and begin to dig. There's something comforting about the familiar smooth surface of the wooden handle. The earth is crusted and starved of moisture, but as each clod breaks open the smell of fresh loam fills my raging heart. I dig until the sweat runs from me, till my back hurts, till my breath is lost in sobs. Leaving the fork upright in the newly turned earth, I stumble to my bench and let myself cry.

I cry for Orla, for Rah, for Jonny but most of all I cry for myself. I know I'm filled to the brim with anger and hate, but I'm frightened of what lies ahead. Can I really torture someone? Even if they're as horrible as Hoyle. In theory, I want to inflict as much pain on him as possible but when it comes to it, can I? Will I? And what about my promise to Rah, can I bring Orla home?

After a while I lean back and gaze into the night sky. Its inky

241

blackness is smeared with lighter clouds, and the moon has grown in a week, fattening from a curved sliver to a solid wedge. As my ragged breath eases I become aware of the pain from my grazes. "Shit," I mutter, inspecting my forearms and knees. Fresh blood leaks from the wounds. I dab them with my t-shirt but it stings like hell. Getting up, I blow my nose and go to find my watering cans.

2023

"…Friday came and we all, one way or another, dressed ourselves in black. Minty looked like he was about to deliver a box of Milk Tray chocolates."

"Sorry, what chocolates?" D.C. Fry asks.

"It was an old T.V. advert, Fry," D.C.I. Logan says dismissively, and for the first time I sense she is just as interested as D.C. Fry.

"Gwen wore the teensiest dress in the world, with her hair all curled and puffed up and her face covered in a thick layer of makeup, complete with false eyelashes, kohl and a slash of sharp red lipstick. She looked horrible, but totally in character. None of us mentioned it.

Herrick was the last to arrive about 8ish. When he turned up, wearing black too, he reminded us that the L.G.O. concert was on Saturday night and that this year it was being played in memory of Orla. He explained it was a sort of last minute decision, in light of the failed court case, to honour Rah and Orla by changing the programme to reflect the oboe's role within the orchestra. He'd supplied them with a photo of Rah and Orla, thinking rightly that we wouldn't want to have been bothered with it all.

Like I explained before, this is a very prestigious event in the musical world's calendar. The tickets are hard to come by, and the fact that the concert was being dedicated to Rah and Orla was no minor thing. Herrick gave us 5 courtesy tickets, one each for Minty, Gwen, Jonny, Rah and myself…"

1998

"Fucking hell, do we really have to do this," I blurt out, unable to

restrain myself.

"I think so," Minty says, almost apologetically. "If we don't go questions will be asked."

"I really don't give a damn what the L.G.O. think of me," I huff.

"Nor do I. But I don't think we should do anything that draws attention to ourselves."

"Jonny?" I say, trying to enlist him onto my side.

"I don't want to go either, Maggs, but Minty has a point. It's a big deal concert and if we don't make an effort to be there it would be weird."

"Fuck," I mutter, knowing they're right.

2023

"…We, of course, had better things to do than go to a concert, but we knew if we didn't go it would just look odd.

At 9:45 Gwen and I gulped down a second large gin before Minty dropped us on Pye Road. The night was windless and still held the day's warmth. I was already sweating, though most of that was from nerves…"

1998

"Gwen," Minty calls, leaning from the car window.

"Don't say anything, Minty," she warns.

"I'll be there all the way, Minty," I reassure him with a confidence I'm not feeling.

"Okay, see you both later." We watch him drive off and Gwen takes my arm, I guess for balance on her stupid shoes but maybe for courage too.

"Let's do it," she says putting a false smile on her face.

2023

"…I knew the others would now be at Jonny's, checking everything before walking down to Godiva Gardens with the wheelchair. At the corner of Pye Road, the lights from the pub flooded through the open windows and the air was filled with a dull, heavy rock beat from a live band.

I watched Gwen bravely straighten her dress and pat her hair before entering the pub, before I snucked into the tiny car park and crouched down between a 4x4 truck and a battered Fiesta. To be frank, I was shaking like a leaf, and I wanted to vomit up the gin and the Shepard's Pie Gwen had made us all eat earlier. After a while though my nerves began to settle, and I found myself fidgeting. On top of that, I hadn't a clue as to what's happening to Gwen, so I decided to edge forward..."

1998

Darting towards the pub's sidewall as though I'm a member of the SAS, I lean back against the building in a pool of darkness. Next to me is a stack of empty beer barrels and crates of used bottles and beyond that a door. Suddenly, it is flung open, casting a dirty yellow light out into the car park. I press harder into the wall and watch a pony-tailed youth dump a crate on top of the others. The glass rattles dangerously, but the boy either doesn't care or knows the strength of the bottles, as he never gives it a backward glance.

"Move," I order myself. Inching around the wall, I see the open windows that face the road. The music drills ever louder, as I creep closer. At the first window, I steel myself and take a quick look, but all I manage to see is a blur of light and colour.

"Hey, are you looking for someone?" a voice says behind me. Letting out a small yell, I swing around, fists tightly clenched.

"Oh God, sorry, I didn't mean to scare you," the man says apologetically.

"No, no you're fine, you just gave me a bit of a start," I pant, un-balling my hands.

"Sorry. Do you want me to find someone in the there for you?" he asks again, gesturing towards the open window.

"Uhmm, no, I was-I was just trying to see the band," I stumble back.

"Yeah, they're great, aren't they? They're playing at The Spotted Dog on Monday."

"Ah, perhaps I'll go. And thanks anyway," I say, backing away

towards the road.

He raises his hand, "no worries," he calls over his shoulder as he heads into the pub.

"No fucking worries, fucking bloody stoners," I shout inwardly.

2023

"…I ended up crossing the road and sitting on a bench at the bus stop opposite the pub…"

1998

"FUCK, if you're like this after that, you're going to be SHIT at kidnapping Hoyle… No, I fucking won't," I argue back at myself belligerently, trying to regain control of my adrenaline-driven heart. "Yes, you fuuucking will. Fuck, shut up and concentrate. It's Gwen you should be worrying about, not yourself, you fucking cowardy custard."

2023

"…I scanned the windows and slowly began to join the dots together and identify shapes. It was actually a much better place to see into the pub and I started to make out different people. Then, I spotted Hoyle leaning on the bar, wearing one of those red, nylon, football shirts and smoking a cigarette…"

1998

"There's the Cunt," I almost shout aloud.

2023

"…He was bent towards someone; I couldn't quite see…"

1998

"It could be Gwen. It could be Wheeler. It could be any fucking one."

2023

"…Then he indicated to the bartender. The bartender handed Hoyle a bottle that looked a lot like whisky. He turned to the unseen somebody, then handed the bartender money…"

1998
"It's got to be Gwen. Blimey, Gwen, that was quick work."

2023
"…I checked my watch again for the umpteenth time and saw it was coming up for 11. The band's vocalist announced the end of their set, the crowd cheered and the bartender called time. I was just estimating that I'd have another hour to wait when the pub door was flung open…"

CHAPTER 42
Fleshy Roll

Maggi
"…And Hoyle stepped out of the pub with Wheeler…"

1998
"Where the hell is Gwen?" I think, jumping to my feet.

2023
"…followed by tiny Gwen, tottering on her high heels…"

1998
"I've got another bottle, Big Boy," Gwen giggles, taking the fat cunt's arm and leaning into him. Wheeler farts loudly, lifting one leg.
"'ang a pearl necklace round the slags neck f' me mate," he shouts, as he walks off up Albert Street.
"You're next on my list, bastard," I think, balling my fists again.
"Well, let's go and fuckin' drink it then," Hoyle says, turning towards Pye Road.

Gwen stumbles slightly, giving her a moment to glance around. I quickly step forward, out of the shadows and I'm pretty sure she's seen me.

2023
"...Wheeler left up Albert Street as Hoyle and Gwen rounded the

corner into Pye Road. I remember hoping that the others were already in position, as we were now an hour earlier than scheduled.

I followed, keeping my distance as the streetlights were numerous and bright in that part of town. Suddenly, Hoyle stopped to urinate …"

1998

"I'm surprised you can find it under that gut," I silently scoff, slipping into a darkened drive way as a great arc of urine hits the brick wall and the cunt sighs loudly. Stepping away from the spreading pool, he pushes his cock back into his jeans.

2023

"…Then, unexpectedly, he grabbed Gwen and shoved her hard against the wall. His huge carcass towered over her tiny frame and he said something like, 'Let's have a feel of your twat, Bitch. I bet you cum like a train.' I wanted to run to her, I wanted to stop him from touching her, but what I did was to keep still and wait. Gwen answered as sweetly as though she was selling jam at a W.I. fete, admiring his prowess. Hoyle called her a, 'horny bitch,' and asked if she wanted to have sex with him against the wall…"

1998

"No, I want to enjoy it back at yours. I bet you're a stallion in bed," Gwen coos.
"Fuckin' right there, take a feel of this bad boy."
"Ugh, nooo," I think as I see him push her hand down onto his crotch.
"Whoa, a big stallion too!" Gwen exclaims, managing to sound impressed. I see him grab her chin and forcing it up as he leans down to kiss her.
"Fuuuck," I think, trying to decide what to do.

2023

"…She cleverly managed to duck out from under his arm. I thought he was about to kick off, when she pulled the whisky bottle out of her bag and offered him a drink. He must've been placated, as he took the bottle and walked off..."

1998

I see Gwen wipe her mouth and glance back towards me. I know she can't see me but I hope she knows I'm here.

2023

"...I let them get ahead before I started trailing again. As I rounded the bend in the road, I caught a dart of movement. I knew it was Rah and I dearly hoped Gwen had seen her too, as I knew it would give her courage. I let Hoyle and Gwen turn into the Gardens before entering myself. It felt pitch black after leaving the lit road, with only a half formed moon for light..."

1998

"Even Blind Pew would find this dark," I think as I strain to see the pathway.

2023

"...Gwen shouted something about the whisky, unnecessarily loud, I guessed to warn the others that they were on their way. I judged from her voice that she was no more than 10 feet in front of me. Hoyle told her to shut up. I quickened my pace, though I was careful to tread softly. Then Gwen started to sing raucously as though she was off her head..."

1998

"Put it, Put it, Put it where you know..."
"Fuckin' shut up, you stupid Bitch," Hoyle snarls, but Gwen bravely sings on.
"I told ya to fuckin' shut ya cake 'ole. Funkin' singing that bender crap."
"What do you want me to sing then, Big Boy?" Gwen asks, still at

full volume.
"Fuck, what's wrong with you, stupid bitch? Shut up."

2023
"…Hoyle had another go at her…"

1998
"Fuckin' shut up and come here, stupid Bitch."
"No," I catch her fear in that one word.
"You want it, Bitch."

2023
"…Then I heard a scuffling of feet on the path ahead. I stopped. Gwen protested saying she didn't want to and I knew she was starting to really panic. Hoyle called her a few choice names and I could tell from the direction of his voice that they were no longer on the footpath but off to my left. I tried to picture the Gardens. I reckoned there was a small grass bank leading to a lawn, and that they must be somewhere down there. A dull thud vibrated through my feet, quickly followed by Gwen screaming my name. I ran like hell, straight down the bank, shouting her name and tripped right over them…"

1998
"WHAT THE FUCK," I hear as I scramble round with adrenaline-fuelled courage and throw myself at the largest shape on the ground. My arms and legs grip tight and I'm rewarded by the feel of nylon under my hands.
"FUCKING CUNT," I yell.
"MINTY, JONNY, HELP," screams Gwen.
"GET OFF OR I FUNKIN' KILL'YA," bawls Hoyle.
"HELP. MINTY, HERE," Gwen screams again and again.
"FUCKING CUNT," I manage one last time before the bastard elbows me in my ribs. The pain shoots through me, I can't catch my breath, "Don't let go," I scream at myself as the reassuring sound of

running feet followed by yells of, "WHERE ARE YOU? GWEN? MAGGI?" comes towards us.

"HERE. HERE. QUICK, HELP MAGGI," Gwen shouts back as I feel myself rolling. My back slams into the ground, jarring my spine. I'm struggling to catch my breath as Hoyle jerks his head back and smacks me across the bridge of my nose.

"Aaargh," I gurgle deep in my throat as an explosion of pain mushrooms through my face, followed by a jarring impact ricocheting through my belly.

Ooph. I feel the breath leave Hoyle's lungs as another massive jolt rings through me.

"Again, Jim Bob," I hear Jonny yell and I know instantly what it is I'm feeling, Jim Bob's punch. I grip harder, squeezing the bastard round his bull-like neck. His legs are pumping as he scrambles up. Ooph. Another dull thwack hits him in the belly but he's regained his strength and is on his knees now. I feel him pull his arm back to lash out and I do the only thing I can think of to do –sink my teeth into the fleshy roll at the back of his neck. It's not a good bite by any standards but I'm rewarded by a howl of pain. Encouraged, I bite harder and using my fingers, I claw into his face.

"GET IT IN, JONNY," Minty roars.

"I"M TR ..." smack. "Fuuuck!" Jonny groans. Jim Bob's next punch must've landed right in Hoyle's diaphragm as I feel the air leave his lungs. He starts to double over, I pull my weight to the left and we tip together, hitting the ground. Someone is on his legs, I feel him fight against the restraint, though I instinctively realise his anger has shifted to panic. I know we are winning. I bite harder.

"HELP ME," Minty yells and more weight falls on the cunt's kicking legs. My left thigh explodes with pain.

"HOLD HIM STILL, JIM BOB," Jonny shouts.

Another massive load crashes down. I think my femur is about to snap. Hoyle struggles, I bite harder. I feel the power ebbing from his body.

"HERRICK, THE OTHER SYRINE," Jonny orders. Suddenly, there's stillness. I don't let go. I can't let go.

"Maggs, Maggs, it's alright, he's out for the count," Jonny says breathlessly.

"Maggs, shh, shh," I feel her familiar touch as she strokes my face. "Stop now, Maggs." I let my jaw slacken; I pull my teeth out of the disgusting flesh. Someone is tugging at my arms. "Let go, Bigster," Jim Bob says calmly. I roll on my back; someone pulls Hoyle off my leg. Then I'm on all fours, choking, crying and gagging. A mixture of salty iron and bile fills my mouth. I spit it out.

"Shh, Maggs, it's done. You were amazing. God, I love you." Rah gently murmurs, kissing me.

2023

"…There was a fight, we got battered, but we eventually managed to hold Hoyle down long enough for Jonny to get the Midazolam into him. Then, Minty warned us there was no time to lose and we needed to get out of the Gardens as quick as possible…"

1998

"Maggi, get up now," orders Minty, "We haven't got time for this. Herrick, get the chair." I struggle to my feet, wiping my face with my t-shirt.

"Gwen?" I murmur.

"I'm right here, Maggi, I'm fine," she answers as Herrick appears with the wheel chair.

"Right, you get the left arm Jim Bob, Jonny the right. Maggi grab one leg, I'll do the other. Norah, Gwen pull the waistband of his jeans from the back as we haul. Herrick hold the chair steady." Minty instructs. The pain in my side almost winds me as hot blood runs down my face, but I manage to lift Hoyle's leg as the others manoeuver him into the chair. He tips forward, Jim Bob rights him. "Let's get out of here before someone decides to come and investigate" Minty commands.

2023

"…We shoved him in the wheelchair and headed back out onto Pye

Road.

Jim Bob took one look at me under the street light and said I was a right mess and to go home and get sorted out, because if we meet anyone it'll be suspicious enough, us pushing Hoyle, without me looking as though I've gone ten rounds in a ring. Both Rah and Gwen decided to come back with me too. At home, Rah made me swallow a large amount of pain killers before insisting I get into a hot shower to wash off the blood."

"The blood?" D.C.I. Logan questions.

"Mine, Hoyle's, I'm not sure, probably both…"

1998

Hot water pounds my body; I breathe deeply and force my face under the jet. My nose screams with pain but it slowly starts to subside. I wash my mouth, scrub under my fingernails, as the idea of that cunt's blood makes me cringe. Dressing quickly, I stuff toilet tissue up my nostrils and go downstairs.

Gwen greets me with a huge hug. "Maggi, you're so brave," she says, "I was so frightened." I pull away from her embrace and look into her sweet face, now stripped of all the make-up and I see tears filling her eyes.

"I wasn't brave, Gwen, I was angry," I tell her truthfully.

CHAPTER 43
A Marriage Made in Heaven

*

Maggi - 2023
"…After showering, Rah and I walked back to Pump Road. Gwen didn't want to come…"

1998

Taking Rah's hand, I feel her excitement and my own heart leaps with the thought that Orla will be coming home soon.

2023
"…When we got to Jonny's, Hoyle was already starting to come round…"

1998

I look at the fat cunt laid out naked on the trolley. His arms are tethered in three places, to the bars with cable ties, his legs in two. Jonny has already got a cannula in one arm and the tourie cuff on the other.

"I'm sorry he's naked, Maggi I know you wanted him in a hospital gown but Jonny thought, and we all agreed, he'd feel more vulnerable uncovered," Minty says, as Hoyle starts to moan loudly, turning his head from side to side. "As soon as he's fully conscious, we'll begin."

"What the FUCK?" Hoyle shouts, trying to twist his body away

from his restraints.

"Shut up, you fat Cunt, and listen to what's going to happen," I tell him, pulling on a pair of latex gloves and snapping them theatrically. The others stand around the trolley, watching silently.
"I'M GOING TO FUCKIN' KILL YOU." Hoyle bellows.
"Yeah, yeah, yeah," I say unconcerned. My voice is derisive and low, and for the first time in ages, I feel in control. Something must've struck a chord as he turns and stares at me. "You're scared," I snarl.
"FUCK OFF." he growls back at me.
"Yeah, pants on fire, Cunt, I can read it in your body, your heart rate, your breath, your pulse. But here's the thing, and I advise you to listen carefully, in the next few minutes you'll experience fear like you've never experienced before...." I let that thought hang, just for a split second, in the air. "Jonny, here, and I don't give a flying fuck if you do know who we are, and I are going to hold your worthless life in our hands."

Lifting his head he aims and spits at my face. Almost in slow motion I manage to sidestep the globule, like some sort of spit-fighting ninja. "I'm guessing you don't believe me. Jonny, Ambu-bag." Stepping forward, Jonny holds up the ventilation mask and bag. "Even a fat twat like you must know what this is for."
"FUCK OFF BITCH," he shouts again.
"Okay, Cunt, here's the deal. Jonny is going to inject you with a drug. One of the drug's most interesting effects is that it will paralyse your lungs and you won't be able to breathe amongst other things. The only way to stop you from suffocating is if I pump air into you."
"I'LL KILL THE FUCKIN' LOT OF YA" Hoyle snarls as Jonny holds the Roc-filled syringe up, in front of his face.
"Once the drug hits your system, you will have approximately 60 seconds left before you die if we do not step in," Jonny explains in a dispassionate voice.
"Don't get us wrong, we've no intention of letting you die just yet, that would be far too easy," I add.

"FUCKIN' BASTARDS," Hoyle repeats over and over again.
"Just give him a dose, then he'll understand," Minty says, ignoring the abuse.
I watch Jonny attach the syringe to the cannula. I almost feel the slight click as the two ends marry up and slip together perfectly.
"A marriage made in heaven," I murmur.

2023

"…With Hoyle conscious again, we explained to him what was going to happen. In his anger he either didn't understand or wouldn't listen, so Minty suggested we give him a round of the Rocuronium…"

1998

"Like Maggs said, you'll have less than 60 seconds," Jonny tells him, looking around at the others. We all nod in agreement.
"FUCKIN' BASTARD," Hoyle hollers back as Jonny depresses the plunger.
"1, 2, 3, 4,5," I count off, staring into Hoyle eyes. They're steady and full of hate. I wish it was fear but I assure myself that will come later. When I reach 35, I'm rewarded by Hoyle's natural urge to draw oxygen into his depleting lungs. By 50, a fleeting desperateness crosses his features, before every muscle starts to slacken into a paralytic state. I look at Jonny, who's observing carefully and counting too. I move to Hoyle's head and hold the Ambu-bag directly over his face so he can see it.
"This represents life and we control it. You have approximately 30 seconds left before your brain cells start to die." I look at Jonny and he nods. Holding the mask over Hoyle's mouth and nose with my left hand to create a seal, I use my right to operate the bag. This is a thing I do every working day, without thought or question, but hate stops my hand from pumping.
"Maggs, now," Jonny orders, "he's lost consciousness anyway and we don't want him dead or incapable of telling us where Orla is."
"Yes, of course, sorry," I say squeezing air into the lungs. We allow

him 10 minutes of respite before I withdraw the mask.

"You're fighting now, Cunt?" I whisper into his ear. "Fighting to breathe." Of course, he just stares blankly ahead, his face and body totally immobile.

After another round of oxygen, I explain to the others, knowing full well he can hear every word. "On top of the obvious agonies of asphyxiation, the Fat Cunt's heart is now struggling; his eyes are burning, his throat is dry and his skin is crawling."

2023

"…Remember how I explained the drug only paralyses and the recipient remains fully conscious throughout the procedure?" The Officers both nod. "Well, though I ensured Hoyle received enough air to maintain his life, it was minimal and he was always on the point of suffocation. On top of this, Rah piped up and asked if it was possible to cut his penis off without killing him. Jonny said we could but he'd have to rig up a urinary track of some sort, though it would be much easier to just castrate him…"

1998

As I start to bag Hoyle one last time before the drug loses its grip on him, I think how Jonny's just saying this to frighten him, though I'm not so sure about Rah.

2023

"…After approximately 30 minutes, Hoyle started to gulp for air as his natural reflexes began working again. Removing the mask, I watched dispassionately as his chest heaved, his eyes ran with tears and he tried to swallow. Slowly his limbs unfroze but his muscles shook and his skin goosed…"

1998

"I see we have you back, Mr Hoyle," Minty says, sounding like he'd just stepped out of a 60s movie.

"Ba..s..tard..s,' pants Hoyle.

"Yes, highly unpleasant I would imagine. But all this will be over for you very quickly, if you take the time to listen to my instructions."

"Fu ..." gasp, "ckin" gasp, "bas ..."

"Save your breath, Mr Hoyle, you are going to need it. So, here's what going to happen.

This time we are going to tourniquet your arm, which basically means the drug will have no effect on this limb. We'll provide you with a piece of paper and place a pen in your hand, which you will use to write your answers to our questions."

"FUC kin', "gasp, "Bas ...tard ...s."

"You can, needless to say, avoid the whole thing by answering our questions now before we inject more Rocuronium into you."

"WHAT," gasp, "FUCKIN' QUESTIONS?" Hoyle slams back, his lungs now nearly recovered.

"Where is Orla Montgomery?"

"WHO THE FUCK?"

"Orla Montgomery. The girl YOU raped and murdered, Mr Hoyle."

"WHAT THE FUCK ARE YOU TALKING ABOUT?"

2023

"…After Hoyle regained control of his body, Minty asked him where Orla was. He refused to answer, though I knew his fear was real because when Minty ordered Jonny to administer another dose of Roc, Hoyle pissed himself..."

1998

"NO, FUCKIN' NO," Hoyle pleads as Jonny picks up the syringe, removes the air bubbles and measures the contents. I attach the tournie to the cuff and switch the machine on. It whirrs into life, sending air into the cuff. I watch as Hoyle's blood vessels bulge, blue and bold, under his skin, before picking up the Ambu-bag. Jonny inserts the syringe into the cannula.

"Last chance, Mr Hoyle," Minty states coldly.

"IT WASN'T ME. I NEVER RAPED ANY BLEEDIN' GIRL."

"Well, we all know that's not true, don't we? Do it Jonny." Jonny

feeds another dose of Roc into Hoyle's vein. I count aloud this time and Jim Bob, Rah and Jonny join in. As the count rises, Hoyle's futile struggles lessen until they are barely perceptible.

"Scared now, aren't you, Cunt?" I crow. "See the mask," I hover it in front of his eyes, "will I wait, or won't I?...Oh, I'll wait Cunt, you can be sure of that." A moment passes.

"Maggs, now," Jonny orders. I bag.

"Mr Hoyle, I'm placing a pen in your hand," Minty instructs. "Write your name or I'll ask Maggi to withdraw the mask." Hoyle's hand frantically scribbles. We all peer at the paper. It would've been hard to read if I hadn't already experienced his crap.

" 'Fuck off' is not going to work for me, Mr Hoyle. Maggi." I stop bagging and watch as Hoyle's chest deflates. Jonny pulls Hoyle's scrotum free from between his legs. "If I make an incision here, I reckon I can pull the testis free and stitch across the perineum," he says objectively, nicking the skin with a scalpel blade. Blood bubbles out of the small wound, mixing with the urine leaking from his penis.

"Careful, Jonny, we don't want the Fat Cunt to lose too much blood at this stage," I say, wanting to scare Hoyle even more, though I know the cut is pretty minor.

"Mr Hoyle, I suggest you write your name this time." Hoyle manages to form a capital aitch followed by a hardly legible o, y,l,e, as I start to bag again. "Now, we are getting somewhere. All we want is Orla's body back, then we will let you go. Just write the location, that's all you have to do." He scribbles again. I slow the bagging to a minimum just enough to trickle air into Hoyle's agonised lungs. It takes minutes for him to form the words. He finishes just as the Roc is ebbing from his system. Minty picks the paper up and reads aloud. "I didn't kill her, I don't know where she is."

"Not good enough, Mr Hoyle."

"Pl ee ...s," he manages to splutter, gasping like a fish out of water. "Pl... ee ...s."

"Where is Orla?" Minty asks, leaning into Hoyle's face.

"Pl ..." gasp, "ee ...s," gasp, "plee ..." gasp, "se," gasp, "pleese I,"

gasp, "I don't," gasp "know," gasp.

"Liar," Rah snarls, stepping forward.

"No, honest," gasp, "ly," gasp, "it wasn't me," gasp, "God's honest truth," gasp, "If I knew, I'd tell you. I'd never heard of her before the police arrested me," gasp. "I was with Wheeler, ask him," gasp.

"Oh, and we'd believe that cunt," I sneer.

2023

"...After the second round of Roc, Hoyle's attitude was markedly changed. He'd lost a lot of his aggression and was seriously scared. He begged us to stop, though he also stuck to his guns and claimed he was innocent. None of us were believing that. Minty told him that we'd give him sometime to think over his alternatives. Spelling out the fact that a prison sentence was a good compromise for him compared to what lay ahead, if he didn't tell us where he'd hidden Orla's remains.

We left him still tied to the trolley, lying in his own blood and piss. In the kitchen, I opened the back door and stood outside. The early morning light was already breaking across the sky, I breathed in deeply and was immediately rewarded with a massive spasm of pain shooting across my battered ribs, making my eyes water and my nose burn. Pulling a packet of painkillers from my pocket, I swallowed a double dose.

Rah came and stood next to me. She took my hand and said she'd thought we'd have known by now where Orla was. I agreed with her and promised I would make the Fat Bastard pay for wasting our time.

Then Herrick came out balancing two mugs of hot coffee. He reminded us it was Saturday and he had the L.G.O. concert at Glass Hall that evening. He asked if we were coming. I really could've done without it, we had bigger fish to fry, but I told him we'd be there. It meant, one way or another, that we needed to deal with Hoyle before 1p.m.

But by mid-day we really weren't getting anywhere. Yes, he'd shit himself, cried like a baby and spilt the beans on his previous crimes, but he still hadn't told us where Orla was…"

CHAPTER 44
Skin Coated Skeleton

*

Maggi - 1998

"What are we going to do with the fat twat?" I ask the others.

"We've got to be dressed and in London by 7."

"He has an arrhythmic heart beat now and he needs fluids too if we are going to keep going," Jonny states.

"Bloody right we are going to keep going," I assert.

"What if Jonny gave him some more Midazolam and we put him back in the wheelchair," Jim Bob suggests. "Then I could give him a drink while you lot go to the concert? Maybe I could play good cop too if you like. You know, be his new bestie, promise I'll do everything to get him released, stop you from cutting his balls off?"

"Sounds like a good plan, Jim Bob," Minty agrees.

"Only thing though, I don't fancy sitting with him with all that shit plastered down his legs. I can hardly stand the smell as it is."

"I'll clean it up," I say.

"I'll help," offers Rah.

"You don't hav…" I begin.

"I do," she says with a smile.

"Okay but we'll do it once he's under; I'm not having him see us clearing his shit up."

2023

"…We had to go and get ready for the L.G.O. concert, so we

decided to leave Hoyle in Jim Bob's charge. We'd tied him in the wheel chair with cable ties around his limbs and duct tape around his chest and thighs…"

1998

"That should do it," I say, standing back and looking at my work. The theatre gown he wears has a spreading pool of blood from the new cuts to his groin, which mixes with his tears, snot and drool dripping from his mouth as his head lolls forward.

"Rah, have you still got that hood you made?" I ask.

"I'll get it," she replies, leaving the room. A moment later she reappears, holding the dark, cloth bag. I take it and shove it on his head.

"Good thinking, Bigster. That'll freak him out when he comes round. Then I'll take it off and it'll freak him even more when he sees all that blood."

Back at Peartree Road, we find soup and fresh bread left by Gwen. I heat the soup while Rah showers and carry it upstairs. In our bedroom, I find her sitting on the floor, dripping wet, staring vacantly at her open wardrobe. Sitting next to her, I pull her into my arms and ask her gently, "What's going on, Rah?"

"I can't think of what to wear, Maggs. What do you wear to a concert in memory of a dead daughter?"

"You wear your best dress," I say getting up and going to her wardrobe. "What about this?" I hold up a beautiful dark blue gown, trimmed with silver. "Orla always loved this one."

"The second Zuki gown you bought me," she says, rising from the floor. I look at her naked body, a body I know so well, and want to cry. Her flesh has all but melted away, leaving a skin-coated skeleton. Every joint protrudes, every rib bulges, every vertebra burls. I turn away, making an excuse to shower but really I don't want her to see my heart is breaking.

After my shower, I dress in what I always wear to Rah's concerts but the waistband of my smart trousers bags dangerously and the shirt hangs like an empty sack.

"Shit, fuck and bugger," I mumble at my reflection in the mirror. There's a small knock at the door.

"Hi, Maggi, can I come in?" asks Gwen.

"Hi Gwe…" looking up at her I'm astonished at her transformation, "wow," I say, genuinely impressed.

"I know, I went to Braxham Wick to the hairdressers and had my hair cut off this morning. I think they've done a nice job and it's such a relief to be rid of the dyed hair," she says, combing her fingers through the short sculptured style.

"You look amazing, Gwen." And she does, dressed in a colourful, embroidered skirt with a delicate black blouse and emerald earnings against her dark skin and short hair. "On the other hand, I don't."

"Clothes too big?" she states knowingly.

"Yeah, I guess. I've lost some weight."

"While I was in town, I took the liberty of picking you up a shirt as I thought you might need a smaller size. I hope you don't mind, and if it's no good, I can easily take it back." Gratitude washes over me and I hug her close. "Oh Gwen, you're so thoughtful, thank you."

"Well it mightn't be any good. Try it on." The shirt is pale blue and goes well with my charcoal suit.

"Now, let me see what I can do about the trousers," and she produces a needle and thread. "Lift the shirt and I'll put a couple of stitches into the waistband."

"Thanks, Gwen," I say, looking in the mirror again. "I think, that'll do." Downstairs, Jonny, who's as drawn and hollow as the rest of us, still looks fabulous in a dark suit. Rah has on the blue dress but someone, and I guess it's Gwen, has hoisted it up with a belt. She still looks fashionable chic in a waif-like manner while Minty, always tall and serene, looks the elegant gentleman.

"I guess we all look okay, not like torturers or anything," I comment.

2023

"…Rah and I travelled to London in Jonny's car, while Minty and Gwen went in theirs. We arrived purposely late so we could evade any small talk. Thoughtfully, someone had allocated us a box and we took our seats just as the lights were dipping. The orchestra entered, followed by the principle players including Herrick, who bowed low before tuning. Lastly, Helena took the rostrum holding her baton. I was grateful she kept her speech short, only giving a brief outline of Orla's life before opening the concert to much applause. I think, the pieces had been chosen to highlight the oboe. The concert started with Tchaikovsky's Symphony No 4, it has the most amazing horn opening, and even though my mind was still in Godlinghoe, it stirred my blood. Rah was slumped against me, her head on my shoulder but that all changed as Herrick played the oboe solo at the beginning of the second movement. His only accompaniment was a plucked violin. Rah suddenly shot up in her seat and engaged with what was going on. Naturally, I thought it was her interest in Herrick's ability to convey the melancholic melody but she sat rigid through the 3rd and 4th movements.

During the interval, I tried to speak to her but she raised her hands and just said she needed more time. I didn't understand, nor did the others but we steered all the well wishes away from her. The second half of the programme was Scheherazade, Rimsky-Korsakov. I must admit, I sat there crying my eyes out from the first violin solo. It was so beautiful. I could see Rah was now on the edge of her seat, her bony shoulders tilted forward, her head angled, her fingers in motion as though playing along. I remember thinking that, perhaps, in some bizarre way, it was a good thing we'd attended the concert when, the first moment ended and the Kalander Prince began. The thieving bassoonist, I told you about yesterday, played her solo beautifully and was then immediately followed by Herrick's oboe. He was only seconds into the passage when Rah grabbed my hand and insisted we leave the auditorium…"

1998
"Maggs, look at me," Rah demands.
"What?" I whisper back.
"We have to go."

265

"What?"

"Now. We have to go now," she says, getting up and tapping Jonny on the shoulder.

"Okay," I mumble, following them out into the corridor, beyond the box. Rah is standing facing Jonny, her hands are out, her eyes wide, her mouth gritted. I hear the box door close behind me and know Minty and Gwen have joined us.

"Rah?" I ask, feeling confused.

She looks at me. "Maggs, I know who took Orla." Her words are precise and clear, though whispered.

"Yeah, so do I. Hoyle," I answer, feeling even more bewildered.

"No," she says, shaking her head, "No, Maggs, it's not Hoyle."

"What?" Jonny mutters.

"Shh," she says, putting her bitten finger to her mouth. "I don't want anyone to hear us. It's not Hoyle…"

"I don't understand," I question quietly, "What do you mean?"

"It was never Hoyle, Maggs. It was Herrick."

CHAPTER 45
Skin Him Alive

*

Maggi - 2023

"…We stood in the dimly-lit corridor, the four of us looking at her and she told us it was Herrick who took Orla."

"Herrick?" D.C. Fry utters in amazement. "But-but why did she think that?"

I look at D.C.I. Logan and for once, her face shows the beginnings of surprise. I know how she feels, because I felt it too, only my surprise was mixed with hate, revulsion and revenge. I say felt, but that's a lie. I still hate, I'm still revolted and I still want revenge.

I look back at D.C. Fry, perched on the edge of his chair. "Do you know, in that minute, none of us questioned it, we just believed her," I answered him. "But what we did have to do, and quickly, was make a plan before the concert ended. It was Gwen who stepped up and organised us all…"

1998

"Jonny, take Norah and Maggi home. Get rid of Hoyle and prepare the Kill Room," Gwen orders firmly. *"Someone needs to stay behind and fob Herrick off, make him think you left because Norah was taken ill."*

"I'll do it," I offer, fists already clenched.

"No, Maggi," Gwen smiles gently at me, *"You'll give the game*

away."

"I won't," I protest.

"You will, Love, and besides, Jonny and Norah need your help at the other end. God knows what you're going to do about Hoyle."

"Don't worry about him, I've already thought of something," Jonny mutters. I look at him, he's as white as a sheet.

"Okay, Minty and I will delay Herrick, take him for a drink at the bar, praise him up, tell him you were swept away with his performance, Norah, and if he's up to it, could he pop by Peartree Road for a late coffee and a chat about the concert. How does that sound?" I look back at Gwen standing in her concert finery, tiny and purposeful, and yet again I'm amazed by her.

2023

"…Jonny, Rah and I left Minty and Gwen to hoodwink Herrick into thinking all was well and slow him up to give us a chance to get home and sort things out. It wasn't till we were speeding out of London that Rah, stiff with horror, told us Herrick had been playing Orla's oboe.

You might remember, I explained to you earlier how special this oboe was to Rah, how she knew it intimately. A bit like a car you love and drive every day, I'd imagine. You can buy the identical make and model, but it won't have the same idiosyncrasies, the same flaws, the same peculiarities. It's the equivalent for musical instruments apparently.

Anyway, Rah told us that Orla's oboe, her oboe, had a slight stickiness on the G key. Obviously, that meant nothing to me and Jonny but she said it was just a quirk and that if you knew the instrument really, really well, you'd know how to prevent it…"

1998

Rah sits in the front seat of the Aston Martin, biting her fingers and crying as she tells us between sobs. "I heard it and knew straight away, it's Orla's oboe, but I needed to be sure. That's why I waited until the first solo in the Kalander Prince. I knew if I was right, the

268

lying fucking bastard wouldn't be able to control the slowed reaction from G, to F♯, to A."

"But surely, Herrick must know this... this G thing," Jonny asks, as I see a traffic camera flash as we fly past.

"Not necessarily. It's just something Orla," and I hear her voice break, "and I know and we know how to compensate for it. It's not something I would have told anyone about and Orla... Oh My God, do you think she was sending us a message? Like a clue?" she moans as another traffic camera registers our speed.

"She could've been Rah, she was always brave and clever," Jonny says, his voice pinched with pain.

"Oh God, what have I done? I made her go round there, I did this," Rah cries pitifully.

"No you didn't, Rah, that sad fuck, Herrick did it and I swear I'm going to skin him alive. The fucking, shitting, fucking bastard," I spit out through clenched teeth, wanting to punch something.

"Not before we have Orla back, then I'm killing him too," Jonny states as the third camera goes off.

2023

"...We made it back to Godlinghoe in just over an hour and skidded to a halt in Pump Road.

Jim Bob greeted us with a look that said he hadn't gotten anywhere with Hoyle. We told him what had happened, quietly outside the Kill Room..."

1998

"Holy Hell," he mutters in disbelief.

"I know, fucking Herrick, I'll fucking have him," I swear.

"First, we need to get rid of Hoyle," Jonny affirms. "Can you stick some Midazolam into him, Maggs, while I ring Seb and Paul?"

"Sure."

"Rah, you bundle up his clothes into a bin bag."

I look at her, she's not fit to pick up a feather but she goes and does as she's told.

2023

"…Then I injected Hoyle with some more Midazolam, and when he was out for the count, we untied him and re-tied his hands behind his back. Jonny had phoned Seb and Paul, who turned up half an hour later in their brand new Mercedes…"

1998

"Hey, Jonny, what's this all about?" Paul asks.
"The less I tell you the better, guys."
"Okay. What do you want us to do?"
"Take this bloke, he's drugged up, so he won't give you any trouble, and dump him somewhere. I'd leave the hood on him just in case though."

Wheeling Hoyle to their car, we haul him in. It's hard, coz he weighs a ton. He lies across the white, leather back seat and farts.
"Fuck," Paul moans.
"Sorry, mate," Jonny apologises.
"Anywhere?" Seb asks.
"Anywhere. And guys, he's a piece of shit, he's just not our piece of shit."

2023

"…They dropped Hoyle at a disused WW2 airfield, out near Little Lessing. He'd come too by then, and they'd dragged him behind an old hut before threatening to leave him tied up if he'd didn't count to a hundred before pulling the hood off. He agreed, but I reckon he was so shit scared by that time, he would've agreed to anything. They dumped his clothes next to him and untied his hands, then drove off. They never asked us why and we never told them.

After getting rid of Hoyle, we left Jonny to load another syringe with Midazolam, Jim Bob grabbed a load of cable ties and Rah sat in the wheelchair as I wheeled her home.

At Peartree, all was still and quiet. I unlocked the front door and left it ajar for Jonny. We dashed upstairs and changed back into our dark gear. Jonny was soon with us and ready to go…"

1998

I look at Jonny wearing his black outfit. And though he's still handsome, he looks disturbingly dangerous. I hope I look the same.

"How are we going to trap the cunt?" I growl.

"Easy," Rah answers, I can tell she is fighting hard now to control her crying. "I'll stand in the kitchen, he'll come walking through, and you two can jump him from behind." Headlights swing in through the open, front door and we all hold our breath as the car engine is switched off.

"It's not Herrick's car," Jonny utters.

2023

"…Minty and Gwen arrived. We told them we'd disposed of Hoyle, and Gwen said Herrick would be here any minute; he'd just popped home to park his car and return the oboe. I glanced at Rah but she said nothing…"

1998

"Rah?"

"Yeah," she whimpers.

"Put your dressing gown on quick to hide your clothes. Make it look like you've been sick and want to go to bed." She tears upstairs and is back in seconds.

"Here." I wipe her tears and kiss her. "Now, stand leaning against the kitchen unit. Good. Jonny, you take the right side of the kitchen door with me, Jim Bob you take the left."

"I better shut the front door or it'll look odd. Then, I'll answer it when Herrick arrives," Gwen says, dashing off.

"And I'll stand with Norah," Minty adds. Minutes tick by. I feel the sweat seeping down my back. I wipe my forehead with my sleeve. I can hear Rah crying softly and want to comfort her.

"You okay, Bigster?" Jim Bob mouths.

"Yeah," I nod, but I want to get on with it. I look at the clock, it's 12:03. "What if he doesn't come?" I panic.

"He'll come," Jonny asserts, his voice full of disgust.

271

"How'd you know?" I ask.

"Because Rah asked him to."

Time passes; I watch the long hand jerk between the clock's digits.

"Breathe, Maggs," Jonny warns. I breathe, I watch, I wait. There's a polite knock at the door.

"The fucker's here," I mutter as I hear Gwen twist the latch.

"Oh hello, Herrick, I'm so pleased you've arrived," she says, all sweetness and light. "Norah's in the kitchen. Do go through, she can't wait to see you." I feel rather than hear the slightest of hesitations and pray Gwen hasn't overcooked the goose.

Rah must've have thought so too, as she calls persuasively to him.

"Herrick."

"Rah," he answers and I hear the pleasure in his sicko voice.

I silently egg him on as I listen to each footfall as he comes down our hallway.

He steps into the kitchen, followed by Gwen.

And I slam the door shut.

CHAPTER 46
Iron Control

*

Maggi - 1998

He looks around. First at me. Then at Jonny, who stands holding a syringe in the air.

"Rah," he begs, turning to her, "what's happening?"

"I know, Herrick," she screams at him, dropping the dressing gown from her ruined body. "You're so fucking stupid playing Orla's oboe, as if I wouldn't know."

I hear Gwen gasp at my side.

"Just tell us where Orla is and this will be over," Minty states coldly. "You'll have the same deal as Hoyle. Prison, but life."

2023

"…When Herrick showed up, he panicked and tried to run but we had him. Jonny got the needle in, and he went down like a sack of shit. We wheeled him to Pump Road and had him striped and on the table by the time he was coming round. He was already pissing himself with fear…"

1998

"It's not what you think, Rah. Please believe me, Rah. Please, Rah. I love you. You know I love you," Herrick pleads pathetically. I hear her whimper from the edge of the room. I turn and see she has slid down the wall and is curled, sobbing, into a ball.

*"Don't fucking call her that you fat, cunting, ginger fuck-twat," I
shriek, punching him as hard as I can. I feel the bone of his nose
shatter as my blow jars up my arm into my torso. It's so satisfying.
Herrick screams, then struggles to draw breath.*

*"Help me, Rah," he manages, before I punch again, with all my
might.*

"You piece of fucking shit, you bag of wank," I scream.

Pulling me away, Jonny shouts, "Maggs, stop."

"Stop," I scream, spittle flying, "I haven't even fucking started."

"Just stop and come with me."

"Come with you," I yell, "what the fuck for?"

*"Now," Jonny demands. He shoves me through the plastic curtain,
out into the hallway, then in to his kitchen. Minty and Jim Bob
follow.*

"Chill, Maggs, and listen."

*"Don't you fucking dare tell me to fucking chill, Jonathan Gifford,"
I slam back in his face.*

*"Bigster, don't," Jim Bob warns gently. My lungs heave as sobs rip
through my chest. He puts his arms around me and I bawl.*

*"Listen," he says, after a while, "The most important thing here is to
find Orla, and beating the crap out of Herrick probably won't help
us do that quickly."*

"Why not, I think it's an excellent idea."

*"Because, it's just making him incoherent. All he's doing is begging
Rah for help, he's not telling us anything."*

"'Kay," I mumble after a while, knowing he's right.

*"I think we have to be clever. He's terrified, he knows what we are
capable of and he's witnessed the effect the Roc has on a person. But
he also knows that Jim Bob, Minty and Gwen will not allow us to kill
him."*

"So?" I sulk.

*"So, it means they can promise him life, promise that they won't let
you or me hurt him or give him the Roc in return for the
whereabouts of Orla," explains Jonny reasonably.*

I look at Jonny, I see the father of a lost child. His face is pinched,

274

his jaw tight, his fury barely contained and I know he's fighting all his instincts not to go into the Kill Room and beat the crap out of Herrick too.

"'Kay," I say, hugging him.

"Good," he breathes.

"Sorry," I mumble.

Minty sighs. "I'll do it," and I can see he's crying too.

"I'll do it with you, he trusts me," says Jim Bob stoically.

"And I need to threaten him with the Roc, so you can save him," Jonny adds.

"And me," I begin.

"No Bigster, you're too volatile. You might lose control."

"I'm not going to be left out," I snap, "but I won't say anything, I promise."

"Right, that's agreed. Now for goodness sake, let's go and help Gwen and Norah," urges Minty.

"Oh God, Rah," I mutter and dash back into the plastic-coated room. Like usual, I'd only been thinking of myself, my own anger, my own pain. She's there, lying on the floor, with Gwen sitting next to her. I kneel and pull her into my arms.

2023

"…Minty and Jim Bob began to question Herrick while Jonny, ignoring Herrick's petrified squeals of fear, calmly inserted a cannula into his arm before picking up a syringe and making a show of filling it with Roc. We—me, Rah and Gwen – just sat on the floor, against the wall and watched. Minty reminded him that we'd all made a pact when we were planning Hoyle's torture not to kill, only to find Orla…"

1998

"Do you remember that, Herrick?" Minty's voice is impressively calm.

"Yes, yes, yes," pants Herrick, his eyes darting between the three men.

275

"So, you know you are safe with me and Jim Bob here, don't you?"

"Yes," he whimpers pathetically. "Help me, Minty, Jim Bob. I swear it's not what you think."

"And I swear I won't let Jonny inject you with the Rocuronium, if you speak to me properly."

"I will, I'll tell you everything," he cries gratefully.

2023

"…With what must've taken an iron control over his emotions, Minty pulled up a chair, sat back and relaxed his body as though he was about to have a nice friendly chat with a good mate.

The other two instinctively drew back from the trolley, while Minty assured Herrick again that he would protect him if he told us everything…"

1998

"Now, why don't you tell me all about it? Why did you take Orla?"

"It's not what you think, Minty I swear it," he wails, blood and snort bubbling out of his nose.

"Why don't you explain it to me then? Make me understand. I'm sure there's a reasonable way out of all this mess."

2023

"…And Herrick sang like a canary…"

1998

"It's all Rah's fault. You see, I love her, she's my life, my everything." I see Minty's throat tighten but he keeps a look of sympathetic understanding on his face. "That's why I moved here, to be close to her. I always hoped she'd see that, see that my love is pure, clean, not tainted and dirty like Maggi's, or perverted like Jonny's," he snarls as he pronounces our names. "See that I could offer her a decent life, make her respectable. You've no idea Minty how people talk about her behind her back. I just wanted to save her. But instead, she chose Maggi." He spits out my name as Rah sits up

with her back against the wall. She's no longer cowering, like a
trapped fox cornered by a packed of hounds, she's listening to every
word he is saying.

"But why take Orla and not Norah?" asks Minty, as though this is
the most rational of questions.

"Haven't you understood anything?" retorts Herrick, his disbelief
momentarily suppressing his fear. "I would never make Rah do
anything she didn't want to. You've no idea how difficult it has been
all these years. Staying silent, watching and waiting as she ruins her
reputation."

"But that doesn't explain why you took Orla?"

"I didn't want to, please believe me, Minty," whines Herrick again,
oscillating between emotions. "But when I saw her playing her oboe,
she was just like my sweet Rah. It's in the eyes, the embouchure, the
expression. I realised in that moment, she's a miniature Rah, a little
kitten, like my Rah, a Rah Kitten that needed my love and guidance."

I hear Minty's deep draw of breath and know he's fighting hard
to nod sympathetically. "It hasn't been easy, Minty, really it hasn't,
I've had to be firm. Tough-love, that's what my mother called it."
My temper shimmers, but Rah reaches her hand out to me to hold me
back.

"Where is Orla now, Herrick?" Minty says, keeping his voice even.

"In the Special Room. I built it for my Rah, but she's such a sweet
little kitten, just like Rah, how could I not let her stay there?"
Choking, I hold my hand in front of my mouth.

"Is this Special Room in your house?"

"I swear to you, I've looked after her, she has everything she wants.
It's not what you think, Minty, it's not. We make music together, just
like Rah and I, just like it should've been if it wasn't for-for Maggi
and Jonny," he sneers again, before continuing. "That first night,
we played an Albinoni concerto to warm up before the Mozart. She
made some terrible mistakes, Minty. You'd think at grade 8, she
would've been better prepared. I had to correct her on a number of
occasions. You can care and love a little kitten but you won't be
doing them any favours if you don't correct their playing. Tough-

love, you see, Minty."

2023

"…I'd known Herrick for years though, truth to tell, I'd never given him much thought, but in all that time he had always come across as reserved, even tempered and pathetic. He was always the same, rain or shine, consistently boring. But it was like the fear stripped him of his outer shell, exposing a melting pot of emotions. He instantly latched onto Minty as some sort of confidant-cum-saviour."

"Like Stockholm Syndrome?" asks D.C.I. Logan.

"Uhm, maybe, but I felt it was more his inability to hide his true feelings. And they were truly fucked up. One minute he'd be whining, the next he'd be affronted, then companionable, as though Minty was his new best friend."

1998

"But I thought you were with Norah that first evening?" Minty queries and for the first time I hear an edge to Minty's voice. I know what's running through his brain. It's the same thoughts that are running through mine and probably everyone else's too. What does tough-love mean?

"I was with Rah, for a short while. She phoned me. I heard the distress in her voice, I heard her need for me. I went to comfort her, to rescue her. How could I not?"

"But I don't understand," Minty's tone wavers again. He pauses and clears his throat.

"Norah was distressed because Orla was missing and you knew where she was. You could have brought her home."

"I'm not stupid, Minty. I realise that but you have to see it from my point of view," snaps Herrick petulantly. "Rah needed me, I was important to her now. It was me who sat with her, comforted her, held her. I sat through that trial, she turned to me when Hoyle was found innocent. It was me who risked everything to kidnap Hoyle. Me that stood by her."

"I appreciate the fact that you've been around for Norah," strains

Minty through gritted teeth, as though he is learning to be a
ventriloquist.

"Why wouldn't I be, Minty? Haven't I explained that? We're soul-
mates, meant for each other."

Minty swallows hard. "When the police called that night and then
Maggi, was Orla with you?"

"Of course, I wouldn't have abandoned her, Minty, I'm not a
monster. I had to slip out to get rid of the bike but I was soon back to
comfort my little, frightened kitten. I'd just tucked her into bed," I'm
rising from the floor, my fists clenched as Jonny lets out a roar, deep
and wounded. I see Jim Bob grab his arm. Herrick flinches, "No,
help me, Minty, it's not what you think, I promise," he cries in
alarm. I stop myself from moving forward.

"You're fine, Buddy," Jim Bob soothes, "You know how strong I am,
I won't let Jonny hurt you." Herrick wobbles and I'm scared we've
lost him. Minty, with a mastery of self-restraint, reaches out and pats
his arm murmuring, "There, there, Herrick." Herrick's eyes flicker
around the room before refocusing on Minty. Minty smiles
benevolently back at him. "You were saying?" he asks sweetly.

"It's not what you think, Minty... I swear it ... I love my little Rah
Kitten. I'd never hurt her. That first night, I'd dressed her in one of
my mother's nightgowns. I'd brushed out her hair and tucked her in,
but she kept on crying, so I was comforting her. Tough-love, Minty,
that's what I told her." Rah moans quietly as I try to hang onto my
own agony. "When the police arrived in the early hours, they came
in briefly and then Maggi, I said she could come in for a cup of
something hot or I'd come and help her search."

"So you got out of bed, in the ...the Special Room," Minty stumbles
very slightly but recovers quickly, "and came downstairs to talk to
the police and then Maggi?" I know what he is doing, he's trying to
hide his real question inside a fake one.

"Yes," Herrick huffs. "Like I said, I was looking after her when the
police came, then Maggi, then I went back to take care of her. She
was frightened, Minty, can't you understand that?" he retorts
exasperatedly. "It was her first time away from home. She was a

279

little frightened Rah Kitten and I needed to coax and pet her. Do you know, Minty, she had a terrible accident the next day, poor, little kitten fell out of bed and knocked herself against the music stands..."

"Oh no, no, no..," I think, remembering the crashes Jonny and I'd heard when we were standing in Herrick's back garden that day.

"I had to bandage her up, you know, Minty, and kiss her better. She's much happier now, no more crying."

I try to ignore the kissing bit and focus on the tense he has used. I repeat the statement in my head, "She's much happier now, no more crying," and a desperate hope fills my mind. Could Orla still be alive?

I see Minty's jaw working before he manages to casually ask, "Is Orla still in the Special Room at your house, Herrick?" I hold my breath.

"Aren't you listening to anything I'm saying, Minty?" snaps Herrick indignantly. "I've said so, haven't I?" I look at Jonny and he looks at me.

"Yes, I'm listening to every word, Herrick, I can assure you," utters Minty gravely but Herrick doesn't seem to notice the change of timbre and carries on, as though they're the best of friends. "It's not been easy you know, looking after Rah and Rah Kitten. It has been very difficult; she can be unmanageable, recalcitrant. You understand, don't you Minty..." I hear him whine as I leave the room.

CHAPTER 47
Beacon of White

*

Maggi - 2023

"…What Herrick told Minty was a grotesque, fucked up version of the truth. He knew right enough that Orla was Orla, not Rah, but I think he saw her as a sort of pet Rah, a toy he could play with."

"What do you mean?" D.C.I. Logan asks.

"It's hard to find the right words to explain… but I think, I mean like a doll. Something he could use to play out his fantasies of Rah with. He called her his …" I don't want to say the name but I know I have to if I want them to understand, "his Rah Kitten," I gulp.

"Rah Kitten?" D.C. Fry repeats incredulously.

"Yeah," I shut my eyes, "a kitten to be played with and taught tricks. Though there was another big pay-off for him."

"What was that?" D.C.I. Logan asks.

"The fact, for the first time, Rah actually needed him. I really don't think that's why he took Orla, I think that was all to do with the miniature Rah Kitten thing. But this was like an unexpected reward, her gratitude, her love, for his support and help.

Anyway, eventually Minty got him to say Orla was being kept in a Special Room, upstairs in his house…"

1998

"Let's go," I mutter, looking at Jonny, who's holding Herrick's front door keys in one hand and his car keys in the other.

2023

"...Jonny and I took the Aston and tore down to Bosuns Road. It was broad daylight but we weren't thinking about covering our tracks, we were only thinking about rescuing Orla.

I rammed Herrick's keys into his front door and shoved it open. Inside, Jonny took the stairs two at a time and I followed. We found ourselves on a landing with four shut doors..."

1998

The corridor is dimly lit by a small window covered in an ancient net curtain, the doors, all made from dark wood, seem to crowd in on us. "Orla," I call as my toes curl in revulsion from the thick, musky carpet beneath my feet.

"Which one?" Jonny asks, not really needing an answer. I pull on the handle of the door nearest me, it clicks open and I push it gingerly with one finger. The room is as ancient as the net curtain, with an old stained enamel bath, a brown-cracked porcelain toilet and a large hand basin.

"Urgh," I shiver as I move to the next door, calling Orla's name. Jonny tries the first door to the right. "Maggs," he calls softly. I go to him and stare into the gloom. Even with the room clocked in darkness, I can see the beacon of white.

"Oh fuck no. No, no, no," I moan.

2023

"...We tried a couple of doors before Jonny found the right one. The room was dark, as the curtains were shut but we could just make out a double bed covered in something brown and a full-sized freezer stood against the far wall..."

1998

"Do you think..." he can't bring himself to complete the question "Fuck," is all I'm able to say. Reaching for the light switch, Jonny clicks it on. A single, un-shaded bulb flickers into life, casting a mottled gloom that barely illuminates the centre of the room. I feel

sick with apprehension and fear as I force myself forward.

"Maggs," Jonny says softly, and I turn and see what he's looking at. It's a small table laid for two, next to a double bed and a couple of music stands.

"What the fuck," I gasp, not really understanding what I'm seeing but instinctively knowing it's something really, really horrible.

We stand in front of the 6ft white cabinet together, like Hansel and Gretel lost in the forest. Dread fills my soul, I want to run away, I don't want to look.

"We'll do it together, Jonny," I say, taking his hand.

"Okay," he breathes, wiping the tears from his eyes.

"But if we find her, let's try and make it better for Rah and the others. Let's try and-and- sort it out somehow."

"Okay," he murmurs again, gripping my hand hard. Neither of us moves.

"I'll open it," I say after a while.

"No, I'll do it, but don't let go of my hand."

"I'm here, all the way." I try to sound composed and brave but my voice wobbles betraying my fears.

We step forward and I see him reach for the shiny handle, his fingers shake as he grasps it. He waits. Then I feel his body tighten as he pulls against the rubber seals.

A harsh, bright light floods out into the tenebrous room and I force my eyes to see.

2023

"…It was Jonny who opened the freezer door. Inside, sat Orla smiling blindly back at us, surrounded by white and sparkling, like an ice princess in a Disney movie."

"I don't understand, if she was dead how was she smiling?" asks D.C. Fry.

"I'm sure you don't, neither did I."

There's a firmness to my voice now. With each word, each explanation, I feel the full force of my anger firing on all four cylinders. It's no longer the pathetic anger I've been shielding myself behind since the start of the confession. It's raw and spiteful. If Hitler had walked in now, I'd have taken the shitting bastard on and beaten his ugly face to a pulp. I'm not sure if Logan felt it, but she leans ever so slightly forward in her seat.

"Jonny and I stood shell-shocked and silent, staring at the apparition that had once been our daughter. And it was then that I heard a low keening, like something an injured animal might make, coming from behind us. I turned to see Rah standing in the doorway with her hands clasped to her mouth. I went to her, calling her name, telling her not to look, but she didn't hear me, she just stumbled forward. I tried to close the freezer door but Rah held her hand against it and said, 'Oh fucking hell no, it's me'…"

1998

Pulling my eyes from Rah I stare at Orla again. Her long, beautiful hair is fastened high on her head and hangs like a river of dark ice down over one shoulder. Around her tiny neck, sparkles a sapphire necklace with matching earrings glinting in each ear, they're identical to the set I bought Rah for her 30th birthday. I stare at the dress, which falls in stiff folds to the white floor. The strong colour peeks through the veil of ice. I know this gown, it's soft silk, it's red swirls against Rah's dark skin, it's the Zuki gown.

Orla's small arms are raised at the elbow; the finger tips and thumbs holding a slim circular wooden pole. "Like an oboe," I say aloud, as Rah's words dawn on me.

2023

"…And she was right. Sweet, innocent Orla had been bastardised and manipulated into a distorted copy of Rah."

"How?" D.C.I. Logan asks.

"She'd been dressed in the Zuki evening gown, the one that we'd thought the bassoonist had nicked, with her hair styled in a manner Rah used for concerts. Her hands were frozen into a position to hold an oboe.

It must've taken me minutes to understand this, because by the time I turned back, Rah was no longer there..."

1998

"Rah?" I murmur and look at Jonny. He's on his hands and knees, there's a pool of vomit next to him. He retches and is sick again.

"Jonny, Oh God Jonny," I say, kneeling next to him and taking him in my arms. "Oh fuck, Jonny."

"I don't understand," he sobs. "Why the fuck would anyone do that?"

"I know. Fuck I know. Shh, shh," I murmur through my tears. We sit bathed in the caustic light, holding each other, looking at our daughter. After a while, Jonny breaks away and wipes his face on his shirt. "What are we going to do, Maggs?" he asks, "you know, what you said about changing her, turning her back into Orla for the others?"

"Oh fuck, Rah," I mutter sniffing up as much snot as possible.

"What?" Jonny mumbles.

"Rah, we have to go and find her. She was here, she saw Orla, didn't you hear what she said?"

"No? What?

"She said Orla has been ...never mind. We have got to find her, Jonny. Shit, what if she's gone back to yours to... "

"Kill Herrick?" he finished for me.

"Yes." I leap up, but before I go, I look, one last time, at the abomination that had been fashioned from our daughter.

"Orla, my Love, my sweet, sweet baby, I'll be back to bring you home, Darling, I promise." Shutting the freezer door gently, I take Jonny's hand. We stumble out onto the landing, down the stairs and out the front door. Jonny's car is gone. I stand dumbstruck and stupefied, staring at the empty space.

Jonny lets go of my hand. "Herrick's keys." A moment later, he's pulling me around to the back garden, then down the path and into the garage. "Come on, Maggs," he shouts, unlocking Herrick's Sierra. Everything inside of me screams in revulsion at the idea of getting into that car. "Get in, Maggs," Jonny orders, turning the key in the ignition. Covering my mouth, I climb in. The smell of leather and stale aftershave makes me heave and I'm sick in the footwell. Jonny ignores me and reverses out, spinning the wheels, turns and accelerates down Lead Lane.

2023

"…Jonny and I left Orla and went after Rah. We'd guessed she'd headed back to Pump Road to take revenge on Herrick. Neither of us gave a flying fuck about the cunt but we did about Rah and Orla. We were still working on the assumption that we'd be ringing the police, that they'd arrest Herrick and we'd be bring Orla home to have a proper burial…"

1998

Slamming the breaks on, we screech to a halt in Pump Road. The Aston, with the driver's door hanging open, sits abandoned in the middle of the street, blocking both lanes. Two other vehicles are queued in front of it, unable to pass.

"Oi, Mate," shouts one of the drivers who is standing, looking at the marooned Aston Martin, rubbing his chin, "Do you know whose car this is?"

"Oh, Jonny, is that you?" calls the other driver, leaning out of her car window. "Would you mind awfully moving your car?"

"Go," Jonny orders me while raising a hand of apology. "Sorry, sorry, I'll move it straight away."

Running to the rear of the house, I fly in through the kitchen door. Minty, Gwen, and Jim Bob look up at me as I dash past. Around the corner, into the hall, I push through the plastic curtain into the Kill Room. Rah is kneeling over Herrick's head, spitting in his face.

"For this, all for this!" she snarls with pure hate. She's naked and her hands are between her legs while the Roc-filled syringe hangs empty out of the cannula.

"For this, you killed her for this," she hisses as I round the trolley and see her pulling her labia apart, displaying her vagina.

"Oh, Rah, no, no, he's not worth it," I moan, putting my arms

around her. Then, Jonny's there, Minty too, followed by Jim Bob and Gwen. "Oh, Rah, no." I pull her from the trolley and cradle her in my arms, rocking her.

I vaguely see Jonny firing up the defibrillator as Jim Bob grabs the Ambu-bag and uselessly pumps air into Herrick's lungs.

"Stand back," hollers Jonny as he presses the paddles to Herrick's chest.

Bang. Nothing. Charge.

Bang. Nothing. Charge.

Bang. Nothing. Charge.

Bang. Nothing. Charge.

Bang. Nothing. Charge.

"Jonny. Jonny, stop," Gwen's gentle voice cuts through the electrical tension filling the room. "Jonny, he's dead. It's over."

CHAPTER 48
Pasty Blubber

*

Maggi - 2023
"…By the time we'd reached Jonny's house, Rah had already killed Herrick."
"How?" both Officers ask in unison.
"She'd injected the Rocuronium into his system and watched him asphyxiate…"

1998
Taking off my jacket, I cover Rah's nakedness, she looks at me tear-stained and crazed.
"I saw him die, Maggs." She articulates each syllable with pure venom. "I saw him struggle. I saw him panic. I looked into his eyes as he suffocated, Maggs, and I saw who I really am."

2023
"…I felt her satisfaction, her vengeance, but I felt her hate too and unlike my own hate, which I directed outwards, hers was personal, hers was against herself."
D.C. Fry's face creases into his next question, "Why?" he asks.
"Because she believed it was her fault Orla died. She blamed herself for mistaking Herrick's friendship as something special, something born from their shared love of oboe music, instead of seeing it as a flawed obsession.

When we all stood in front of that freezer and saw Orla dressed as a macabre version of Rah, Jonny and I didn't get it, well, not in the way Rah did. She interpreted it as her own failing that she'd allowed this monster in, that she'd encouraged his love without fulfilling her role by giving him what he wanted, her body. So he'd taken the next best thing, her child's body."

"But that's..." D.C. Fry pauses.

I know he's searching for the right adjective, just as I know there isn't one. So I finish the sentence for him.

"Mad. I understand it doesn't make sense to you, as it didn't to Jonny or me. But that's who Rah was. Jonny and I suffered, we still do, you only have to look at the Christmas trees to know the truth in that. But for Rah it was different, so much worse. Her imagination took her to places we could never perceive.

I didn't and still don't blame her for killing Herrick, to be honest, I would probably have done it anyway as I'm sure Jonny would have too."

"Be careful what you say, Maggi," D.C.I. Logan warns gently.

"Thanks," I smile, "but I'm beyond caring for myself and I'm pretty sure no one is going to bother with Jonny..."

1998

I look up at the others; they're as stunned and shocked as me.

"Jonny, we have to save Rah, we have to ..."

"No, Orla must be rescued," demands Rah.

"Yes. We'll get rid of the body somehow. Maybe burn the house down."

"Or cut him up," I blurt out.

"No, too much blood, too much evidence," utters Jim Bob.

"Dump him then," I bargain.

"No, Orla. It doesn't matter about me," Rah insists.

"Just stop." I look at Minty standing there, tall and elegant in his evening suit, next to the ginger topped mound of pasty blubber. "We need to think, but not here, not with that thing," he nods towards the body, "it's clouding our judgements, making us rash."

"Rash, I think we're a bit passed rash now, Minty," but I keep my mouth shut.

"Maggi," he continues, "take Norah home in Jonny's car. Gwen, Jim Bob walk back calmly to Peartree Road while Jonny and I lock this house up and return Herrick's car and make sure his house is secure. We don't want anyone poking around in there. Then, and only then, will we come up with something."

Gwen picks up Rah's black t-shirt. "Here, Norah, let me help you," she says. I pull Rah gently to her feet and Gwen slips it over her head. "Now, the leggings." She brushes her daughter's crop hair with her fingers and wipes her face on the corner of her own skirt. "There," she murmurs, "that'll do, just the shoes now."

"Mum…" Rah begins.

"We'll deal with that later, Norah, but first let's get rid of the body and bring our Orla home, safe and sound."

Jonny hands me his car keys. "Here, I'll see you later."

"Yeah," I say, hugging him hard.

Jim Bob takes Gwen's arm. "We'll go first, Bigster." I look at the two of them, a most unlikely pair. Gwen in her finery, Jim Bob still dressed in black, both exhausted, both devastated, both involved in a crime that they hadn't chosen to commit.

They push through the plastic curtain and then out the front door. I glance at the body, hate consumes me and I punch it as hard as I can, then again, and again and again, sobbing loudly.

"That's enough, Maggi," Minty says, stopping my fist. "Take Rah home." I turn and look at her, waif like and marooned in her grief. She looks at me, her eyes large and glassy. I take her hand, gripping the keys hard in the other, hurting my palm. Nodding to the others, I leave.

An hour later, Jonny and Minty appear. Both look grey and drawn, both look determined. "So, Minty and I think we should try to get rid of the body before we consider involving the police."

"Okay," I agree, "But Bro, I think you should go home, you shouldn't be here for this, then that way you can't be connected to Herrick's murder if the police find out."

"I'm not going anywhere, Bigster, so forget it," he states flatly. "Anyway, you'll need help lifting that fat bastard."

"But what about Orla? I'd rather go to jail for murder than leave Orla where she is," Rah cries.

"I won't leave her there, I made her a promise," I tell her sincerely.

"I've had an idea." We all look at Gwen.

2023

"…We decided it was worth trying to get rid of Herrick's body to protect Rah. Though I'd already made a secret pact with myself to take the blame, if need be. There was no way I was going to let Rah go to prison and I reasoned that Jonny and Gwen wouldn't have fared much better either. Minty and Jim Bob might have managed but, why should they? Orla was my daughter and like I said, I was going to kill Herrick anyway.

It was Gwen who came up with the idea of secretly laying Orla to rest here, in the garden…"

1998

"It seems to me," Gwen begins, "whatever we do about Herrick, one way or another Orla needs to have a proper burial, a proper grave. And I can't see why it should really matter where that is, as long as we can all visit it. So, I was thinking, perhaps, we could bury her here."

"Yes," Rah smiles through her tears.

"What about in the wildflower meadow she helped me sow? Jonny, what do you think?" I ask, turning to him.

He smiles sadly back. "I think that's perfect. But I want to get rid of that fucking bastard first. I want him gone from our lives before we lay our daughter to rest. Like Jim Bob said, he's no lightweight. Has anyone got any idea about what we should do with him?"

"Bury him, that's got to be the easiest option," asserts Jim Bob as though he has had years of practice at disposing of bodies.

"Please, not here," Rah begs.

"No, not here, but I suppose we could burying him at mine," Jonny

offers, "under the floor boards or in the garden. That way, we won't have to move him far."

"Nah, too obvious. If there's an investigation your house will be one of the first to be searched," states Jim Bob confidently again.

"At his?" I suggest.

"Nah again, Bigster. Too obvious and the neighbours will question what we are doing. Also, we might have to sell the house, then where would we be?"

"Herrick's house," murmurs Rah. I look at her chewing her fingers and know she's not thinking about Herrick but about how Orla's been there all this time.

"Okay, it'll have to be away from the houses but that means shifting the body. It's got to be somewhere where digging and moving soil isn't suspicious," Minty lists sequentially, "somewhere that's easily accessible, somewhere that we kno…"

"I know where," I cut across him.

"Where, Bigster?"

"My allotment."

"No, Maggs, that's not fair, it will destroy it for you. It's your sanctuary, your refuge from all this shit," Rah jumps in.

"Rah's right, Maggs," Jonny agrees. "It's your place."

"Yes, but it's perfect. I can dig the hole, stack the earth, disperse the surplus and no one will question it."

"It's perfect, especially if you dig the grave inside the shed," adds Gwen.

"Is that possible, Maggi? Minty asks.

CHAPTER 49
Pale Starlight and Inky Heavens

Maggi - 2023

"…And, as you know, we decided to bury Herrick under the allotment shed. It was easy enough as far as disposing of a body goes.

That afternoon I went to the allotment on my own and tidied my shed, putting my stuff in my barrow and wheeling it home. In the evening I went back with Jim Bob and we raised the wooden floor and began to dig. We bagged the soil and stacked it outside, by the compost bins. About 2 o'clock in the morning Jonny and Minty turned up and took over…"

1998

Jim Bob leaves for a shower, food and some sleep but I'm too full of hurt and hate, so I lay down between my runner bean rows and watch the pale starlight against the inky heavens.

"FUCK," I scream silently as I remember how I'd stood at Herrick's front door that first night, so wrapped up in my own pain that I couldn't see what was in-front of me. It makes me cry with the senselessness of it all. Eventually my tears turned to sleep because the next thing I know someone is shaking me awake.

"Maggs."

"What? What?" I shout, fists ready to strike.

"Maggs, you're fine, it's me Jonny."

293

"Fuck," I breathe. "What is it?"

"We've finished. Come and look, see what you think." Light is creeping across the eastern sky as I climb out from under the beans. I can smell their sweet freshness; I know I will never eat anything from here again. Inside my shed there's a great, dark cavernous hole.

"How deep do you reckon it is?" I ask.

"I'm over 6ft and it's above my head," Jonny answers, "though there's one problem."

"Oh?"

"We can't widen it without the walls collapsing," Minty sighs tiredly, leaning on my spade.

"In that case we'll just have to bend the cunt over to bury him," I mutter.

"Yeah, that's what we thought. Can you check everything looks normal outside, Maggi before we go? I would hate anyone to snoop around." I take a look, move a few bags and tidy some soil before locking the shed door and putting the key back under my water butt.

2023

"…We'd finished digging by dawn and trudged home through the silent streets, all of us dog-tired. I was deep in thought when Minty asked us if we'd had any ideas on how we were going to organise Orla's funeral.

To be honest, I was so focussed on getting rid of the fat turd laying at Jonny's that I'd pushed Orla's funeral to the back of my mind. But that wasn't the whole story. The whole story was now that the police weren't going to be involved, I was scared of what else we'd find when we went back to Herrick's."

"In what way?" asks D.C. Fry.

"Mainly, I guess, the evidence that was bound to be on Orla's body. What he'd done to her, what he'd made her do, how she'd suffered, how'd she'd died. I wanted to run away from the truth, I didn't want to see it or have to deal with it.

So I told Minty I'd not really thought about it. He said he and

Gwen had had a chat and they'd thought of a way to have Orla's committal without attracting too much attention.

Their idea was to hire a small wedding marquee, with a covered tunnel leading from the house. Something large enough to dig beneath and something a coffin could be carried through unseen. Also, if asked, something that could be explained as a family gathering in memory of Orla..."

1998

"That's brilliant, Minty," I say, genuinely grateful for the idea. "What does Rah think?"

"She likes it. Jonny?"

"Yeah, it's fine by me," he agrees wearily.

"I'll get on and order it as soon as possible then."

2023

"...Minty also said that they thought it was only right to let Arthur and Amelia, Rah's brother and sister, know Orla had been found and whether I thought I should tell my parents too..."

1998

"Really, Minty, do you think that's a good idea?" snaps Jonny, too tired to try and hide his irritation. "And I'll tell you something for nothing, don't even think about asking me to tell my parents."

"I have no intention of mentioning Herrick to them," Minty retorts in a voice that's equally fucked off, "but I'm sure Arthur and Amelia will want to know that we've found Orla."

Jonny doesn't answer and I just keep putting one tired foot in front of another.

"We'll talk about it some more when we've got rid of the body," Minty adds grumpily.

"The body," I ponder silently as I plod along and after a while, I say, "There's something I've been thinking we should get before the day's out."

"What?" they both ask turning on me.

2023

"...Back home, Rah, Jim Bob and Gwen were all flaked out in the sitting room. You might wonder how any of us could sleep with Herrick on the trolley at Jonny's and our sweet Orla still frozen in her world of horror. But we'd been on a rollercoaster of torture and death for nearly three days and we were exhausted, both mentally and physically.

Jonny set about making us all food while I drove to the hospital to break into the new transplant suite. I pretty much expected it to be closed for the Bank Holiday weekend, as no one rich enough to buy organs needed to schedule an operation during a holiday. Jonny offered to come too, but unlike me he hadn't slept.

At the hospital no one gave me a second glance as I headed for the top floor..."

1998

The lift clanks softly to a stop and the doors slide open. Shades of pastel greens surround an unmanned reception desk. I step out onto a thick carpet and look around. All is quiet and ordered. To my left, is a seating area with leather sofas, fashion magazines and potted plants. Turning right, I pass the consulting rooms and single-bed wards. Glancing in, I can see they are stocked with the latest in medical technology and media entertainment.
"Fucking Conservatives," I mutter as my anger, never far away, surfaces at the thought of the barely adequate wards below.

Farther along I see what I'm looking for, a pair of rubber sealed doors with 'No entry unless authorised,' written above it. Praying my security code works in the private sector, I swipe my I.D. card and push against one of the doors. It pops open and I find myself in familiar territory. Clinical and clean, no carpets, no potted plants and no soothing greens.

A wide-berthed lift stands open, it's brand new and shiny and I know instinctively which floor it drops to, floor 9, where the sleeping dead wait to be harvested. I shudder and move on through the next set of sealed doors into a layout that I know well. Anaesthetic room, scrub room, two theatres, recovery room and store cupboard.

2023

"…And found what I was looking for, the supply cupboard that held the body bags for the new transplant theatres…"

1998

"Knew it," I mutter as I grab one of the vacuum-packed parcels. Driving home, I find the others up and eating spaghetti Bolognese, they hand me a bowl, I eat it standing up, not wanting to waste any more time.

CHAPTER 50
Game Face

Maggi - 2023

"...Back at Jonny's, I dumped the body bag on the floor. The plastic sheeting at the window diluted the strong sun but already the room had begun to smell of decay. I looked at Herrick lying in his own shit and watched a fly walk across one of his eyeballs while another crawled into his gaping mouth.

Rah came to my side and slipped her small hand into mine. She asked if I was angry with her for killing Herrick. I told her, no, not one little tiny bit, which was true. Then Jonny and I gloved up and washed the body down, shoving a hospital gown on him while the others began to dismantle the room."

"Why did you bother to wash him?" D.C. Fry asks.

"I didn't want Rah's DNA to be found on his body if it was discovered. Jonny opened the body bag on the floor and all of us lugged Herrick and his clothes in and zipped it shut.

After that we tried bending the bag double and securing it with duct tape but it just won't hold. In the end Jonny came up with the solution. He went and got a couple of climbing ropes."

"Were they red? The climbing ropes, I mean," D.C. Fry asks.

"Yes, maybe, I don't really remember. Anyway, Jonny made a sort of noose, which we eased over the bag, feeling for the knee and neck joints. Then pulling the rope tight, he wrapped it around several times. He did the same thing with the other rope but in the opposite direction before tying it off with one of his climbing knots."

"A Grapevine Bend," D.C. Fry states knowingly.

1998

Any ideas on how we're going to get him to the allotment?" I sigh, already feeling drained.

"Trolley, we can put him back on the trolley, cover it with a sheet and stick him in the transit van. If we do it sort of casually, the neighbours won't even register what we're up to." Jim Bob suggests.

"What? In broad day light?" I say, astonished as I stare at the massive, black lump tied up with red ropes in a neat knot.

"Why not? What have we got to lose, Bigster? We're in it up to our necks anyway and while we are on the matter, there's no way you are taking the rap for this on your own."

"No one said anything to me about Maggi taking the blame. I didn't agree to that," interjects Gwen.

"Fucking not," I mutter.

"I know you, Bigster, so forget it."

"Maggs? What's he saying?" Rah asks in alarm.

"Fucking nothing, forget it, Rah," I snap back at her, my anger spilling over.

"No I won't, Maggs, and if anyone is going to suffer for what I've done, it's me ... and me alone."

"Leave it you three, now's not the time," bridles Jonny.

"Well you're not doing it either," Rah retorts.

"Fucking right there, you'd not last a minute with your pretty boy's arse," I fling out, "And another thing, Minty, I agree with Jonny, it's a fucking twatty idea telling Arthur and Amelia."

"What the hell? Dad? You can't be serious?"

"Holy frigging smoke, I never signed up for broadcasting that we'd murder someone. Are you for real?" Jim Bob demands.

"Okay, that's enough," Gwen says quietly. "Let's focus on getting rid of the body. In some ways I can see that Jim Bob's suggestion is quite sensible."

"You would," I say sulkily.

"It would look more suspicious if we were loading the van in the dark whereas in daylight who's going to question it?" I stomp out of the room, through the kitchen and out the door. I'm thankful Jonny's garden is overgrown, as I find a secluded spot and burst into tears.

A moment later I feel his big hand on my back. "Bigster, I'm sorry. That was stupid of me to blurt your plan out."

"How'd you know?"

"How'd I know that you always wanted to be an Native American rather than a Cowboy, that you love chocolate and hate jelly, and that you're scared of snakes but like insects. I've known and loved you all my life, why wouldn't I know? Besides, you were taking great care to bleach Herrick's face and chest."

"Oh," I mutter.

"Yeah, oh." He hands me a tissue and I blow my nose loudly.

"Better?"

"Yeah, better," I say.

"Come on, get your game face on, Bigster, and let's go and commit another crime together."

2023

"…Jim Bob came up with the idea of moving Herrick in daylight to avoid looking too suspicious."

"Impressive," D.C. Fry expresses, earning him a look from his senior officer.

"I know, right, especially when I added in my idea to it."

"Which was?" asks D.C.I. Logan.

"That we should move him in my wheelbarrow."

"In the wheelbarrow?" D.C. Fry echoes, even more impressed.

"Yes," I smile. "The others weren't that keen but as it turned out, it was a brilliant idea. I went home and collected the barrow with some garden tools and a few burlap sacks and wheeled it into Jonny's back garden.

We managed to drag Herrick to the back door and haul him into the barrow. I covered the body bag with some soil and the sacks, then tested the load. It actually wasn't too bad, though really heavy.

Jim Bob and Jonny picked up the tools and we set off, leaving the others to clear the rest up.

The streets were quiet and hot; the afternoon still. A few flies buzzed around our load as I made it to the end of Pump Road before Jim Bob took over, then Jonny before it was my turn again. By the time we reached the allotment side gate, on Blind Lane, we'd only seen four people, a man teaching his son to ride a bike and two dog walkers. They all gave us a passing hello, though one of the dogs was really interested..."

1998

At the side gate, I look at the lock.

"Shit, I haven't brought the gate key," I mutter through clenched teeth.

"I'll go and get it," Jonny offers.

"No, I'll go. I'll know where to look. Are you two going to be okay?"

"Bigster, I'm sure Jonny and I can manage just as well on our own and if a passing police officer does decide to inspect our load, I'm sure we can do a...Oh My Garrrd...a body, officer! I don't know where that came from." The parody of Jonny at his campiest makes us all burst out laughing.

"Fuck off," I say between giggles, "And don't say body."

"What, like there's anybody here," Jim Bob grins.

"Hello, Maggi, forgot your keys?" Mr Peterson asks from the other side of the gate, making us all jump.

"No. Yes, yes, I have, Mr Peterson," I splutter.

"No worries, I'll let you in but I'm afraid you'll have to leave via the main gate and walk the long way home."

"That's fine, thank you, Mr Peterson." Jim Bob, pressing his lips tight together, pushes the barrow through the gate and along the path. Jonny follows as I see Mr Peterson out and thank him again.

"Fuck," I chuckle when I catch up with them.

"You can say that again, Bigster."

"I think I'm going to be sick," Jonny gulps and throws up.

2023

"…There was only a couple of people at the allotment, pottering around their own plots. They both raised their hands in greeting but neither spoke. I think since I'd told old Mr Andrews to, 'piss off,' a lot of them were wary of talking to me.

We wheeled the barrow to the shed. I found the key under the water butt and unlocked the door. Jonny and I stepped in and stood on either side of the hole. We grabbed the end of the body bag and guided it as Jim Bob tipped the barrow up. It sort of hovered for a split second before toppling in. Jim Bob and Jonny collected the soil bags from outside and I heaved them onto the body bag. When it was as good as covered, I jumped down and stamped the air out of the earth…"

1998

"You fucking, cunting, bastard," I chant under my breath, to the beat of my stamping feet.

2023

"…It didn't take long before we pretty much had a flat surface again. We re-laid the floor not bothering to nail it back in place. I knew I could do that at a later date, though I did park the barrow over the top of it and rearrange the tools. Outside, there was still a massive pile of earth and several more soil sacks but I wasn't bothered, as I knew no one would question it.

Back at Pump Road, the others were having a major discussion over the disposal of the equipment. Minty wanted to buy a metal cutter and chop it up and dump it. Gwen and Rah thought it would be better to return it to the hospital. At first, I thought they were bonkers, but the more I listened to their reasoning, the more sense it made.

"It what way?" D.C. Fry asks.

"Their argument was that if parts of medical equipment started showing up on dump sites, questions could be asked as to where it had come from, whereas nobody was going to take much notice of a trolley etc sitting in a disused hospital corridor. So we washed and repacked the equipment in the cardboard and loaded the van. By the time we had manoeuvred the trolley back into the hallway, the day was drawing in. The smell of barbecues was strong as Jonny covered the trolley in a sheet and Minty and I rolled it back out to the van.

Obviously, we didn't have Herrick this time and to say we were tired was an understatement, but it actually went really smoothly. At the hospital, Jonny pushed Rah in the wheelchair holding the Ambubag, heart machine and defibrillator, while I returned the trolley and the tournie, to the dark basement corridor. 30 minutes later we were back at Jonny's, packing up the last of the plastic..."

CHAPTER 51
My Sister My Heart

*

Maggi - 1998

"Fuck, I'm tired," I think as I pull the duct tape up from the floor and begin rolling up the plastic sheeting. When I get to where the wheelchair had sat there's a small pool of dried blood, cracked and mottled like old ceramics. "Hoyle's blood," I mutter as a feeling of spiteful satisfaction momentarily pushes aside my tiredness. "He deserved it."

Finding the bleach, I scrub it up.

"What shall we do with the bin bags?" Gwen asks. I look tiredly at the eight waste bags, wishing they'd just disappear.

"Why not just leave them out for the bin truck. With the holiday and all there's bound to be extra rubbish for them to pick up," suggests Jim Bob.

"I'll take a couple back to ours," I volunteer.

"I can take three to London," Jim Bob adds.

Gwen holds her hand up. "We'll take one."

"Okay, and I'll put the other two out with my rubbish," Jonny says.

I wake on Tuesday morning to the sound of the bin truck taking the rubbish bags and feel relieved that the plastic sheeting is on its way to the rubbish dump.

The garden is already filled with birdsong and sunlight as I thread my way towards the kitchen.

"Today," I tell the birds, "I can keep my promise to Orla." The bi-folding doors stand open, the others are sitting around the table.
"Morning, Bigster."
"Hey, Bro," I say, kissing his head.
"Maggs," Rah smiles at me as I sit next to her.
"Coffee?" Jonny asks as he goes to the kitchen to get my mug.
"Yeah," I yawn.
"And breakfast, I think, for all of us," Minty adds firmly.

2023

"…The following day, we talked about the thing that we all wanted to decide upon more than anything else, how we were going to bring Orla home. Minty ordered the marquee but the earliest they could do was Friday, the 11th of September. So we set the date for Orla's funeral for Saturday, the 12th of September, that meant we could start the process of bringing her home on the Wednesday before…"

1998

"I don't see why she can't come home now," demands Rah.
"Think about it, Sweetheart, we've nowhere to keep her," explains Gwen.
"I understand what you are saying, but why can't we bring the whole freeze here?"
"That would be really tricky. It's going to be suspicious enough collecting Orla as it is, without lugging a freeze out too," Jonny reasons. I hadn't really thought about it, I'd just presumed, like Rah, we'd go and get her as soon as we'd got rid of Herrick but now I can see how weird it would look if we all troop in and out of the fat twat's house, shifting his things about, without him being there. Huffing slightly, I say, "I think Jonny's got a point, Rah. We can't just bowl up, let ourselves into Herrick's house willy-nilly and take his stuff without attracting attention."
"And that's another thing," Minty adds, "We need to keep a low profile around his house. We need to think carefully about how and when we go there."

"Going in the back door would be the most discreet. Lead Lane is dark at night, no one will see us enter or leave if we are careful," I suggest, shuddering slightly at the memory of how dark and deserted it was the night Jonny and I searched it.

"Okay, so we need to get the back-door key then. Also, I think we should check out his bills and mortgage," Gwen advises.

"He doesn't have a mortgage, Mum, he bought the house right after his mother died."

"He might have borrowed against it," Jim Bob says.

Rah shakes her head, "Not him."

"Too much of a hoarding miser," I mutter.

2023

"…We also discussed how we were going to cover Herrick's absence up. After a few suggestions, from burning his house down to faking his suicide, we decided to write a letter from him to LGO saying a fictitious elderly German aunt had fallen ill and he, being her only living relative, had to travel to Germany to assist her. As September is the annual break for the orchestra, the timing couldn't have been better.

Minty and Jonny volunteered to go back to Herrick's house that night and riffle through his paper work and collect samples of his hand writing and signature, his bills, bank statements, cheque books etc…"

1998

"You're on your own for this one, guys, I've got to go back to work, but I'll see you all next week. I'll take annual leave and come down after work on Tuesday evening," says Jim Bob, getting up from the table.

"Thanks, Bro," I say hugging him hard.

"Jim Bob, how do I begin to say thank you?" Rah murmurs, hugging him too. Then the others join in. We sort of cling to each other bounded now by more than just grief.

Later, when half the world is still and all sane people are asleep

in bed, Minty and Jonny get themselves ready to go.
"Jonny," I say, catching him in the hallway, "will you…"
"No, I'll not go upstairs, unless I have to."

2023

"…In the morning, Jonny, impersonating Herrick, contacted his water, phone, and gas suppliers and cancelled his accounts asking them to send through their final bills. For obvious reasons, we left the electrical supply on."

I see D.C. Fry beginning to question this but D.C.I. Logan softly says, "The freezer."

"Yeah, sorry," he mumbles.

"It's fine, there's no need to apologise. Rah proved to be our best counterfeiter and she composed something she knew wouldn't be questioned by the LGO.

As the week wore on, my nerves frayed ever thinner as I fretted over what waited for us in Herrick's house. Jonny and I worked, booking time off for the following week. On Saturday, we cleared the music room and set up a table in there, covering the floor and table in yet more plastic sheeting, but this time with a multitude of towels. Gwen went shopping and bought a stack of hot water bottles and other stuff.

We'd just finished when Amelia turned up. I don't know Amelia that well but I'd recognise her anywhere. She looks a lot like Minty, tall and slim, though she has Gwen's warm skin tones and dark eyes… Rah and Orla's eyes.

She'd come bearing gifts…"

1998

"Norah," she murmurs, hugging Rah, "My sister, my heart." I look daggers, first at Minty then, at Gwen.

"Amelia, how come?" Rah asks bewildered.

"Don't worry dearest, Dad and Mum haven't told me anything, only that Orla will be coming home. I'll be here Friday evening on my own; I'll not say anything to Simon. Arthur is flying in on Saturday

morning too. He's due to land at 7a.m. our time, so he should be here by mid-day.

Come Norah, come and see what I have brought Orla, see if you think it will do." Taking her sister's hand, she leads Rah out of our front door to the back of her large car. I follow with Minty, Gwen and Jonny in tow. Raising the rear door, Amelia steps back and I see a look of wonderment break across Rah's face.

"It's beautiful, Amelia, thank you," Rah smiles. Stepping forward, I glance in. A wicker casket, woven with bleached willow, sits in the back of the car.

"Oh, Amelia, it is beautiful," I murmur in agreement. Gwen smiles at me and I know she is in on it too.

"I will bring the flowers on Friday evening, Norah, and we'll weave them, with our love, into the wicker."

2023

"...She'd brought Orla a coffin, one made from willow. It was a beautiful thing with plaited edges, white rope handles and a deep bed of pure white cotton. And I loved her for what she'd done for her sister. When she left, I walked out to her car with her and thanked her again. But she must've seen my troubled look, as she told me she and Arthur knew nothing of what had happened to Orla or how we'd found her and she assured me that they would never ask. She also promised me that they would never tell anyone where Orla was to be buried. And I believed her..."

1998

"Remember, Maggi, I've two children of my own and I'd do anything, anything, for them."

CHAPTER 52
Small Life

*

Maggi - 2023

"…That night, thunder rolled across Godlinghoe, threatening to break the heat wave.

Rah woke up screaming. She wanted to go to Herrick's and be with Orla but, instead, we went out into the garden. We watched the lightening crack in the southern sky but no rain fell. By the morning we'd marked out where our daughter was to lie.

The following days were just as desperate for Rah. I wanted more than anything to go and rescue Orla too but, as you know, my want, unlike Rah's, was edged with fear. Finally, Wednesday came…"

1998

Driving down Bosuns Road, Jim Bob turns right into Lead Lane. I lean forward from the back seat. "Switch your lights off from here, Bro." We creep along, keeping the engine in a low gear. At Herrick's we roll to a stop. My heart rate doubles its beat and I feel sweat prick my armpits.

"Rah, are you sure you want to do this?" Jonny whispers, turning to her.

"Yes," she says firmly.

"Okay, give me 5 minutes to open the back door before you two come," he whispers, switching off the interior lights, so when the car door is opened no light will show.

"Right," I murmur as Jonny quietly opens the front nearside door and clicks it gently closed. I see his dark shape pull on the rucksack and move to the side wall of Herrick's garage. I check my watch. The minutes tick slowly by, before I say, "Okay Bro, see you in a bit."

"Bigster..."

"Yeah?"

"Nothing. Just take care."

"I will," I say, touching his shoulder as Rah lifts the car door handle and slips her slight frame out of the vehicle. I make more of a pig's ear of it before finding her leaning against the garage wall. She takes my hand and squeezes it reassuringly.

I look towards the back door. The swollen moon hangs pale above the row of houses, casting dappled shadows across the garden. I swallow my fear and follow Rah along the path. She reaches the back steps, climbs and pushes gently against the door. It opens. I see her steal through. I touch the doorjamb and step in. Jonny's there. He takes Rah's hand and she mine, then we weave our way through the cluttered house to the stairs.

Each tread creaks as we climb. At the top we turn into the dingy corridor. I can smell the old, musky carpet beneath my feet, making me feel sick. Jonny reaches the door and opens it. We step in. I hear the low hum from the freezer; it vibrates up through my feet. The room is pitch black. I stand stock still, though my heart hammers against my ribs. I feel Rah's urge to run forward.

"Wait," I whisper. Jonny switches on his torch, covering the beam. He swings it slowly around the room, its narrow shaft of light catching objects, the bed, the table, the music stands, the freezer. He aims it towards the curtains. They're shut. He turns to the wall and switches the light on. I sense movement ahead. Something furry, caught in the dirty, yellow gloom from the single overhead bulb, darts into an unlit corner.

I jump, "Fuck," I mutter.

"Shut up, Maggs, it's only a rat," whispers Jonny as he switches the torch off. Rah leaves my side and walks towards the freezer. Pulling

the handle, she releases the door catch. A sliver of sharp light escapes from between the seals.

"Okay," Jonny breathes. I swallow my nausea down. I'm not looking at the bed, I'm not looking at the table, I'm not looking at the music stands, I'm not looking at the freezer. I'm just watching Jonny pull the dark green blanket from his rucksack and lay it out on the floor with the torch next to it.

"Now," he says. Rah pulls the freezer door right back, Jonny and I step forward into the flooding brilliance. I try not to see what's in front of me. I try only to think about the job I need to do. But I can't help myself, I look into her sweet, sweet face. A sob escapes my lips.

"Now, Maggs," orders Jonny quietly, but his voice is stern.

Rah's voice reaches out to me, soft and controlled. "Maggs, it's alright, I'm here."

I stretch out my hands. I touch her cold, cold shoulder and her cold, cold knee.

"Now," he orders again. I feel his warm body pressed taut against mine. I grip and we lift together.

She does not come alone. The chair she sits on rolls forward, the front ice-chilled wheels bump down the lip of the freezer. I look at Jonny. I see his jaw tighten; I see tears roll down his face. "Pull," he commands. We do. The chair trundles forward. Rah, remaining silent, shuts the freezer door, killing the penetrating light.

"Only look for the strapping, Maggs, do not think about anything else," he instructs, and I'm sure he is directing himself as much as he is directing me. Picking up the torch, I switch it on and aim the beam. Three bungee cords at her hips, waist and chest secure her to the back of the chair but cable ties hold her neck to a sort of metal brace. This time, there's no stopping my reflex, I retch remembering it was Herrick's suggestion to use cable ties for Hoyle's capture.

"Bastard, fucking shi ..." I start to hiss.

"Shut up, Maggs. I'm going to the kitchen to find a knife or scissors, her arms are secured with cable ties," whispers Jonny.

"I'll go," Rah murmurs and I see her disappear from the room.

"Jonny," I whimper, clicking off the torch.

"I know. Don't think, Maggs, and try not to speak, the quieter we are, the better."

I stand in the gloom as bitter tears roll down my face. "This house is more like a mausoleum or a dungeon, no one's going to hear us in here. No one heard Orla," I mutter.

"Don't you think I know that, but we agreed to keep any noise and light to a minimum, so let's just do it," he counters in a fierce, low whisper.

I feel like screaming, instead I stare at Orla's child-like arms, turned white with death and cold. Slowly I make out the structure that holds them in place, a wooden frame built with precision and attached to the back of the chair. I lean closer and see her fingers have been forced into shapes with wires. I swallow, I gag, I pant, I gag, I can't breathe.

"Maggs, no," Jonny warns firmly, "I need you. Stay with me." I shut my eyes and swallow again. Panic steals my breath. My lungs feel rigid; they won't inflate.

Rah touches me lightly. "Shh, Maggs, I'm here now. Just breathe, in, out, in, out. That's it," she says soothingly before handing me a pair of scissors and Jonny a knife.

I watch her reach out and hold her daughter, "I've got you now, Sweetheart," she murmurs, kissing her head. My heart is breaking, breaking for all the people I love. My throat tightens, I gasp.

"Breathe, Maggs, stay with us, we need you," Jonny warns again. Pulling air into my lungs, I go to the back of the chair, unclip the bungee cords and help Jonny cut the arm straps.

Eventually Orla's ridged body comes away. We lower her onto the blanket and wrap her in. Jonny picks her up; her frozen shape is awkward in his arms. Putting the torch back into the rucksack, I tug it onto my back while Rah switches off the overhead light, plunging us back into darkness. I hear the hum and scuttle of small life over my thudding heart and shallow breaths.

"Jonny, can you feel my hand?" asks Rah quietly.

"Yes," he answers.

"I'll guide you. Maggs, hold Jonny from the back." I grasp his shirt,

it's wet with sweat. I feel him move forward. Out in the corridor, we edge towards the stairs. The wood creaks as Rah steps down onto the stairs and Jonny follows. I hold tight. Each stair-tread groans as we descend.

"Last one, Jonny," I hear Rah whisper and I feel him descend. Then I'm on ground level too. Rah guides us as we thread our way through to the back door.

She stops. "Go, I'll lock the door." I step out first. The moon is shockingly bright. It feels like a trap, a searchlight. I move back.

"Maggs?" Jonny whispers, bumping into me.

"It's so bright out there," I pant.

"Okay. Calm, breathe. You go first and wait for me by the garage." I squeeze his arm, breathe and go. Weaving between the moonbeams, almost bent double, I sprint down the path. A stupid rhythm runs through my head with each step.

"In and out the dusty blue bells. Shut up," I shout silently at myself as I make it to the garage and lean against its shadowed wall. Nothing moves, all's quiet. Then I hear Jonny's footfalls. He too leans against the garage wall, blowing like an animal smelling slaughter. We wait. Silence. I feel rather than hear Rah's arrival.

"Maggs, Rah, go and get into the back seat and I'll pass her to you," Jonny orders, but I can tell from his voice, he is on the edge. Rah inches forward, staying within the shadows, I follow. At the car, she eases the back door open and disappears into the dark interior. I pull the rucksack from my back and climb in after her. Jim Bob says nothing but I see his hands gripped tight on the steering wheel. Jonny steps out. He tries to ease Orla through the door but it's not going to work.

"Put her in the front seat," directs Jim Bob. "Bigster, hold her from behind." Cold immediately bites into my hands, burning my flesh as I grasp her tiny shoulders. I feel Jonny climb in next to Rah and the door clicks shut.

"Go," Jonny orders. Jim Bob starts the engine. The noise is almost deafening. Shifting the gear stick into first, he lifts the clutch and we slowly creep forward. I feel every bump and every rut. I cling to the

icy form, keeping her upright. At the top of Lead Lane, Jim Bob turns on the headlights, pushes the car through the gears and soon we are back on Peartree Road and pulling into our driveway.

Jim Bob parks and kills the engine. I breathe. Jonny's out of the car, Rah moves. I feel hands take Orla. Gwen's at the side gate. Minty behind.

"Here," they call quietly into the moonlit night.

CHAPTER 53
Sky Lanterns

*

Maggi - 2023

"…We brought Orla back here and laid her on the table in the music room. Gwen and Minty placed hot water bottles and hot towels around her body and, slowly, the ice began to melt. When Rah's Zuki Gown was semi pliable we cut the fabric." My voice is strong, my hate focussed. I don't want there to be any mistake here. I don't want them to think Orla's death was some sort of accident. "Under the dress, there was an old-fashioned, corseted back brace, something that a medical museum might exhibit. It was structured from stiff fabric and bone with a metal rod that rose up the spine ending in adjustment screws and a cupping device around the occipital bone, the back of the head. It must've once had chin straps, but these were cut away and, instead, Herrick had used more cable ties to fix it around Orla's neck. The corset was laced on so tight, I could hardly get a knife under the cordage." I pause for a moment, I want them to absorb the full horror of what I'm saying before I continue. "Her elbows were secured to her restricted waist by an old, leather belt. She wore Rah's underwear and Rah's evening shoes, cable tied to her feet. As her flesh thawed ligature marks became visible around her ankles, mouth and hands.

None of us needed to be told that these injuries were sustained in life." I carefully articulate each word, though I hug Lobo and feel him, ever loyal, pressed against me. "When, after hours of washing

315

her with hot water we were able to straighten out her damaged body, Gwen began her face, releasing her eye lids and her mouth."

I stop again. I want them to recognise the full cruelty of what I'm about to describe. "In her mouth was a wedge of wood, cut from what looked like an old door stop, and her lips had been lifted at the corners by small fishing hooks, that bit into the flesh. The hooks were attached to a nylon thread that ran over the top of her ears and around the parietal bone, the back of her head. Gwen never said a word as I passed her hot cloth after hot cloth but we both cried silently as we worked..."

1998

"This is our time now, Minty," Gwen tells him gently. "Take Jonny and Jim Bob and go."

He nods his acceptance and leaves with the other two. We three women stand and look at Orla's adolescent nakedness laid out before us. Her barely budding breasts and downy pubis.

"Norah, Maggi, I want hot, scented water, shampoo, scented soap, new towels and flannels. You will find them ready in the kitchen."

The timbre of Gwen's voice is firm. I know her well enough to understand that she is not going to allow her emotions to interfere with the preparational rites of her granddaughter's body.

We do as she asks, carrying back bowls of hot water laced with lavender and rose and bales of new towels.

"First, we will wash her hair," Gwen directs. We work together removing all the hairspray, pins and clips. As Orla's hair is released it becomes obvious how dirty it is. We soak, shampoo, rinse and condition. Then we do it all again and again until we can comb her long, dark tresses free.

"Now, her body," instructs Gwen.

Gently we wash and cry and wash. Her flesh is mottled badly from the corset restraints, her small breasts bruised, her mouth torn. All three of us recognise that her child-like genitals have been badly damaged. Rah and Gwen gently cleanse her as I wash and dry her small feet.

316

"What shall we dress her in?" Gwen asks, her voice soft.

"Something that is hers, something she loved," I say between my tears.

"I know," Rah smiles, "the outfit I bought her for Christmas." She goes and returns, carrying bags of clothes I've never seen. We cover Orla's vandalised body, dressing her in the clothes she would've loved. We shut her eyes and dry her hair, plaiting it over her shoulder. Then we call the others who lay her, oh so carefully, into her casket.

As we clear the room of every scrap of evidence, every wet towel, every hot water bottle, Jonny takes my arm and quietly asks, "Was she..." For a split second, I consider lying to him, but we are way past that now.

"Yes," I confirm.

2023

"Were there any signs of sexual abuse?" D.C.I. Logan asks, her voice betraying her emotions.

"I think that goes without saying. I don't know how long he kept her alive or how she died but from the state of her, I guess it was sometime.

The sick thing is that I'd hoped and prayed we'd find her alive but after seeing what the bastard had done to her, I wished I'd prayed for her death."

"That's-that's really sad," D.C. Fry says. I look at him, his eyes are glassy and sincere and I think for the hundredth time, "you're not really cut out for this line of work."

"It's all sad and it's not true when they say it gets easier as time goes by, it doesn't. You just get better at hiding it.

Later, after Orla was clean, dressed and laid at peace in her coffin, I left Rah asleep on the floor next to her and walked to the allotment, opened the shed door, shut it and screamed hate into the floor.

Friday came. The marquee was erected under Minty's guidance and I began to dig..."

317

1998

The earth, starved of water, is hard to break open. It hurts my back, it hurts my arms but I welcome the pain, it fuels my anger, it drives me on. The others offer to help but I want to dig alone.

Evening comes, streaking the sky blood red. I dig on. Sometime later, Jim Bob sits with his legs dangling down the shear sides of my trench. We talk some, we cry some and then, at last, I let him help me.

2023

"...Amelia was as good as her word. She arrived bearing sunflowers, gerberas and large-headed daisies. Rah and her spent the night singing and weaving the flowers into wicker. Then they tied long, white, silk ribbons to the handles. In the morning, we all showered and dressed.

I was going to wear my concert clothes but in the end, I couldn't, so I just wore my jeans and sandals. Gwen, Amelia and Norah wore beautiful summer dress, Minty and Jim Bob, both wore suits but, Jonny, dressed in dark trousers with a matching waist coat and a pure white shirt, outshone us all. Rah's brother, Arthur, arrived from America tanned and suited and, lastly, Seb and Paul.

There was no real plan for the day but, as if on cue, Arthur brought out his classical guitar..."

1998

"Norah, will you play with us?" he asks his sister gently.
My eyes fill with tears as she murmurs, "Yes."
Jonny, Minty, Jim Bob and I each take one of the rope handles and stand under the covered tunnel.
A lone, sweet, soprano voice rises out of the afternoon air, "Thy hand Belinda, darkness shades me…" and I know it's Amelia who's soon joined by Arthur's guitar. Then, I hear her oboe. Tears flow unchecked down my face.
"When I am Laid in the Earth, Dido's Lament. How fitting," Minty murmurs, as we start our walk, carrying our child to her grave.

2023

"…And Rah joined him and Amelia in the garden. It was the last time she ever played…"

1998

That night we go to the seashore and light sky lanterns.
Crying, I light the last lantern and hold it for a moment until the warmed air takes it from my fingers. Rah leans against me and I put my arms around her emaciated body.

She's so thin that I can feel the moment when she fills her lungs and begins to sing. Amelia's perfect soprano quickly joins her, followed by Arthur, blending seamlessly with his sisters' harmonic ranges.

I watch the lantern join the scattered line of beacons sailing into the night but I cannot find my voice, my throat is strangled with pain. I keep my eyes firmly fixed on my last offering of love. And, even when the light dims and eventually disappears into the darkness, I cannot bring myself to stop searching the heavens. I feel Jonny stir at my side.
"It's like Orla," he murmurs through his tears, "she's the light we can no longer see."

CHAPTER 54
Deaf Dumb and Blind

Maggi - 2023

I lay my head in my arms and cry. I don't try to stop my tears now, there's no point. I think if they haven't understood then there's no more I can do to explain my hate, Jonny's hurt and Rah's revenge. "Maggi," D.C.I. Logan says gently, "It's way past lunch time, you are entitled to a break."

"No," I mumble back through my sobs, "I need to finish this now, before Jonny comes home."

"Okay, if you're sure." I pull my head up off the table and look at her. I can see through my tears she's as composed and professional as ever, though I think some of the sternness has left her face. D.C. Fry, on the other hand, is visibly shaken. I blow my nose, set my shoulders, reach for Lobo, who, ever faithful, has laid his head in my lap and begin again.

"Rah changed in the weeks following Orla's funeral. At first I was so wrapped up in my own anger and grief that I didn't notice it. It wasn't until Gwen spoke to me about her concerns that I started to see it. As you know, after Orla disappeared Rah almost held her breath waiting for her return. During the trial and kidnap of Hoyle her hope surfaced but with Herrick's confession, her hatred ignited and burnt deep.

You might think, so what… And you know my hate was furnace hot, and there's no way that you cannot know Jonny too was consumed by revenge. But Rah's hate was different from ours. Mine and Jonny's was aimed full blast at Herrick and anyone who got in our way, while Rah's was aimed solely at herself.

Before, when she'd stopped eating, it was because she couldn't stomach any food, but now it had become a punishment. I began to see large bruises bloom on her malnourished flesh and sweeping cuts across her scalp where she shaved her head. I'd find her blue with cold standing naked in the garden or burning red as she stood under a scolding shower. None of us knew what to do.

Jonny and I had returned to work, I needed the money and we needed to look normal... well, as normal as possible. Gwen and Minty would watch her while I was on shift or at the allotment."

"You still went to the allotment?" D.C. Fry asks.

"Yes. First to mend the floor and disperse the soil but then it became my place to wallow in my grief and lick my wounds. I'd lose hours standing over Herrick's body, damning his soul to hell.

Then, one day, I came home and found Rah on the floor of her studio.

1998

"Oh fuck, no, no, no, no, Rah, what have you done?" I moan, staring down at her naked body lying in a growing pool of bright red blood. I kneel next to her and feel for a pulse. It's faint, but there. I try to see where the blood is coming from. Finding two large slices cut deep into each breast, I quickly strip off my long-sleeved t-shirt and try to bind the cuts.

"Fuuuck," I cry as I watch the blood still spreading around her.

I run my hands over her. Reaching her legs, I see great, red sways arcing her inner thighs. I open them and sob. She's cut away one side of her labia and attacked the other. "Oh Rah, no." Looking wildly about, I see her painting apron hanging on the door, next to Orla's. I grab it and thrust it between her legs, shutting them to hold it in place.

Downstairs, I snatch the phone from the cradle and dial Jonny's number.

"Jonny. Fuck, Jonny. Quickly. It's Rah."

"I'm coming, Maggs." I click the receiver off and dial 999. When I'm through, I screech into the handset, "Ambulance, ambulance, quick. My friend, she's bleeding out."

"Address please?"

"33 Peartree Road, Godlinghoe. Please, she's dying, I can't stop the blood," I plead through rasping sobs.

"They're on their way. Can you give me her name?"

"Norah Montgomery. Hurry, please," I beg.

"And what has happened to Norah?"

"Maggs, where is she?" Jonny asks, coming through the door.

"Studio." he tears up the stairs, I drop the phone and follow.

"Shit," he mutters as he bends down and applies pressure on her chest wounds. "Do the same to her vulva," he orders. I'm crying. I'm praying to any God who will listen. I'm swearing that I'll kill the ambulance medics if they do get here soon. Time ticks by. The apron turns red. I see blood welling up between my fingers.

"Hello, ambulance here, can we come in?" calls a female voice from below.

"Yes, upstairs," Jonny calls back. I hear them treading on the stairway and can't believe anyone can walk so slowly.

"In here," I shout, trying to transmit a sense of urgency. After what feels like forever, two medics walk through the studio door.

2023

"…The ambulance medics saw what Rah had done to herself and set too, saving her life."

"What had she done?" asks D.C. Fry, his face creased with concern.

"She'd cut herself…badly."

"Was it a cry for help?" D.C.I. Logan asks.

"No, not a cry for help, nor a suicide attempt," I reply resignedly. "Maybe, in fairness, I've not given you enough details to understand Rah, how she ticked, and then, how she was undone. I'm not sure I've understood it completely, Jonny seemed to get it better than me, but it's no good asking him anything now. So, I'll try to describe what I think was going on in her head that day.

She'd been painting her hate...hate's not quite the right word here ...uhm ...more like her disgust, her loathing of herself." Articulating these adjectives, I try to capture and convey the truth about Rah's mental state. "Though, to be more precise, against her body."

"Her body?" D.C. Fry questions.

"I know that sounds weird, but by then, Rah was regarding her body as a separate entity from herself. She saw it as her enemy; something that had given life to Orla and something that should have protected Orla to the last drop of blood, instead of betraying her daughter by denying Herrick his desires.

The psychologist at the hospital labelled it Body Dysmorphic Disorder but I thought it was more like all-out war. Anyway, she'd painted her hate by cutting her body and using her blood as paint." I see D.C. Fry's expression turn from one of disbelief to horror, and even D.C.I. Logan looks stunned.

"Damn," he murmurs.

"She spent some time in the hospital, healing, before being shipped off to a Psych Unit. It took Jonny and me weeks to persuade them to release her into our custody. That's when Jonny shut his house up and moved into the music room, so I could give up work. Gwen and Minty helped of course, but in the end, we all knew it was hopeless.

1998

The pot of stew is thickening nicely on the stove, filling the kitchen with a sense of home. I'm rolling dumplings and trying not to let my mind dwell on tomorrow, the first anniversary of Orla's disappearance, with little success. I've left Rah in the sitting room, in front of the telly, curled under a blanket. She's bone thin and mad. I'm not even sure she's aware of the time of year, let alone the approaching day.

I switch the kitchen lights on, pushing back the heavy rain-filled skies outside and try to sing along to the music coming from my radio. I hear the slightest of clicks and easily imagine Orla coming out of her bedroom, before thundering down the stairs and bursting into the kitchen. I file the sound, along with my other nightmares, into the box that I refuse to look in, and sing more loudly.

Finishing the dumplings, I lay them onto the simmering surface of the stew. I wash the flour from my hands and look across at the table covered in not very inspiring gifts I've bought for Christmas. Next to them is a new jumper for Jonny's birthday.

"I'll check on Rah and see if I can get her to drink something, then I'll do some wrapping," I say to the little Christmas tree, trying to keep myself from slipping into places I don't need to go. Leaving the kitchen, I can hear the telly, a lunchtime show where women are politely being rude to each other. I see the blanket mound and call her name.

"Rah?" there's no answer, but then there never is. I sit next to her and reach out to touch her shoulder. The blanket collapses under my hand. She's not there.

"Rah," I call through the house. Nothing. I search the garden, expecting to find her laid out cold and naked on Orla's grave, but no. Worry edges my thoughts. "Where are you? Where would you go?" Pulling on my coat and hat, I start hunting for her on Peartree Road.

Minutes pass, my worry deepens.

"Hi Maggi, cold today." I look up at the man; it's nice Mr Peterson. Memories of standing on one side of the allotment gate with Herrick's body in my barrow while Mr Peterson stands on the other, comes flooding back to me.

"Oh, hi,' I mumble.

"If you don't mind me saying, I've just seen your friend, Norah isn't it? Not looking all that well dressed for this weather."

"Where, Mr Peterson? Which way? She's not well and I've lost her," I say, trying not to cry.

"Heading towards the town centre. Not well you say, yes, I thought perhaps something wasn't right. I'll help you look."

"Thanks, Mr Peterson." Walking fast towards the town centre, we start checking the roads. Nothing.

"Mr Peterson, was Norah wearing anything? And I don't mean a coat."

"Yes, she had a long t-shirt and socks on but no shoes or outside clothing. I thought it was strange that's why I was on my way to knock on your door."

In the town centre, several people have already spotted her. I suppose she's not hard to miss being nearly naked and completely bonkers. They all point towards the sea front.

We follow. The green promenade is deserted. The children's swings, where I'd once pushed Orla as a small child, sway in the biting wind coming off the sea. We weave our way through the brightly coloured beach huts onto the esplanade. Driven by the wind, the iron-grey waves roar ferociously against the rotting, wooden groynes.

"Rah, where are you?" I shout desperately at the top of my voice. Mr Peterson shouts too as he starts walking along the wall looking first at the sea, then between the huts. I copy, not knowing what else to do.

"RAH." I scream as each crashing wave stings my face with cold, salt water.

"Maggi, Maggi, over here." Looking, I see Mr Peterson waving his arms. I run.

"What?" I ask, hardly able to breathe.

"There, Maggi, in the water."

"Oh my God, no, Rah." Stripping off my coat, I climb over the wall and ease my way down to the sea, never taking my eyes from the slight body surfing the tumbling waves. I slip on the thick weed that clings to the concrete and fall into the water. The cold snatches my breath. Standing, I start to wade. The sea slaps against my waist, chilling me to the bone.

Like the stuff of nightmares, every time I think I can reach her she slips away on another wave.

At last, my fingers grasp the t-shirt and I pull her to me. Turning her over in my arms, I cradle her ice-cold body to my chest.

"No, Rah, I can't do it without you. Don't you know you're my life? Oh God, help me,"

But the Gods were always deaf, dumb and blind to my prayers.

2023

"…She drowned herself in the sea. By the time I found her, she was dead." Laying my head back into my arms, I cry softly. I don't have to remember the feel of that icy water as it slapped violently against my body while I cradled her uselessly in my arms. I re-live it in some form or other every night. The cold, the emptiness, the hopelessness, the fear. I feel it now swimming up from the place where I store all my hate, it saturates my senses.

I look up at D.C.I. Logan knowing I will reveal the last of my lies. A fabrication, an untruth, that I've carefully nurtured for years and hidden behind.

"Beautiful Rah," I tell her, "she was sensitive and fragile, and I thought she needed my protection. But what I realised in that terrible moment, standing in the sea with her lying lifeless in my arms, is it was never her that was the weak one, it was always me."

CHAPTER 55
Slicks of Dark Slime

*

Logan

The old dog lets out a low whimper as Logan waits for Maggi's tears to pass.

"Maggi, do you still have the keys to 16 Bosuns Road," she asks.

"Yes, both front and back doors," Maggi answers, blowing her nose.

"Why did you keep them?" Fry asks.

"I don't know, because none of us have ever gone back there. Perhaps, it's because it was the last place Orla was alive, or, maybe, because I hate Herrick so much. I know that doesn't make any more sense than hunting for a child that you know is dead, but, somehow, I just couldn't let go."

"Okay. We'll need the front door key to verify your story before we…" Logan stops herself from saying, excavate Orla's remains, instead she changes it to, "I.D. Butler's remains."

Maggi wearily climbs to her feet and with the dog glued to her side she leaves the room. Logan can see her stout figure disappearing into the cupboard under the stairs before re-emerging moments later. Back at the table, she puts a single Yale key down on the wooden surface.

"Thanks," Logan says, picking it up and pocketing it. "We'll be back tomorrow. But be aware Maggi, we will be arresting you. Please be prepared."

Outside, the afternoon light is overcast. "Are we going to the house now, Boss?" Fry asks nervously.

"Tomorrow," Logan replies, not wanting to face it so late in the day.

The following morning the conversation in the car is minimal. Logan hates this part of the job. She's not scared as such, just apprehensive. She's sure Fry is feeling it too. Reaching Bosuns Road, she drives slowly along until they are outside 16.

"There's no mistaking that," Fry comments as she parks.

Getting out of the car they study the forlorn looking house sitting in an overgrown, rubbish-filled garden. The front door, with a tide of creeping filth, is flanked on either side by mould-incrusted, curtain-covered, windows. Above, the guano splattered roof has created an eco-system of its own, with flora and fauna sprouting from between broken tiles and sagging gutters, while vertical slicks of dark slime decorate the Victorian brick work. Everything about the house makes Logan's skin crawl.

"Oh, my days," Fry murmurs at her side.

"You don't have to come in Fry, I'm only going to take a quick look just to confirm Maggi's story before I send for forensics."

"It's okay, I'll come."

"Oil lubricant and gloves then," she says, going to the boot of her car and pulling two pairs of latex gloves from a box and picking up a small spray can.

Unlatching the front gate sends a flock of squalling seagulls airborne, while a tabby cat hisses a warning. Taking no notice of the defensive feline, Logan sprays the lubricant into the corroded lock and over the key before forcing the tumblers to open. Using her shoulder, she shoves hard. The resisting door judders but moves by inches. The stench of decades of decay leaks out as Logan squeezes her body through the partly opened doorway, followed by Fry.

The atmosphere is thick and the floor gives beneath her feet. "Torch," Fry instructs his Noc and she looks down to see what they're standing on. Through a haze of dust motes, she can just make out heaps of old newspapers, coloured flyers and letters filling the narrow space.

"Blimey, Boss, it stinks," coughs Fry, instinctively trying to cover his mouth and nose with his sleeve.

"Fuuuck doesn't it." She breathes out, trying not to gag. Gingerly moving forward, she pushes against the first door, wishing she had her baton, though pleased she's got her gloves on. It creeks back on rusted hinges and Fry sweeps the room beyond with his Noc, catching objects in its beam. Like a scene from Satis House, the ancient piano, thick with dust, looms out of the crepuscular gloom. A large mantle piece with indistinguishable, conoid-shaped objects dominates the far wall while a music stand takes centre stage.

Something long leaps from the rotted cloth of the piano stool, making them both jump.

"Let's move on," Logan says through gritted teeth and walks down the hall into the kitchen. Daylight filters through a dirt-encrusted window, illuminating the room. Worktops, strewn with strange rotting shapes, edge the walls, while an old metal saucepan and the corpse of a long-dead rat sit on the hob.

In the sitting room, torn and tattered soft furnishings bear witness to generations of nesting creatures, while papers spill from draws that teeter on the edge of falling from a grimy bureau.

They climb the carpeted staircase, disturbing years of thickly laid dust. Each wooden tread groans under their weight, making Logan wonder how safe it really is. On the landing, a net curtain, mottled with mould, covers a small window.

"Do you remember which room it is?" Logan asks, fighting the urge to run away.

"Maggi never said," Fry mumbles from behind his sleeve. They turn to their left and push open the far door. A decomposing bed and an old wooden wardrobe fill the space.

"I don't think it's this one," Logan states, before trying the next door.

"Bathroom," Fry observes, after quickly flicking the Noc light across a claw-footed bath and another dead rat. Turning back along the corridor, Logan pushes open a third door and Fry lifts the light. A cold shiver runs down her spine as the torch beam hits the tall, white freezer that seems untouched by dirt and time.

"Okay," she mutters more for herself than Fry as she steps into the room. Fry moves the light slowly around the perimeter. It picks up a double bed, a table, a chair, two music-stands and a strange wooden structure lying next to an overturned, office-type chair.

"There's a weird smell in here, Boss. I know the whole house stinks but there's something else in here."

She knows what he means, she can smell it too. "Shine the light over here," she says, walking towards the bed. "Decaying rubber."

"What?"

"Do you remember when Maggi described the room, she said the bed was covered in something brown?"

"Yeah."

"It's a rubber sheet. Really old fashioned, the sort used to protect mattresses from bed wetting back in the 50s. The smell is rotting rubber."

"Why would there be a rubber sheet on the bed?"

"I'd imagine it's got something to do with frozen flesh defrosting."

"Damn," Fry mutters and Logan knows he is trying hard to keep his emotions in check, as she is trying to do the same thing to.

"I think we've seen enough to bare out Maggi's story, let's leave it to forensics now."

Outside in the warm May day, away from the claustrophobic festering history, they strip off their gloves and breathe deeply. Fry shuts his eyes. "That was bad in there."

"Yeah," Logan agrees. "I did one like that years back and I think it's the smell more than anything that stayed with me."

"Excuse me, are you from the council?" A rotund, middle-aged woman stands at the front gate.

"No, Chelmsford Police," Logan answers, trying to sound professional.

"Have you come to do something about this house? Only it's been empty now for goodness knows how long and it's a health hazard. I've been onto the council a number of times, that's why I thought you might be the council. It's the rats, someone needs to do something about the rats."

"And you are?" Logan enquires, stepping back into her professional role.

"Mrs Wormold, I live two doors down, number 20. It's an accident waiting to happen and, quite frankly, it's an eyesore too. It brings our little community's standards down."

"Have you lived here long, Mrs Wormold?"

"Since 2001. When we moved in, this house was already empty. You'd think it would belong to someone but no one remembers who, though Kenny at 49 thinks it was a Nazi, but then he thinks everyone is a Nazi on account of his father's war experiences. He's away with the fairies, if you know what I mean," she says, making a twirling gesture with her forefinger.

"Thank you, Mrs Wormold," Logan replies, dismissing the woman and walking towards her car.

But Mrs Wormold is not that easily put off. "So, are you going to do anything about it then?" she persists, following them.

"All I can tell you is that, at the moment, we're looking into it," Logan answers, spraying disinfectant onto her hands before passing the bottle to Fry.

"Well, you need to do something, and soon, before someone dies of a nasty disease like the Black Death," she tells them before marching off.

"Can people still die from the Black Death?" Fry asks as they drive away.

"I very much doubt it but I'm not surprised the neighbours are upset, I wouldn't want to live next to that house."

"Me neither, it's horrible. Do you think there'll be much left in there for forensics to find?"

"I don't know, it's been awhile, but I'm hoping there will be D.N.A. to prove Waxy is Herrick Butler and that Orla Montgomery was held there."

Chapter 56
A Ham Toasty and a Cup of Tea

*

Logan

At Peartree Road, Maggi opens the door and Logan sees her examine Fry's face before commenting, "Bad then?" Fry just nods grimly at her. "Come," Maggi says to him, leading the way through the house, "Jonny is here, he'll make you feel better. He's in the garden; just follow the path. I'll make coffee and bring it out. But please don't say anything about where you have been." Fry nods again and makes for the garden.

"Maggi," Logan says, staying behind in the kitchen, "you know why we are here, don't you?"

"To arrest me D.C.I. Logan, but there's no reason not to have coffee with Jonny first," she answers calmly, though Logan sees her hand shake as she pours hot water into the coffee pot.

"I should be getting on with this," Logan thinks as she finds herself, against her better judgement, following Maggi and Lobo along a path and under a honeysuckle archway before entering a small, grassy meadow.

"Hello, Jonny," she hears Fry say to the old man sitting on the veranda of a wooden summerhouse.

"Hello, have you come to play with Orla? Don't mind me, I'm a bit wiggledy. Do you know, I think there might be some cake."

"Yes, Maggi is bringing drinks and cake now."

"Maggs, yes…cake. Have you seen Orla? I've just got to check if the

Christmas tree lights are on."

"The Christmas tree lights are on, I've just seen them," Maggi reassures him, putting the tray down on a small table.

"Is there any cake?" Jonny asks brightly.

"Coffee and walnut today," Maggi replies, adding, "There's chairs in the summerhouse, D.C.I. Logan." Crossing into the hut, Logan sees an old potter's wheel standing in the corner next to a shelf of clay objects, paints and brushes and knows this was once Norah's pottery studio. She takes a chair and sits next to Fry on the veranda.

"This is where they're buried," she thinks, taking in the tiny, wildflower meadow bordered by trees in full blossom. Her eyes are naturally drawn to the full-sized bronze sculpture of a woman and child, hand in hand, looking back across their shoulders to where she now sits.

"Coffee and walnut… Maggs, I think there's something wrong," Jonny says in a puzzled voice.

"Everything is fine, Jonny," Maggi answers lightly, pouring the coffee.

"If you don't count the fact that I'm about to arrest you," Logan thinks and sees Fry look down at his shoes.

"But something… something ... Maggs, where's Orla?"

"Orla is with Rah, they are safe and sound."

"Safe and sound."

"Yes, safe and sound. Now, how about a slice of cake? It's coffee and walnut today."

They chat about nothing more important than the garden. Logan sips her coffee, it tastes good but she can't bring herself to take a bite of the cake. The very thought of it makes her feel sick. "Probably not the cake," she thinks, "more likely what you are about to do."

But it's Maggi who speaks of it first. "Can you give me until tomorrow afternoon? You know I'm not going anywhere."

"Where are you going, Maggs?" Jonny asks, his face creased with concern.

"Nowhere, Jonny," she smiles back at him before turning back to Logan. "It's just that I need to make sure the others are ..." she

333

stutters for the briefest of moments, "are looked after. I've made arrangements with Fellowfield House, that's why I've kept him home today. Just one more day together," she says, looking at the old man and Logan sees her eyes shine with unshed tears.

"And Lobo?" Fry chokes, making the dog look up.

"Ah, Lobo." Maggi pauses, touching her fingers to her lips and Logan knows she is fighting for control. "Lobo and I have an appointment with the vet tomorrow morning."

Fry's eyes widen with hurt. "Jeezes," Logan thinks weakly, "what am I going to do about you?"

"Maggs, what's wrong?" Jonny asks, Logan hears the note of panic puncturing his words. "Maggs, is Julia coming? Quick, we must hide Lobo, she'll kill him." He begins to cry and tries to struggle out of his chair.

"Jonny," Maggi says, placing her hand on his, "Julia is not coming here, I won't let her, I promise you and you know how strong I am, I won't let anyone hurt Lobo," but Logan can see Maggi can't hold back her tears and knows the lie must be ripping her soul apart.

"But, Maggs, you're crying," Jonny wails, clearly terrified.

"My eyes are just watering because of the sun," Maggi continues lightly, "I should've brought my sunglasses out. Lobo is as safe as houses, I promise you, Jonny."

"Safe as houses?"

"Yes, safe as houses."

"Jonny, I like chocolate cake do, you? Though, this cake is nice too." Fry pipes in, his voice rising slightly.

"Chocolate cake?" Jonny repeats with a look of confusion on his face.

"Yes, chocolate cake, that's my favourite. Can we have chocolate cake tomorrow, Maggi?" Fry asks and Logan stares at him, unable to hide her incredulity.

"Chocolate cake, yes, can we have chocolate cake tomorrow, Maggs?" Jonny asks too.

"That's a good idea. I'll bake a chocolate cake tonight."

"What the fuck am I doing here?" Logan thinks, and unable to stand it anymore, she gets up from the table.

"Tomorrow afternoon, at 2." she states laconically. Maggi nods her acknowledgement while Fry pats Jonny on the shoulder as he passes.

"Be ready," Logan warns as she walks away.

In the car Fry is quiet. After a while Logan asks him to check the emails, more to break the silence than needing to know.

"One in from your friend Ron," he tells her.

"What does it say?"

"**...Hi Lo, nice to hear from you. Family's good, thanks. I've dug around on those names you gave me. Virtually nothing of note for some, more on others. Anyway, hope it helps. Cheers Ron...**He's attached a file underneath. Do you want me to open it?"

"Nah, I'm taking the afternoon off, I'll take it home with me. You should go early too, most people are, what with the launch tonight."

"Yeah, think I will." Logan hears his despondency, and though she is still irritated by his chocolate cake comment, she knows how he feels. She also knows there's nothing she can say that he can't reason out for himself, though when she gets back to the station, she catches up with Grim.

"Hey, Top Cat, ready for blast off?"

"Actually, I'm sharing blast off with someone else tonight."

"Fuck off," he laughs. "Who's the poor bastard?"

"Greyson," and much to her annoyance she feels her cheeks begin to flush.

"Ho, ho, ho, you'll be in for some fun with him."

"It's not like that."

"Yeah, fucking right it's not."

"Anyway, two things. I think I've got an I.D. for Waxy."

"Think or know?"

"Know, but ..."

"Go on."

"It's one of those ones where you wish to God it wasn't so."

"One of those, huh. Are you charging anyone?"

"Yep."

"Done it yet?"

"Nope, I've given her till tomorrow to sort stuff out."

"Okay, what's the other thing?"

"Fry."

"What about him?"

"I don't think he's got the personality to be a copper."

"Has he fucked up?"

She thinks briefly about the cake episode. "No, he's intelligent, enthusiastic, got guts and is very able, but he's got an innocence about him that mars his judgement."

"Lo, don't knock his chances. We were all innocent once. Jeezes, there was no one more wet behind the ears than me."

"S'pose... anyway, I'm off. Have fun with the lads."

"Not as much fun as you're going to have with Dr Greyson Stonewalker."

"Fuck off," she smiles, punching his arm.

Alone in her car, she has an uncomfortable prickling at the back of her mind. She knows what it is; she'd let her guard down by not arresting Maggi. At home she changes into her running gear and tries to run it off. A couple of hours later, after a hard workout and a hot shower, she persuades herself she's feeling better. Making a ham toasty and a cup of tea, she opens Ron's file. The Noc projects the writing into the air and she reads while munching on her sandwich.

Name: Matthew (known as Minty) Credence Montgomery
DOB: 7.9.1923
DOD: 11.12.2009
Father: Rev. Credence John Montgomery
Mother: Isabel Louise Montgomery nee. Mistle
Siblings: N/A
Spouse: Gwendolen Kyoko Montgomery nee McMara (m.1953)
Children: Arthur Credence Montgomery 1956 - Norah Kyoko Montgomery 1958-98 - Amelia Louise Coleman nee Montgomery 1960.
Profession: Professor of Music, Royal College of Music
Census 1971, 1981, 1991, 2001, Address: 42 Oyster Lane, Godlinghoe, Essex. CO7 8DY

Name: Gwendolen Kyoko Montgomery nee McMara
DOB: 6.1.1934
DOD: 4.1.2021
Father: Thomas Albert McMara
Mother: Kyoko Aina McMara nee. Katsumata
Siblings: N/A
Spouse: see above
Children: see above.
Profession: Professor of Music, Royal School of Music.
Census 1971, 1981,1991, 2001, Address: 42 Oyster Lane,
Godlinghoe, Essex. CO7 8DY with spouse.
Census 2011, same address but spouse deceased.
Name: Norah Kyoko Montgomery
DOB: 06.06.1958
DOD: 21.12 .1998
Father: see above.
Mother: see above.
Siblings: see above.
Children: Orla Éowyn Faith Montgomery 6.9.1984.
Profession: Musician. Principle oboist with the London Glass
Orchestra.
Census 1991 has Norah living with Margret Katherine Drew and
Orla Éowyn Faith Montgomery at 33 Peartree Road Godlinghoe
Essex CO7 0JK.
Jonathan Gerald Gifford is registered as Orla's biological father
but, interestingly, Margret Drew is also registered as a non-
biological mother.
Sadly, Orla Éowyn Faith Montgomery was reported missing on
22.12.1997. Cold Case, No, MF-6934565-97, have marked her as
presumed dead, though her remains have never been found. The
case remains open.
Name: Orla Éowyn Faith Montgomery
DOB: 06.09.1984
DOD: was reported missing on 22.12.1997- presumed dead.
Father: Jonathan Gerald Gifford

Mother: (bio) Norah Kyoko Montgomery
Mother: (non-bio) Margret Katherine Drew
Census 1991: Orla Éowyn Faith Montgomery, 33 Peartree Road, Godlinghoe, Essex CO7 0JK, lives with Norah Montgomery and Margret Drew.
Orla Éowyn Faith Montgomery was reported missing on 22.12.1997. After a large police enquiry, Hamilton Hoyle was arrested and charged with her abduction and murder. Her remains were never found, though she has always been considered as deceased. Hoyle pleaded not guilty and it went to trial. He was found innocent.
Cold Case No. MF-6934565-97 remains open.
Name: Margret Katherine Drew
DOB 21.07.1955
DOD: N/A
Father: David James Drew
Mother: Katherine Stella Drew nee. Webb.
Siblings: Jim Bob Drew (1976-2014)
Spouse: N/A
Children: (non-bio) Orla Éowyn Faith Montgomery (See above)
Profession: Operation Department Practitioner
Census: 1991, 33 Peartree Road Godlinghoe Essex CO7 0JK with Norah Montgomery, Orla Éowyn Faith Montgomery.
Census: 2001, 2011, 2021, residing with Jonathan Gerald Gifford
Name: Jim Bob Drew
DOB: 19.6.1974
DOD: 2.2.2014 (California USA)
Father: David James Drew
Mother: Katherine Stella Drew nee. Webb.
Siblings: Margret Katherine Drew (see above)
Spouse: N/A
Children: N/A
Profession: Computer Forensic Engineer.
Census: 1981, 1991, 56 Freya Road, Bexleyheath, DA4 6TP.
Left U.K. in 2000 for California.

Name: Jonathan Gerald Gifford
DOB: 24.12.51
DOD: N/A
Father: Edmund George Gifford
Mother: Hon Julia Henrietta Charlotte Gifford nee Portmann
Siblings: Georgina Henrietta Diana Downpatrick nee Gifford, Charlotte Victoria Helen Wallace nee Gifford
Children: Orla Éowyn Faith Montgomery (See above)
Profession: Senior Nurse
Census: 1991, address 27 Pump Road, Godlinghoe Essex. CO7 0TS
Census: 2001, 2011, 2021 residing with Margret Katherine Drew, 33 Peartree Road Godlinghoe Essex CO7 0JK.
Name: Herrick Richard Butler
DOB: 05 .01.1956
Father: Richard Burton Butler. 1931-1969.
Bandmaster with the British Army 1948-1953. Stationed, Aden, Germany, England.
Mother: Adelaide Ada Butler, nee Köhler 1923-1982, piano teacher.
Siblings: None
Profession: Musician/teacher.
Spouse: None
Children: None
Census 1970 has Herrick Richard Butler and his mother Adelaide Ada Butler living in Bristol, (father Richard Burton Butler deceased -1969). 98 Shortland Drive, Bristol. BR2 0EL.
Census 1991: 16 Bosuns Road Godlinghoe Essex. BR7 0KD
Seems to have disappeared off the radar after that. Nothing on the 2001 census and no tax recorded after October 1998.
Two other notes of interest:
After the death of his father, there seems to have been some sort of incident concerning the daughter of the local Anglican vicar. It's not clear what occurred, the records are very vague, probably to do with underage protection, but the outcome was

that the Anglican Church recommended Butler to be educated as a boarder at the Western School of Music at their expense. The music school took him and that seemed to be an end to it. The second anomaly is the death/suicide of his mother, Adelaide Ada Butler. She died from asphyxiation by hanging. The Coroner passed an Open Verdict, as he was not completely satisfied by the findings of the court, though the report states there was a suicide note found claiming that Adelaide had never got over the loss of her husband.

Herrick Richard Butler was her only beneficiary.

Photo as requested is taken from a publicity shoot for the London Glass Orchestra.

Name: Hamilton Matthew Hoyle.

DOB: 1964

DOD: 2017

Spouse: Kenzey Hoyle nee Cresswell (m. 1983 d. 93)

Children: Matthew Hoyle - 1983, Kieron - 1985, Dianel-1990

Profession: Security guard for nightclubs.

Hoyle has a considerable criminal record, starting with a couple of spells in Borstal for car theft and GBH, 1978-79, 1980-82.

1986, convicted of burglary with GBH, served 3 years in adult male prison.

1995, stood trial on 3 counts: abduction of a minor over the age of thirteen and under the age of sixteen, false imprisonment and rape of said minor. The jury failed to reach a verdict. He was released and relocated to Essex to protect the child involved. (His wife divorced him and there has been no contact with his biological children.)

1998, stood trial on 4 counts: abduction of a minor over the age of thirteen and under the age of sixteen, false imprisonment, rape and murder of said minor. He was found not guilty.

2009, convicted on 3 counts: abduction of a minor over the age of sixteen, false imprisonment and rape of said minor. He served 4 years and 3 months.

Died in 2017 of natural causes.

Interestingly, there is a note added by D.S. Crumble, the investigating officer for the '98 investigation into missing teenager, Orla Montgomery. He stated that Hoyle came to him with claims that he was abducted and tortured by Orla's parents. Crumble seems to have strongly advised him to drop the allegation, which, for all intents and purposes, he did.

Logan examines the photo of Herrick, sighs, closes her Noc and goes to get ready for the first date she's had in years.

CHAPTER 57
Two Horses

*

Tristan Fry – 11:40 pm
Sitting behind their telescope in the back garden, Fry and Frank stare up at the inky, clear, night sky. A 3D projection streams from Fry's Noc showing the crew of five, now horizontally seated and strapped in. Fry feels his belly tighten with nervous excitement. He keeps his eyes focussed on Major Asha Blackthorne, going through her final checks as she instructs her team for the first leg of their journey to the International Space Station. He feels immensely proud that she has beaten the odds to win this chance to be included in the first human mission to land on Mars.

Logan
Logan clasps a mug of hot, mulled wine between her gloved hands. She too feels an overwhelming sense of excitement and pride as she watches the live-feed. The camera pans out as dawn fills the Indian sky at Satish Dhawan World Space Station. Maya-Daughter stands vertically, silhouetted against the morning light.

Earlier, as she'd driven to Greyson's cottage, she'd felt she was almost entering outer space too. The road had petered ever smaller until she'd found herself bumping along a dirt track. Her Noc had told her to keep going, that her destination was near, but all she could see was arable farmland and wooded copses. Darkness had crept in and she'd switched on her headlights. But still the track went on.

"How much farther?" she asked the Noc.

"Destination 40 meters."

"Really?" she answered sarcastically, looking into the headlight beam and seeing only a tree-lined track.

"Correct. 38.4 meters."

"Go mute." she'd pursed. Eventually the track ended in a T-junction. The Noc read right. She turned and rounding yet another bend, she saw lights ahead.

"Wow," she thought, pulling up and gazing at a thatched cottage that looked as though it had been plucked from a fairy tale. A moment later, Greyson was there.

"Fuck, he looks good," she'd murmured, smiling to herself and grabbing the wine she'd got out of her car.

The cottage had been as magical inside as it was without. Next to an open log fire, they'd eaten food she'd never heard of, but knew from the first mouthful she'd want to eat it again. Then carrying mugs of steaming, spiced wine, Greyson had taken her hand and led her deep into his garden. He'd opened a small door in a curved, wooden hut and ducked inside. She'd followed and found herself in another world full of star charts, electronic equipment, deep seats, warm, thick blankets, and a huge telescope.

"If you sit here, I'll set it up," he'd told her and she'd sat, warm and comfortable, watching him instruct, first the live-feed projection, then the view from the telescope.

Tristan Fry

Frank grins at Fry. "T-10 will start in precisely...3 minutes, Tris."

"5:27 Indian time and counting," Fry grins back at his grandfather. "We'll be there next year, Tris, standing right where Maya-Daughter stands now." They both stare in awe at her sleek, cylindrical sides, gleaming now as the first rays from the rising sun catch her fuselage. "It'll be something else," Fry says and he means it too, but the thought of Jonny, Maggi and Lobo prods persistently at the back of his mind. "Frank, have you ever had to do something that you know

343

is procedure but just doesn't feel right?"

"How'd you mean, Tris?"

"Like ... say, if you were in the army and you were ordered to do something but you felt it was wrong."

"Is this to do with work?"

"Yeah."

"Tell me," Frank says, watching the feed but listening carefully to Fry.

"Tomorrow we've got to arrest a woman for a crime that will more than likely lead to a prison sentence."

"Do you think she's guilty?"

"Yes."

"Do you like her?"

"She's bad tempered and angry but yes, I really like her. Though, that's not why I'm concerned."

"Oh?"

"It's more to do with the fact that she is responsible for two other lives and without her, they won't survive. Also, I can't help but feel her crime was justified, that she was just protecting her family and she shouldn't be punished for it."

"Is there a victim to consider here?"

"The victim is dead and if ever there was a case of 'good riddance to bad rubbish', this is it."

"Is she a danger to society?"

"No, far from it. It's really a matter of law."

"Law is sometimes a devilishly difficult thing to interpret. I always think, if you can't ride two horses at the same time you shouldn't be in the circus."

Fry gazes into the night sky before asking, "What would you need to light a fire with, say if you wanted to burn a building down?"

"I'd probably use dry, combustible material as a foundation."

"Like?"

"Oh, I don't know…uhmm, maybe paper, but lightweight, easily flammable."

"Old newspapers?"

"Exactly, though they're as rare as hen's teeth," Frank chuckles. "And, perhaps a bit of cardboard too, the sort I keep in the shed for bonfires. But I'd soak it all in petrol from the cans in my shed, though, to get a good flame, I'd make sure there was a ready supply of oxygen available too. Oxygen can feed a fire and really get it going… Oh, look the countdown is about to begin."

Logan

Logan listens to Greyson explaining what's happening as the seconds disappear and the four boosters begin to glow. There's a last shot of Asha Blackthorne giving an order to the other four astronauts before Maya-Daughter's boosters explode into downward streaks of fiery light and the supporting frames fall from her sides. Exhilaration shimmers through Logan, she can hardly breathe. Grabbing Greyson's hand, she holds tight as she watches Maya-Daughter hover for a minuscule moment before the force of her four rockets drives her up into the new, morning light.

Later, after having crossed the Blue Halo into the darkness beyond, Maya-Daughter orbits the earth as Logan lies Greyson's arms after the best sex she's had in years… while Fry phones Maggi.

Tristan Fry

His Noc rings twice before she answers. "Hello," Fry hears her say. There's nothing sleepy about her voice as he knew there wouldn't be, even though it's past 2 in the morning.
"Hi, Maggi, it's me, Tris Fry."
"Hello, Tris."
"Maggi, I need to see you. I can be at yours by 3, if I push it."
"Don't push it, Tris, I'll be here waiting for you, whatever time you arrive." In Frank's shed, Fry pockets a small hammer and a battery torch before sniffing various cans. Finding what he wants, he puts them in his car and drives to the police station. Swiping himself in, the desk sergeant greets him, his 3D projection of Maya-Daughter performing a Hohmann Transfer hovers over his desk.
"Did you see the launch?"

"Yeah, brilliant, wasn't it?"

"I'll say. They're about to burn again. You can watch it with me if you like," he offers.

"Thanks, mate, but I'll catch it later." Fry says, swiping the security door and letting himself in.

He's waited years for this night. He and Frank had planned it down to the last minute, but now he's left his grandfather to watch it alone on his Noc while he enters Logan's office and types in the code for the SafeCage. The metal door pings open and he pulls out the Cam.

Back on the road, he drives to Godlinghoe. As he pulls in at 33 Peartree Road, he is welcomed by the Christmas tree lights and Maggi, with Lobo at her side.

"Hi, Tris, Jonny and I are just having hot chocolate, we're watching Maya-Daughter," she greets him without asking why he has come. He shuts the front door behind him and touches her arm gently. She looks up at him, her face immediately creases and he can easily read her fears. He knows he's about to increase those fears a thousand fold, "but now," he tells himself, "is not the moment to think about that."

"Maggi," he says quietly, "I came over to say that I'll take Lobo and give him a home for as long as he needs one." He watches her hand rise to her mouth, see her old eyes fill with tears.

"Are you sure?" she implores.

"I'm sure," he answers.

She puts out her arms and pulls him to her, "Thank you, Tris," she murmurs. He finds her embrace unexpectedly comforting, it makes him realise how easy it would be to run away from his own troubles, just leave and let the law do its work. "But Maggi," he says, pulling away from her embrace, "there's something else."

"Yes?"

"It's a hypothetical question if you like."

"Go on."

"The D.N.A. at Bosuns Road is the only tangible evidence to link Butler to the body found at the allotment. If, hypothetically, say, someone had the back-door key and sprayed it and the lock with an oil lubricant, then entered the property with a can of petrol, soaked the upstairs carpet before pouring the rest of the petrol down the stairs and on the cardboard and paper in the hallway before setting it alight with a box of matches, I reckon the house and all its contents, all it's evidence, would go up like a booster rocket."

"I remember the house as damp," she says tremulously.

"It is damp, but only on the edges. The stairs are as dry as a bone, they creak like holy hell." He watches as her hand clasps her neck, he can hear the rhythm of her breathing changing to a shallow pull. "The trick to this," he continues, trying to sound self-assured, trying to infuse her with confidence, "is to create a draft by opening the landing window and the back door. The oxygen will fuel the fire and burn the interior, the evidence, before the Fire Brigade have a chance to put it out."

"But I've made a confession, you recorded it," she pants, ever so slightly.

"The Cam can easily have an accident. But that's not the question here, Maggi. The question is, hypothetically, whether you'd be willing to deny everything and risk a much longer prison sentence, if Logan wants to take it further."

"That's easy to answer. Going to prison will upset Jonny and seeing as he has no sense of time, it doesn't matter how long I go for. So, yes, I'd risk it. But what about you? You could get into so much trouble for this, Tris."

"Me," he smiles warmly at her, "Don't worry about me, I'm fine."

"I can't go out and leave Jonny on his own. Will you stay with him?"

"We'll watch telly together." He sees her hesitate; her breathing is ragged and fitful. "It's your call, Maggi, but Jonny and Lobo need you here, not in prison."

"Yes," she mutters, "You're right."

"And, Maggi, there's a torch, a spray can of oil, cardboard and a can of petrol in the porch, next to the Christmas tree."

"Okay," and he sees her steel herself.

CHAPTER 58
The Virgin Mary's Veil

*

4:20 a.m. 12th May 2023

Logan and Greyson lie on their backs, snuggled deep into soft pillows and warm blankets, watching Maya-Daughter swing round to face the ISS before docking to Maya-Mother... while Fry checks the time.

"You are clever, Tris, knowing all about the space ship. I think I remember when they went to the moon, or have I made that up?"

"You're right, Jonny, we went to the moon in 1969." Lobo pricks his ears and Fry hears the back door open.

"I won't be a moment, Jonny," he explains, getting up and patting the old man's shoulder. Jonny reaches up and reciprocates the gesture. "Take your time, me and Lobo are just dandy."

In the kitchen, he finds Maggi leaning against the sink, rasping for breath. The smell of petrol and fire seeps from her clothes.

"Maggi?"

"I'll be okay," she pants.

"I can't stay, I need to go." She nods, fighting for breath, her hand in front of her mouth, her lined skin bleached white. "I'll see you later. But remember, I was here to discuss Lobo," he reminds her.

"Yes," she manages.

"Okay. The matches, can I have them?" She riffles in her pocket and pulls them out.

"See you later," he says, leaving through the front door.

348

Picking up the torch, the oil spray and the empty petrol can from the porch, he puts them back into the boot of his car, next to the full can. He is about to get in, but something makes him stop. He turns his face upwards and feels fine drops of rain, then he catches something else. Smoke. He smiles and hopes that Maggi has managed to build a fire big enough to gut 16 Bosuns Road before either the rain or the fire brigade have time to extinguish it.

Forty minutes later, Fry drives past his house before entering the smaller Victorian backstreets of Chelmsford, where no road cameras are mounted. He knows these roads well, he and his mates used them as teenagers, skateboarding at night. After a while, he parks his car on a deserted stretch of wasteland, next to River Chelmer. Watching his windscreen wipers for a moment, he tries to be philosophical, gives up and gets out.

Taking the Cam, Fry pulls out the memory stick and pockets it before smashing it to pieces. It hurts his heart to see such an amazing piece of technology ruined and just hopes it going to be worth it. Chucking the pieces back into the car, he smashes the driver's side window inward, then wrapping his hand in a plastic evidence bag, he collects the shattered shards from the ground.

Back in the car he pulls the electrical leads from the steering column before uncapping the second can of petrol and pouring it carefully over the seats. After throwing the empty can into the car, he stands back and looks at his beloved machine. Sighing resignedly, he pulls Maggi's matches out of his pocket and studies the box. He understands the theory, though he's never used them before. Removing one of the pink-tipped shafts of wood, he holds it against the strike. Trying to mimic the action he saw Maggi use, he flicks hard. The pink tip bursts into flames making him drop the match. "Dammit," he mutters, taking out another. This time he's ready for the flare but the rain puts it out.

"Double dammit." He gingerly leans into the car. He wants to shut his eyes but knows that's just stupid. Holding his breath, he strikes a third match. A massive ball of orange fills the space and he jumps back. Soon the interior is engulfed in flames. Satisfied the car will burn, he walks towards the riverbank. A pale, rain-filled light is already starting to smear the sky as he pulls the memory stick from his pocket and throws it into the dark current. He watches the indestructible sliver bob away. Soon it will reach the Blackwater before entering the North Sea and from there, "goodness only knows," he thinks.

Taking a last look at his beloved car, he turns for the camera-free maze of backstreets and alleyways and begins his run home.

Maggi

Dressed in warm, sweet smelling clothes, with Jonny safely tucked up in bed, I make a pot of coffee and with Lobo padding along behind me, I make my way through the garden. I can smell smoke on the early morning air and as the first birds break the dawn silence they are accompanied by the distinct sound of fire engines roaring towards the village. I shut my eyes and pray to a God who has never listened to me. "Just this once, for Jonny, for Lobo and …okay, if I'm truthful, for me… let the fire have done its work."

At the summerhouse I open the doors and sit just out of the rain, watching it fall on the wooden planks of the veranda and the garden beyond.

"I never thought I'd go there again," I tell my daughter and my best friend as I shudder at the memory of forcing myself to unlock that back door and step in. All my instincts had screamed at me to leave as I pushed my feet up the stairs, to the room. I stood in the doorway, looking at the freezer. Petrol can in my hand. Cardboard under my arm. I felt swamped by my revulsion, my love, my hate. For twenty-five years, I'd lived with it, containing it, covering it, first for Rah then for Jonny. But standing again in that evil place was like ripping the Virgin Mary's veil away and finding only mortal flesh. There was never going to be any fairy tales, myths, prayers or wishes that were going to make any of this better.

I sniffed deeply and hawked up all the phlegm I could muster from the back of my throat and spat my hatred into the gloomy darkness. Then opening the can, I trailed petrol over the upstairs rooms and landing before coming down the stairs.

I could tell that the can was virtually empty. I began to panic and hyperventilate, it had taken all my will to calm my diaphragm and breathe properly. I looked about, forced myself to think. Saw the door to the cupboard under the stairs, opened it and shone Fry's torch into the recess. He'd been right, it was bone dry apart from the petrol that was now dripping through the treads.

Dragging my foot across the disintegrating newspapers, letters and flyers, I balled some together and pushed them into the cupboard. Making a second pile at the bottom of the staircase, I ripped the cardboard and scattered it around the paper mounds before dousing it with the last of the petrol.

"Is it enough to save Jonny and Lobo?" I fretted, standing there, looking at my handy-work with the smell of petrol clogging the air. I trawled my brain to remember what Tris had told me. "Oxygen," I sobbed, knowing I would need to re-climb the stairs. I forced myself back up and stood in front of the window but I just couldn't make myself reach out and touch that vile, net curtain. I looked down and saw I still had the can, taking it in both hands, I heaved it at the glass and smashed it through the curtain.

The noise echoed out into the night but I'd already turned and taken the stairs, running for the back door, which stood slightly ajar. "Just fucking do it," I yelled at myself. Putting down the can, I grabbed it with both hands and wrenched it open. The fresh air hit me hard, it helped me breathe, it made me feel sane. I nearly stepped out into the overgrown garden, but I knew if I did I'd never go back in again.

Pulling the matches from my pocket, I saw something scurry past me across the kitchen worktop.
"You better get out," I warned as I struck the first match. It flared brightly as I carried it to the cupboard and laid it against the paper. It caught. The petrol ignited. The paper burnt. I struck another, throwing onto the hallway pile. It went up too.

Smoke quickly filled the narrow space. I covered my mouth and nose as I watched the flames grow, spreading and sprouting, as they rose viciously licking the walls. The old paintwork started to blister and melt, the wallpaper curled and caught. A stench of burning dirt and decay mixed with smoke wafted from the blaze, it made me retch and cough. I backed away just as a small breeze swept in from the door, curled around my ankles and hit the fire. Like a ship's flare, the flames soared upwards, igniting the petrol-soaked stairs. A roar of heat forced me back into the kitchen, I turned, one last time, and saw the carpet ignite.

Back home, after Tris left, I stripped myself naked and stuffed all my things, including my shoes, into the washing machine. In the shower, I scrubbed my skin and hair hard. I could've spent the rest of the night under the hot, cleansing water trying to wash the immovable filth from my body, but that, like my anger, would've been futile and a pointless waste of time.

Getting up now, I walk out into the gentle rain and watch the droplets roll lazily down the sculptured bodies, deepening their colour to a darker bronze. With my finger I trace the features of the little girl and her mother, their almond shaped eyes, their neat nose, their high cheekbones. My heart feels the familiar ache of emptiness and longing as I make my useless wish.
"Just one more day." Lobo nudges my thigh. I reach for him, burying my head in his short fur and feel, again, the over whelming relief that now, come what may, I will no longer have to kill him.
"But Jonny, what do I do about Jonny?" I ask the three of them. Today was the day I'd arranged for him to move into Fellowfield House. "He'll hate it, I know he will. He'll cry in the night, be frightened and I'll not be there to comfort him. Maybe I could put it off, maybe Mr Trudy will hold the room for just a bit longer and maybe, just maybe, Tris's plan will work."

CHAPTER 59
Born to be Hanged

*

Logan

Logan feels the taut muscles of Greyson's torso as he slowly enters hers. Sighing with pure pleasure, she widens her thighs, wrapping her heels around his buttocks, drawing him in. She feels his breath on her face, his lips on her skin, his rigid cock pushing her open as she senses his excitement and feels her own mounting need to have him deep inside of her. Slowly, slowly, he rhythmically moves against the early morning light making her ache, making her body beg. Her conscious mind wants to hold on, for just a moment longer, but her body begins to crown with thundering waves of immeasurable sweetness that come crashing through her.

"That was sooo good," she thinks, catching her breath and gathering her thoughts. She wonders how, yet again, they'd managed to cum together. "Either we are a match made in heaven or it's true what they say about him, he is the best fuck in town."

Tristan Fry

Fry, reaching home, empties the evidence bag of glass chips into the gutter where he usually parks his car. Pocketing the bag, he unlatches the garden gate and opens the back door.

"Is that you, Tris?" Frank calls from the kitchen table.

"Yeah, only me. How's it going?"

"Fantastic. Maya-Complete is nearly operational. Asha has given her

353

first live interview, I have to say it was very moving." Fry comes and rests his hands on his Grandfather's shoulders. The Noc shows Maya-Complete spreading her solar arrays, preparing for her maiden voyage to meet the IMS Mars orbiter. "But more to the point, how are you, Tris?"

"I'm good. What you said earlier about riding two horses, well, I think, you're right. Only problem is, I've had my car stolen."

"Oh?"

"Yeah, I got home about 5:40, parked as normal, went to bed, got up and now it's gone."

"Will you report it?"

"Yeah, I'll have to. I had the Cam in the front seat."

"Fancy a cuppa?"

"Defo and a blooming, great, bacon sarnie too. I'm starving."

"Tell you what, give me your clothes and I'll get them into the machine, jump in the shower and I'll whizz us up something. Your mother's still at Leroy's, no need to give nuts to people without teeth."

"Thanks," Fry says, leaving the kitchen.

"And, Tris."

"Yeah?" he turns back in the doorway and looks at his grandfather.

"Just remember, if you're born to be hanged, you'll never drown."

Logan

Sipping fresh coffee in Greyson's warm kitchen, Logan can see the sky beyond the cottage windows is misty and grey. She can't remember a time when she has felt so whole, so at ease with herself, her body, her nature. She's loved every minute of it. The way he touched her, the way he moved against her, inside of her. His sexual energy, his giving, his taking.

"So, D.C.I. Logan, are we doing this again?" Greyson asks, smiling at her across the granite counter.

"God, yes," she replies, smiling back as her Noc vibrates. She picks it up, two messages.

Fry: **Hey Boss, any chance of a lift?**

She types back: **Pick you up on my way, 11 ish.**

Fry: **Cheers.**

The other message is from Andrea.

Andrea: **Thought you should know, on the local news there was a report of a house fire last night in Godlinghoe, Bosuns Road. Not sure of the house number.** Logan stares at the screen.

"Everything okay?" Greyson asks.

"Yeah, just work."

"Waxy?"

"Yeah, there's been nothing straight forward about this case."

"Isn't that the nature of murder?"

"Sometimes, most times. But this… it's challenging. It's taking me to places I don't want to go."

"Ethically or lawfully?"

"Ethically, I guess."

"Do you know Britten's opera, Billy Budd?"

"Nah, I'm not that clued-up on opera."

"Billy Budd is a story of homosexual violence and discrimination muddled up with an allegory of Jesus Christ's Passion. It's symbolistic, metaphoric and political but, above all, it's a tale of a moral judgement versus a lawful one. The Captain, in the story, clearly 'does the right thing' as the law dictates but his verdict still troubles him many years later."

"Okay, but how is this relevant?" She smiles slightly.

"You're smiling."

"Yeah, that reminds me of the last time I asked that question, and fuck was it relevant."

"Well the relevance here, sexy Logan…" he says softly, coming around the counter and touching her face, making her want to forget all about work, "is, I often find myself using the analogies in Billy Budd when I've a moral decision to make. If you like, I'll tell you the story tonight?"

"Is that a date?" she asks, raising an eyebrow.

"God, yes," he answers, mimicking her earlier response, before kissing her very willing mouth.

CHAPTER 60
Godspeed

*

Logan
At home, Logan jumps in the shower. She can still smell Greyson on her body and it makes her want to laugh out loud.

Tristan Fry
Fry and Frank munch their way through their breakfast, watching Major Asha Blackthorne and her crew waiting for their first timed blast to send them on a trajectory to Mars.
"This is Satish Dhawan actual. Godspeed, Maya-Complete."
"This is Maya-Complete actual. Thank you, Satish Dhawan."

Maggi
The doorbell rings and Lobo attempts a woof from his basket.
"Maggs, there's someone at the door," Jonny says, trying to lever himself up.
"It's only Anya, Jonny, I'll go."
"Anya? Is that Orla's friend? Is Orla here? Are the Christmas trees lights on? Maggs, where's Orla and Rah?"
"Orla and Rah are safe and sound Jonny, I promise you."
"Safe and sound," Jonny repeats.
"Safe and sound. And all the Christmas lights are on. Doesn't the little one on the table look pretty?"
    Out in the hallway, I look at the three suitcases packed and ready

to go before opening the front door.

"Hi Maggi, I hear there's been a change of plan?" Anya says, with her usual brightness.

"Hello, Anya. Yeah, sorry to mess you around. I spoke to Mr Trudy earlier and I've arranged for Jonny to just attend as normal today, then see how it goes."

"I must warn you, Mr Trudy won't hold Jonny's room for longer than a week, Maggi. I think he's only doing this as a favour, as Jonny is one of our regulars."

"I know, it's really kind of him, but I'm not ready…"

"Maggs, whose bags are these? Is someone coming to stay? Anya, are you coming to stay? There may be some cake if you're lucky," Jonny says, coming into the hall with Lobo at his side.

"Hello, Jonny, I've come to take you out for tea and cake."

"Ooh lovely, I'll just get my coat."

Logan

"So, what's the story? Engine trouble?" Logan asks as Fry gets into her car.

"Nah, it was stolen," he answers, buckling his seatbelt. Ever since she'd read Andrea's text, she'd felt uneasy, as though something wasn't going to add up. She'd tried pushing it aside blaming her day ahead, which, whatever way she looked at it, was bound to be shitty. Now this. She hopes to God that Fry isn't going to be involved in anything weird.

"What, from here?"

"Yeah, would you believe it."

"You loved that car."

"Yeah, but hey-ho, Frank and I have got our eyes on one of those new Eoes. Every cloud and all that."

"Nice," she comments, trying to ignore the obvious.

"There's just one problem, Boss, the Cam was in the car."

"Fuckin' hell, Fry," she swears knowing the obvious is just not going to lie down and play dead. "What have you done?"

"Nothing, Boss," he replies with such innocence.

357

She pulls over and stops the car. "Tell me, Fry," she demands.

"Really, there's nothing much to tell."

"Try me anyway," she snarls.

Tristan Fry

Even though he'd practiced this moment in the bathroom mirror and was feeling pretty confident with his performance, he starts to feel a bit edgy. He hates the thought of lying to Logan, but even more he hates the thought of Jonny and Maggi being punished unjustly. Looking down at his hands, his heartbeat begins to quicken. He braces himself and looks up at her. "Frank and I watched the launch, did you see it? It was really…"

"Don't…," she warns him.

He sighs resignedly. "We watched the launch, but I couldn't help worrying about what was going to happen to Jonny and Lobo when we arrest Maggi today. I had a chat with Frank and I decided the best thing I could do was offer Lobo a home, so Maggi wouldn't have to put him to sleep."

"Jeezes, Fry," she snaps, shaking her head in dismay. "That infringes so many fucking rules."

"Yeah, I know, so that's why I went to the station to get the Cam, so I could record the conversation, so, you know, it won't look that bad if I ended up owning a convicted criminal's dog. And that's about it."

"About it! You've got to be joking. Why did you go in the middle of the fucking night? Did she know you were coming?"

"Okay." He swallows hard, feeling as though he's standing in a wind tunnel and someone has just turned up the dial. "Like I said, I was worried, so I called Maggi and told her I was coming. I didn't want to leave it just in case she went to the vets first thing in the morning."

"First thing… What, like 3 fucking o'clock in the morning? It doesn't open till at least 8, I'm sure you could've waited."

"Probably, but I was worried, so I phoned her and when I got there, we talked about Lobo and she was really relieved. Then I headed home. Got back about 5:40, went to bed and when I got up, the car, with the Cam, was gone."

"And the fire?" she asks, with her head tilted and her eyebrows raised.

"What fire?"

"Fuck you, Fry. And I suppose when we turn up to arrest Maggi, she'll deny the whole thing. And by-on digging up Orla's body we've got no proof anymore."

"Orla's body won't really give us any proof and anyway we don't know where the body is, Boss, Maggi never exactly told us that."

"No, but I could make a good fucking guess at it. Jeezes, fucking Christ, Fry." Gripping the steering wheel, she stares ahead.

"Boss?"

"Don't Boss me," she mutters, then taking a breath, she says, "You'll have to report the car and the Cam stolen, then I suggest you go home and give me a chance to think this through."

"Okay," Fry murmurs, feeling sick.

As they drive through the streets of Chelmsford, he can't help but check the traffic cameras. He's sure that the footage and times will bear out any minor investigation, as it will show him heading to the police station, driving to Godlinghoe, then returning. What it won't show is his extra curricula street running activities. As if Logan has read his thoughts, she suddenly says,

"They'll check the cameras, Fry."

Maggi

Pottering around the kitchen, I try to stay focussed on making tomato sauce and pizza bread. But my mind keeps pulling me to the overnight bag that sits on the table. Every so often I think of something essential and put it in, only to rethink it and take it out again. Lobo, aware of my unease, watches wide-eyed from his basket.

Logan

At the station, Logan leaves Fry to file his report and angrily stabs at the lift button. It doesn't respond.

"Fucking lift," she mutters, pressing it again and again. If she's honest, it's not the loss of the Cam that really bothers her, though that's bad enough, it's the thought of Fry getting into trouble. She really likes him and wonders how far she'll push the boundaries to shield him.

"Not beaten by a lift are you, Top Cunt?" comes an acerbic voice from behind her.

"Fuck, that's all I need," she thinks before answering brusquely, "Go away, Trev."

"No Officer Dibble to back you up, Top Cunt? What? Is he at home with his pinny on?"

Sighing deeply, she turns to face him. "I've decided to take half of the house; if you check out the current prices, you'll know what I'm expecting to be paid. If not, it'll be on the market next week."

Bing, the lift arrives. Getting in she presses 3 and looks back at Trev. "The divorce papers are with my solicitor, who'll be contacting yours, Jodie Lewis, I presume at Slater, Cooke and Penninghams." She sees his expression, she knows that look only too well. A mixture of shock and hurt, the same look he gave her every month, when she told him she wasn't pregnant. He begins to say something; she cuts him off, "In future, only contact me through my solicitor." The door slides shut, the lift jerks once, then it's on its way up. She leans back against the metal wall and breathes out.

At the 2nd floor, Andrea gets in. "Hi Boss."

"Hi Andrea," she says, putting away her personal life.

"That fire I texted you about?"

"Yeah?"

"It was 16 Bosuns Road. I recognised the address as belonging to one of the people Fry asked me to check out, Herrick Butler."

"Of course it fucking was. Jeezes, Fry, what the fuck have you done?" she thinks with a sinking heart before thanking Andrea as the lift halts and they both get out. She turns and finds herself walking into Grim's office.

"Hey."

"Hey," she answers, flinging herself into a chair.

"Good night?" he asks over the rim of his glasses.

"Yeah," and even though she feels the weight of the world on her shoulders, a smile cracks across her lips.

"That's good. They always say Greyson's the man," he grins at her.

"And *they*, whoever *they* are, would be right," she grins back.

"*They* are probably an eclectic mix of interesting people knowing Greyson."

"Well, I've just joined the interesting people's club."

"Will you be renewing your membership?"

"This very evening. How was your night?"

"Bloody brilliant, loved every minute of it. That Asha Blackthorne is a woman and a half. I'd marry her any day."

"She'd be a fool to turn you down."

"That's clinched it, I'll ask her as soon as she gets home. Anyway, what brings you to my door, D.C.I. Logan?"

"Two things. Firstly, I need a good solicitor."

"Bloody hell, he must have some powerful spunk if we're talking divorce papers."

"Fuck off," she grins again.

"I'd try Victoria Dunmow at Dunmow and Sons. Second?"

"It's the Waxy case. I thought I had a solid I.D. but now it seems to have disintegrated."

"Uh, one of those. Who's in your line-up?"

"It could be one of two people. The most likely is Herrick Butler. No record. Never been missed, no family, no friends. The other is Victor Martin, whose family is desperate to have him back."

"Any D.N.A. for either man?"

"No."

"Any witnesses?"

"I suspect not."

"P.M. report?"

"Both men could fit the classifications."

"What's your gut instinct?"

"I know it's Butler, but I haven't got any proof."

"Is there more to this than you're saying?

"Yeah, a heap more. But it's all conjecture, all messy and a bit fucked up."

"If you told me, would it tie your hands?"

"Almost certainly."

"You could name the body and add a proviso to the effect that the I.D. is only supposition based on post-mortem findings and date analysis."

"Would that hold up if there was a further investigation?"

"As long as you make it clear that it's guesstimated. Or, if you're that uncertain, just mark the body as a John Doe and file it with Cold Case. Oh, and don't forget that pro-ass report on Fry, I need it by Monday tops.

CHAPTER 61
Snorting with Fear

*

Logan

Leaving Grim's office, Logan suddenly feels claustrophobic with the thought of being stuck in the Station for the afternoon, trying to write up Fry's assessment. Taking the lift back down, she gets into her car and is in Godlinghoe within the hour, looking at the blackened remains of 16 Bosuns Road.

The house still smokes ominously as a crew of weary fire-fighters douse down the scorched walls and singed roof beams.

"You made a bloody good job of that, Fry," she thinks sarcastically as she avoids stepping into a continuous stream of murky water running from the garden into the road gutter.

"I told you it was a health hazard." Turning towards the voice, she sees a middle-aged woman, arms crossed and slippers on, fronting a small band of people standing on the other side of the police tape. "I only said the other day it was an accident waiting to happen."

Logan knows the face and hunts her mind for a name. "Good afternoon, Mrs Wormold, you live two doors down, don't you?" she says, going over to the group.

"Yes, number 20. We warned the council and what did they do?"

"Nothing," supplies another slipper-shod gang member.

"I could've been burnt in my bed, for all you lot care," proclaims Mrs Wormold, huffing her large bosoms in the air with her crossed arms while the muled members nod in agreement.

363

Logan feels her eyebrows wanting to rise in an expression of, "Really…coz that would've taken a miracle," instead, she controls herself and asks, "Did you see or hear anything last night, Mrs Wormold?"

"Yes, it was me that called the Fire Brigade. I was awake due to my back, I'm a martyr to it, though you never hear me complain." The slipper crew confirm this with their now synchronised nodding.

"What alerted you to call the emergency services, Mrs Wormold?" Logan inquires, trying to keep her tone professional.

"I smelt something fishy, well not fishy… smoky. I went out to have a look and Lord Above, 16 was on fire."

"What time was that?"

"Just after 5, though I'd been up since 3. I had to take painkillers, and then I just couldn't get back off. I suffer from insomnia too."

"5, that sounds about right," Logan thinks, calculating the time it would've taken, after the launch, for Fry to get to Godlinghoe and set a fire. "Did you notice anything unusual before you called the Fire Brigade? Any noises? Any cars?" she asks.

"I'm not one of those who spends my time peeking through my nets, you know," Mrs Wormold states self-righteously, huffing her sagging boulders up again.

Logan knows her irritation at the whole situation is getting the better of her when she retorts, "I'll take that as a no then."

"Yes, it is a no, because I would've said, wouldn't I, if I'd seen anyone lurking about up to no good?" Mrs Wormold replies and Logan feels the eyes of the slipper squad bore belligerently into her.

"You've lost them now," she silently reprimands herself before saying, "Okay, well if you do remember anything, however small or insignificant, please can you phone Chelmsford Police and ask for D.C.I. Logan." Then bobbing under the tape barrier, she pretends not to see the shared look of scornful incredulity that passes between them.

At her car, she changes into wellies before walking back to the charred house. Stepping through the front door into the blackened remains of the hallway, she can see that the stairs have all but

364

disappeared, only the shaped brickwork hints at where they'd once stood. Carefully, she threads her way across the unstable floor till she reaches the solid, concrete surface of the kitchen. Looking up, she can see the pale grey sky between the charred rafters.

"Hey, you can't come in here." She turns to find the towering figure of a fire-fighter bearing down on her.

"Sorry, I should've said I was here. Chelmsford CID, D.C.I. Logan."

"I couldn't give a monkey's whether you're the Queen of Sheba, it's not safe and you shouldn't be in here."

"I just wanted to check out the damage."

"Those joists could go at any time and you haven't even got a hard hat on."

"Yeah, sorry. Is the interior complete destroyed?"

"I'd say, the place will have to be bulldozed for sure, nothing salvageable here."

"What do you think started it?"

"I'd pretty much stake my career on it being petrol," he answers and she can feel him warming to his subject.

"Arson then?"

"I reckon."

"Where was the fire set?"

"My guess... around the staircase. The back door was open, that's what fuelled it. But, and here's the interesting thing, the fire spread through the upstairs first. It's gutted, unlike down here."

"Why's that?"

"Someone put down an ignitant up there, petrol most probably. Took out the first floor before dropping through. Now I must insist you leave," he says, indicating towards the back door.

"Thanks for your help," she replies, stepping out into the scorched, wet garden.

"I've got a couple more things to check out and then I'll write up my report," he says, ushering her along.

"Okay. I think, I'll go and check out the track that runs behind these houses," she replies, lifting her hand in goodbye and heading along the path.

At the garage, she peers through the dirty glass and can just make out the shape of a large old-fashioned car, the sort of thing her Dad would've liked. Walking on, she briefly stands in Lead Lane and imagines Maggi and Jonny's terrifying hunt along this over-grown track in the pitch black looking for their lost daughter. Logan shivers and strides back to her car.

After changing her shoes, she drives to Peartree Road. Now she's gotten use to the Christmas trees, she finds them strangely welcoming in the dull grey afternoon light. Knocking on the door, she hears a single woof echo in the passageway followed by Maggi's broad frame.

"D.C.I. Logan, come in." Stepping over the threshold, Logan notices the suitcases in the hallway and then the half-packed bag on the kitchen table, next to the little Christmas tree.

"No D.C. Fry?" Maggi asks.

"No," Logan answers, watching the old woman. Her stance is strong like her body and Logan finds herself thinking, "you're brave."

"Are you going to arrest me?" Maggi asks assertively.

"I think the real question should be…" Logan replies matching Maggi's tone, "do you know who was buried in your allotment?" Logan knows she needn't have come, she knows she could have done this on the phone but she wants to see Maggi's face, wants to know how well this old woman is going to lie.

"No, I have no idea." Maggi's voice remains even and reserved.

"And do you have any idea how he got to be under your shed?"

"Again, no idea."

Logan stares at her opponent, willing her to crumble but Maggi holds her gaze and stands her ground. "This won't make it go away," Logan states flatly and walks out of the front door.

Driving home, the sun starts to break through the cloud, its rays glint off the side of a huge metallic juggernaut that Logan is passing. Baby-soft, pink-tinged muzzles peek through the metal vents, snorting with fear.

"Fuck," she mutters and puts her foot down.

CHAPTER 62
Principle Players

*

Logan - December 2023

"This is Maya-Complete actual…contact and capture achieved."

"This is International Mars Station actual…hook-docks lined and ready for locking."

"This is Satish Dhawan actual… International Mars Station, please finalise procedure."

Greyson lays his hand on Logan's belly as they watch the docking of Maya-Complete to the International Mars Station. He feels the baby move, stretching her muscles, finding her limbs.

"Did you feel that?" Logan smiles, lying propped up on pillows and blankets in Greyson's observatory.

"Yes," he smiles back. "Any idea what you are going to call her?"

"I thought...maybe ... Maya," she says shyly. It's the first time she's spoken the name out loud to someone else.

"Maya," he smiles again, "Maya because she can reach the stars. I like that." A mixture of relief and pleasure fills her. She's pleased he likes it, though she knows he would never challenge her decision. Watching the two spacecrafts dock in Mars' orbit, she thinks back on those weeks after the launch.

It had been a rollercoaster ride for her following the Bosuns Road fire. It hadn't helped that she'd started to feel a bit under the weather. She'd put it down to the stress and worry over Fry – that and pure tiredness from the late nights and early morning in

Greyson's huge bed.

When she'd left Maggi on that fateful day, she'd driven to Fry's. He'd made her tea and they'd sat in his kitchen.

"Off the record," she'd said to him, "are you really going to be able to deny Maggi's confession?"

"It's not about denying what I heard, it's more about denying Butler two more lives. Jonny would never survive without Maggi, she's his rock in his dementia-riddled brain. Butler has already ripped their souls apart and I'm dammed if I'm going to let that monster kill again," Fry had declared passionately before pausing and running his hand through his hair. "Anyway, if you don't ask me the question, Boss, I won't have to lie."

Logan had pursed irritably. "For fuck sake, Fry, you could face criminal charges, you know that, don't you?"

"Yeah, I know it," he'd answered resignedly.

Later that night, after Greyson had told her the tale of beautiful, stammering Billy Budd and troubled precisianistic Captain Vere, she'd done something she'd only ever done with Grim. She'd confided in him. He'd listened as she'd told him the whole sorry tale of Maggi, Norah and Jonny, the murder of Orla, the torture of Hoyle, the killing of Butler and, finally, her terrible suspicion that Fry had destroyed the evidence.

He'd thought for a while as he lay naked next to her, one arm curved around her, the other behind his head. She'd waited, her hand resting on his warm, smooth skin, watching the even rise and fell of his chest. After a moment, he'd said, "Do you know where Orla is buried?"

"Not exactly, but I gathered it's in the garden at Peartree Road."

"And what would be gained by exhuming the body?"

"That it would confirm her death. That her remains had been hidden. It might even show she was murdered."

"That could be difficult after 25 years unless her bones were broken and, from the description Maggi gave you, it doesn't sound as though they were. More likely asphyxiation of some sort. It would fit with Butler's M.O. to own, dominate and control. And Maggi is the only one left to answer for the murder of Butler and the torture of Hoyle?"

"Yes. The others are either dead or incapacitated."

"Is Hoyle alive?"

"No, died in 2017 from natural causes. Ron sent me his file, he was a nasty piece of work by all accounts."

"And Maggi didn't actually kill anyone?"

"No, but she has concealed two bodies, Butler's and Orla's."

"This other guy you mentioned a couple of weeks ago, Victor Martin, was it?"

"Fuck, you've got a good memory. But yes, Victor Martin."

"Tomorrow, send me over the files on both men and I'll let you know how the science adds up. But I have to say, using Rocuronium bromide... it's inspired! I think I'd like Jonny and Maggi."

"Yeah, that about says it all and it brings me to my biggest fucking headache, Fry."

"Ah there it is, the Billy Budd predicament. How about I do the calcs on your two principle players before you make a decision about Fry?".

"Okay," she'd said, relieved for the lifeline even though she thought it was probably too flimsy to hold her weight.

She'd left Greyson's warm body just as the sun was rising and had wound her way back through the sleepy lanes into Little Marney before hitting the A12. She'd told her Noc to connect to the car speakers and play, at full blast, Grim's remix 70's hits. Singing along to Donna Summer's Love to Love you Baby, she'd remembered the last time she'd sung this song. She'd been full of hurt at Trev's betrayal.

"It's amazing what a good fuck can do," she'd thought as the Jackson Five kicked in.

At the station, she'd opened her Computer and brought up Victor Martin's original missing file and Ron's report on Herrick Butler. She'd selected one photo from each of the files and sat for some time, looking at the two men.

"There's something... what? Something TV...Ah-ha." Searching for a third photo, she asked the computer for American detective shows. Running through the list, she'd touched one and selected an image of Tom Selleck as Thomas Magnum P.I. and placed it between the other two photos.

"Bingo," she'd smiled, staring at the three men in their mid-30s. Selleck was dark haired and healthy, unlike Butler and Martin who were both ginger haired with bulging waist lines but what really tied them all together, was the unmistakable bushy Thomas Magnum moustaches. And, as if to corroborate her hypothesis, Victor Martin was sporting a brightly patterned Hawaiian type shirt.

"Noc, phone Christina Martin."

"Hello," came a timid voice Logan recognised it.

"Hello, Christina, this is D.C.I. Logan from Chelmsford Police. I wondered if I may ask you a couple of questions about Victor?"

"Yes," Christina answered and Logan heard the note of hope in that one word.

"Did Victor like the TV detective program, Magnum P.I?"

"Oh yes, it was his favourite. We actually had a family holiday in Oahu, Hawaii."

"And, Christina, by any chance, did Victor like to chew gum?"

"Yes," and this time Christina's tone holds not only hope but astonishment too. "How did you know that?"

"Just a lucky guess."

After the phone call, Logan added this information to Victor Martin's file before emailing both Butler's and Martin's files to Greyson.

CHAPTER 63
Tossing and Turning

*

Logan

By Monday afternoon, Greyson had sent his reply. She'd been in her office with the door shut for most of the day. She'd known Fry and Grim were both around but, for very different reasons, she hadn't wanted to speak to either of them. She'd opened the email on her Noc. Somehow, it had felt less complicit than if she'd read it plastered in the air above her desk.

So, here's what I think.

Herrick Butler's profile is tailor-made for Waxy but… if I had no one else in the line-up, I might have considered Victor Martin as a possible match. There's a fair amount of corresponding info, however, as the distinctive muscle stress in the jaw and upper body doesn't equate, I'd probably be wary of confirming this I.D. (Nice try on the chewing gum front though)

"Fuck," she'd muttered.

Still…without DNA there's nothing solid here either way.

I'm with the Eddy Paths this week, be back Friday if you fancy supper.

Greyson

"Fuck again," she'd said, surprising herself about how much she minded that he was away.

Shutting the computer, she'd left the office. At home, she'd changed into her running gear and made for the farm track. The May afternoon was still warm and buzzing with life but Logan thought she might as well have been wading through mud, as her legs felt like dead weights, her lungs rigid and her muscles tight.

"Pocket back, pocket back," she'd muttered, trying to keep her mind on her stride. At the end of the farm track, she'd bent and caught her breath.

"Jeezes, what's wrong with me?" she'd asked herself. "Oh, let's see... you're about to screw up Fry's life, let alone Maggi Drew, Jonny Gifford and Christina Martin's, to say nothing of the druggy son." Suddenly, without warning, she'd found herself crying.

"What the...?" she'd thought and wiping the tears away on her sleeve, she'd forced herself to run home, hard. After showering, she'd sat and filled in Fry's Pro-Ass and emailed it to Grim. Next, she'd typed up her case notes on Waxy, deleted them, wrote them again, deleted them again, gave up and went to bed. She'd fully expected to spend the night tossing and turning, instead, she'd slept like the dead.

On Tuesday, she'd heard Grim come bowling down the corridor, laughing with Daff before putting his head around her office door. "You look like crap," he'd said, grinning at her as he'd leaned against the door frame with his arms crossed.

"Thanks," she'd said light-heartedly, though she'd felt a tiny prick of hurt.

"Greyson not up to it?" Grim had continued in true police banter.

"Fuck off. Anyway, he's in Edinburgh this week," she'd responded in kind.

"Ah, that accounts for it. You must be pining."

"And fuck off again," she'd said, forcing herself to grin back at him. "Did you get hold of Victoria Dunmow?"

"The solicitor, yeah. She reckons it will be pretty straight forward, only the house to agree on," she'd answered, relieved by the change in subject.

"Do you want the house?"

"Nah, can't wait to move back to town. Somehow country living is not my thing."

"You can always kip on my couch until you get a place," he'd said and again she'd found herself wanting to overreact, as though he'd offered her one of his kidneys.

"Cheers," she'd mumbled back.

"Oh, and nice Pro-Ass on Fry. How's things going with Waxy?"

"Slowly," she'd sighed, and, much to her irritation, she'd felt her eyes start to sting with tears.

"Right," Grim had paused, tapping his thumbs against his elbows. "Curry and beers at mine and let's thrash this fucker out. I've got work backing up, I want you on the Jasper Lane burglary."

"Fine, but one thing," she'd replied, shuffling stuff around as though tidying her desk so she could avoid looking at him.

"What?"

"I want you to reassign Fry to another team. I reckon he'd do okay with Beverly Garrow's lot."

Again, she'd heard the thumb tapping. "And who do you want as a replacement?" he'd said after a while.

"Anyone," she'd replied casually, as though it meant nothing to her.

"Anyone? What, even Tinpot?"

"Yeah, he'll do."

"Fffuuuck," Grim breathed out, not even bothering to hide what he thought of that.

"I'll tell you later," she'd said, shutting the conversation down.

"Oookay … see you about 7," he'd said and walked off.

They'd cracked a couple of beers open and eaten a takeaway. Grim sat in his usual Lazy Boy and she was sprawled across the black, leather sofa.

"God, I'm stuffed," she'd moaned, undoing her trouser button starting to feel herself again.

"Yeah, me too. I promised the doc I'd cut down on the carbs but when duty calls, you've just got to go for it," he'd said, rubbing his belly.

"What's the problem?"

"Apparently, I drink too much and my cholesterol's high, can you believe it? Me an Adonis of a man… I could give Ajax a run for his money any day of the week."

"Have you been playing Greek Boys again?" she'd asked, smiling at him.

"Might've," he'd smiled back before saying, "So, spill the beans, what've you got stashed in your wooden horse?"

"Off the record?"

"Off the record." And for the second time, within five days, she'd related Maggi's story.

"Whoa, that's a humdinger," he'd responded, tapping out a tune on his beer can before doing what she knew he would do, tell her one of his allegorical stories.

"I've probably mentioned Bolly before. He was one of my first D.C.I.'s, a right tough fuck always temperamental, rude but as loyal as a British Bulldog with his own brand of morals, which, truth be told, often differed from the policing manual. He wasn't above metering out his own sort o' justice, if you get what I mean. I could say he taught me everything I know but that would be a fucking lie, but what he did teach me was that you always have a choice.

So, here goes…It was the winter of '82 and one major crime was dominating the Met, a series of armoured van raids across the city. They were well coordinated and executed, professional like, and the bill was stacking up. The banks involved were spitting fire at the chiefs and they were spiting fire at us mere mortals.

It was overtime all round, everyone out greasing their grasses. Well, that was until a couple of Toms turned up dead. Both had been mutilated, strangled and dumped, not even hidden, just dumped, like rubbish. Now this was a crime Bolly couldn't stand. Battering women, as he saw it and, I have to agree, just trying to earn themselves an honest living. You've got to remember this was before all that sex slave and pedo stuff came to light. Anyway, Bolly was incensed when he was told to look the other way and stay with the armoured van investigation. It was like a red rag to a bull with 'fucking this' and 'bastard that' but he did his duty until a third working girl showed up murdered like the other two. Then, he did the complete opposite. He kept a couple of useless twats on the bank vans and the rest of us were sent chasing the perv."

"Did you nab him?"

"Fucking right we did, stupid little cunt. You know the type, weedy little mummy's boy trying to prove himself by killing vulnerable woman. Cried like a baby when he coughed. Dead now, jail justice, knifed in Parkie, I do believe."

"What about the armoured vans?"

"The gang turned over a couple more and disappeared into the ether, well, probably more like Costa del Crime, but same difference. But here's the thing... Bolly knew if he'd nicked them, he would've been king pin with a fat promo, just as he knew that catching the perv would only earn him a bollocking."

"And the moral of this story is..." she said with theatrical innocence, "don't nick the perv if you want to collect the bounty?"

"Do you know what Lo..."

"Fuck off?" she added for him jokingly.

"Hole in one," he'd chuckled back. "But seriously...the point here is Bolly had options. I don't mean the illegal crap, forget that. I mean there are always choices, however small, as long as they're legit. And yeah... sometimes, it's not all about pomp and glory, it can be about principles."

"Thanks," she'd acknowledged.

"Having said all that... can you move your fucking arse and get Waxy Boy sorted, I've a stack of work that needs seeing too."

"I'll start on the Jasper Lane burglary tomorrow, but I still need some more time."

"Don't take too long."

"By the way, who've you assigned me?"

"Roberta Leopard."

"So, not Tinpot?" she'd smiled, raising an eyebrow.

"Even I wouldn't inflict that tosspot on you," he'd laughed.

CHAPTER 64
Smashed to Smithereens

*

Logan

Logan's following three weeks had been taken up by the Jasper Lane burglary, a stabbing at Tall Tom's nightclub and a violent assault, as well as Greyson. Roberta Leopard proved to be competent and capable but she couldn't help missing Fry's friendly enthusiasm, though the thought of him made her tetchy and irritable.

At the beginning of June, the 'under the weather' feeling developed into full-blown sickness. One morning, after dragging herself to work, she'd tried to drink a Latte Roberta had bought her, and had promptly thrown it up in the bin.
"Eww, perhaps you should go home, Boss?" Roberta had said, her face a picture of revulsion, which would've made her smile if she hadn't thought she was going to be sick again.
"I'll be..." she'd managed, before pushing past Roberta and running for the loos.

After emptying the contents of her stomach, she'd rinsed her mouth and looked at herself in the mirror over the sink.
"Jeezes, you look bad," she'd told herself, examining her washed-out face and bloodshot eyes. The door swung open and P.C. Rowena Wilkinson strolled in, accompanied by an overpowering scent of body spray that sent Logan dashing for a cubicle again. With nothing left to chuck up, her body had jerked and retched spasmodically, squeezing out the last of her bitter tasting bile. Back at the sink, she

was rinsing her mouth again when she'd caught Rowena looking at her through the mirror.

"You okay, gal?" Rowena had asked briskly.

"Yeah-yeah ... fine." she'd answered, hanging onto the rim of the sink.

"You've been looking rough for a while, haven't you?" Rowena had stated pragmatically.

"Don't hold back, Rowena," Logan had thought as she said, "What do you mean?"

"Just that… you've been looking crock for a couple of weeks now. The whole station's running a book on it. People are betting on whether you're either cracking up because of the divorce or you're up the duff. I've put my money on the baby, coz I reckon even you know Trevor Dillsworthy ain't worth it."

Dumbfounded, Logan tried to think of a witty response but all she could manage was, "Sorry, Rowena, you're about to lose your dosh because I can't-I can't conceive," and a familiar stab of pain nearly smothered her.

"You think? Have you had tests and that done, from the Docs? Coz my cousin tried and tried for a baby with her fella and in the end, they went to one of those fancy clinics up London, cost them a bomb, and used donor sperm. It must o' been powerful coz bingo, next minute she's up the duff. And from what I've heard, you've been shagging Greyson Stonewalker. Well, if ever a fella's going to have magic sperm it's bound to be him with a name like Greyson Stonewalker. Is that really his name? Coz it sounds like he's stepped right out of one of those sci-fi movies my Steve watches."

Staring back at Rowena through the glass, Logan thought she'd probably be on the floor if she wasn't hanging on so hard to the sink.

"Yeah, that's his real name," she'd mumbled back, feeling sicker than ever.

"What was his parents thinking o'? Mind you, not as bad as some I've heard. I nicked a girl the other day called Cherrie Pie. Can you believe it?"

"Umm."

"Do a test, Love, and let me know, coz I've got a tenner on it," Rowena had said with a smile and left.

"Ffffuck," Logan muttered at herself in the mirror before following her out. Rowena was still in the corridor, chatting to Daff. "Probably reviewing her fucking bet," she thought and headed for Grim's office.

"Hey," he'd said as she'd plonked herself in a chair.

"You never guess what's just happened to me. I was in the loos and Rowena came in and told me there's a fucking book running on whether I'm going crackers or I'm pregnant. Jeezes Christ, can you believe it?"

"Yeah, I heard."

"What?"

"Yeah, the odds are quite good. I'm toying with the idea of putting a score down." He'd grinned at her.

"What the fuck on? Me cracking up or being pregnancy?"

"Seeing as I have inside info, it's not going to be the cracking up, is it?"

"Are you saying you think I might be pregnant after all that shit with Trev?"

"You're the detective, D.C.I. Logan."

"Well I'm fucking not, so that just leaves me being shipped off to the looney bin," she'd snapped uncharacteristically back at him, before bursting into tears.

"Oh Lo, sorry," he said, coming round his desk and sitting next to her. "It's just the usual crap, you know, no one means it. We run a book on every bloody thing. There's even one on whether Tinpot will make Chief Super."

"What've you put on for that?" she'd asked, blowing her nose and smiling through her tears.

"Dead cert," he'd said smiling back. "Listen, seriously. I think you should take the morning off and do a pregnancy test."

"That's just-just... fucked up and stupid."

"What if you are?"

"What if I'm not?" she'd slammed back.

"What if what, it doesn't matter." he'd said with a shrug. "Look, give me five minutes and I'll come with you. We'll buy it and go to mine."

She'd stared at him, "Are you bonkers?"

"Yes. See you in 5."

In the town centre, they'd bought a test then headed to Grim's flat. She'd fannied about, trying to drink a coffee, trying to put off the inevitable until he'd said, "For fuck sake, Lo, go and get on with it, the suspense is killing me."

Opening the packet in the bathroom, she hadn't bothered to look at the instructions, because every word was already imprinted across her heart. Weeing on the stick, she'd waited a moment before coming out and looking at Grim.

"And?" he'd said, thumbs tapping.

"Yes...fucking hell, yes. Oh my God! Yes."

He'd leaped out of his chair and grabbed her and they'd danced round his sitting room like teenagers, her shouting, "Yes," and him shouting, "I fucking knew it!"

When they'd stopped, she'd looked at him and seen tears glistening in his eyes.

"Grim?"

"Fuck, it's nothing-nothing," he'd said, turning away.

"It's not nothing. Tell me?

"It's stupid."

"Go on."

"It's just, I never thought I'd have a baby...I know it's not my baby biologically, but I will be the best goddamn uncle... dad... superhero it could ever wish for."

"Aww, Grim, that's brilliant," she'd said, hugging him hard.

Walking to the station, she'd felt more alive than she had in months, even with the constant nausea lurking under her happiness.

"Bloody got to put a ton down now on that bet," Grim had laughed.

"Me too," she'd laughed back.

"By the way, how close are you to finishing the Allotment Body investigation?" he'd asked.

"I'm there with it," she'd told him, and that was true. It's just that she hadn't been able to commit it to words.

"When can I expect it, Lo?"

"Today. Just got to write it up."

Back in her office, she'd shut the door, dictated her report, watched her words appear on the computer screen, read it through, signed it electronically before e-mailing the file to Grim. Feeling sicker than ever, and knowing it wasn't all due to the pregnancy, she'd asked her Noc to dial Christina Martin's number. Each ring made her nausea deepen.

"Hello," came the hesitant voice that she knew was Christina's.

"Hi Christina, it's D.C.I. Logan, Chelmsford Police. I have some news for you."

"Yes?" And the hope she heard had brought tears to her eyes.

"I'm sorry, Christina, the body isn't your husband's, it isn't Victor." She'd tried to sound firm, and reassuringly professional, but her own voice quivered with emotion.

"Oh, I had hoped." Logan heard her words bathed in pain.

"Victor's name will stay on our files, Christina, and I'm sure it will come up again." It was all she could tell this woman, whose hopes and dreams she'd just smashed to smithereens, it was all she had to offer.

Later, Grim had texted.

Hey Lo, thanks for the Waxy report. If you're sure, I'll file it.

File it, she messaged back.

CHAPTER 65
Mists of Nausea Waves of Joy

*

Logan

The early June weather was warm that weekend and Logan felt the sun on her back as she'd weaved her way along the path to Greyson's allotment. She'd stopped short of the entrance and, still hidden by the vegetation, she'd watched him digging.

He was dressed in a t-shirt and cotton trousers, the type hikers wear and she could easily make out the body, she'd begun to know so well, beneath the clothes. Slim, strong, long-limbed with knotted muscles. His dark hair, cropped stylishly short, caught the sunlight, while his skin was already tanned. No one would describe him as good looking but he had an energy that transcended his physical form that she, like many others, found desirable.

"Your father," she'd thought, touching her belly. She wasn't in the market for any kind of long term relationship and she was pretty sure Greyson would never give up his lifestyle for her or a child anyway, but she liked their easy friendship and was happy to tell him about the baby.

Stepping out, she'd called to him and he'd turned, smiling.

"Lo, good to see you. Fancy a cuppa? I've even made biscuits." They'd sat in the afternoon sun, talking, eating and drinking.

After a while she'd said, "By the way, I'm pregnant." He'd looked at her and for a split second she had no idea what he was feeling until, slowly, a huge smile cracked across his face.

"Wow, that's fan-bloody-tastic, Lo. When's the baby due?"

"8th of Feb," she'd smiled back, pleased he was pleased.

"Wah-hooo," he'd exclaimed. "Can I be there?

"I'll think about it."

"If not, Grim and I can pace the corridors together."

"That sounds like a plan."

"I bet Grim's over the moon."

"Yeah, he's really pleased."

"Is there anything I can do… you know, to help? You can move into the cottage if you like or I'll…"

"Thanks, but that'd never work for either of us, though it's really kind of you to offer. I'm moving back to Chelmsford, I miss city life."

"Great, I'll put some money in too, I've got a bloody great inheritance just sitting in a bank doing nothing. And I'm a whizz with a paintbrush…Wow, a Dad," he'd mused. "God, that's awesome."

The summer weeks had rolled by in a mist of nausea, broken only by sudden waves of joy. By the end of July her sickness had abated, her divorce had gone through and Trev was in the process of buying her out. She'd known she could have got more money on the open housing market than he was offering but it would've taken longer and "besides," she'd thought, "the house was always his choice anyway."

She'd been cleaning and boxing up her few possessions when Grim had messaged.

Flat for sale in my block, I can arrange viewing if you like, Mother of Dragons. Xx

Sounds good, but Mother of what? Xx, she'd texted back.

I'll get the box set out and educate your heathen soul. Xx

That afternoon, she'd taken a quick look around with Grim in tow. The flat, a floor above him, was much more substantial, with three bedrooms, en suite, family bathroom and a wrap-around balcony. Though it was in desperate need of modernisation and a lick of paint, the light, when the thick net curtains were pulled aside, was incredible.

"I'll help you clean and decorate it," Grim had offered and she'd bought it on the spot.

It was that week too when Fry had knocked on her office door and asked to have a word.

"Yeah, sure," she'd said, though her tone had been far from friendly.

"I just wanted to thank you for my Progression Review."

"That's okay," she'd muttered back.

"It's given me the opportunity for promotion."

"Good," she muttered again.

"But I've decided to hand in my notice."

"Oh?"

"Yeah, I don't think I'm made for a career in the Police Force." For a moment, she'd thought of saying something along the lines of that being a shame but decided not to lie.

Instead, she'd said, "What are you going to do?"

"I've got an apprenticeship at Strong and Co Engineers, it's where Frank used to work. I know I'm a bit old to start at the bottom again, but I think I'll make a better greaser than I ever would a copper."

She'd smiled at him then, seeing again the D.C. she'd enjoyed working with rather than the person who'd trapped her between her principles and her heart. "That's a really good decision, Fry, I think you'll be much happier."

"Cheers, Boss," he'd said with a smile. "And ... good luck with the baby."

"Thanks," she'd said automatically, dropping her hand protectively to her swollen belly.

CHAPTER 66
A Hair's Breadth

*

Maggi - August 2029

Easing my stiff legs over the side of the bed, I slip my feet into my worn slippers. I'm relieved to be awake and not still locked in the spiralling waters of my nightmares, where cold seas tug at me, where Rah drowns, where Jim Bob's face is smashed to pieces, where Orla is a shapeless form of ephemeral light, always a hair's breadth out of my reach before getting lost again in a busy street or a crowded shop.

"Lobo," I call into the darkness, "Lobo, old boy, let's go and put the kettle on." There's no reply, no soft padding across the room, as Lobo has been dead these past three years but I still find comfort in the idea of his ghostly presence. It's not that I'm any great believer in an afterlife, a Valhalla, or, for that matter, a bearded man in biblical dress sending my soul to burn in hell, for surely that's where I'll find Rah and Orla. Rah, for committing murder and Orla for being born from sin. But sometimes, just sometimes, I imagine a nudge against my leg. It's more than a memory though in what way, I can't tell. Then, there's the smell, a whiff of wet dog or Rive perfume. And sometimes, before the sun rises, as I sit dozing in the summerhouse, I'll feel a small hand press against mine.

Ignoring the spreading ache through my hips, I walk out onto the landing. Passing Orla's bedroom, I glance in through the open door.

The faded posters of the Spice Girls, still declaring 'girl power', decorate the pale pink walls. Ever so often the thinning paper, on one or another of the posters, will give way and a tattered corner will billow over. Through the years, I've lovingly patched each one of the pictures and rehung them back onto the pink walls.

"Orla, I love you," I whisper into the moonlit room as I slowly pass.

The next bedroom door belongs to Tris. "He'll be fast asleep, no need for night duty tonight with Jonny at Fellowfield," I muse.

It'd been a major decision letting Jonny go and it had only come after he'd taken a fall in the night, because I wasn't quick enough to reach him in time. I'd known he'd found it hard living at Fellowfield even though Anya had reassured me. It had been Tris who'd made all the difference, stepping in and helping me at night. It'd meant that Jonny could at least come home at the weekends. He'd stabilised for a while, dwelling less on his fears, until Lobo had died, then he'd fallen into a dark pit of depression.

"Stupidly," Tris had commented one morning, as we'd sat in the kitchen, nursing mugs of coffee, after getting Jonny back to bed, "I used to think people with dementia didn't feel the same as they once did, because they couldn't remember what caused them to feel like that in the first place."

"I think it's worse," I'd answered, thinking about Jonny's earlier frantic search for something he knew was lost. He'd been trying to climb into his wardrobe, calling out and crying, when we'd found him. "Jonny's pain is as undiminished as mine but he, unlike myself, doesn't understanding why he hurts so much." It was after that episode Tris had come up with the brilliant idea of rebuilding Jonny's Aston Martin. He'd cleared the garage out with Frank's help and pushed the car in. Then the three of them had set about cleaning the old engine while singing along to Frank's battered radio.

At the stairs, I grasp the banister and slide my right foot slowly down the riser. With it firmly planted on the tread, I move my left foot forward. My slipper scuffs the carpet, making me topple very slightly. Instinctively I go to tighten my grip on the banister but in that reflexive split second my world augments, distorting all know scientific principles and laws like sand hovering, motionless, in a turned hourglass.

Within this time lapse I see, as clear as day, two choices. Two roads, unequal and uneven. One long, undulating, pitted track bathed in light, the other short, dark and straight as a die. I know they both lead to the same destination. I make my choice and let go of the banister. Tumbling effortlessly forward into the abyss.

After, when time has righted itself, there's darkness, a strong sense of pain and a desperate voice calling my name.

"Maggi, Maggi hang on. The ambulance is on its way. Goddamn it, don't you give up on me Maggi." I feel him leave my side, hear him shout, "In here," his voice full of tears, but below, way, way below, there's a growing warmth, a weight across my body. Sinking into the sensation, it solidifies.

"Lobo," I think as I feel again the comfort of his body. A smell of Rive surrounds me as a small hand slips into mine and then… another on the other side.

"Be brave, Maggi Drew. Straight ahead," I tell myself as a feeling of blissful contentment fills my broken heart… whilst someone… somewhere… says, "Sorry, mate, she's gone."

CHAPTER 67
Steady as She Goes

*

Logan

Logan sits at the round table. She lets her fingers rest on the old, dark wood and remembers the week, six years ago, when she'd sat here, with Fry, listening to Maggi's story.

"They were sad days," she thinks as she reaches a hand up to smoothen her long hair tied in a neat ponytail.

"Hey, you okay?" asks Fry, pulling her back from her memories.

"Just remembering," she answers, glancing across at the small, incongruous Christmas tree. "Still have the trees then."

"Yeah," he smiles. "Not the same ones, of course. I've changed them over the years, when they've conked out."

"Does Jonny notice?"

"Not really, though to be fair, I think sometimes he knows something's different, especially with the little one on the table. That's always the hardest to source. I had to send to Canada for this last tree. I ended up buying two more for back up."

"It's pretty, Maya would love it."

"Where is Maya today?"

"With Grim. He's meant to be helping her with her school work but I definitely heard the words ice cream and something about who can eat a bowl the fastest as I was leaving," she says, shaking her head.

"That sounds like fun. Shall we?"

"Sure." Pulling her satchel-type handbag over her head, she follows him into the garden. The shrubs and trees are in full summer leaf, shading the pathway from the hot August sun.

"It looks lovely," she tells him.

"I try to keep it in good order without losing that 'devil-may-care unkempt-look' Maggi was so keen on." This makes her smile as she walks behind him. The air suddenly thickens with a redolence of honeysuckle as she passes under the vine-covered arch into the open space of the small meadow, that throngs with wildflowers and insect life. A neatly mown path winds its way past the bronze sculpture to the summerhouse.

Logan can see the doors stand open with a table set for afternoon tea. In one of the four easy chairs sits an elderly man, fast asleep. "How is Jonny?" Logan asks quietly as she walks past the bronze sculpture. She glances at the smaller of the two figures and an unexpected spike of pain knells in her heart. Since Maya's birth, she's found it almost impossible to remain objective in any crime that involves a child.

"Old, confused. Can't understand where Maggi and Lobo are but can't quite remember who they are anyway."

"Does he live here still?" she says, sitting at the table.

"No, mainly at Fellowfield. Maggi eventually let him move in, about four years ago. I think it was more for Jonny's safety; she really wasn't coping very well with his care. I moved in around that time, so he could spend the weekends at home. Tea?"

"Yes, thanks. Milk, no sugar."

"No sugar, that's new," he smiles at her.

"Yeah, you know, motherhood and all that. I've got to set a good example now. Maggi?"

"I'll bury her ashes by the bronze."

"Are they there?"

"Yes, but we always knew that, didn't we?" he says, handing her a pottery mug. "Maggi and I buried Lobo there too. Cake?"

"Cake?" comes a sleepy voice.

"Yes, cake, Jonny. Want a slice? It's chocolate, your favourite," asks Fry brightly.

"Hello Jonny," Logan says, employing the same timbre she uses to greet Maya at the end of a school day.

"Oh, hello. Are you Tris's Mum? Have you come to pick him up? Don't mind me, I can be a little bit higgledy. There's cake you know, would you like some?"

"Yes, that would be very nice."

"Nice. Yes, nice," Jonny nods as Fry tucks a napkin under his chin and offers him a bowl of mouth-size pieces.

"Where's Maggs? She'll want cake," Jonny asks, looking around.

"Oh, she'll be along soon, Jonny. I'll keep her a nice, big slice," reassures Fry.

"A nice, big slice," Jonny repeats contentedly, eating his cake. After a couple of mouthfuls, Fry helps him with a sip of tea before he starts to drift off again.

"Does he sleep a lot?" Logan asks.

"Yes, thankfully. Though he does have some terrible nightmares, but Maggi taught me the best way of dealing with them. I miss her, you know, and Lobo too. The house is empty without them. I'm just grateful Jonny's about at weekends."

"What about Frank and your Mum?"

"She married Leroy last year and moved to Devon. Frank still lives in Chelmsford but he spends quite a bit of time here with Jonny and me. The three of us are restoring a classic car. Been fiddling around with it for years, it's the sort of job you never really want to finish."

"I've never had a job like that, especially now. I'm always rushing here, there and everywhere between work and Maya."

"How's Grim enjoying retirement?"

"Loves it, though there's not much in the way of golf or bowls. He's either looking after Maya or is at the pub with Daff."

"And talking of bowls, how's Greyson?" Fry asks tentatively.

"Greyson," she smiles knowingly. "Oh, we love Greyson, he's the best father anyone could have. He's always taking Maya on adventures, teaching her amazing things. He'd buy her the world if I let him, but he's still the Greyson you knew, living life to the full."

"So, are you still... you know, living life to the full with him? Or

389

have you met someone else?"

"No, single, if you don't count Grim. How about yourself?"

"Same, single. I don't seem to meet many women who are interested in spending their weekends under the bonnet of an Aston Martin."

"You know you don't have to, Fry, you have a choice."

"That was the deal. Maggi left me everything on the understanding I would take care of Jonny and the graves. I would never have agreed to it if I hadn't wanted to. And that kind o' brings me to why I invited you here for tea."

"Okay?"

"I wondered if you wanted to know more about them... Maggi, Jonny, Norah and Orla?"

"In what way?"

"This," he said, getting up and going to the back of the summerhouse before returning with a folder.

"What is it?"

"Just stuff. I'm going to bury it with Maggi but I thought, before I did, you might like to read it first. If you don't want to, it doesn't matter," he states, putting the folder on the table between them.

"Will it compromise..." she begins hesitantly.

"No, nothing like that. I just thought it might close a door for you."

"Okay," she answers, reaching for the folder.

"Wait," he says, nodding towards Jonny. "I'll take him inside first, he doesn't need to see it."

"Okay," she replies again, though this time she is less certain and wonders whether it would be prudent not to look. "You know you will though," she tells herself.

"Jonny," Fry calls gently, shaking the old man's shoulder.

"Yes, yes, I'm here. What's wrong? Is it Orla? Are the Christmas tree lights on? She needs them to see her way home."

"All the lights are on, Jonny, I've check them myself," Fry tells him.

"Where's Maggs? Orla?... something bad... something really bad."

Logan can hear the rising panic in the old man's voice as he tries desperately to struggle out of the chair.

"Jonny," Fry's voice remains calm but assertive. He doesn't hurry his words as he makes clear statements. "Orla's fine. She's safe and sound. She's with Maggs and Rah."

"Maggs and Rah?"

"Yes. They are all safe and sound. I promise you."

"Safe and sound," Jonny repeats.

"Yes. Safe and sound.

"Safe and sound."

"But I need help clearing these tea things up," Fry says, reverting back to his sunnier tone.

"Tea things? Yes," Jonny offers.

"I was hoping you'd help me. Here," and taking Jonny's arm, he helps him up gently before handing him a cup. "I'll take the teapot. There. All steam ahead. Steady as she goes, Captain Jonny."

"Steady as she goes," Jonny repeats with a little chuckle.

Logan watches them make slow progress across the tiny meadow, stopping briefly at the bronze sculpture, so Jonny can touch each figure in turn before shuffling onward. She hears them long after they have disappeared under the honeysuckle archway, singing a rendition of the Drunken Sailor.

CHAPTER 68
The Songs of The Dead

*

Logan

Picking up the folder, Logan opens it. She knows instantly what she is looking at. A set of photos the sculpture's design was taken from. The first is a full-length picture of Norah and Orla holding hands and walking away from the camera. Bare-footed and dressed in sleeveless frocks, with their long, black hair hanging plaited down their backs. They both lean slightly inward as they look back across their shoulders, smiling at the photographer.

Logan can tell that the picture was taken right here, though the trees are still immature and the small wildflower meadow hardly grown. The next two photos are close ups, taken from the original. Logan studies the faces. Their fine-boned, dark-eyed Japanese ancestry dominates their D.N.A.

"IC 5 and IC 1," she thinks, ever the police officer.

The next photo is, in many ways, more startling for her then the previous three. It's Jonny as a young man. When Maggi had described Jonny, Logan had pictured him as a Greyson-type person, charismatically magnetic but not necessarily good looking. What she hadn't expected to see was true beauty; the sort only mythical gods are made from.

The last photo is of the four of them; Orla can be no older than Maya is now. The stab of fear Logan had felt earlier, as she'd passed the sculpture, returns and she quickly turns the photo over.

Picking up what she presumes is a concert programme, two much smaller photos fall out. One is of a large group of people, some holding instruments. The other is of four people who are also sombrely attired. Three of the people carry their eastern lineage while the fourth is a tall, elderly, white man.

"Minty, Gwen, Amelia and Arthur," she presumes.

Opening the programme, she realises it is not a concert programme at all, but an Order of Service for Norah's funeral. She tries to read the lists of musical pieces and amazes herself by recognising Gorecki's Symphony of Sorrowful Songs, movement 2.

She searches for the memory, and then wishes she hadn't. It had been a school thing, a guest speaker on Auschwitz. The talk had ended with this piece of music being performed within the camp as a reminder of the Nazi's use of music as yet another form of torture. The piece, the speaker had explained, was taken from a prayer scratched into a cell wall in a Gestapo prison by a frightened girl. Logan had been deeply affected by the girl's story and the haunting music.

"Move on," she tells herself, putting the order of service back into the pile.

Two envelopes remain. Logan picks up the larger of the two and empties the contents onto the table. Out falls a tiny pair of sparkly socks, a set of pink mittens, a package of pale-pink, translucent tissue papers with a lock of soft, black baby hair carefully enfolded inside, a child's painting of four stick figures, three tall, one small with a huge, golden sun and a backdrop of primary-coloured flowers. 13 birthday cards, the first decorated in bright scribbles, the last in fluorescent pink bubble writing.

"Fuck," she mumbles under her breath as she quickly gathers the objects together and returns them to the envelope.

She hesitates before opening the much smaller envelope, not wanting to see any more evidence of a murdered child's life. Gingerly, she slips the piece of paper out. Its texture is fragile but the writing, mature and well formed, slopes slightly forward and is easy to read.

Maggs, my heart, my love, it's nearly time to say goodbye. We both know I cannot live with what I have done, that I traded my body for the life of our child. I don't know when it will be but I know it will be soon. If I can, I will find her, love her and, this time, protect her, I promise. And when I do and all is well, we will be waiting for you. Just look straight ahead, Maggs, do not be afraid, we will be looking back towards you. Xxx

Slipping her sandals off, Logan walks over to the bronze. She lets her finger trace the child's woven metal plait before placing herself in their line of sight. She'd thought she'd understood the significance of the sculpture but now, trying to see it through Maggi's eyes, she catches its true meaning.

"I always thought it represented loss," Fry comments. She looks up and sees him standing in the arch of honeysuckle. "That is until I found Norah's letter. Now I think it's more to do with what is to come, rather than what has been."

"Yes," murmurs Logan, still staring into the cast faces, "I think you're right."

"Do you mind if I ask why you wrote that report?"

"You mean on Waxy?"

"Yeah."

"Because it was the truth. Because that's who I am, a copper through and through."

"I understand why you decided against identifying the body as Victor Martin but why name it at all? Why I.D. it as Herrick Butler?"

She turns sharply, drawing her slight frame to attention like a soldier called to arms. Though she wears jeans and a t-shirt, not the ubiquitous dark C.I.D. suit, she's battle ready.

"You took a gamble, Fry, when you destroyed that evidence," she retorts. "You bet against my feelings for you. You knew I liked you and you used that."

"It was nothing to do with you," he replies calmly enough, but she hears the edge of something hard in his voice too. "You know it was

394

all about Jonny and Maggi, it was never about you."

"You jeopardised my career with your-your... nefarious act, who did you think you were? Some bloody, fucking medieval knight in shining fucking armour?"

"Nefarious? That's a bit strong."

"A bit fucking strong, Fry? Jeezes Christ. I trusted you and you put me in a really shitty position."

"No, I didn't. You put yourself in that position. What I did was for the sake of justice."

"Justice? And who the fuck are you to decide what's just and what isn't?"

Fry runs his hand through his hair and sighs. "That's just it, Lo, I am who I am. I didn't do it as some sort of altruistic, shining, horse charging, damsel rescuing deed, I did it for my own selfish need. It wasn't to hurt you, it was to save me." He smiles, surrendering to her by lifting his shoulders and spreading his hands.

"Fucking Billy Budd," she mutters.

"Billy Budd?" he questions.

"Nothing," she snaps. "What do you mean *to save you*?"

"Frank said to me, not long after the fire and while I was still waiting to see which way you'd jump..."

"Which way I'd jump?" she flings back.

"Sorry, that came out wrong, I didn't mean to sound flippant and I certainly wasn't feeling flippant either. Far from it, I was really worried. Scared I'd be facing criminal charges. And in truth, I knew I'd placed you in a difficult position too."

"Huh, you think?" she huffs.

"I'd not said much to Frank but he knew what I'd done and how I was feeling, and he did that thing he always does to me. He makes a little statement or says a little saying and moves on. And by the time I've worked out what he means, he's off doing something completely different."

"And what wise words of wisdom did he impart to you?" she purses sarcastically.

"I was standing in the kitchen, staring down the garden and he came up behind me and said, 'It's only when you stand in the light, Tris, can you see your own darkness'. And like usual, he was right. That fire freed me, it made me understand I was never going to fill my father's shoes, never going to be the copper he was or the son I'd imagined he'd be proud of.

That's when I handed in my notice."

She sighs, her anger slipping from her like sand through a sieve.

"Yeah, I see that. And if I'm truthful, my choice wasn't totally by the book. Grim left me an open door and I walked right through it."

"How come?"

"I told him the whole story of Orla's murder and he gave me a long, winded version on how we always have options, however watertight a case maybe."

"Really?"

"Nah, not in that way, Grim's as straight as an arrow. What he meant was, as lead on the case, I had a choice between taking a moral line or seeking the status and promotion through solving a child murder.

I had to name Herrick Butler. What else could I do? Not only did I categorically know that Waxy was Herrick Butler but Greyson's P.M. report fitted his profile like a glove and Victor Martin's didn't. But I chose not to state how Herrick Butler's name came to my notice. I left it to Grim to decide whether to investigate Butler's death or close the file."

"And Grim closed the file, no questions asked," Fry finishes.

"Yeah, that's about the truth of it."

"For what it's worth... thank you."

Logan shrugs and returning to the table, she slips her sandals on and picks up her handbag before walking back along the mown path.

"So, how's the engineering business?" she asks, wanting to change the subject.

"Great, I love tinkering around with equations and lumps of steel," he answers, leading her through the garden to the front of the house.

"I'm pleased you came today," he tells her as they stand by her car.

"So am I," she answers honestly. "Say goodbye to Jonny for me."

"I will, not that he'll remember who you are," he smiles.

Getting into the car, she takes the Noc from her bag. "Connect to speakers. Grim's Remix. Shuffle. Play."

As the first melodic chords of 'Heart of Gold' fill her mind, she pulls out of 33 Peartree Road, leaving the songs of the dead behind.

Made in the USA
Columbia, SC
26 December 2017